# THE ID PARADOX

Jan Notzon

© 2017 Jan Notzon
All rights reserved.
ISBN: 1545501378
ISBN 13: 9781545501375
Library of Congress Control Number: 2017906317
CreateSpace Independent Publishing Platform
North Charleston, South Carolina

*For the best friend a man could ask for:*

*Memo Benavides*


"There are people who *only* respond to violence."

—Claude Alexander Notzon

*"Move over!"*

*His big brother Frank stood just outside the open rear door of the family station wagon and gave the order. His tone was the slap of a barber's razor against a strop. There was no mistaking its intention. It was meant to belittle, to demean, to squeeze the rag of self-worth dry. Although the boy knew well its purpose—to establish dominance, to make him feel as small and powerless as possible, to strip from him whatever morsel of dignity he might still possess—he had not the vocabulary to give it a name.*

*The humiliation turned his face the color of a bloody sunrise. Rancid anger ate away at his insides. He hesitated. But the truth was he was afraid of Frank. There was something beyond the fact that he was bigger, two and a half years older, and already post-puberty. There was something in himself, something that his immature mind could not name, that held him back—even with his peers. And it was a quality he instinctively knew was lacking in his brother. He only knew the name everyone else gave it.*

*And that word filled him with shame.*

*A thought hovering moth to flame told him that standing up to his brother and taking the pain and humiliation of a beating would probably put an end to the torment. But acting on such knowledge requires a crumb of self-respect— something shorn from him long before.*

*Head bowed in mortification, teeth grinding away a layer of enamel, he slid across the seat to the opposite window.*

*But submission to bullying never appeases. It only encourages. His brother exited the car, walked around the back to the other side, opened the door, and in an even louder and surlier tone repeated the command.* "Move over!"

*Fear and shame prickled his entire body with needles of fire. His cheeks burned with anger and self-scorn. He could not succumb to this added humiliation. A shaky, trembling "No" escaped his lips. There was an awesome silence, the tension of a rubber band stretched to the point of snapping. The boy waited, trying to control the trembling that wracked his bones. What would be the result of his defiance? A push? A slap? What would he do in response?*

*But his brother Frank was not alone in his insatiable urge to teach his spoiled, snot-nosed kid brother his place.* "Oh, you brat, move over!" *came like a Greek chorus from his two big sisters up front.*

*What the boy at that tender age simply couldn't understand was that as he did everything in his power to be like his older siblings—to talk like them, to act like them, to sneer at the gross stupidity of others as they did—it only alienated them further. And so he would redouble his efforts, straining to mimic their timbre of voice with each sarcastic remark, their posture of condescension, their arrogant dismissal of the small-town mentality that surrounded them, in the hope that some combination might gain their acceptance—perhaps even their approval. And the cycle would begin anew.*

*Outsized and outnumbered, this time he quickly slid across the seat, and the disgrace stooped his shoulders one inch further to the ground.*

# 1

There are people in your life that stick with you. In the listening quiet of memory, they serve in small measure to order the chaos of life's blitzkrieg. The reasons they linger are as varied as the people themselves. Portraits of evil are as memorable as paragons of humanity—often more so. Both can give you insight into this curious thing called life that we share: with apologies to Winston Churchill, a mystery, clothed in a riddle, wrapped up in an enigma (except for those who have hewn it into some shape that gives them the comfort of certainty). These individuals may have inspired you to love, to hate, or to vomit. But you do not love for what is done for you. You love for what you do. Love is not a state of mind. It is an action.

Why I was thinking about that now—under the fearsome assault of the Rio Grande Valley sun, harvesting cantaloupes for seventy-four cents a crate, with sweat and sunscreen dripping into my eyes and stinging like a hive of yellow jackets—is another mystery.

"Oye Licenciado, ése no. I awready esplain it to jou: when thee tallo, thee estem, comienza a separarse. Da's when thee melon ees maduro—reep."

"Ripe."

Luís, the *capataz*—foreman—was affectionately impatient with me. He seemed rather bemused that this gringo ex-lawyer and ex-teacher would be working alongside his fellow migrant farmworkers as a day-laborer. He'd obviously been at it a long time, his rawhide skin burned a rusty, coffee-colored almost ebony. There it sat atop muscle unyielding as monks to temptation. Rivers of sweat poured down the shriveled, cracked, blood-dried mess. His manner was of another age: humility and kindness beneath a gentle teasing that gloved the fist of criticism. "Okei, okei, *raeep*. You teash me Eengleesh, I teash you melones, eh?"

"That's a deal." I left the one he'd cautioned me against and shot a quick glance at him as I moved to pick another and place it in my crate.

"Ése si. Estás aprendiendo. Jou learning, jou learning." The gently ironic smile cloaked beneath paternal impatience.

Late afternoon light burned yellow-white and relentless on this citrus/melon farm just outside McAllen, Texas. It lay a desultory two hours down the Rio Grande from Aguagria, the home of my birth. The third spray of the day meant to keep the fruit from sunburn had evaporated in the time it took to recommence the harvest. I was about to pick a melon that looked ripe but then noticed it hadn't started separating from the stem.

"Muy bien, Licenciado. Jou learning, man." Luís had come up behind me, making sure I followed his instructions. I tried to straighten my back, spasm-hardened with stooping. "Jou back hurt?"

"Me está matando." Luís just laughed and went on to check another peon's full crate.

The sun beat down like an implacable enemy, soulless and homicidal. A plea for a breeze to wick some of the heat away from my body was insolently denied. Only a dry, calid gust now and then ground through the trachea and down to lungs on fire with resentment. Fine grit sidled into my nostrils and throat and then colluded with sweat to make a dirty brown nest around my neck. It crawled beneath my contacts, deliciously grating against my eyeballs. I tried to tear them out, which only invited gnats, moisture-starved and needling, to congregate there. I'd inhaled a host of them already, tried to snort them out and only succeeded in expelling a honker of gnat-ridden snot. (I sincerely hope you don't get that particular cantaloupe.)

Pointless, backbreaking work. And a certain comfort in that.

I stretched again, the muscles in my back creaking open like pretzeled guy-wire. I then looked out over the flat dusty fields and beyond. On the edge of the Wild-Horse Desert, the Lower Rio Grande Valley was once the exclusive habitation of whitetail and rattlesnake, scrub brush and horned toad. You can still see the occasional armadillo, elder statesman of atavism, leprosy-carrying relict of antiquity. But ancient serpentine meanders of the river, when it could still make claim to the moniker "Great," were pinched off into oxbow lakes or resacas. When upriver obstructions came to cut off their water supply, they left a deep loamy-rich soil. There, citrus thrives, and melon seeds, with a tender drip of irrigation, sprout and fructify.

It is not really a valley at all but a floodplain from olden times when the river occasionally roared in changed courses. It is a constant battle to maintain that part that has been tamed by irrigation and modern transport. The rugged, harsh beauty of desert wildness shrugs its shoulders at civilization, biding its time until the forces of domesticity weary. Just beneath the surface of these islands of cultivation lie the seeds of the untamed and primordial: creeping gray-green squawbush, crucifixion thorn, and *huisachillo*, primitively spiked for self-defense in a universe of godless savagery.

A cold, threatening voice snapped me out of my reverie. "Oye, gringo, aquí no. Éstos son míos." The voice is accompanied by cobra-cool eyes and a mouth sculpted out of granite. I'd moved to another eighty-inch bed and hadn't realized it was already occupied by one of my more hostile co-workers. I'd been warned already that I would be viewed as an interloper here and might have to defend my presence. But I knew there was no rule about who could pick where.

"I don't see your name on them. No veo tu nombre encima."

He stood and squared off. "Thees ees my caja. Muévete pa'lla."

This was the moment I'd been dreading. It had been made clear by both Luís and Mr. Langhorne, the owner, that ducking a challenge would be an invitation to continued mistreatment. I could feel the fear welling up in me. But this time, I couldn't back down.

For a reason I couldn't quite articulate, I needed this job—this mindless, monotonous, slave-wage job, under the skin-flaying Texas sun, with minimal skills required and no future. Maybe it was because I had no stake in the outcome. It allowed me, perhaps for the first time in my life, not to interpret a correction as an attack on my self-worth. Then again, maybe it was because it entailed not a single moral question to parse. Perhaps both.

I stood and faced my rival. Here was to be the most primal of endeavors: man versus man in physical combat. As I questioned whether keeping the job was worth it, a passage from Shakespeare rattled rudely in my brain: "Rightly to be great / Is not to stir without great argument, / But greatly to find quarrel in a straw / When honor's at the stake." Internally shaking, but with a firmness that surprised me, I quietly answered: "No."

I was unprepared for his quickness, however, and the first blow met full blush with the bridge of my nose. It sent blood and snot spurting down my upper lip. *Um, salty,* I thought, as for a split second all started to go black. I caught myself before going down, however, and moved back to shake away the cobwebs. Pain shot through my head and radiated outward like the spider-webbing of a cracked mirror. There followed a fusillade of blows that I was more or less able to fend off, only one or two glancing off my temple and ear.

I threw a weak-kneed left jab that made partial contact but only drew more savage blows. What was it that held me back? *Defend yourself, Jakie!*

My antagonist ever-so-briefly paused, and we semi-circled each other, which allowed me to hear the words of encouragement from our fellow day-laborers. "Ahor-a! Ahor-a! Ahor-a!" The cheers didn't seem to be for either one of us, just for the sheer pleasure they took in the entertainment.

He charged forward, swinging wildly. Out of instinct, I suppose, I moved sideways and used my weight to encourage his progress down into the dirt and cantaloupes. When he came up, I could see murder in his eyes—not for any physical pain I'd caused him but rather the indignity in the eyes of his peers.

"Éso, Licenciado! Éso!" It appeared I at least had one fellow gladiator rooting for me.

I'd read that how much a person feels physical pain varies from individual to individual. All I knew was that a piercing ache was shooting through my nose and forehead and radiating across my whole cranium. Where were those endorphins that make you oblivious to pain? I was spitting out blood and snot, and the torrent seemed endless.

As I prepared to meet his next charge, I could see out of the corner of my eye money changing hands. The crowd circled. He charged again, feinting high and then tackling me low. This at least gave me the opportunity to wrestle. Being longer and lankier, I had an advantage there. As we rolled around on the ground, short punches, elbows and knees were thrown that rarely made contact with any vulnerable body part. We were now caked with sweat-based mud and dust, snot and blood, all of which I was trying to spit out of my mouth.

Then, as he broke free and stood facing me, relief finally raised its merciful head. "Ahí viene el patrón! El patrón!" All heads snapped and eyes squinted westward at the gate separating the farm from the Langhorne home. Two mismatched riders on horseback approached it. One was unmistakably the wiry, born-in-the-saddle figure of the boss, his crown of white hair barely visible under a straw hat. The other was his polar opposite: tall, so stiff in the saddle he might have been seated on a cactus. My fellow combatant then turned back to me. The look of bloodlust on his face was quickly replaced by a sly smile.

Immediately, the order came from Luís: "Descansen. Descansen. Agua. Water breik!" Suddenly, a sheepish quiet enveloped the afternoon. My adrenaline-inspired frenzy recorded every sound. There was the lonely, broken rumble of a jet in the distance, the monotonous electrical buzz of cicadas, the haunting coo of white-winged doves, feet shuffling in embarrassment.

Broken lines formed at the water barrels, and Luís came toward me with the last small piece of ice left in one of them. He pulled my bandana from my neck, wrapped up the niggardly piece of ice in it and placed it on my forehead just above my nose. "Manténgalo ahí, between jour ice." Quickly, the flow of blood stopped. Then, as I approached the line before one of the watercoolers, Luís handed me a cup. I downed it in one gulp and stood in line for more. "Peleastes bien, Licenciado. He won' bother jou no more."

I was skeptical. I knew I'd fought like a water lily in a typhoon. I shot a glance at him—a feeler to get the spirit in which he'd offered his congratulations. His look was enigmatic. There seemed to be some sincerity in his praise, perhaps for my not having backed down. Looking back on it now—and I can still see that look so clearly—there was a quarter teaspoon of condescension. It seemed to judge me lacking in whatever it takes to meet aggression on its own terms—to use the only measures it understands or respects.

A rite of passage completed, I suppose. But I'll never understand the thrill some get from a fistfight. For as long as I could remember, they'd always left me with a profound feeling of emptiness—the pointlessness of empty space where galaxies collide. I just had to avoid giving in to tears—not out of fear or pain but rather a piercing sense of alienation and loneliness.

As was his custom, Mr. Langhorne didn't dismount to open the gate. From atop his horse, he slid the rope off, backed his mount up to open the gate and bridle-slapped his lanky companion's horse through. The awkward stranger bounced up and down like a Ken doll. Mr. Langhorne then came through himself and closed and roped the gate in one smooth motion. The two riders gradually came into focus out of billowing heat waves.

Apparently, it was quite an occasion for the boss to come out to the fields, as Luís didn't give the order to return to work. Instead, he went forward to meet him and his awkward fellow rider, decked in suit pants and a tie loosened at the collar. Completing the ensemble,

Mr. Langhorne had obviously lent him one of his hats. It was a few sizes too small and sat precariously on his head, bobbling side to side.

From atop his horse, Mr. Langhorne conferred with his foreman. While Luís and El Patrón parleyed out of earshot, there was a lot of uneasy muttering among the workers. What I could pick up consisted of a nervous questioning of the purpose of the meeting. Is there some problem? Is the harvest going to stop for some reason? Will there be work? Who is the tall *güero* in the tie with the hat two sizes too small? Could he be *la migra?* Some I knew to be here illegally shot furtive glances in all directions, eyeing possible escape routes.

Then I noticed Mr. Langhorne cast a glance at me. I looked from him to the tall blond stranger. The latter's attention seemed fixed on me, only occasionally tossing a word or two to Mr. Langhorne. Who is this greenhorn, and what could he possibly have to do with me? Why does he look familiar?

A disquieting thought bubbled up from my gut: Don't tell me the public defender's office in Austin sent someone after me. Hah! Delusions of grandeur, Jake: no one cares about a third-year PD who ups and quits. And it's been over two years, now. Just as likely he's from the New York City school system looking for a lost second-year teacher. But then why the hell is he studying me that way? And why the hell is he not even trying to hide it?

Without a word to the rest of us, Mr. Langhorne turned his horse around and started back to the house. The other horseman—and I use the term loosely—sat perplexed until Luís pulled the old nag around by the bridle and slapped her rump to get her going. She followed the boss's horse like an old married couple.

"Bueno, todo terminado. ¡A trabajar!" Luís gave the order to return to work. He stopped me and pulled me aside. "Como te sientes, Licenciado? Can jou work?" I just nodded my assent. "Yoost a leetle light lef'; media-hora no más. Usa el agua de la hielera para to clean jourself. Cool jou, too. Todavía está fresca."

The sun had already secreted itself below the western horizon when quitting time was called. The sleepy yellow of dusk settled supinely over awakening night creatures as we made our way to the showers. The heat was in no way assuaged, however, and I was aching for the comfort of the coldest water I could nurse from those ancient calcified pipes. I let it pour on my aching nose and head, allowing it to soak up some of the poison of the day's battle. Then, ravenous, to supper: chicken mole, rice, guacamole and refried beans with mounds of steaming corn tortillas that disappeared as quickly as they were placed on the table.

Afterward, as we emerged from our tin-roofed, cinder-block housing, the last vestiges of daylight were slowly swallowed into the sublime mystery of night. Cloaked in the quiet of crickets and katydids, it spread its soothing blanket over the trouble of day. There, it wove its brick-oven heat into the apron folds of tomorrow. The watery trill of a poorwill accompanied—disembodied threnody of fantasy and yearning. One lone coyote howled the surrounding feral anarchy. Above, the astral silence of nighthawks floated through the cast-off light of naked bulbs.

Since the heat of the south-Texas sun still radiated down from those naked tin roofs, most of us abandoned them to sit or stand beneath a sea of stars. They barked out their sparkle, clear and cold as creation. They then faded in the milk-pale light of the city, or above in the liquid pearl of a courtly half-moon. Randy fireflies caught by children clicked in anguish to be set free. The ache of a child's wonder at power over nature cut through the gathering darkness.

A gently strummed guitar echoed liquidly between the cinder-block structures, high-E string a quarter tone or so off pitch. But notwithstanding that petty fault, it was soothing as spiced apple cider on a cold winter night. A song of lost love accompanied it, tender as the twilight, wistful as the smell of new-mown hay. It filled the evening with illusions of gentility and grace, riding on airs of absolution.

A languid whisper blew out of the south, hinting at the sea's patient moisture. It wafted tentative and a touch morose, as though breathing only out of habit. Then, as the cries of migrant children playing make-believe pricked the evening with hope, it sighed out a gentle caress of seafoam and promise.

"Oiga, Licenciado," Ezequiel, a fellow melon-picker, called, thankfully wrenching me from my rapture, "we have Eengleesh lesson tonight?"

"Maybe not tonight, Ezequiel. I'm recuperating. Me estoy recuperando."

A knowing, close-lipped smile was his only answer. He wandered away, swallowed into the night.

I started to rise to walk out into the soothing cocoon of darkness. But just then, my antagonist from the afternoon appeared at my side. He leaned back against the wall of the bunkhouse next to the plastic chair I sat in, one foot lifted against it in a relaxed pose. He stood alarmingly still, his gaze pasted forward into the anarchy of night. After a quick glance, I trained my eyes star-wise as well, saying nothing. The hair on the back of my neck stood up, as fight-or-flight hormones coursed through my body. They bristled a thin coat of sweat to my skin, and my heart pounded.

Out of the corner of my eye, I saw him reach behind him. I jumped up and backed away, anticipating some kind of weapon. As I turned toward him, however, I saw him shake a cigarette out of a pack of Lucky Strikes. It lay curved and flattened from its berth in his back pocket.

I looked up to his face. Though it seemed calm and expressionless as the night, there was some subtle discourse in his eyes. It was too cryptic for me to read fully. There was a vague suggestion of comradeship, but a critical element, too—a cool but at the same time scathing...condescension perhaps? An urging? To what, I wondered.

I'd started smoking again after my surrender to the forces of barbarism in Austin and continued, off and on, during my brief stint in the New York City school system. During my hospital stay after an assault by my students, I was forced to quit—smoking, not to mention teaching. Bruised and battered, I made my way back home to

Aguagria. I suppose that was what this mindless, menial job was about. Perhaps having no mysteries to solve other than whether or not the fruit before me is ripe might ease my way back to sanity.

But here was a peace offering I couldn't refuse without insulting the tempter. (Or was that just my rationalization?) Whatever the case, I accepted, and the curved cancer-stick dangled sumptuously from my lips. My onetime enemy pulled a battle-scarred Zippo out of the coin pocket of his jeans and lit my cancer-stick and then his own. Then he relaxed against the wall.

That first shot of nicotine when you haven't smoked for weeks is the devil's hook. All the sharp edges of self-recrimination seem to melt away. Pricks of purposelessness float heavenward to oblivion. Nerves and muscles knotted by a world that refuses to conform to your ideal suddenly relax into the gentle folds of grandma's quilt. As it swaddles you in memory, her soothing hand strokes your back in consolation. And there you lie, protected from life's contradictions.

The only problem is the one with all drugs, all escapes from the realities of this existence: as the body becomes accustomed and comes to crave it, those pleasures prove more and more elusive. And then all that is left is the ever-deepening need, satisfaction shrinking to bare alleviation.

"Gracias."

The only answer he gave was a long exhalation of smoke. Suddenly, I could feel him tense up as another figure to my left emerged from the darkness. It was the awkwardly mounted stranger from the afternoon. As I turned back to my fellow pugilist, he had slithered into the night as silently as a water snake.

"Hello, Mr. Kazmareck," the stranger greeted me in a manner that reeked of bureaucrat. It was as out of place here as a tuxedo at a rodeo. He indicated the backless wooden chair next to mine. "May I join you?"

There was nothing threatening in his manner. Quite the opposite, in fact. But still, a host of sand fleas crawled up my flesh. My invitation wasn't particularly friendly. "Help yourself."

He sat as though he were at a meeting with the president, his back hard and straight as a plank of composite board. "I'm sorry if I scared your friend away. I suppose he was afraid I might be from immigration."

"Are you?"

"No. Although I did nothing to disabuse Mr. Langhorne of that impression. That's why he was willing to escort me out to the fields this afternoon." A moment passed as he looked out into the vast expanse like it was an old friend. "I'm sure I looked pretty silly on that horse."

"As silly as you look right here." He was now fully suited with collar buttoned and tie tightened. "So what is it brings you out here?"

"You. I had your boss bring me out to make sure it was you."

There was something familiar in his attitude that set my teeth on edge. It was clear from his saber-cut delivery that he managed calculations at machine-gun pace. The smoothness of it made an assessment of his character elusive. It might have been an oily grace, but something told me there was substance beneath his polished-glass demeanor. There was an aura of politics about him, an air of organization but not command—a general's aide-de-camp, perhaps. I was sure I'd seen him before...somewhere. "Do I know you?"

"Actually, we have a friend in common."

Something in the way he pronounced the word *friend* sent a chill up my spine. There was some subtle qualifier that made the term almost sound like its opposite. "I don't have any friends who'd chase me way out here." Suddenly, it dawned. "You were at my father's funeral."

"Yes. I hope I didn't distract from the proceedings. And you did a pretty fair job of disappearing afterward. Although finding you wasn't all that difficult. You have family that care deeply about you— one sister, in particular."

The thought of my little sister suddenly focused my attention. "What the hell is this about?"

"I have a message from our mutual friend."

A light suddenly switched on in my head. It sent a flood of nausea through me. "Connors McLain." His cool, steady gaze confirmed my suspicion. "Connors McLain has no friends. Only sycophants."

In the silent moment that followed, I could tell that I'd pricked a tiny hole in his bureaucratic armor. Coolly, he replied, "Connors McLain is the most popular politician in the state of Texas. Though I work for him, I consider him my friend."

"The popularity of a politician is proof positive that if he ever had friends, he doesn't anymore."

A razor-thin smile made it clear that my response was anticipated. "He assumed that that would be your reaction. He said to tell you that it concerns your mutual friend, Artie Cavazos."

I felt violently ripped out of air and space. Connors McLain and Artie Cavazos: the feelings those two names inspired sucked the air out of my lungs. "His name on the lips of Connors McLain is sacrilege."

"He's alive."

I felt a prickling sensation as though my flesh were pulling off my body. The chair I was sitting in seemed to tilt forward like some kind of carnival ride. The earth rose at a sheer angle and teetered side to side. "You're a liar."

The patient smirk reappeared, and a puff of air escaped his nose. "Mr. Kazmareck, I may be many things. Often, in my line of work, I have to put things in a certain light. But when it comes to Connors McLain, or anyone close to him, I would never, ever lie." He pulled a few battle-scarred browning pages from his well-used briefcase and placed them on my lap.

"What's this?"

"It's the manifest of inmates at a prison in Tlaquetillo, Coahuila, Mexico. Please look at the second page, fourth name from the top."

I locked my eyes on him as he patiently attended to the night sky. I wondered what kind of game Connors might be playing. But as I look back on it now, I was also pierced with a flicker of hope. I'd long since despaired of ever finding out what happened to my long-lost friend. I reluctantly turned to the document before me, and as I came to the place he'd indicated, I saw the name *Cavazos Linares, Arturo Miguel.*

"That's not an unusual name in Mexico." As I was about to continue my protest, he pulled a battle-worn photograph from his attaché and placed it on top of the registry. It was taken from a distance, and it took me a moment to recognize the person in it, but I was finally able to make out the emaciated figure of Artie Cavazos. He had a lengthy stubble and a vacant look that seemed as foreign to him as the craters of the moon.

"Where'd you get this?"

"How I came by it is not as important as what it means. Wouldn't you agree?"

I pored over his face for signs of smugness. I found none. "How in the name of God..."

"I think that's a matter for you to take up with Mr. McClain." I started to voice my objections, but before I could, he placed an airline ticket on top of the pile. It was a flight from McAllen to Austin. "Mr. McClain is expecting you at his office tomorrow morning. Our flight leaves at six-o-nine. Better get some sleep. I already cleared it with your boss—former boss."

"What the hell makes you think I'll go?"

He closed his briefcase and stood, leaving the documents. "Either you will or you won't. I'll be by at four-thirty. Nice shiner, by the way."

I pawed and scraped at sleep that night. What could my former friend be up to? Artie alive? It's got to be one of Connors's tricks, one of his little ruses to bend people to his will. But what would he want with me now? The possibilities pinged through my mind like a schizophrenic pinball.

Artie Cavazos and Connors McLain: my inseparable friends from whom I'd been violently separated. We were the three musketeers, searching for adventure and braving all challenges. They were the brothers I had lost hope of finding in my own family, though my relationship with Connors had always shared aspects of that family torment.

Ah, but together we explored the banks of the Rio Grande and took sustenance from its prey. We camped beneath a blanket of stars as the day's desert fire gave place to Aguagria's sable night canopy. We passed days and even weeks grazing on prickly pear and feasting on catfish, bass, jabalina and even, on occasion, the infrequent rattlesnake.

Although I could fieldstrip any game that my two cohorts brought down, that was always the extent of my participation. I was often faced with the necessary precursor violence, Connors's rifle rudely clapped into my hands. My aim was true, as long as the target was inanimate. But place a living, breathing creature in my sights, and the fever came upon me. Beads of sweat would flow down my temples, and my hands would start to tremble, the barrel dancing in rebellion.

"Jake, what's the matter with you?" Connors would fiercely whisper. "He's right there! He's yours! For God's sakes, shoot!"

I did everything I could think of: try to imagine it a statue, take a deep breath, tighten, loosen…but it was hopeless. The ribbing I took from Connors was always merciless. And he never stopped slapping his .300 Savage into my reluctant grip. Obviously because the chance to torture me afterward was so appealing. There was never a word from Artie. He'd just raise his rifle and, with an aim as sure as the sunrise, bring down the beast. Usually with one shot.

So on this night, I lay in my bunk with these memories mercilessly stabbing, snores of my fellow bunkmates wracking the rafters. The possibilities knotted my stomach muscles into bands of steel. My mind began to amble along roads of memory.

Connors was always larger than life, six-feet-four-inches tall, full of stories of adventures he'd never taken and anecdotes of people he'd never known. But he told them in such an entertaining way, with such a panache and self-important affability, that they placed him on a pedestal of popularity. He was student-body president two years running, full of invented studies and fabricated testimony in debate.

Artie, by contrast, was as tight-lipped and mysterious as Connors was extravagant. I don't think anyone, not his girlfriend or mother or sister, really knew Artie. There seemed to be a gangrenous part of him buried under a calm self-assuredness. He was a dormant volcano beneath the placid waters of a mountain lake.

Never much at academics, he seemed to know and be able to do everything else. He could tear apart a car engine, grind out the cylinders and put it back together the way someone else might hang his coat on a rack. He taught me how to strip game, prepare snake meat and hook, bait and set a line to catch myriad species of fish. He could build or repair anything with a sneeze and a smile.

His family crossed the border from Mexico when he was nine or ten. Although he would only talk about it dismissively, his older sister told me that the family came with no possessions and no money. They lived for years by the side of the Rio Grande—the first few months in a dugout. His father and he kept the family fed by fishing and trapping in and around its waters. Then one of the river's infrequent floods made finding new accommodations necessary.

There was a legend, perhaps apocryphal, that seemed to drape across his shoulders and broaden them in the minds of all who knew him. It was that the family was forced to flee from their home in Mexico because Artie had killed a cop who was trying to rape his big sister—hacked him to death with his father's machete. I somehow knew never to ask about it. What would I have done in his place?

Amid these memories and speculations, I finally drifted into a fitful slumber.

It felt like bare minutes later that a car pulled up behind the bunkhouse and wrenched me awake. I sat up, my back strongly protesting. As I yanked a clean T-shirt over my head, its brushing across my nose reminded me of yesterday's events. I had to hold a moment for the pain to temper. I finished dressing and stuffed my one tattered gray shoulder bag with the few clean clothes I had. I exited into the pitch of predawn, only that moment realizing that I'd actually decided to go the minute I'd seen that picture of Artie. Connors's acolyte had not even bothered to exit the car to come get me.

I felt vaguely shanghaied as we boarded the plane to Austin. "So, do you have a name, or do you just go by *Connors McClain's minion?*"

"My name is Trevor DeGrassi, Mr. Kazmareck. I'm Mr. McClain's personal assistant. I started law school a few years after the two of you graduated. I recognized his talent from the very beginning, worked on his campaign and then clerked for him the whole time he was district attorney for Travis County. I now serve him as attorney general and will when he becomes governor."

"Attached yourself to his rising star, huh?"

Nothing beyond a darkening in his eyes betrayed the prick my suggestion provoked. "What the present attorney general can and will do for the state of Texas, and eventually for this country, is something I think all of us should recognize. I have no idea what caused the rift in your relationship, Mr. Kazmareck. My supposition is that it has to do with your mutual friend, Artie Cavazos. But that my boss is the best hope for the future of this state and nation, I have no doubt."

It was no surprise that Connors McClain could inspire such loyalty. He had charisma that exploded from him like Fourth of July fireworks. But, as has happened so often in my life, I realized that I had underestimated this young man. He was not just bewitched by Connors's charms; he truly believed in him. And I could now sense a penetrating intelligence and ferocious sense of honor I had overlooked—probably as a result of my feelings toward his boss.

"Artie, he...he's alive?"

"It would appear so."

"I *saw* him. I saw him down."

"Did you?"

"I..."

I recognized now in his gentle smile not self-satisfaction but patience, a sense of understanding that startled me in one so young. "Sometimes what we think we see and what actually transpires are at considerable odds—especially in exigent circumstances.

"At any rate, Mr. Kazmareck, I suggest you save those questions for the attorney general. I only know what I've shown you. I know little of the past the three of you shared, what brought you together or what tore you apart. I'm just the messenger with no knowledge of the message's meaning."

And so we passed the rest of the short flight to Austin in silence, and I stared at the picture of my long-lost friend with a bizarre combination of wondrous hope and piercing dread. And, drifting into a delayed, troubled sleep, remembered...

# 2

"If we're gonna do this, we've got to get them across Wednesday night, Christmas Eve," Artie said in his usual wrought-iron undertone. As he continued, his voice dropped further. "That's when a big shipment from Chiapas is coming in." He cast a furtive glance at Connors. "Your sources across the river confirmed that, right?"

"Right."

"So my uncle's supposed to be there to help unload and distri—" He stopped himself short as a pool player crossed behind us to take a cue from the rack.

It seems a lifetime ago as I recall that fateful Christmas. Connors and I were home from our respective law schools for the holidays, and the three of us were sitting at Bob's, the Iturbide Club. Telltale sounds of racks obstreperously splintered, Mexican polka music beating a snare drum to submission, and the squeak of chalk on pool cues provided cover for our secret confab.

We had met there to firm up our plans to sneak Artie's Uncle Teo and his family across the Rio Grande and away from the drug cartel that had forced him to work for it. The viscous odors of beer, sweat, cheap cologne and cigarette smoke clung like ivy to every breath of air. It served as counterpoint to the ever-present sense of danger that made it so attractive to the young bucks we were then—or, in my case, were trying to be. There was always a brawl only a disrespectful word or lingering look away.

"Christmas Eve, huh? And I was so looking forward to Midnight Mass," Connors quipped. "How do we know once we get them here they'll be safe? The cartel has goons on this side of the border too."

"I've got an idea on where to send them. Best if you two don't know anything about it."

"What about you, Artie?" I asked. "They're bound to know his relatives over here. What're you gonna do?"

"You two guys worry about yourselves. You both'll be graduating from law school soon, and I want—"

"Yeah, well, Jakie's graduatin' in May. I may still be there when we're old and gray."

"Neither of you will graduate at all if we get caught. You're gonna be breaking some major federal laws helping me." Then he looked at both of us with a deadly seriousness that cast a chill over the table. "I wanna say again, I don't expect your help in this. I can do it by myself."

Connors was first to jump on that. "Of course we're going to help you, Artie. We're brothers. And neither of us is forgetting how you saved our *pellejos* on that canoe trip through Big Bend."

"Hey, you guys don't owe me anything for that. We all saved each other, anyway."

"Yeah, right," I scoffed. "If it had been just Connors and I, we wouldn't be here to help you at all."

Connors sat back expansively, extending his monstrous arms around the two of us. "That's right, *hermano*. We're in this together. Even if Mr. Grammar here says 'Connors and *I*' instead of 'Connors and *me*.'"

Artie quietly sighed. "I wish there was another way." He nodded at Connors. "I really appreciated your father getting them on the waiting list, but you know how long that can take. And my uncle's getting in deeper and deeper. None of the coyotes will touch anybody working for the cartels. They'd be dead before they hit the river. Most of them are working for some cartel nowadays, anyway. And they have all kinds of spies at the bridges. My uncle doesn't know the river, and I can't afford to leave the canoe sitting there for anybody to take while I go looking for them."

"Yeah, that's something I checked out," Connors confirmed. "This is the only way."

A brooding silence fell over the three of us. It seemed to carry across the pool hall, interrupted only by a few vacant tips and clicks of bank and soft shots. It was then suddenly shattered by the sharp crack of tight rack split open in big-bang ebullience.

Artie heaved another sigh. It was short and incisive like the air that jets from a tire stem when you release pressure. "I've always been grateful for the sanctuary this country's given my family. I always said I'd respect its laws."

"Artie," Connors said, placing a firm brotherly grip on his shoulder, "this is not your fault. This is family. This is a screwed-up world, and you do what you have to for family. There's no question that sometimes, to do what's right, you have to break the law."

Artie just let out a clipped "Yeah" of resignation. He then looked at the two of us again with a steady, commanding gaze. "All right, you guys. You promise me—*promise me*—that if anything goes wrong, if the cartel gets wind of this, or the Border Patrol, if there's *any shooting*, you guys blend into the cattails, and you stay facedown till the danger's passed."

A pause vacuumed the air out of our discussion. Connors and I glanced uneasily at each other. Artie leaned in and pulled our faces to him. "Hey, if you two guys don't swear, *right now*, that you're gonna hightail it at the first sign of trouble, I'm doing this on my own." Though he spoke in the plural, he gaze was fixed on me "¡En serio, vatos!" He paused slightly to make sure he had made an impression, something Artie could never fail to do if he tried. "Now, do I have your word?"

I was the first to nod my head, being the least adventurous. Then Connors followed with a quiet "Awright."

"OK. Let's get out to the river. My spidey sense is tingling here. I just remembered where I'd seen the guy who passed by us to get a stick. It was across the river. He had his own personal cue then. Yeah, he whipped ass too."

So, after stopping at Artie's place on a gravel road off Iturbide Street, we made the trip to reconnoiter the area he'd chosen for our rescue attempt. As we stumbled our way down the modest cliff to the bank of the river, fear and excitement battled within me for primacy.

The cacophony of crickets, frogs and rushing water snaked through the night air, awash in the pure and primeval. A waxing, three-quarter moon shimmered off the water, dreamlike and insouciant. Perhaps more out of reverence than caution, I almost whispered to our leader, "You sure this is where you want to cross, Artie? It looks awfully open."

"Follow me." We swished down a tiny trail in the tall grass and brush. I was aware that Artie knew that part of the Rio Grande down to its eddies and caprices. His family's first home, the dugout I'd mentioned earlier, must have been cut in a high bank much like this one.

"Hey, Artie," Connors teased, "isn't the mansion where you and your family spent your first few months around here somewhere?"

"We put it on the market in case you're interested. But I doubt you and Andie could afford it," he answered, making reference to Connors's then fiancée. "Now, look across, Jake. You see that area where the bank on the other side has a kind of hiccup?"

"Looks more like a burp to me," Connors offered.

"It seems like the bank kind of overlaps or something." I tried to see in the stark moonlight.

"It's not much more in the daytime—that's why I picked it. Since this area is so open, the Border Patrol tends to just check it every now and then. And if we send them on a rabbit trail way on the other side of the main bridges, they'll be short over here. What you're looking at is actually a tiny inlet, perfect for hiding the canoe.

"Why not just walk across, Artie? The river's not that deep," I suggested.

"'Cause it's not pleasant walking through a latrine," Connors said.

"Yeah, and all the really shallow parts are covered by *la migra*. Plus, it'll be way up by Wednesday. It's been raining like hell around here and snowing up north. They're already releasing water from the dams." Artie's tone darkened as he paused. What came out of him next seemed to ooze with tragedy. "Besides, the mud sucks you down like quicksand."

The change cast a pall over us and muted Connors and me. Artie quickly recovered, as though he'd revealed something he hadn't meant to. "Now, from here, that little cove doesn't look like anything at all. As far as I know, the BP isn't even aware of it."

He put his hands on my shoulders. "But Jake, you keep this in mind. When the river's up at all, it gets treacherous. And the reservoirs in Mexico are full to overflowing. Like I said, they've already started releasing water."

He pulled me to his side and drew a line in the air across the river with his other hand. "You need to follow this course across, from this willow straight across to the inlet. Make sure you're looking back to be certain of staying on that exact path. The river bottom is more even here. Outside this direct heading, there're sandbars and deep spots, and all hell breaks loose. I'll steer the way back. But if anything happens to me, follow the same course back."

A reverent silence ensued that Connors and I somehow knew to respect. It was peculiar, the way Artie felt, or better said, the feeling I got from Artie whenever we were at the river. There was something beyond the sense of kinship I assumed he felt from having lived on it—something deeply ambivalent. It was another thing I knew never to ask about.

"Yeah, this river gave me and my family life for a good while." He turned back to me with his arms on my shoulders, hands clasped behind my head. "But Jake, there's no kindness in it. Believe me, there's a...a...what was that word you used in English class? When we were talking about that poem? Uh, 'Turning and turning in the gyre...' Something like that.

"'The Second Coming.' William Butler Yeats."

"Yeah. What was the word you used? *Mal...mal...*"

"*Malevolence?*"

"*Malevolence.* I know this river...like an evil twin. So be careful. And follow this direct line, all right?"

"Yeah, yeah, OK." I was a bit taken aback by the gravity of his manner. "Uh...where's the canoe gonna be?"

Artie said nothing but just pulled a willow branch and some tall grass back to reveal an old, familiar buddy: that old aluminum canoe, still with its marks and dents from our earlier voyage down another part of the river, now painted black.

We all fell silent as the sight of that old tub inspired a reverential pause. It's extraordinary how a familiar object can teleport you back in time. Waves of nostalgia wrenched me slewing and jerking to our near-death adventure seven years ago in Big Bend National Park. Images of grandeur together with sensations of abject terror to jubilation rifled through me like an electric current. In that weather-beaten canoe was contained an ordeal that had bound us together in knots of brotherhood.

But rooting around the underbelly of those feelings, at least for me, there was a distant tremor. Something dark and discomfiting slithered through them. They sent a shudder to my body that registered in my companions. "Boy that brings back memories."

"Miracle it's still in one piece," Connors said. "That gonna hold Teo's whole family?"

"It'll have to. If not, I'll have to make a second pass across the river."

Connors and I said nothing, as the prospect of a second trip magnified the danger by a factor of a thousand.

We suddenly had to duck down in the tall grass and weeds as the headlights of an SUV screamed above us from the top of the bank. "Border Patrol?" I whispered. Artie just held up his hand to quiet me until the sound of the car faded into the cricket-frog-water rush symphony of night.

We slowly stood and took a breath. Then, Artie continued. "They usually make a pass around this time of night, though they try to vary it. On Christmas Eve they won't be as vigilant as they usually are." He turned to me. "As soon as they make their pass, you call in the tip to let them know there's a group coming over with coyotes on the other side of Zapata Bridge. Wait for the BP car to pass, or for them to take off if they've stopped, then cast off across the river. *And make sure you're following the direct line.* The river's a little narrower here, so it'll be quicker across, but that makes the current stronger, the water deeper, and the crosscurrents trickier, so follow *this exact path.* Hide the canoe in the inlet and just wait."

"You inspire me with confidence."

"Miren vatos, anytime you want out, you just tell me."

"I'm fine, Artie. I'm just kidding."

Connors jumped on the opening. "Yeah, as long as he doesn't have to shoot anything, he's good."

"Your contacts across the river gonna come through?" Artie asked Connors as we threaded our way back up the riverbank.

"I got someone to give the false tip, but my father's influence is dwarfed by the bottomless reservoir of cash and fear the cartel can throw around. We're better off depending on the element of surprise."

"Right. Just you and your people monitor the area from over there—*at a distance.* Three warning shots if there's trouble. Then disappear. Got it?

"Got it."

"Jake, you swear to me that if you hear those shots, you'll turn right around and head back to shore."

"Yeah, OK."

"Swear it."

"OK, OK, I swear."

"We don't have to actually delay the shipment from Chiapas. We just need the cartel to think there's a hitch."

A brooding silence overcame us as we walked the desolate quarter mile or so back to Connors's truck. Tree frogs, crickets and katydids dueled in the crisp night air, bleating and croaking in competition for a mate. The mustiness of the river verdure gradually gave place to the sterile sting of arid plain: dirt, dry mesquite and cactus. An idle wind made the faintest whisper now and again across leaf and branch.

Artie finally broke the spell. "Hopefully, the goons in charge of delivering the shipment will be celebrating *la Noche Buena* and be too drunk and coked up to notice."

"Right," Connors answered.

Something about the uncharacteristic terseness of Connors's reply sent a wave of dread through me, and I shuddered.

"You cold?" Artie asked. But I felt like he knew it was a tremble of apprehension.

"A little."

After a few moments of walking in silence, he quietly asked, "How's Grace?" The subject of my little sister was always a touchy one for my two companions. It never seemed to stop slightly rankling, like an old cactus thorn you never were able to remove that last tiny bit of. A hypersensitive soul with an artist's temperament, Gracie was the butt of ceaseless ridicule in school. In particular, there was a group of studs that called themselves "the gods" that always had her in their sights.

I think Artie had been the first to realize that her treatment had been shameful—cruel, in fact, as kids can often be with someone deemed *different*. I suppose that was why he had the courage to ask. At the mention of her name, Connors slammed shut like a mussel. He drifted off ahead and out of earshot. I could not look at either one of them when the topic turned to my little sister.

"Okay, I guess. About as well as can be expected, anyway."

We walked a few more minutes in silence. "Is she playing?" Only Artie would have gone this far. He was the one of the group who usually limited himself to an occasional uncomfortable laugh at the remarks of the others, chiefly Connors.

"For family, for friends."

And so we walked, pondering the danger of our undertaking, and trying to overcome the uneasiness the mention of my sister had created. "Jake," Artie continued, and by the hushed way he began, I knew the bleeding topic he was about to address, "have you seen Dolores?"

Connors walked ahead, trying to absent himself from a subject that stabbed like a board of nails in your foot.

"Just before heading down here," I answered without looking up.

"Did she say anything?"

"No."

# 3

The canoe trip in Big Bend National Park we'd mentioned took place several years earlier, immediately following our graduation from high school. And despite Artie's inherent modesty, I most certainly would not be here to recount this story if not for him. We were three young bucks, without a scintilla of doubt about our immortality, brash, bold and eager to prove ourselves—as hormone-poisoned adolescents tend to be.

Anabel and Andie, respectively Artie's and Connors's girlfriends, would drive us up to our embarkation point. That was just downriver from El Mulato, a small village on the Mexican side of the river.

Flowing out the tail end of Colorado Canyon, the river there cuts a path through the last rusty red escarpments of brash igneous rock. Their iron-tinged wonder is adorned with the dirty-snow-colored formations of welded tuff, ancient volcanic ash heated, compressed over millennia and then weathered into pockmarked shapes only Mother Nature could confect.

The cliffs then surrender to a broad plain of lacy feminine willows, arching lime-green cottonwoods, cattails and bulrush that winds its way a fair hike above the Santa Elena Canyon. The river then meanders past the tiny settlement of Lajitas on the Texas side just outside the park's boundaries.

We had chosen this entry point so that we could avoid the hassle and expense of coming in through the national park. Nothing so tame and conventional for these three intrepid pioneers, no, sir! We also knew that firearms were verboten in the country's national parks, and we had no intention of making the trip unarmed. The women would pick us up at the tiny settlement of Santa Elena in three days' time.

Connors and I had had grand illusions of canoeing the whole park, putting in at Manuel Ojinaga above the Colorado. But fortunately, Artie quickly dismissed such overweening hubris. We took plenty of fishing gear and a rifle hermetically sealed in plastic wrap, plus all the braggadocio and steaming cockiness of testosterone-envenomed teenagers.

Explaining my stag presence on the car trip up involves touching on a subject that would become a raw, aching pustule in the not-too-distant future. Dolores, my girlfriend at the time, couldn't join us. "I'm afraid to go, Jacob, to even ask." I could hear worry mixed with a dash curiosity in her voice. "Ever since my mother heard about it, she's been so...I don't know...it's hard to explain. It's like she's distant but kind of clinging at the same time. She wants to know everything I've done—at school, with you, with Gracie. But every time I bring up the trip, it seems to send her into a...like a *despair*. Maybe it's the fact that we'd have to go into Mexico with the way it's been getting lately, but...well, I just don't think I can go."

Sigrid Martínez, Dolores's mother, though always welcoming of Grace and me, had been exceedingly careful with her only child—tied to her with reeds that seemed to choke and smother. Would I had known then what I know now, looking back over the great expanses of south Texas and my life. But as it was, only the five of us made our way to the three musketeers' grand adventure.

As we started out, I thought I had exclusive information. "Hey guys, I got a report that Mexico released a ton of water from their dams upriver, so we'll have plenty of water to work with." We would drive north through west Texas to take in the mountains and then south to cross at Ojinaga before heading down to El Mulato.

"Yeah, I got that yesterday. That's why we're gonna be able to do the Santa Elena," Artie confirmed.

"I should've figured you'd know these things before I did." Artie just laughed, and Connors couldn't help but rub it in: "Yeah, you know Jake just informed me that the Vietnam War is over?"

"You boys behave yourselves," Andie admonished.

"Sí, pórtense bien, niños," Anabel added. Anabel struck me as the perfect match for Artie. She was originally from a small village outside of Culiacán, Sinaloa, on the Pacific coast of Mexico. Her entire family was killed when she was twelve. They had been small-time marijuana farmers and were ostensibly the victims of a family feud, although she claims it was just a case of a large producer eliminating competition. How she managed to escape was something she'd never shared. Too painful a subject, I imagine. From there she made her way by herself to the border and across, coming to live with an aunt in Aguagria.

She learned English from television and amazingly had none of the accent so prevalent on the border. And ironically enough, she'd served as interpreter for her aunt and family a short time after coming to live with them. She was rather tall and slender and had a self-assuredness that dovetailed perfectly with Artie's. I wondered if there weren't some German or Catalan in her ancestry, her skin pale and freckled. "I really wish you'd go through the park system so they can be on the lookout for you," she continued.

Connors question was a statement: "What would be the fun in that. Since Jakie and I are gonna be lawyers, we have to learn how to evade the law. I think that's one of the first things they teach you in law school."

Andie just shook her head and sighed. Andie was short, pert and full of energy with huge brown eyes and a rather booming voice. She was from a prominent Aguagria family but had none of the airs that often attend such a position.

The first leg of our hegira from Aguagria to Del Rio passed in the unremarkable sameness of mesquite, huisache and prickly pear. As far as the eye could see, dull flatness was rarely interrupted by a gradual rise that faded once again into dusty subservience.

Then we crossed Lake Amistad, liquid turquoise captured in striated, sand-colored cliffs. As we did, the gnarly eye-level brush of semiarid shrubbery yielded to the vast expanse of an even starker complexion. Suddenly, desiccant shrubs lowered and scattered in obeisance to the unflinching remains of shell and coral, silt and volcanic effluvia and the preciously meager moisture the heavens afforded. They were defiant survivors of the arrant hostility of juiceless heat and unyielding hardness, clinging to life through sheer will.

Incredibly, the muscular sky expanded to even greater reaches and stretched its glory to the limits of fancy. Here and there, it was patched with vacant puffs of cottony down that shed the occasional faint shadow on the land.

From horizon to horizon, sharp, tonsured mountains jutted skyward in dromedary peaks and buttes. Jutting chins of limestone proudly proclaimed their survival from ocean's retreat eons before. The blue mountain horizon at the seeming end of the earth ached of solitude—forlorn but mighty and majestic amid scrub brush and heartache. The air was painfully clear and hard as a diamond cut, sharp and mean and precious. Pollarded mesas stretched in the distance and were layered up to extending flatness, so noble, august and permanent.

We crossed the Pecos River, a shock of malachite green cut in ancient smooth limestone dusted up to blackened cuts of water's niellate stain. The solitary two-lane on which we traveled was occasionally hewn into mason-like sand-colored rock strata that yielded musky maroon highlights—errant iron blotches amid the dusty ocher stone.

We stopped at an overlook to gorge ourselves on the water's and this vast country's sublime grandeur, turning our faces into the virile west-Texas wind. It whispered a dirge of eternity through obliging mesquite leaves. The anhydrous sirocco whined of the ancient travails of pioneers and Indian raids and Spanish quests for gold—of the necessary savagery meeting savagery.

Whirling dust devils that so briefly danced and died were reborn, only to dissipate once again into the ether of memory. In their ephemeral but ever-imminent existence was contained the immanence of the Almighty.

"Oh my God, it's so...!" Anabel could find no word or phrase that might contain the grandness of what we were witnessing.

"That it is," was all I could manage. "That it is."

Even Connors was muted into reverence—but only momentarily, of course. "This looks like the ideal place for you, Jakie. Seems like you could go days around here without finding anything to shoot at."

"I could always shoot you."

"Boys, boys," Andie scolded.

And so in silence we absorbed nature's majesty.

We continued on our way, and as we approached the next town, I casually asked, "Anyone know how Langtry got its name?"

Connors was, of course, at the ready. "Everybody, take out your notebooks! It's time for a Jake Kazmareck history lesson."

"Except Connors. We all know knowledge is anathema to him."

"Is *what*?" Anabel demanded.

"And as a bonus, we get a vocabulary lesson."

Andie came to my rescue. "You could certainly use some lessons on both counts. How, Jake?"

"The infamous Judge Roy Bean. Lilly Langtry was his favorite actress/chanteuse. He named it after her. There's a museum here. Maybe we can stop on the way home."

"We planned on coming back through Mexico," Artie reminded us, "but if you guys want to come back this way, that's fine with me."

"No, no, I'd forgotten. Yeah, let's come back through Mexico. It's another part of the country, or another part of another country, I haven't seen."

Anabel had qualms about the idea. "I don't know, guys. Mexico's getting kinda dangerous these days." We were just on the cusp of the drug-cartel era.

"Not that part, not along the Big Bend." Artie's word was always so rare as to be taken for gospel. "We'll cross back at Ciudad Acuña."

We spent the rest of the trip reminiscing, with some verbal repartee between Connors and me and just commenting in wonder at nature's handiwork. We passed Dryden, Sanderson, veritable ghost towns, and, after a seemingly infinite stretch of desert solitude, Marathon.

Turning west into the Davis Mountains, striking in their stark beauty, we once again arrived at civilization in Alpine. At Marfa, we turned south, past the Cuesta del Burro, through the Chinati Mountains. On the way we passed more chalk-white mounds of welded tuff, the ancient memory of angry volcanoes now quieted to oblivion.

We saw the Mule's Ears formation in the distance, a pair of sharply curved rocks stretching heavenward, which the Mexicans call *Cuernos del Diablo*. "They look more like great-horned owls' ears to me," I suggested.

Connors, of course, couldn't resist. "Well, maybe you should make a formal petition for a name change, Jakie."

On our way to Presidio—such an uninviting name, Spanish for *prison*—Carousel Mountain rose as a brown nipple atop a squared platform of ancient rock. Then we passed another flattened toad-face formation sticking out its tongue from one smallish peak. In the distance lay Apache Canyon, where Indians primitively mined chert, limestone transformed to jasper, chalcedony and agate through prehistoric diagenesis into the raw material of their arrowheads, tools and jewelry. Finally reaching the border, we crossed into Mexico and were forced onto a dirt road as the only path leading to El Mulato. There, our adventure would begin.

In moments of quiet, the jagged open landscape, in its vastness the progenitor of contemplation, engendered in me thoughts of

Dolores and of the life we might share—of Grace, her best friend and my beloved baby sister, and the glorious music she was then still making. And in those days I still had hopes that I could somehow nurse her back into sharing her incredible gift with the world at large.

But buried beneath, under the soothing blanket of good friends, impossible plans for an impossibly successful future and this awaiting grand adventure, there was still a barely nettlesome burr, like a tiny pebble in one's shoe. It was a faint and troubling echo, the sound of a coyote's howl over unknown hills and plaintive: "Grace is a walking mistake." But it was far away and faint in those heady days. And I could then, with some mild effort, banish it from consciousness.

It shyly blended into the Sierra del Carmen Mountains in the western distance. They were cast in shadow by the setting sun, distant and amorphous in a cloud of blue to verbena dust and pensiveness.

Andie and Anabel would drop us off at the riverside just outside town. It was actually more of a tiny settlement of a few ramshackle huts and one dirt street we were fortunate enough to be able to travel over in Andie's four-by-four. As we passed, children playing in the dirt, some naked as the day they were born, stopped to gawk. I waved and called out "Hola." One little girl in a soiled muslin dress with raven hair dangling to the small of her back worked up the courage to lift a hand in tenuous salutation.

A wizened *anciano* in a donkey-driven cart stared as we passed. I could tell that from his perspective we might well be from the moon. We were strangers from a century yet to come—one of assumptions and concerns that might have bewildered him, of star travel and exotic modes of communication.

We unloaded all our gear at the river. The women would head back to Terlingua and stay in a motel for two nights. Then, the afternoon of the third day, they would pick us up at Santa Elena just across the border from Castolon.

"Where're you gonna to stay tonight?" Andie asked.

"Right here," Connors answered. "This is where Artie feels most comfortable. This is his *milieu*. I learned that word from Jake. You like that, *milieu*?"

"We're gonna be camping on the river anyway on the trip. No hay hoteles," Artie said.

"Right."

"What if you're not there when we come?" Anabel asked.

"If we're not there by sundown Monday, go back to Terlingua and come the next day."

"Ohhhkay..." was Anabel's uncertain reply.

"We'll be fine," Connors assured them both in his usual blustery manner. "No se preocupen. We'll see you in three days. We're 'the gods,' remember? Well, two of us are, anyway," he had to add, making reference to my tangential affiliation with the group.

I thought I'd begun to feel a certain coolness coming from Artie when Connors mentioned that elite clique at school. There was nothing overt, and no one else seemed to notice. Consequently, as I was still in my days of mordant self-doubt, I thought it might have been just my imagination. Now as I relate this story, I realize that the group that I was always just on the margins of was beginning to hold some vague discomfort for Artie. Even Connors seemed to be referring to it less. Perhaps the realization that the group would be dissolving now that we'd graduated, added to the fact that he would be nobody at the university next year, was beginning to temper his arrogance. Then again, maybe we were all just starting to grow up a little.

"If we're not there Tuesday, there's a river access ramp just a little past the mouth of the canyon. Look for us there," Artie noted.

"You really *assuage* our fears," Andie answered. "I learned that word from Jake. The irony, too."

A kiss and a hug, and they were off.

It was early June, and the blast-furnace heat seemed to curl the toes of your shoes. Artie had made sure we each had a broad-brimmed straw hat, and I'd brought enough sunscreen for the three of us. Before we set up camp, he told us to wet ourselves in the river. "As the water evaporates, it'll act as natural air-conditioning, absorbing heat from our bodies. And hydrate. Don't let yourselves get thirsty."

"Tú mandas, Mami," Connors quipped.

Beside a thick rush of tule, unjustly lush and virid among the competitors for river's moisture, we laid down our sleeping mats and built a small fire. As the sun set, we looked to the east over Texas. There the pastel pinks to purples of low-lying clouds embraced the sky, shedding their dancing colors on the Chisos Mountains. And those peaks' saddlebacks and stegosaurus saw-teeth glowed in the stippled majesty of dusk. Almost bald, they had a thin stubble of brush, like a day or two's growth of beard on the tanned, leathery skin of an old vaquero. As the sun set, they turned a dirty blue, and then maroonish purple as though cooling from the fire kiln of day.

As night fell, sudden, like the claws of a bear trap, their outlines traced the spilled diamond majesty of night. Venus gleamed moist and feminine, like a delicate bauble hanging from Cassiopeia's ear. The Saptarishi of the Great Bear ladled the unbearable mystery of darkness and the agony of knowing. The Seven Sisters pleaded patience, blushing to nonexistence at the effrontery of those who seek to ogle them directly. And the great hunter stood proud and certain and bold, his arrow poised to seek the prey of elusive divinity.

We ate an Olympian supper, adolescent appetites honed to bottomless pits by eagerness for the adventure that awaited us. As darkness enveloped us in its womb, the lullaby of the gently rushing river soothed every jangled nerve with its delicate riffle and purl. The rapture was only interrupted by the occasional stinging bite of a hungry horsefly—noisome reminders of Eden lost. Mosquito repellant is no match for these voracious insects, but as night absorbed the land in blackness and a muscular wind arose, deliverance descended in thunder-whispering calm.

Artie rolled a cigarette as he directed our attention north. There, sheets of lightning behind billowing gray-green clouds betokened a distant storm. It reminded me that, as a child, I thought it was called *sheep* lightning and wondered if that was for its white and woolly aspect. "Looks like rain upriver," he observed. "That might mean even more water and a stronger current. Let me finish this cigarette, and then we'll move up farther away from the river and pitch the tent. Rain might move this way."

"Artie, you worry too much," Connors protested, blissfully supine on his sleeping mat. "I'm too comfortable to move."

"I'm not worried, just prepared. Remember I lived on the river for more than a year. And it's tame around Aguagria. Tricky when it's up, but nothing compared to here."

"Oh, stop being a worrywart and roll me a cigarette."

Artie threw his tobacco and papers to him. "Be a good lesson for the trip if you learned to do something for yourself."

Connors reluctantly did so. Then the two lit up and inhaled the soothing nicotine from the nipple substitutes, lighting their faces as they drew. Each time one of their faces became visible, I wondered, could it have been he who uttered that hateful phrase about my sister Grace? Or he? If it were either, how could they remain my friends? Finally, Artie finished his coffin nail, rose and pulled our diminutive tent from the canoe.

"I'll give you a hand."

"Thanks, Jake. We need to rouse *el flojo* over there, too. Up, Connie."

"Now you know too many cooks…"

"Up. If we need to set it up on the trip in a hurry, we all need to be familiar with it."

With a protesting sigh, Connors acquiesced.

# 4

O f course, when we awoke the next morning to a perfectly dry campsite, Connors couldn't help but take advantage. "Boy, I'm sure glad we stayed in the tent last night. If not, I'm sure we woulda been just swept away by the deluge." It was still before dawn, and the darkness seemed to sharpen his mockery.

"We were lucky," Artie said without any sign of defensiveness. "You guys see how much the river's up?"

"Is it?" I asked. "I can't tell."

"Looks the same to me." Connors stood at the water's edge, letting Artie and me take down the tent.

"You see this stick?" Artie walked over to a healthy twig with its tip sticking out of the water. It was barely visible in the early-morning gloom. "I put it at the water's edge last night. It's up over a foot already, and the rain lasted most of the night, so that's probably just the beginning. Not to mention that it was raining in Mexico, which probably means they'll be releasing more water from their dams. That's gonna factor in when we hit rapids."

"Should we walk to Santa Elena?" Connors sniped as we stumbled around in the dark.

I banged my shin into the canoe. "Ah!"

"Careful, Gra…" Connors started but stopped himself before saying the name. There was an awkward silence as Artie and I continued breaking camp. I wondered if his hesitation was an acknowledgment of his mistreatment of my sister.

To break the tension, I followed up on Artie's observation. "What kind of rapids we talkin' about?"

"From what I hear, normally class two to three, maybe four or five in the Rockslide. If the river rises much more, we could be facing fives and sixes."

"*Rockslide*—that sounds ominous."

"In Mexico, it's known as *El Antro de Perdición*, the Room of Doom. Tons of fallen rock in the river. A good piece of the canyon wall just collapsed. The limestone's really brittle."

"Hey, you been on this trip before?" Connors asked.

"No, Connie. I just do my homework."

"You know, if you paid that much attention to your schoolwork, you might be going with us to the university."

"Then I'd have to still be putting up with you, Dios me salve. You'll have to content yourself with just annoying Jake up there."

"Oh, come on, you know you're gonna miss me. Who do you know as entertaining as I am?"

"That prickly pear you're standing next to," Connors started to answer, but Artie cut him off.

"Just help load the canoe, will you?"

As we started our adventure down the great river, we were serenaded by the eerie, creaking whistle of an eastern screech owl in the early gray of predawn. The sky, a sheet of pure pewter, was slowly parted by a blood-colored sun peeping shyly over the horizon. Then, as the morning warmed, the plaintive cooing of white-winged doves echoed languidly through the hills. A shock of scarlet on black announced the mischievous frolic of red-winged blackbirds in the bulrush, with a plunking two-note prelude to their hoarse, reedy trill.

With unparalleled grace, a great blue heron soundlessly took flight before us. A few expansive waves of its wings swept it forward in sumptuous elegance. We played chase with it a few times as it flew down the river a short distance to put space between us. Finally, it winged its way from the river and our unwelcome intrusion on its home. A belted kingfisher nervously tittered as he darted up the river above us, trolling the waters for sustenance. Then, all sound bowed before the aching, rusty screech of a red-tailed hawk, a primeval cry of mastery and timelessness.

On the river's banks, dull-green tamarisk trees, an invasive species and infamous water hog, competed for the river's moisture with delicate willows, ocotillo and purple-padded prickly pear. A startled covey of scaled quail took whistling flight from behind them through mesquite, paloverde and up the whiskered mountainsides. Aromas of willow and cottonwood, echoing life and freshness, were eventually subsumed by the dank, cloying odors of river and bulrush. Light and sound and smell were tender in the morning air, though they crackled with the promise of adventure.

Artie steered from the back, and I manned the second paddle up front. "King" Connors sat in the middle, his only contribution most of the first day an endless monologue on topics ranging from the meaning of life to why he parted his hair on the right rather than the left. In moments of quiet—when we could get him to shut up—the soothing cadence of the river hummed a tune of eternity, taking well-earned pride in its handiwork sculpting the mountains its artfully sinuous way.

It was shortly after dawn, the flaming copper of the sun's rise now slowly melting into the virginal blue of a pristine west-Texas sky. After an hour or two's leisurely journey, an authoritative instruction came from Artie: "You guys remember to hydrate."

"*Migrate?* What do we look like, whooping cranes?" Connors smart-assed as he reached for his water bottle. Then he added as an afterthought, "Or unemployed Mexicans?"

I looked around to see a patient half-smile on Artie's face as I took a drink myself.

"Rapids coming up," he alerted us. "Doesn't look like much. Let's steer to the right where it's calmer and keep ourselves off rocks as much as possible. If we hit anything big, look for a triangle that's made between rocks—that's the safest passage."

In his best southern-drawl falsetto, Connors lilted, "Ohhh, you big strong boys do make a lady feel safe!"

We made it through our first rather modest rapids with only a few bumps and jostles, and then through a second later in the morning that was even gentler than the first. "My, my, this terrible white water is enough to scare a lady to death!"

Shortly after, we slid through a graceful bend in the river. And then before us, the placid waters seemed of a sudden to be swallowed by monstrous castle walls, great monoliths of primordial limestone scraping the sapphirine sky. They were black in shadow, with a thin band of the water's chalky stain at river's edge. The palisades thrust upward to heights of Olympian myth and rendered the three of us spellbound. They were mighty, towering and immovable, cut by millennial water's ceaseless ablation. The huge faces of rock rose and closed us in like a giant womb. "My God!" was all I could murmur.

Connors, of course, was at the ready. "That's one of your more articulate descriptions, Jakie." But even his sarcasm was spoken in hushed tones of reverence.

As we were swallowed into the walls of water's ancient chisel work, even he was finally hushed. That patient, laborious river had succeeded over millennia in wearing through the mighty mountains that had thought themselves impervious. In turn, the hearty limestone had had a hand in determining the river's course, yielding at selected points to bend it to its will. Those stone parapets stretched to the porches of heaven. They spoke in the hallowed bass baritone of the infinite and eternal.

The majesty of what we beheld aroused—in me, at least—a hunger for the everlasting, these very walls' immutability. And I marveled at the feeling. Perhaps it was the timelessness of their formation, each layer of shell and sand and coral pressed under the sea's primordial weight. This was then followed by the ocean's molasses-in-January retreat and finally, over millennia, the sedimentary's painstaking wear by the river's patient sculpture. Or maybe it was the impenetrability of their substance, standing tall and straight in fearsome pride, an azure strip of heaven peaking down from between their summits.

All, all—far beyond any sacred ceremony or preacher's exhortation—placed me in the terrible yet gently cupped hands of the Almighty. I felt an impulse to kneel in gratitude for this opportunity to witness the magnificence of His craft. For the joyous wonder of life seemed to grow straight out of these walls' surfaces. From the parapets' dizzying heights to water's edge, prickly pear flourished. And alongside sprouted hardy lechuguilla, called shin-daggers for the penetrating thorns at the ends of their leaves. False agave, dense masses of candelilla and scores of plants more clung to life and thrived in spite of the rocks' seemingly soilless integument. In all directions, sometimes jutting horizontally, they endured, undefeated by nature's dearth.

We forged ahead, eyes agape in wonder. Another hour or two and a couple of dicier rapids later, the sun finally crept into view between those immense partitions of stone. With it, the canyon walls came alive with the shades of primeval history: burnt yellow and dried-blood maroon, with bat droppings a triangular black outlining the ashen blemishes at river's edge.

The only sounds were the river's rolling rondelet and the titter-squeak of colorful cliff swallows echoing between the canyon walls. They flitted from mud nests plastered under ledges that jutted out from the crevasse's flanks. Once airborne, they darted and danced in the air above us, seeking insect meals to feed their young. Then they would deftly slip into their earthen homes like the bird in a cuckoo clock.

High above the cliffs, vultures circled on updrafts that gently rocked them side to side. They were graceful, obtuse Ws against the azure majesty above, gliding on updrafts and wind's caprices.

As the descending whistle of a canyon wren ended in its grating gargle, a pair of white-throated swifts skimmed the waters before us. We spent our time mostly in silence, devouring the magnificence of nature's grace. Of course, our reverie was frequently interrupted by Connors's bombastic, but, I must admit, entertaining disquisitions on what we beheld. I suppose I should have been grateful that it was a topic other than himself.

We stopped for lunch, munching on trail mix, cereal bars and some jerky Artie had personally dried and salted. He also plucked the leaves from a mesquite tree and boiled them into a spinach-like concoction. "Gotta eat your greens."

As usual, Connors had the smart reply: "Sí, Mami."

We continued on, Connors and I switching places. As we made our way farther into the canyon, the bits of dark brooding igneous rock amid the dominant sedimentary gradually faded into oblivion. When the sun once again hit the limestone walls, they came alive in neatly chiseled strata of coarse ocher. The river, in the open flood-plain we'd left behind reflecting the bordering greenery, now took on the mud-brown tint of its natural color.

Artie finally spoke: "Water's still rising."

"How can you tell, Artie?" I asked.

"Look at the cliff-sides at the water's edge. Remember the whitish water stains? They're gone, completely submerged."

Connors did his best horror-movie impression, creepy as the haunting wail of the common loon: "Oooooh, I feel it riiisin' all around me! What is it? What could it be? It's alive! It's alive! It's aliiiiive!" And his mockery darted to and fro between the canyon walls.

As I look back on it now, I realize that this was Connors's way of dealing with the competing emotions that worked to chip away at teenage egomania. First, there was awe at the timelessness of nature's artistry. It seemed to shrink one's sense of self-importance—if that were possible for Connors. At the same time, there was stress produced by the rising waters and our growing sense of isolation. And I do believe now that, of the three of us, he was the most unnerved by Artie's warnings. But given his basic personality and, of course, the unfailing bravado of testosterone-tainted male adolescence, all had to be buried under the cloak of braggadocio.

He was the de facto and de jure leader of "the gods" in our school, the group that had in its sights for ceaseless ridicule the academics, the nonconfrontational, the unathletic. It was the typical band of young toughs and wannabes who bragged of sexual exploits exaggerated to the point of caricature, fistfights that would leave a normal person quadriplegic and bouts with the bottle that would make Sir John Falstaff blush. My one ticket to the group's penumbra was my athletic ability, though it was always undermined by a potent lack of self-confidence—a trait Connors took full advantage of.

From the vantage point of history, I can now see that that need to demean those high achievers was born of the insecurity that most children seem to suffer: the need to belong and the desperate need to deny it. I was Connors's only available target when it was just the three of us. And the need to emphasize my unworthiness grew as well from his displacement as top dog whenever we were away from his sycophantic clique.

I believed then that the only reason he kept company with me was that Artie insisted I come along. His resistance, however, had seemed to be softening somewhat in our senior year. Though he continued to tease me, there wasn't quite the viciousness there had been in the past. Perhaps he was just growing up? Or was it some change in me? Might I—perish the thought—be developing a thicker skin?

I wondered if it might be Artie's influence. Two years older than Connors and I and in our class because he'd started late, he was our unquestioned leader when the three of us were by ourselves. Looking back on it now, I realize that Connors, in moments not crucial, always tried to assert himself. When push came to shove, however, it was Artie who took command.

But it was not age that made Artie so. Rather, it was a quiet confidence and superior knowledge of all things survivalist. Though he could drink with the best of them, he seldom had the adolescents' need to ballyhoo it. And he never had to fight once he came to Saint James, because of the reputation of his fists and an aura of indomitable toughness.

Perhaps it was that self-assuredness that explained why he rarely partook in youth's seemingly insatiable need to tear down others in order to build oneself up. I say rarely, not never. But he seemed to forsake it at an earlier age.

At least to me, there was always something mysterious about Artie. There seemed to be a small, or better said, distant ache in him. I wonder if his experience of being homeless might have afforded him some empathy for those on the margins of society. Or perhaps the legend concerning his family's flight from Mexico was true. I knew better than to pry into the private life of Artie Cavazos.

"Is the river coming up that fast?" I asked with some uneasiness.

"It's rising pretty quick. I'd say it's running above seven thousand cubic feet per second. To give you guys an idea, flood stage is about eight thousand CFS." When we came to a rocky in-swell on the river, he gave the order. "Let's pull over to that shoal on the right. I want to do some scouting downstream. You guys can dig through our provisions till I get back. It's getting on to time for supper. This'll be a good place to camp."

"What's on the menu, garçon?" Connors asked.

"That's you guys' job," he tossed over his shoulder as he headed downstream.

"Hey, I thought we were gonna have our meals catered!" Ignored by Artie, the tall one turned to me. "All right, Julia Child, break out the fine china and crystal. I expect a gourmet meal."

During our ample dinner of *aguacate*, potatoes we baked in the coals and three of the steaks we'd brought, I was reminded of the river's rise when our canoe was almost taken by the current. Luckily, I saw it before it had gotten far.

"Now you see what I mean about the river rising?"

"Yeah. I'm starting to pay more attention. Think I'm getting a handle on it."

"He's such an obedient, attentive child," Connors teased as he stuffed his mouth with the last of his potato.

Ignoring him, I continued with Artie, "What'd you find downstream?"

"Not much, but look up."

Connors and I lifted our heads to see billowing cumulous clouds. "Oh, you've gotta be kiddin'!" Connors exclaimed. "We're in the desert, for God's sakes! It can't rain two days in a row!"

"The one sure thing about the desert is that it's full of surprises. You know that, Connie."

"Yeah, I know that."

As dusk quietly settled over the canyon, Artie hushed us when we heard a rustling in the brush upriver. Moving in catlike quietness, he raised the rifle he had recently taken from its plastic wrapping. The shot reported through the ravine like a series of small explosions. A small juvenile jabalina was the prize, and I slathered on the bug repellant to avoid the nasty bite of the fleas this species invariably carries. I quickly gutted, skinned and butchered it and then set our kill to marinate in the smoke of mesquite wood. "Well, we won't lack for meat on this journey."

# 5

As we continued our expedition the next morning, the river's soothing rush set my mind adrift. I wondered about the friendship between my two companions. Connors had apparently known Artie for some time before the latter came to Saint James. He'd been an outdoorsman from the time he was a child, exploring the river and what, for some reason, we called Vajalio Indio. That first word must have been Tex-Mex as I'd never seen it in any Spanish dictionary. It was a shallow arroyo that as kids we thought the Grand Canyon. It girded the normally dry Pollito Creek bed. On rare occasions when it was kind enough to rain, it served as a pitiful tributary to the lower Rio Grande.

I'd recently learned that they had met there, on the river, shortly after Artie's family's flight from Mexico. A few years later, Artie's father was caught and deported. Once back in his village, he disappeared from the face of the earth. According to Artie's uncle Teo, the police had taken their revenge. That gave credence to the legend. So Artie, his mother and sister went to live for a time in the two-room cabana behind the McClain family home.

Now I understood the fierce bond between them. I suppose the contrast in their personalities worked for them as well. Artie had a taciturnity that ached to me of some distant trauma. Connors, on the other hand, was full of grandiloquent self-promotion, feats of conquest and audacious derring-do—at least in his own telling. I had not yet reached a level of sophistication to realize that it served as compensation for some worm of self-doubt in him.

"You wanna try steering for a while, Jake?" Artie asked. For some reason it didn't surprise me that he asked me rather than Connors.

Connors, of course, had to make the compulsory crack. "What, you want to get us killed?"

"Yeah, OK. Maybe I can arrange for at least one of us to get killed."

"You stay up front, Connie. I can use a break." I doubted seriously that he was really tired. It was rather an opportunity to give the two of us some experience and for him to appreciate at leisure the grandeur that surrounded us.

"Hmph, out front fully exposed with Jakie drivin', and *I'm* the one who'll get broken."

"A benefit to all mankind," I answered.

As if our banter was just background noise, Artie continued with his instructions. "If anything big comes up, I'll take over. Just remember to paddle deep into the water, and if you need to make a quick turn, Jake, backward and deep on the side you want to go to."

"Got it."

"And remember the triangle formed by the water between rocks in rapids."

We continued on through calm waters but a seemingly ever stronger current. Clouds in the narrow slit between the canyon walls billowed and passed, billowed and passed. I steered us through another moderate rapid with Artie's patient—and sometimes slightly impatient—instruction.

We passed a jabalina sow and her litter on one of the infrequent banks we passed. She took umbrage at our presence and skittered away with her brood up a ravine. On another, we encountered a gathering of cattle amid paloverdes, thick clumps of candelilla and a tree with leaves that looked like miniature tobacco.

The waters calmed. I could feel a breeze of serenity pass through the three of us. Even Connors's discourses tempered to digestible

commentaries. I was rather captivated by Artie's reaction to what surrounded us. This was the first time I could remember seeing him so
enraptured. He seemed transported to another dimension, mesmerized by the beauty. But still, through the rapture, I could feel that distant ache in him. There were times he seemed a thousand miles away.

Our attention so distracted, no one noticed the murmur in the
distance that grew as we approached. It was at first a low, aching moan
barely noticeable beneath Connors's bombast, the natural hum of
the river and the titter and squeak of cliff swallows. Ever so slowly, it
managed to shake us to consciousness.

But not soon enough.

We pulled around a sharp bend, and there the giant roar drowned
out all other sound. "Man, that sounds scary." I doubt I was even
heard beneath the clamor.

"Pull over, Jake. Pull over." Artie was finally pulled out of his
rapture. Before us as we rounded the bend, water crashed and spat
in white waves against huge masses of ponderous stone. Some were
rounded and impenetrable, others sharp and flat and pointed, all
massive and stridently proclaiming, *You shall not pass!*

"Which side?" I screamed at the top of my lungs.

"Any side! Just pull over!" Though he turned and yelled for all he
was worth, I could barely hear him above the thundering bray.

I judged that the Mexican side was our safest bet and dug backward into the now-raging waters to steer us to the scant piece of sand
and rock.

Connors, however, had not heard Artie's directive over the roar.
"What the hell are you doing, Jake!" He could barely be heard as we
entered the turgid waters of the infamous Rockslide. In confusion,
he pushed off an exposed rock with his paddle to lead us back toward
a mass of boulders and white water splashing murderously high.

"No, Connie!" Artie screamed just above the thunder of the waters. But our working against each other sent the canoe widthwise
into the first series of rapids. I managed to straighten us just enough
to avoid our smashing sideways into a huge sharp-edged piece of

cliff. The current, however, sloshed and teetered, spitting and whirling high above our heads with a deafening roar, spinning us fully around and banging us against the myriad underlying and above-surface rocks.

There were screamed directions as the jostling and pounding of the rapids' bluster concussed like cannons. Desperate and barely heard cries squeaked above the din as we fought to keep from being thrown from our craft. We then shot skyward over another towering fountain we were fortunate enough to hit with the back end of the canoe and so traverse lengthwise.

The rapids bellowed like a mile-wide tornado, slapping and caterwauling in fury. Artie had grabbed the paddle from me to try steering from the middle, but the current whirled and whipped with such ferocity that trying to direct our craft was now a vague supplication to God.

We spun once again a full 360 degrees and then back again, bounding and cascading over rock and white water, slamming against debris so forcefully that I wondered how in the world we weren't tossed from our vessel.

At the next collision, I was thrown like a weightless piece of Styrofoam out and ricocheted off a huge boulder, a blow I had just enough presence of mind to cushion with my hands and arms. Then I was mercifully tossed back into the canoe. The thundering drone and chaos were now all that could be heard as I fought from the vessel's belly to regain my seat.

Thoughts were fleeting, helter-skelter, prayers for deliverance and moment-to-moment flashes of groping for anchorage. In the midst of despair, we were providentially whirled back again to be slammed into and crudely lodged between a massive boulder on our right and a mostly submerged piece of water-honed scree on our left. The force of the impact sent Connors halfway over the side, and a panicked "Ayeeeee!" could be heard above the rapids' din. Only Artie's quick hands saved him from incurring on his body the punishment our canoe had suffered.

For a considerable time that seemed no more than a moment, the three of us, even Artie, just sat in a state of shock. The waters bellowed and cursed all around us. We sat. We gripped the sides of the canoe with white-knuckled fists. Our eyes bulged outward doubting that we were still alive. Perhaps we'd been launched into some twilight zone of postmortem calm. I shook so mightily that I was afraid I might loosen the canoe from its mooring. No word was said. No glance was exchanged. We were trembling, hard-breathing statues.

After what seemed an eternity, Artie at last came to life. He turned to look at me and then turned back to Connors. "Is everybody all right?" he yelled above the blustering howl.

As he turned back to me, I exhaled in a monotone, "I'm-m…I'm awright."

"Connie…?"

Connors turned his face, the color of the chalky residue at river's edge. "I think I'm ready to go home now."

I was amazed at Connors's ability to find his sense of humor at this moment, and his comment wrested a reluctant half-smile from my face. Artie was engaged in figuring how we could extract ourselves from this monumental obstacle.

We had taken on a good bit of water, and many of our supplies raced downstream in the torrent. We were now an immovable object subject to the almost-irresistible force of the river's current. Connors had lost his paddle in the chaos and sat gripping the sides of the craft, trying to steady himself.

"Jake, can you manage to get out onto that rock on the left?" Artie finally asked.

"Uh…yeah, I think so."

"OK, one foot at a time, and make sure—absolutely *certain*—that you're out of the current before you put any weight down. Even a couple of inches could sweep you right off your feet."

"If anybody can sweep me off my feet, it's Jakie," Connors quipped. I think I'd been right about his use of humor to cover fear, as he was violently trembling despite the irony.

"OK, Jake," Artie directed, "one foot on the rock first and holding on to the canoe. Then the other."

I carefully followed his instructions and made my deliberate way onto the rock. Before he followed me, Artie quickly doffed his life jacket and shirt and tied the sleeve of the latter to the rearmost cross-bar of the canoe. "Give me your shirt, Connie," he ordered as in one swift motion he put on and reattached his life jacket.

"You always expect the shirt off my back."

"What're you doing, Artie?" I asked.

"When and if we pull the canoe loose, it'll give us something to hang on to, to keep it from being taken by the current. If it holds, that is."

"We lost the rope?"

Artie didn't even bother to answer. It was among the debris speeding downriver. He then tied Connors's shirt to his and ginger-ly stepped onto the rock next to me. Connors followed only after Artie's directive: "Life jacket first." There was, by the grace of God, just enough room for the three of us. Just then, of all things, a pow-erful wind kicked up, and it began to pour down rain. Artie could just reach the back edge of the canoe from his place on the rock and handed the shirt-rope he'd fashioned to Connors and me.

Owing to the ballast we'd lost in the form of many of our sup-plies and despite the water it had taken on, the canoe was lighter than it had been. Consequently, we were surprised at being able to dislodge it on our first good tug. We had not accurately judged the force of the current, however, and it pulled the boat with such herculean might that Artie immediately lost his grip—fortunately, I assume, because otherwise it would have pulled him straight into the raging waters.

Connors, however, was yanked into a teetering position on our rock perch, which he announced with a piercing cry. On bare in-stinct, I caught his outstretched right hand and yanked us back to collapse and cling for dear life to the rock. Unfortunately in order to do so, I had to let go of the shirt-connection to our canoe. It flew away, banging between huge boulders, and soared and flipped over the raging white water downriver and away from us.

"The canoe!" I screamed and started in its direction.

"No, Jake!" Artie grabbed me at the last minute before I went heedlessly after it.

"But what…?"

"It's not worth it. Not now."

The three of us sat on the rock, stunned to abject silence, staring at the escaping canoe. It bounded through rapids clunking against rock and twirling like a majorette's baton. Then it finally righted itself and glided effortlessly away on the river's powerful current. We sat for a moment in a stupor.

After what seemed like an eternity, I found my voice: "My God. What the hell do we do now?"

Artie took a deep breath and made a quick visual survey of the area. "That way." He pointed to our left around a large rock directly in front and a series of smaller ledges where the current was not so fierce. "Now are you glad we all wore life jackets? If we're lucky, we'll find the canoe downriver. If not…well then," he nodded faintly, staring down the river, "we've got a real adventure on our hands."

# 6

We reached the less treacherous left bank, made it beyond the rapids and proceeded down the river. The rain had suddenly stopped when we reached the edge of the canyon, and the thin strip of sky above us blazed again in blue pimpernel calm. The banks were in short measure completely swallowed by the sheerness of the cliffs, so that we had to swim or, rather, let the current sweep us along.

Slowly, the earlier adrenaline rush dissipated, and the relative calm allowed each of us to take stock of our situation. It cast a pall of gloom over us, or at least over me, all my adolescent swagger now vanished. But Artie's frequent instructions on safety while floating—feet facing downriver in case of rapids or shallowing waters—along with survival tips and directions on scouting for our equipment, kept my mind occupied.

As we went, we found, scattered here and there, a few of our quondam provisions. First we discovered a savior container of water caught in the branches of a willow leaning out over the bank. A while later, we came upon some fishing line that was not ours strewn through a mesquite tree. By the grace of God, it had an old rusty hook still attached. The tree also had some edible beans clinging to it. We harvested those and carefully unwound the plastic line.

We also found our rifle, or what was left of it, completely destroyed by its journey downriver. Now all we needed was a pole and something to use as bait. Any of the three of us could fashion something, but I imagined Artie would devise the most serviceable contrivance.

We continued on through the day, not even stopping for lunch, our anxiousness to reach our destination muting hunger pangs. As the afternoon progressed, a rare bank of earth here and there granted some distraction from the canyon walls' immensity. Birdsong and the rippling grace of the river were often the only sounds we heard as the precariousness of our situation muted us all. After a few more hours, we happened upon one of our sleeping pads caught between rocks that split the river in two.

"What the hell are we gonna use that for?" Connors protested against its rescue.

"You never know," Artie answered. "For one thing, it's buoyant. Might come in handy if one of us is injured."

"Well, if I have to rescue it, I get to sleep on it."

"We'll take turns. If we get out of the canyon in two days, we'll be lucky."

"Why don't we just climb up one of the side ravines?"

"'Cause we have no idea what's on the other side other than blistering desert. We have shade most of the time here, little danger of heatstroke and easier access to food sources."

"Know-it-all," Connors groused as he pulled the pad back to the bank.

Just at that moment, the sun, now low in the western sky over Mexico, glanced off a bend in the canyon before us. Despite my apprehension concerning our present state—and I'm not ashamed to admit I was pretty scared—I was entranced by the exploding colors that the sun's rays touched off on the canyon walls. A stately wine cerise at its base grew wide to a small band of delicate canary yellow at the cliff's peak. "God, that's beautiful."

Connors turned to us with a face that looked like he'd just eaten a handful of Aguagria dirt. "Only Jake would notice something like that at this point. If we can't eat it or drink it, I don't wanna hear about it, all right?"

"If worse comes to worst, we could eat you."

"Ohhh, I love it when you talk dirty."

"Come on," Artie broke us out of our repartee. "That bank on the left looks like a good place to camp. It's got trees and grass. Keep your eyes open for insects and isolated pools of water along the banks where there's no current. There're three varieties of catfish in these waters and a bunch of other edible ones. The best bait'll be frogs, if we can find any. I'll dig for worms, but we can use anything that wiggles or flutters, anything that's alive."

"Guess that excludes harvesting a piece of Connors's brain."

"Maybe Jakie'd contribute the tip of one of his toes. I bet the catfish'd really go for that—nice and stinky."

"Or maybe the tip of something of yours. You're not circumcised, are you—yet?"

When we made it to the bank, we knew we only had an hour or so of light left, so we immediately went to work. Artie cut a branch from a likely willow at the waterside to use as a fishing pole. He expertly notched one end to hold the fishing line in place, and within a few minutes, we were ready to catch our supper. I caught a beetle and a tiny lizard and wondered where I might keep them.

"Improvise," Artie answered as he cut leaves from an endemic sotol plant. We all carried a good-size hunting knife on our adventures.

"What're you doing?" The sotol leaves didn't look particularly appetizing.

"You'll see in a minute. Use the lizard for bait. Let Connors fish while you look for more insects and frogs." Connors was a fisherman with considerable experience. I was the expert at scaling, gutting and cleaning—or skinning in the case of catfish. "See if you can find some flint too."

"I don't remember what flint looks like."

"It's usually embedded in the limestone, but it's harder and usually darker and looks glassy, or kinda waxy. You got your knife?"

"I had it in my bag."

"Connors, lend Jake your knife!"

Connors lifted his pant leg, pulled his knife from its scabbard and threw it to me. He stood at a pool of almost-standing water created by a back curve in the river. "The blade and end are steel," Artie continued. "Hit it against any likely rocks you find. If you get a spark, it's flint. You gotta be patient, though."

I searched and searched. I tried every combination of rocks I could find, but not one would produce a spark. I finally found a piece of marly-looking stone that had the hard, cloudy aspect Artie had mentioned. I struck the blade against the rock. Nothing. I tried again and again. By this time, hunger and exhaustion exacerbated by incipient panic had gnawed my nerves raw. "Aw, come on, come *on!* Spark, dammit!"

"There you go, Jakie. Yell at it. That ought to make it work."

"Looks like I'm having about as much success as you are catching our dinner." There was now an incisive edge to our banter as the afternoon took on the trappings of evening. Connors started to make another smart remark but then just turned in silence. I could sense that for both of us desperation was oozing in with the approaching darkness.

I caught a dragonfly and another beetle and then fortunately discovered a plastic bag caught in reeds at the river's edge. I kept the pieces of milky, hard mineral and guarded a few of them in my pockets. The largest piece I had to just carry in my hand. This was just in case the problem was not the material but my technique.

Finally, I came upon a pool of stagnant water, and tiny kerplunks betokened the presence of frogs. I silently placed the rock on the ground and turned myself into a statue, trying to see if there weren't some I hadn't chased into hiding. *There* were the tiny amphibians, just a few on the far side of the little pool. I spied out a silent path toward my prey—one step and freeze and then another and another. A few more of the tiny morsels dove into the slime-green pool. But I was there. So, with a swift motion I plunged my hand down and caught two of the oozy creatures, together with a gob of muck and miry green algae.

Success! I was a wily, intrepid hunter! I had captured the sought-after prey! I put one in my plastic bag with a bit of water, and the other I took to Connors, who immediately pulled in his line and baited it with the wiggling, slippery insectivore. He seemed to be gearing up for another smart remark but then hesitated and turned away. A gradual transformation seemed to come over him. "Thanks, Jake. I wasn't havin' much luck with the lizard."

I was caught a little off guard, trying to decipher whether this was sincere or simply a ruse to entice me into a greater taunt. I tested the waters: "I've got another one when you need it."

He turned around and looked me in the eye. *Here it comes*, I thought. "That's great, Jake. Thanks."

I made my way toward Artie in wonder at the miracles adversity can produce. I noticed that there were also tons of ants scurrying through the sand. "Artie, you want me to catch these little ants?"

"Catch every living thing you can find, short of bobcats and mountain lions."

"I was afraid you'd say that." Luckily in my vagaries on the bank, I had found a small plastic flask buried in the dirt and used it to capture the ants, which I then transferred to the plastic bag. The only problem was they seemed to take offense at being trapped and were very artful at escaping, finding the hand that had trapped them an apt target for their burning sting. I quickly learned to stomp them dead before collecting them. "Artie, how in the hell can we use ants for bait?"

"That's not what they're for," he said as he turned around with an object he'd made out of the leaves of the sotol plant. They were woven into what looked like the backing for a piece of wicker furniture.

"What the heck is that for?"

"I'll show you. Take me to where you found the frogs."

"How'd you know—? Never mind." We made the short trek to the stagnant pool. He silently motioned me in a wide berth around to the other side as he carefully approached the slightly oversize mud puddle. He then quickly slid his contraption down into what was the pool's bottom and snapped it up, and in and jumping out of it were more tiny frogs and some minnows. I managed to grab a few of the escapees and put them in my bag.

"Man, that's ingenious."

"You learn a few tricks living on the river."

Just at that moment came an ebullient expression of triumph and relief from Connors: "Got one! Got one! It's a flathead!" He then put on his deific voice: "I have, out of my mighty hand, brought us sustenance!"

"That's great, Connie," Artie encouraged. "We've got more and better bait too." We made our way over to him and provided him with another tiny frog, which he immediately hooked and plunged back into the water.

A flathead catfish: great eating, but only when cooked! Consequently, my search for flint was now even more urgent. "Artie, it's almost dark, and these are the only pieces I could find that resemble what you described."

He took the one that was fairly sizable and hit it with considerable force against a large piece of outcropping. It broke into three pieces, the insides of which had the same waxy, glazed appearance. "You got it. Keep these pieces in your pockets."

"But I couldn't get a spark to save my life."

"It's really hard with a blade. You have to be really patient and hit it just right." He unsheathed his own knife and pulled out a rounded file from one side. "It's easier with something rough like this." With the second strike, a tiny spark emerged, more visible because of the increasing darkness. "I've got a pile of tinder up where I made the sieve. Come on. On our way, be looking for the tiniest dry twigs you can find. I've got a good supply of *leña* ready to go." As he led the way back, we scavenged for kindling.

There was, fortunately, an abundance of dry, dead grass. It didn't seem to have rained at all on this part of the river. Of course everything in west Texas dries in a heartbeat. And there's a joke about the wind: it stopped blowing once, and all the chickens fell over. Artie made quick work of gathering the tinder into a neat pile. Time after time, he struck the piece of flint he'd chosen for the job, sending sparks down into the tiny mound he'd formed.

I cleaned and gutted the catfish, saving the entrails to use as bait or, if worse came to worst, for food. Back home, I'd use a pair of pliers to pull off the skin, but as tough as catfish skin is, I knew we'd need every scrap of nutrition it could provide.

As Artie worked on starting the fire, I grew more anxious with every failed effort. Finally, just as I was about to voice my concerns, he began to gently blow on the tinder. As he did, a wanton flame emerged from the piled grass. Quickly, he added more he had already mixed with the tiny twigs we'd accumulated. I sat back with a sigh of relief as the fire grew. Connors made his way to us in the growing darkness, another flathead on his line.

"How'd you guys get a fire going? I was hoping we wouldn't have to eat the fish raw." He handed me the second catfish he'd caught.

"Flint Jake found."

"Jake found it? Wonders never cease." I assumed the catch and the warmth of the fire had comforted Connors enough that he felt he could return to his teasing ways. Then he suddenly stopped stone-statue as if something had struck him. Both Artie and I braced for some terrible revelation. "Wait a minute." He reached into his pocket and pulled out the lighter he'd borrowed from Artie to light the cigarettes they'd smoked along the way.

"Oh my God." I sat back in consternation.

"That's all right," Artie reassured. "That lighter's been in his pocket in the water for hours. We don't know if it'll even work."

Connors struck the flint of the lighter, then again, then a third time and a fourth. Finally, after multiple failures, a faint spark emerged. After about three more tries, the butane finally ignited into a tiny flame. "All right," Artie cautioned, "now we have two ways to make a fire. It's always good to have a backup. We should figure out some way to keep it dry." Connors thought for a second and then slipped it in the band of my hat. I was the only one who hadn't lost his in the tumult.

"Good idea. But let's wrap it in a piece of the plastic bag and then stick it back in there. I'm glad you got the kind with strings and a slip-bead."

I'd made a spit out of the green limb of an acacia, and we roasted and ate our meager dinner. "Hey, Artie, if the ants weren't for bait, what are they for?" I asked as I lay back against a piece of driftwood, exhausted.

As he reclined to go to sleep himself, he just mumbled, "Insects are a good source of protein."

# 7

The next morning, we awoke ravenous and shared the half of the second catfish we'd saved for breakfast, along with some of the mesquite beans we'd harvested. I was surprised to find the beans rather sweet.

"That's why they call it a honey mesquite," Artie said. "I can remember my mother gathering them as they ripened and started to fall. She'd dry them in the sun and then grind them into a coarse flour and bake with it. They're kinda starchy too, so with the sugar, they ought to calm the hunger pangs, at least for a while."

"And here I thought of mesquite as just another pest like Jakie."

"I bet it's great for cooking with—just like you'd be if we ground you up, nice 'n' greasy."

A night's rest, the start of a new day and a bit of food in our stomachs had calmed the fears that had subtly changed the dynamics of our relationship. I was surprised to find myself rather relieved. The banter at my expense Connors used to deal with his own uneasiness seemed now to have a somewhat calming effect on me. It took my mind off the tenuousness of our situation.

As I think back on it now, I realize that we all have a tendency to choose what's familiar. Did I actually invite that kind of treatment?

Each of us took a swig of water from the water bottle, which was now about three-quarters empty. One-quarter full did not inspire me with optimism. "Can we drink the river water?"

"Not unless we have to," Artie cautioned. "Have to let it settle to get out as much of the sediment as possible and then boil it a good while. If we're really lucky, we might find some discarded screen we could use as a sieve, but that's *poco probable*. It'd have to be awfully fine, anyway." He carefully extracted the fishing line from the pole, hooked the hook through one belt loop at the back of my shorts and looped the line around his hand and slipped it into one of my back pockets.

We would fashion another pole at whatever site we found to camp for the night. There was an abundance of prickly pear, and we harvested some of its fruit, although we had to scrounge for ones that were ripe enough to eat. "What about the *nopalitos*?" I asked and then remembered the prickly pear's profusion in this area. "Well, I guess they're pretty ubiquitous around here."

Connors was at the ready. "Oh darn, a new vocabulary lesson and not a piece of paper or pen in sight."

I stowed the prickly-pear fruit away in the plastic bag along with the insects and frogs and tied it as tight as I could to one of my side belt loops. The frogs were still alive and kicked against my leg. I hoped they would last us through at least one more fishing session. Connors tied the water bottle securely to one of his belt loops with a bit of the extra fishing line, and we started down the river.

Artie gave us our marching orders. "The river looks pretty shallow here. You guys try to stay behind me and follow my lead. When we come to rapids, get to the side. We walk those." And so, we started to float and occasionally scrape our way down the river. "Be on the lookout for side ravines. There are tinajas in the Big Bend, so there's got to be fresh spring water coming from somewhere to feed them."

We made our way mostly in silence at first, with a few odd directions from Artie as we came upon some mild rapids or parts of fallen cliffside. As the sun crept over the Texas-side canyon wall, it shed a narrow band of light across the dark topping of the opposite palisade. Though our breakfast was meager, our minds were so focused on the task of survival that no one was struck with hunger for a considerable time.

I smiled at myself for the comfort that came with Connors's recuperation of his sense of humor, singing Creedence Clearwater Revival's "Proud Mary," as he slapped his hands on the water's surface. "Rollin', rollin', rollin' on the river!" The sound was magnified as it reverberated between the canyon walls. Artie didn't discourage him despite it being an extra expenditure of energy. I suppose he thought the release of stress might outweigh the need to conserve.

The cliff swallows continued their melodic twittering, and we disturbed a pair of drab Mexican ducks that squawked away in astonishment at these three unlikely beings floating through their habitat. I pointed out the dizzying acrobatics of a kite as it swooped and fluttered, dove and abruptly dashed upward in pursuit of cicadas and other insects it ate while still in flight.

"Unless you're gonna sprout wings and catch it for lunch, I'm not interested, Jakie."

Though it was mildly irritating, I continued to find comfort in Connors's renewed ribbing. It seemed to betoken a sense of calm coming over us as we floated down the muddy waterway—though the raw seedpods and mesquite leaves were not sitting particularly well on my stomach. We didn't stop to eat but only drink as the sun crossed over and disappeared behind the western wall, betokening afternoon hours. Our canteen was now empty.

After what seemed like several hours but was probably less, hunger and thirst began to breed a creeping anxiety in me. As time wore on, it metastasized into incipient panic. Connors's renewed silence augured ill as well, and a cloud of doom seemed to descend on us. I judged it to be mid to late afternoon, and the niggardly breakfast we'd eaten had long since been used up by our bodies. I was thin to emaciate in those days and, I only realized much later in life, hypogly-cemic. Consequently, as my blood sugar dropped to dangerously low levels, my panic and irritability increased exponentially.

A renewed sense of dread began to work through us as day aged into the long, acute-angled rays of late afternoon. I watched Artie scouring the still-towering ramparts for a ravine that might provide freshwater, hoping his eagle eye would ferret it out.

"Artie, I think we need to stop and eat some of the prickly-pear fruit and mesquite pods we have left. There's some moisture in them. Maybe find some barrel cactus. I'm dying of thirst." Then I added with a question that came out like an accusation, "The river water can't be that bad, can it?"

Quietly, Connors murmured, "Yeah, I second the motion."

"You guys hang on. We'll stop soon."

The time dragged on and on. I was lightheaded from hunger, driven to desperation by the aching emptiness that radiated through my body. My mouth was dry as coal ash, and I teetered on the edge of delirium. I remembered the lines from *The Rime of the Ancient Mariner,* and the irony filled me with rage: "Water, water everywhere nor e'er the ship did sink. Water, water everywhere nor any drop to drink." *Wait a minute, is that right? But why am I so in need of quoting it verbatim? Why can't I focus?*

My head sank lower and lower in temptation to reach down and slake my thirst with river water. Each time, like Caesar rejecting the emperor's garland, I would raise my head more reluctantly and, each time, less and less distance from the cooling flow. Then, just as my lips began to part to let in the tainted relief, we came around a bend to see a small gathering of horses on the Mexican side at the bottom of a ravine. As Artie spoke, I spat out the bare trickle that had made its way into my mouth.

"Let's stop here and see if there's freshwater anywhere. The hors-es are a good sign."

As we approached, I was struck by the presence of a cattle egret in all its snowy glory seated on the rump of a black dun a bit away from the water's edge. In my present state, nerves on point like a sea urchin, I wondered if I was hallucinating. The horses nervously eyed us coming toward them, snorting and shuffling, which caused the egret to take flight up the ravine. *Ah, it must be real*, I thought. The horses followed quickly after.

Somehow the hope of relief brought me back into some possession of myself. We trudged through gelatinous mud as we made our way up the bank toward dry land. The muck swallowed our legs almost up to our knees, and I had to rescue a shoe from the sludge.

When we were all safe on more solid ground, Artie stopped us. "You guys hear that?" I tried to listen over the twittering of the swallows and the now-gentle lullaby of the river. There was a faint trickle, but I wondered if I could yet trust my senses. "See the lime-green moss on the rocks up there? That's the sight and sound of spring water."

I marveled at the euphoria Artie's words kindled in me as we made our way up the large limestone outcroppings. There, like manna from heaven, was freshwater dripping down moss-covered boulders. I sucked up a tiny pool at its base as Connors placed his mouth beneath the fastest drip. Artie rescued the water bottle from Connors's waist and put it under another one. I then took out the plastic flask I'd found the night before, washed it out and set it under the faster stream once Connors sat back from it. We took turns greedily guzzling down each bare mouthful as it appeared in the cup.

"This'll get us out of the canyon if we're smart with it." Those words from Artie evoked such a sigh of relief from Connors and me that we both laughed out loud. It was the first time we'd done so since the Rockslide.

As he quickly fashioned another fishing pole, Artie began assigning tasks. "Connie, after the fish." He then began plucking the pods from a paloverde at the water's edge. "The water's fairly still here in the cove, so you should have some luck. Jake and I'll explore up the ravine and see what we can find."

"Those are edible too?" I asked as I pulled a couple of frogs from my bag and handed them to Connors.

"It's a good thing they're still green. Retama beans eventually get too hard to chew and digest."

"Huh, unlike the mesquite pods my stomach fought with all morning."

Connors slipped the hook neatly through one of the frogs and then asked in a bit of consternation, "What am I supposed to do with the other one?"

"Improvise," I tossed over my shoulder as Artie and I commenced our scavenging tour. Up the mountain crevasse we went, finding first a pool or small tinaja of freshwater, a cholla with edible buds we greedily harvested and some more fairly ripe prickly-pear fruit, called *tunas* in Spanish. "Hey, can't we just fill the receptacles here?"

"It'd probably be all right, but this isn't flowing. As long as we've got moving spring water, we'll stick to that. Keep your eyes peeled for something we can boil water in. We can eat the pods and buds raw if we have to, but they're a lot easier to digest if they're cooked."

We squeezed up through a tight hole in the limestone made by years of water's steady sculpture. Then we scurried up narrow ledges and into a cave we had to bend and then go on hands and knees to explore. We found an old tin piece of what might have been a mess kit. It was badly banged up and caked with dirt but usable. As the cave narrowed to become impassable, we made our way back.

As we crawled, something on the cave walls caught my eye. "Wow! Look at this." Ancient pictographs were barely visible as we approached the cave's entrance. "Man, I wonder about the Indian that painted these. I wonder how old they are. Prehistoric, I bet."

But Artie's eye was on something else as he exited the cavern. About twenty to thirty feet above us, sitting on a ledge, was a small flock of white-winged doves. "How's your pitching arm, Jake?" he whispered, referring to the fact that I was in times past a Little League pitcher. Without another word, he handed me a nearly fist-size stone, and as quietly as I could, I took a stance that would allow me a good throw.

I hesitated a moment as an image of another bird from my youth fluttered across my memory. But this time, I couldn't flinch. I reared back and threw. Their bunching close together should have made connecting with a target fairly easy. But either from being out of practice, or as a result of images from my past, I held on to the missile a hairbreadth too long. The stone hit a few centimeters below the bevy. They scattered in a fusillade of whistling wings.

"Sorry, Artie."

"Hey, it was a long shot at best. You came pretty close."

"Yeah, you know what they say about close and rabbits."

It appeared that ants were on the menu tonight. I wished we at least had a chocolate covering to make them palatable.

When we made our way back down, the water bottle was about half-full. Artie stopped at the pool, washed out the tin plate we'd found, filled it and carefully carried it the few feet back down to the riverbank. Connors had caught one blue catfish this time and had baited line in the water after more. "What was that explosion of squawking I heard?"

"Jake almost bagged us a whitewing with a rock."

"¡No me digas! Well, Jakie, you can no longer claim your virginal status. You've actually made an attempt at a kill. Congratulations. I know you'll be going straight to confession as soon as we get back to civilization, but I think God will forgive you in this case."

"I bet He'd *reward* me if I killed you. But I thought you thought you *were* God."

Artie started a fire—this time with the lighter he plucked out of my hatband. First, he boiled away the water in the pan we'd found. I assume that was to more or less sterilize it. He then got more water, and when it started to boil, he placed the prickly-pear fruit and retama seeds in to simmer. The plate was shallow, so we had to turn the harvest frequently to ensure they were completely cooked. I then cut another limb from the paloverde to make a spit for today's catch.

While the greens were cooking, Artie took small slices of a cactus pad, split them open and put the fleshy parts on Connors's nose, upper cheeks and shoulders and then did the same to himself.

"Sunburn?"

"Just a little, but we don't want to take any chances. Once we get out of the canyon, we don't know what kind of sun we'll be facing. You're lucky you've still got a shirt and hat."

Connors continued to fish into the evening as he ate the meager victuals Artie and I prepared. But all he was able to hook was a diminutive carp, so what we had already eaten had to suffice.

As we lay down to retire for the night, our bellies somewhat calmed from their earlier distress, I turned to my two *camaradas*. "Hey, we're gonna be all right, guys. We've got enough water to get us out of the canyon, and Andie and Anabel are gonna alert the authorities if they don't find us tomorrow." I probably said it more for myself than for them. "The human body can go without food for days without any permanent damage, and we've got a full water bottle."

"Yeah, we're gonna be fine," Artie confirmed. "We'll have better luck fishing in the morning, and there's plenty of prickly pear and mesquite to tide us over. I hear wild plums grow in this area as well. They'll be green but edible."

But the quiet and darkness of night descended like a blanket of doom, interrupted only by the echolocative squeaks of bats. They kindly feasted on tiny creatures that would otherwise feast on us. The river's flow now sang a dirge of isolation. Thoughts of mortality and the naked fragility of life wove a web of uneasiness. Images of my mother and father, my brothers and sisters waltzed gently through my mind. Then one heavy beat of a bass drum struck me at the image of Dolores and the future we might forfeit if nature managed to defeat us.

But the most potent and lasting ache arose at thoughts of my beloved little sister. Gracie—so vulnerable to the ravages of a hostile world! Who will take care of you, who will protect you, if my father grows old and I am gone? And what vile slanderer was so heartless as to hasten your retreat from it?

I felt myself and my two companions frail and lost in the awesome fist of the Almighty. How can that be? I'd given up my faith in the Divine, in anything beyond the pantheist belief in the universe as progenitor of itself. But the tautological contradiction in that credo had escaped me. This—this here and now—was not rational discourse. This was pure, blind need. "There's no such thing as an atheist in a foxhole" was an aphorism I had eschewed in the smug arrogance of adolescence.

But here I was, looking up at the vast sequined pattern of the firmament. And offset within it, a smiling quarter moon of sweet silver with its ghostly penumbral outline hung above the coruscated cliffs. It shone like a mighty scythe harvesting those dainty sparkles of light. And on those rough canyon walls, from water's edge to towering cliff's summit, I could see the faint outlines of life. Intrepid life burgeoned out of its flinty surface in noble defiance. It stood abandoned in the rarefied moonlight. It cried to me and to all creation, "I will live! I will live! No matter the heartache, no matter the trial, I will live!"

And so my obstinate lips melted into an earnest prayer: "Take us, Lord. And please hold my world-weary baby sister in your loving embrace."

And so I drifted into a fitful sleep.

# 8

I was the first one up in the morning and in the cool, faint morning light went in search of wood and creatures that could be used as bait. The comforting odor of last night's fire overwhelmed most others, but I detected a delicate sweet smell of some late-blooming flower I couldn't identify. I noted by the stick Artie had put at the river's edge the night before that the waters were still receding.

I hoped our fire might still have a live coal or two beneath the ash but, to be safe, also gathered tinder and kindling. I was able to nab two grasshoppers to use as bait or—and I was surprised to find that I hardly winced at the thought—for food if the need arose. When I returned, Artie had the fire going, and Connors was busy with baited hook and line in the water. We had set our two water-storage devices under the dripping rock, drank them dry and put them back to refill.

Artie cautioned quiet so as not to disturb the fish, and so, as silently as possible, he and I made our way up the ravine to forage for more food. He had set the cholla buds to soak overnight, and I started to collect more together with prickly-pear fruit. "We'll get those on the way back down. Let's go up a little higher and see if we can find a piñon. They make an edible nut that's high in protein and calories, and we can make tea with the leaves. If I remember right, they're a good source of vitamin C and A. While we're climbing, just remember how brittle the limestone is."

We searched and searched, climbing up on treacherous ledges, finding only more of the edible plants we had already foraged. When footing afforded the opportunity, we split, traversing separate paths in search of the elusive evergreen. Then we came together again at points higher up. There was omnipresent lechuguilla, one sprouting a stalk festooned with its purplish buds. I wondered if that was what I'd smelled this morning. Its almost-twin false agave was also abundant, and there was one scrawny tree with seedpods that twirled around themselves in Shirley Temple curls. We stuffed our pockets full of them. There was every plant I'd read about that grew on these limestone cliffs: *sangre de drago*, creosote and tarbush, alongside the occasional ocotillo. But the object of our expedition continued to elude us.

Then finally, about a third of the way up the ravine, there it was: one lone piñon pine—which is actually redundant since *piñon* is Spanish for *pine nut*. I watched Artie pull off a cone and strip it down to a smallish tan nut. The tree had produced only a few other cones, and we greedily stripped away the outer covering and placed the nuts in our pockets. "Well, it's better than nothing. And with the rest, and if Connors has any luck, we'll be all right. We gotta be real careful going back down. You done any rock-climbing?"

"Just at Vajalio Indio. But I'm pretty surefooted. Lemme go first, Artie, and I'll talk you down."

"Ándale."

We made our way down the rugged shale, the handiwork of the ocean's retreat millennia before. No human hand could create such sublime artistry. But as we neared the place where the ravine leveled off somewhat, the reason rock-climbers avoided these cliffs became poignantly clear. A healthy ledge on which I'd placed my right foot and the lion's share of my weight gave way, and I was suddenly sliding down the last few meters, scraping skin off myriad parts of my body.

A fearful "Oh!" followed me as I went. When I finally hit a large boulder to break my fall, it was unfortunately split down the middle, and my right foot hit the ridge at an angle that wrenched it with all the force of the more-than-three-meter drop.

"Jake!" Artie yelled and started quickly down the cliff.

"I'm all right! I'm all right! Don't rush. We don't need both of us bunged up!"

"Don't move till I get there. Stay put," he ordered as he made his quick but careful way down. When he got to me, he went straight to work. "Anything broken?"

"No, I don't think so. My right ankle hurts a bit."

"Can you move it?"

I rotated and moved my foot up and down, biting my lip as I did.

"Good. That's good. You're pretty scraped up, though. I don't like the idea of open wounds in that river. We're gonna have to disinfect and bind them up."

"With what?"

"Creosote. Oughta do the trick—at least for a while." He thought a moment. "Well, Jake, you're gonna be shirtless like Connors and me. I gotta use part of it to bind your ankle and the rest as bandages."

"I think my shirt's dirtier than the river at this point."

He took another moment to consider. "We'll boil it in what's called mormon tea—lotta tannic acid—ought to sterilize it pretty good." He tore off a sleeve and used it to bind my ankle.

"How do you know all this stuff, Artie?"

"My parents grew up in the Chihuahuan Desert. And I spent my first nine years there."

"Thank God for that."

I was able to hobble down the rest of the way to our camp, leaning on Artie when the terrain allowed and then with the help of a walking stick he'd cut and fashioned. When we got there, Connors pulled the gizzard shad he'd caught out of the water and turned around to hand it to me for scaling, gutting and cooking. "What the hell happened to you?" he quietly mouthed.

"Fall from the upper cliff," Artie answered. "Ledge gave way."

Connors shook his head and snorted out a puff of air. "You coulda never been a god, Jakie."

"Ask me if I ever wanted to." That was a bald-faced lie. If there was anything I craved during my teen years, it was acceptance into that confederation of school studs. He answered with another dismissive snort. The mention of that group and my tangential affiliation with it always resurrected feelings of resentment. Almost-visible waves of animosity pulsed between us. And, probably because of the stress associated with our present situation, they now seemed sharper and more intense. As time wore on and hunger and fear wound the spring of panic tighter, it grated on nerves worn thin as moonbeam.

While we were waiting for our containers to fill with water, Artie boiled the stalks of mormon tea with water from the pool. He then added more water, and once it came back to a boil, he allowed it to cool a bit and mixed it with creosote juice to rinse out my wounds, which stung like the devil.

"That's a good sign—means it's disinfecting." He then brought it to a boil again and placed the strips he'd torn my shirt into in the mix as best he could, doing it a strip at a time. Finally, he split open some prickly-pear pads and placed them over the more serious scrapes, put the parts of my shirt on top and tied them tight with the leaves of a sotol plant. We'd harvested the heart of the plant the night before and left it in the coals to bake. We had that, cholla buds, retama pods and a few bites of shad for breakfast.

"We'll save the piñon nuts for later. We don't have a lot, but they're pretty filling—last a good while," Artie directed.

In the midmorning quiet of the rustling river, we continued our journey. Few words were spoken. Those that were carried a veneer of amiability that only feebly covered mounting tension. As the day wore on, the brooding silence cast a veil of desperation and irascibility.

Down the endless canyon waters, we floated through seemingly interminable hours of isolation. I scoured every square inch of the immense walls of rock for any sign of life, of deliverance, of relief from despair. Our hunger came upon us faster and harder, like a creeping hand of doom. It set our nerves on edge. We bristled like the spines of a porcupine, jagged and truculent.

We stopped to walk through some rapids. "Is this goddamn canyon ever gonna end?" Connors's complaint echoed to and fro between the flinty ramparts. There was no humor now, no teasing, good-natured or mean. There was now only a honed edge of despondency. "Why the hell didn't you pull us over before we hit the Rockslide, dammit?" he spat out at Artie and then immediately followed with a new accusation: "We might've found somebody on the other side of that ravine."

Artie took a moment before responding. I could feel him fighting with himself for control. "Connie, look at the canyon walls. Look at the angle of the water stains. See the downslope?"

I did as Artie suggested. It looked like we were descending at an extraordinary angle. I had read in my research on the Big Bend that this was an illusion caused by the southwest lean of the mesas. I was about to mention it when Artie tossed a look at me that demanded discretion. He pulled over to the water's edge, and the two of us followed.

He took two pine nuts from his pocket and gave them to Connors. "There's nothing that exaggerates panic like hunger. Jake, eat two of the ones you've got." I then noticed that he took two more out of his pocket but only put one in his mouth, deftly palming the other and returning it to his pants pocket. "How's the ankle, Jake?"

"Not bad. I banged it a little when we went through that shallow patch a while back, but it was nothing much. I heal pretty quick."

"Don't take any chances."

"No."

"The scrapes?"

"They're fine. No worries."

"We gotta keep an eye on 'em. Some of them were pretty deep."

The pine nuts had not yet worked their magic on Connors. "Hey, why don't we worry a little more about getting out of this damn canyon and less about Jakie's little bumps and bruises, huh?"

The ice-pick sharpness of the look Artie cast at Connors sent a chill down my spine. This was the first time I heard him raise his voice. "Hey, our worst enemy here is panic. We either stick together, or we don't make it. You understand that?" The last three words echoed across the ravine with an authority cubical and sharp edged.

Connors's jaw muscles rippled through his cheeks, undulating in fury. He looked away and stared straight down the river's flow. I might have expected the water to boil from the heat emanating from his eyes. There was no answer. One was tacit finally, in the way he turned his head and looked upriver. "You're right. The river is going down at a hell of an angle."

This, the proud man's *sorry*.

We float-skidded down the river through bend after claustrophobic bend. The sugar content from the mesquite pods we chewed and sucked on, together with the fat from the piñon nuts, gradually calmed frayed nerves. There was a wonderland of bird and other life, but the tenuousness of our circumstances wrenched the joy from it.

As we continued on, our bodies quickly used up the meager lunch we'd consumed. The stone barriers on either side of us, stretching to a dizzying altitude, took on the trappings of prison walls. They were rough, hard and impenetrable. The scar-hewn rock slashed mercilessly at the soul. The tiny slit of sky between them only intensified their claustrophobic menace. The canyon seemed to narrow, robbing us of air, threatening to crush us between its obdurate flanks. A few bone-dry coulees ripped them apart now and then, taunting us with water's promise forsaken.

Now the home of Aguagria we treated with such disdain seemed a paradise we longed for without compunction. How adversity can give you perspective: where this trip was one of escape from the monotony of our sleepy little town on the Mexican border, it was now these walls from which we sought deliverance.

We reached another narrow bank by late afternoon and pulled over to camp for the night. The predusk heat pounded pitilessly, with air as calm as a corpse's breath. Connors, shut-mouthed, went immediately to fishing. Artie and I foraged for the scant amount of wood and provisions the area afforded. The parched air quickly sucked all moisture from us, letting the afternoon kiln our emaciating bodies.

There was, of course, a prickly pear growing out of the side of the canyon within reach with a few edible fruit and pads. We would, I assumed, have to eat them raw or baked on the tin plate, since this stop afforded no freshwater. We'd have to husband what we had for the hydration of our bodies.

Owing to the dearth of fuel for a fire, we waited for the fisherman to provide us with something to cook. The added heat would be as welcome as a toothache. This seemed to increase Connors's impatience, as he started to grumble, "Come on, dammit! Bite!"

Even Artie's efforts to calm had a jagged edge: "Connie, the last thing you can be as a fisherman is desperate. You know that. Cálmate, OK? They'll come, but only if you're patient."

"Well, here then!" he shoved the pole against Artie's chest. "You're the expert. You do it!"

"Come on, Connors!" I spat out myself. "Getting pissed off isn't gonna help anything."

"Oh, you're the one to talk about getting pissed off, Mr. Temper Tantrum!"

It was true that my greatest failing was the short fuse I was famous for. Panic had chewed through my nerves. The insult shot my body up. I took one step toward him but was cut off by Artie. "¡Cálmense los dos! We've got enough water for tomorrow, and I can tell we're getting close to the end of the canyon. We've still got piñon nuts and tunas and nopales to eat. Once we're out of the canyon, we only have about four or five miles to the pickup point. And the girls will already have notified the authorities. So let's *calm down!*"

In the screaming quiet that followed, a bevy of jays screeched like banshees up the ravine. I picked up a rock and flung it at them with all my panic-inspired hate. An explosion of wings and feathers chevroned out of the brush and up the ax-hewn gorge. It seemed to at least temporarily assuage the rising choler in us.

I realize now, looking back, that our old-world reptilian brains were in fight-or-flight mode, our nerves as ragged as the walls that entombed us. I felt the hideous beast that lurked beneath pleasantries fighting for release. It struggled to be given free rein to work its evil. Mounting hunger was exacerbating mordant panic, and each expression of anger or impatience was getting harder and harder to not answer in kind. I resumed my rock seat facing downriver, and Connors paced on the little bit of bank available.

After a moment, Artie continued in a calm but critical tone, "Connie, you all right?"

Connors just exhaled a breath signaling the affirmative. "Then here." Artie extended the fishing pole back in his direction. He hesitated for a moment and then walked over, took it and pulled in the line. I handed him the last of the frogs for bait.

This time he didn't give the slightest of acknowledgments. He just hooked it, dropped the line into the stillest water there to be found and, after twenty or thirty minutes, pulled in a blue catfish. Supper was sparse but succeeded in taking a bit of the edge off our frayed nerves—at least for the time being.

As the evening star waddled tenderly over the top of the canyon wall, darkness swaddled us once again in its shroud. The warble-creak of randy crickets serenaded with solitude: a lonely, friendless sound. Bats flitted in and out of the moon's uterine light, hairy winged, staccato-flapping. Bullfrogs croaked in broken murmur—a hoarse, guttural timbre, sumptuous but craven. The nervous, rasping rustle of creatures scuttling through brush and dead leaves, out on their nightly hunting junkets. They sought prey that preyed on grass, weeds and despair.

A breathless wind whispered from the distant past, permanent yet mutable, its somber austerity predicated on the impermanence of life. It is companionless too, out of the west, dry and hard as rattlesnake breath. It threads down the coombe above, rising in pitch as it passes through the long, thin fronds of paloverdes.

I tell my mind not to dream tonight. It will not listen. It laughs at my command. The moon gracefully but meanly bows behind the canyon wall. The darkness oozes thick as syrup. A coyote howls its plaintive call, far in the distance over mountain and valley. It is painfully comforting. It is the same mournful evensong of home, of family, of a beloved sister and girlfriend. It stabs remorselessly.

So in defense against the mounting dread, stretching a fleeting thought toward heaven's door, I sing an ancient lullaby:

> *Es-tre-lli-ta de le-JAAA-no cie-lo*
> *Tú sabes mi dolor*
> *Tú mi-ras mi sufrir*
>
> *Ven y dime si me QUIEEE-re un poco*
> *Po-orque yo ya no pue-e-do*
> *Sin su amor, vi-viiiirrr*
>
> (Little star in the distant heaven
> You know my heartache
> You see my suffering)
>
> (Come and tell me
> If she still cares for me just a little
> For I can no longer live
> Without her love)

Artie turns. Connors shuffles. Home. Gracie. Dolores. Home. And the silence of the universe was more than one could bear.

# 9

The next morning passed in monosyllabic grunts. Each cut with straight-razor keenness. We were all, even Artie now, fighting the mounting panic of isolation and despair exacerbated by gnawing hunger. Our callous prison walls leaned in and sucked the sky away to a rumor of breath. We shunned eye contact for the most part and ate our crumbs in testy silence. The sound of the rushing river was now the agonizing hum of impending doom. We longed to silence the swallows that chirped above. The cheery whistles of a summer tanager seemed to mock our desperation. And those hovering carrion-feeders in the sky, whose shadows wobbled eerily on the water, were the harbingers of our inevitable fate.

As we walked around a set of rapids, Connors spat out, "Don't we have any of those pine nuts left?"

"We need to save them for later," Artie answered in the sheared-off tone of the cliff face. "I've got two. Jake?

"I've got two."

A testy silence and then: "And why the hell you guys get to keep them, I'd like to know."

Connors's tone was like a rusty nail stabbing into my heel. "Because, in case you forgot, we found them!"

"Yeah, like you caught the fish we ate! How 'bout the whitewing you could've bagged but didn't, huh? I bet you missed it on purpose, didn't you? Because you're such a damn pantywaist when it comes to what it really takes to survive!"

Artie was rather drowned out as he cautioned us, "Hey, dammit, both of you, shut up!"

"Oh man, such a banquet you caught!" We were now squared off, with Artie roughly holding us apart and yelling above us to stop. "It just filled me with contentment!"

"Hey, screw you, loser! You're a damn crybaby, you know that, Jake? A friggin' crybaby! The only reason you're with us is because Artie feels sorry for you!"

"Hey, Connie, you speak for yourself, dammit!" Artie tried to squeeze in on top of Connors's demand: "I wanna see those pine nuts! I wanna see 'em now!" He glared at me, and I at him, with such a venomous hatred that it obliterated whatever memory we had of the companions we'd been.

"Oh, you asshole! You actually think we're holding out on you? Here, you son of a bitch. Look!" I sputtered, fumbling in my pockets and then yanking them out in such a fury that one of the prized morsels dropped in the water. I immediately scrounged desperately for it, yelling all the while. "Damn you, Connors! Damn you! You see what you did?"

"Hey, I can't help it if you're a bumbling numbnuts!"

Finally fishing the piñon nut out of the shallow water, I took both and went straight at him on the bank. "Here, you son of a bitch! You want 'em?" I threw them straight in his face. "I hope you choke on 'em!"

Our nerves raw as roadkill, that was all it took to unleash the atavistic monster in us, the primordial beast that millennia of organized society only manages to dress in the trappings of civilization. Connors started toward me with the same murderous impulse that overwhelmed all inhibitions in me. His eyes were blazing slits of primeval bloodlust, bent on slaughter.

It seems now a moment frozen in time. From somewhere deep in our saurian past arose a feral urge that was beyond anger, beyond hate, beyond human. It was something so primitive and monstrous that even now I shudder at it. Gone was the reserve that had always held me back in the few fistfights I had at Saint James. There had always been some hesitation that pulled my punches. It was a reserve that always seemed to be lacking in my adversaries.

And I never felt the sense of release or excitement I saw in many of my classmates. Rather, they always made me desperately sad. It was for that reason that I inevitably wound up getting the hell beat out of me. But back then, the objective was only to dominate or to release the pent-up frustrations of adolescent hormone-induced psychosis. This was murder, pure and simple.

And I question that that troglodytic impulse came only from the gnawing hunger and fear of death. I have to now acknowledge in myself an abiding malice toward Connors McClain. It was born of the incessant ridicule of my beloved little sister and, I must confess, of me—indeed, of all those deemed by his "godly" clique as unworthy, odd and uncool.

There is a point at which teasing becomes cruel and is a manifestation of some inveterate antipathy. I was not only Connors's intellectual superior. I was also a better athlete and usually beat him at almost all one-on-ones that involved something beyond brute force. But did that envy only travel in one direction? No, I must recognize in myself an abiding jealousy for his popularity.

Whatever its origin, the only thing that stopped the pending bloodletting was Artie coming between us. "Calm down, you two! Dammit, Connie!" Artie ordered as he stiff-armed his taller now adversary.

"Get the hell outta my way!" he roared as he pushed at Artie and launched a blow over his head. It glanced off my cheekbone, but as a result of the awkward direction from which it was thrown, it didn't do a lot of damage. At the same time, I threw a right directed at the side of his face with all the built-up hate and searing adrenaline that had brought my blood to a boil. In it was all the destructive intent of Cain's blow against Abel, instinctual and rabid, thoughtless as a crab at a scrap of rotting meat.

Lunging over Artie and up to reach my taller target, however, left me with my long, eel-skinny frame sprawled over Artie's shoulders and upper back. As I was off my feet, Artie easily snapped me back with the weight of his body, and I flew backward and down, my back making violent contact with a large piece of outcropping. It knocked the wind and, as a result, the fight out of me.

"Dammit to hell, Connie, Jake, stop!" Artie yelled as he pushed Connors back. As Connors again made his murderous way forward, Artie delivered a sledgehammer blow that found its mark directly on Connors's chin. The straight right cross toppled him like a mighty oak. Though Artie was not particularly tall, he had the mesomorphic broad shoulders and thick torso that screamed of punching power.

Suddenly, all was quiet. The struggle to regain my breath likewise quickly restored my self-control. I became aware of the now-quiet flow of the rushing river, the chortling squeak of swallows and the hoarse gargle of a cactus wren. The heavy breathing of the three of us mingled in a shameful melody.

As the adrenaline subsided, I became aware of the sheer stupidity of what had just occurred. Shame and embarrassment replaced the rage that had overwhelmed me. A bolt of regret for my antagonist as he rose from the sand further sapped the fight from me. He slowly placed himself on all fours and then turned to face the river as he stood.

After a moment, Artie spat out in disgust, "Dammit, you two, what the hell is wrong with you?" After a calming breath and a bow of the head, he continued, "Now both of you, look! We're gonna get out of this. But we *have to work together*, not..." He picked up the pine nuts that had fallen on the ground and handed them to me. "Put your fight into fighting this desert, this...damned situation!"

Connors had walked to the far side of the riverbank. Without a word, he attached the water bottle to his belt, now a little less than a quarter full, put on his life jacket and started in the water.

After a brief moment, Artie exhaled a calming sigh and quickly donned his life jacket. "Come on, Jake. Let's get going." And so we continued in silence down the river.

The sky was now cloudless and blue as a robin's egg. But its azure purity brought no comfort, only fear of the sun's burning rays. The now-sunless walls turned the moribund charcoal gray of some monstrous dungeon. They seemed to press in and narrow like the torture room of some B-horror movie.

I spotted a lone aoudad ram atop the Texas wall to our left, austere and self-sufficient. I watched it climb the sheer cliffs in jealousy at its nimbleness, wishing myself so agile. I envied as well its ability to live off those cliffs' scraggly vegetation, its lack of thought beyond survival.

I felt so alone and insignificant in a universe as grand and awesome as it was indifferent—its amorality manifest in the towering cliff face that imprisoned us. I longed for Dolores's loving embrace and vowed that I would never again complain at the lack of the consummation of our relationship. And even beyond that, the potent ache at the thought of enveloping my wounded sister in a protective embrace and shielding her from all the injuries and insults of so hostile a world.

For the first time in my life, a question swirled languidly through my mind. Only now, looking back from my perch above Aguagria, can I find words to express it: *What lies beneath?* It insisted on being asked. How can we turn on each other in such a homicidal rage? How can our civilized selves in moments of fear unleash those destructive monsters of the id?

I'm not sure why it seemed such a revelation to me. But I think I was just beginning to see myself as part of some grand design, a small player in the great drama/comedy of life. It wasn't something I was at all prepared to answer or even articulate. But the question posed itself with dogged persistence. And now the words are clear as desert air: *What lies beneath?*

It was at that very moment, as that thought popped the bubble of my egocentrism, when a sudden sense of calm—euphoria, even— seemed to wash over me. We floated, like any piece of flotsam, down the turbid course of the river. Might it only have been the high that attends approaching starvation? Was it simply the fanciful musings of one anticipating his death? Do the pangs of desperation stimulate the brain to produce endorphins to ease that feared transition from life to eternity? Would it be eternity or simply a return to nothingness?

If I die here, I thought, that hideous impulse dies with me. And my body will serve to feed the hungry beasts and flora, those with no thought of right and wrong, good and evil, so that the glorious dance of creation might continue. This, this is the natural law of creative destruction that reigns supreme in the delicate teleological balance of the universe—down to the tiniest protozoan, to the finest grain of sand. *May it do them great good!*

I had lost all concept of time, but I now realized that the sun had appeared and then hidden once again behind the western palisade. The river had appreciably deepened. I could not touch its bed with my feet. It now seemed as bottomless as endless. There were no banks now, no ravines, only implacable rock stretching from water to sky.

We had stopped, I now remembered, and eaten. Was it a pine nut apiece? Some boiled and preserved prickly-pear fruit? Yes, and dragonflies, beetles and ants. I now felt myself one with the mighty stream that ferried me down its torrent. I said a prayer of thanks to the mesquite, the cholla, the paloverde and the fish that had calmed the aching hunger—that hunger that now faded into the blankness of whimsy.

I could now return the favor and slip from my body the life jacket that buoyed me. And thereby, I might sink to sleep in its abiding refuge. I began to slow my progress, putting greater and greater distance between me and my two—what? Could I now call them companions? I felt now more at one with the earth, with death and resurrection—resurrection not as self but as a bundle of chemicals to fertilize this satellite three places from the sun. Those two beings now moving farther and farther ahead of me seemed to lose reality as they faded from sight.

I loosened one snap and fought against the current to hold my position as they and all living creatures dissolved from consciousness. Then another unsnapping brought me closer to the totality of instance. There came over me a palpable ecstasy at the thought: no longer would I have to endlessly struggle to contain the murderous beast within me. Nevermore would I be forced to fight the gruesome horror that abides beneath the facade of civility. Now could I repay this earth, her breast ever at the ready to feed us thankless creatures.

I loosened the final snap. Now could I return to her bosom and gently rock in the cradle of her womb.

But just as I began to slip loose the one impediment to my reunion with the great nurturer, a startling sight appeared before my eyes. Ahead the mighty ramparts of the endless canyon began to fall, and the sun appeared once again in majesty, illuminating and inspiriting the earth with grandeur. At that precise moment, shouts of triumph and deliverance woke me from my reverie.

"Eeee-haaaah!" Connors's conquering bellow bounded off the ravine walls. "We made it, brothers! We made it! We are here! A-ja-ja-ja-ja-jaiii!" he let out a Mexican yell of triumph, and the sound reverberated as though to fill the universe with jubilation.

The defile's end was as sudden as its origin so many miles and seeming lives ago. Amid whoops and howls of celebration, I swam forward faster than the river's current to join my two companions. As I reached them, the three of us made our way to the shore.

"My God in heaven, has anything ever looked so beautiful!" I exclaimed, as we came together and shamelessly hugged. Even in Artie I saw a rare moment of exultation and, for the only time I can ever remember, laughter and cries of elation.

"We'll be there in no time," he finally judged. "Let's get going." We were too ecstatic to feel the hunger pangs that had earlier played at mumblety-peg with our nerves. We floated down the now-rapid current unconcerned with the sun's punishing rays, knowing that in a matter of hours we would arrive at our destination and rescue.

The river opened up into a broad floodplain to our right on the Mexican side covered with grass and shrubs and livestock. It seemed the whole earth had held its breath in the confines of the dungeon walls we'd left behind. Now its lungs, the massive weight of confinement finally lifted, filled with the pure, sweet air of salvation. We were flanked on our left by reeds and tule thick as a jungle and serenaded by a bullfrog with a bass-baritone croak deeper than the lowest note of a tuba.

Then ahead, something glinting in the sun from the river's middle caught my eye. It seemed to be coming at an angle toward us. It was cutting diagonally across the water like you do to go upriver against the current. "What the hell is that?" Connors demanded. The current was powerful and swept us toward whatever it was.

Before I could make it out, Artie exhaled a barely audible "Oh my God."

It was then I recognized our canoe working its way toward us. I could just make out Anabel's tall frame paddling from the back.

"Anabel!" Artie yelled. "Quédate, ahí! Stay there; we'll come to you!" I doubted she could hear above the rush of the river. At any rate, she kept on fighting her way forward, cutting diagonally across the river to ford upstream.

Just as we met on the Mexican side of the river with fierce hugs from Anabel, a helicopter burst from between the cliffs and came to hover over us. Apparently, when we failed to make our appointed rounds, the women had indeed called for rescue. We alternately waved in ecstatic gratitude and paddled our way down the river to the ramp.

Once on land, questions abounded. "What the hell...? Where did you find the canoe? Why the hell did you...?"

Words bubbled out of Andie through sobs. "We saw it trapped on an island in the middle of the river. Oh God! We thought...!"

She couldn't continue and just bear-hugged her towering boyfriend, burying her face in his chest.

I was surprised at how contained Anabel was. "I was just tall enough to walk through the water and grab it."

"In this current?" I marveled.

"Yeah. It wasn't easy. I had to brace myself against the rocks on the riverbed and walk at an angle into it. It was over Andie's head. She'd found this broken paddle thrown away at the ramp." There was a heavy pause. "We weren't sure what we'd find." She and Artie wrapped their arms around each other. This was the one time I saw a look of amazement on his face.

So, starving, filthy, depleted and worn, we waited for the helicopter to land. Once it did, we were treated to a stern lecture and then immediately hustled off to the park office. There, my cuts and scrapes were appropriately treated and the three of us thoroughly checked over. There was considerable amazement that my wounds showed little sign of infection.

"What the *hell* were you boys thinkin'?" the head park ranger asked without a hint of humor. "Don't ever, *ever* do anything that foolish again, you hear me?"

It was Connors who found the fortitude to speak. "No, sir, I promise. We won't."

It seems an important lesson for the young to learn: that one is not immortal, not invulnerable to the awesome power of nature. We must each of us discover the fragility and preciousness of life. But I wonder also, can we truly appreciate its worth if we've never exposed it to possible loss? Is to never risk to be dead in life?

But beyond that, after a hearty meal and a shower, I had to reckon with the altered state that had led me to the brink of surrendering that life. I cannot say it was in a fit of depression or even sadness. Quite the contrary: as best as I could recall, there was a strange sense of elation. I was overtaken by a feeling of liberation from the oppressive confines of this physical mass and, likewise, from the darker parts of our nature—the horror, perhaps, of our very humanity. I had never felt more alive than I did on that trip. And if I am truly honest with myself, it was precisely at that very moment of savage confrontation with Connors.

How is this possible? Those seconds of hate I felt, and saw reflected in Connors's eyes, was not the product of mere boyhood petulance. No, there was murderous, primeval rage. There was, for the briefest instant, some biblical monster loosed from the chains of moral compunction.

But there abided with it something even more hideous. It crept in the slimy ooze of self-revelation. It lay buried like a dormant retrovirus, waiting for a moment of weakness to strike and consume its host. It was that such a moment of horror carried with it an overwhelming flash of—I hesitate to say, but yes—exhilaration. And why do I connect it so directly with the even greater ecstasy I felt at my dalliance with self-slaughter?

These questions, these reflections, only occur to me now. They weave together like a choking parasitic vine with other even more damning self-revelations. But then I must pause to consider: memory is such a sinkhole of delusion. Were there really those homicidal impulses in that moment of confrontation? Or have the vicissitudes of my journey since then only made it so in my mind?

That terrible question recurs: what lies beneath?

# 10

Several years and untold heartaches later, that particular Christmas Eve was uncommonly cold for Aguagria and San Benito County. On this, the night of our intended rescue of Artie's uncle and family from the clutches of a Mexican drug cartel, the air was crisp as a candle flame. Standing at the river's edge, I shivered at the cold—but perhaps even more at the immensity of our undertaking.

I found the canoe in nearly a foot of water and had to wade out to the tree it was tied to. I pulled it back and retied it to one further up the bank. Just as Artie had predicted, the river had risen at an enormous pace. Now wet feet and ankles worked in synergy with solitude and anxiety to exacerbate my trembling.

As I'd learned from him on our earlier adventure, I took a sturdy twig of mesquite and shoved it into the mud at water's edge. Waiting for the Border Patrol to make its pass, I paced along the riverbank. My wet feet now stung in the cold.

Perhaps it was that feeling of utter solitude that made me reflect on all the events that had led me to this pass: the adventures and misadventures that had bonded the three of us—I thought then, eternally; the despair I felt of ever finding that kind of kinship in my own family—at least until Cousin Gracie came to live with us. And what of the possibility that Connors was responsible for the cutting remark that had ushered in her retreat from the world? What of my own contribution to that family strife?

My one wish, if I had a wish, would be to have it to do over again, knowing what I know now. But unlike the games of childhood, life offers no do-overs. But the truth of that fantasy is that, given the opportunity, whatever one might correct in that second chance could still be corrected, still improved. And even on a third try and a fourth. Yes, no matter how many redos you got, there would always be more *If I had onlys...*

The night was a crystalline wonder, oppressive in its vastness. The firmament spread out against the sky in sequined majesty. Starlight from uncountable ages past rippled gently through the silken threads of a waxing moon. I had not felt this cosmologically alone since my flirtation with life's inexorable end a few short years ago. Here, beside brotherly waters, I again felt the deafening solitude of that moment. Every sound of creature rustling through brush, fish flopping in the water and river's fevered rush peppered my flesh with goose pimples.

There is nothing to do in the stillness of night but think. *Think, Jake, not of your yesterdays but of tomorrows...and tomorrows and tomorrows...* But I remembered broken promises, guillotined hopes and challenges evaded.

I paced. And paced. And thought. And thought.

After some treasonous passage of time, I checked the water level on the stick I'd planted. The knot by which I'd gauged it, a good four inches above the surface, was now almost underwater. The river was rising at a monstrous pace. It whipped and winnowed, stripping leaf from branch and abusing both in angry whirlpools. The moon moaned in the sharp night air, my breath ominously visible in its pallor.

I was rudely yanked from my rapture as the rising waters again wrenched the canoe from its moorings. I pulled it farther up the bank and tied it to another tree. *Oh God, it might be visible now? Please let the Border Patrol stay above! It's painted black, Jake, calm down.*

Now thoughts of how this exploit might end burrowed down to a place between my ribs. Incarceration? Illness? Death? Another story searching for a teller to tell it? Biting cold radiated upward from frozen feet and colluded with the chill of my fears. Rather than attorney for the defense, I saw myself as defendant.

And what would become of my precious sister? I'd already lost the only other person who truly filled my life—and to what monstrous succubus was shrouded in mystery. Though my faith had lost some luster since those fearful nights in the Big Bend, I mouthed a silent prayer. As if in answer, a screech owl's whistle severed the calm of night.

As its eerie warble faded, I heard a vehicle approaching above me and quickly crouched in the tall grass and willows. The car whined higher and shriller than the one the night before. Was it the Border Patrol or not? Despite the increasing cold, my hands started to sweat, robbing them of friction as I rubbed them together. My heartbeat quickened from a nervous trot to a gallop.

*Do I make the call?*

I sat momentarily paralyzed when suddenly a blood-curdling, high-pitched squeal to my left burst the artery of the night. It shot me to my feet, and I twisted in all directions seeking its source. Then, remembering the car above, I quickly hunkered down again, bracing myself for the attack of a hungry cougar or rabid raccoon.

Then, in the pale moonlight, I saw the screech owl I'd heard earlier making his silent-winged way across the river. From its talons hung what looked like a river rat. I remembered once before hearing the nightmarish cry of a rabbit caught and ripped apart by a great horned owl. I gave quick thanks I was not on the menu that night.

Odd thoughts began to flit through my mind. *The way of the world: some must die that others may live.* So why could I accept the fruits of slaughter but not be able to participate in its necessary barbarity? I tried to retard my wildly thumping heart. But the chemicals that coursed through my body from that rat's wheedle were too overwhelming.

Quickly, I flashed a peek at my measuring stick. It was now three-quarters covered. How can the river be rising this fast? I tried to calm myself, but quivers of terror accompanied waves of adrenaline-rush heat.

How much time had passed? It seemed a millennium, but I knew how solitude and the dead of night played tricks on one's sense of sequence. I pressed the button on the side of my watch to make it visible: 12:42 a.m. *Oh God, Artie, please be delayed!*

I reached for the bulky cell phone of that era hanging from my belt. This was Connors's provision—at the time a relatively new technology. It took several error-prone starts before my quaking finger could finally enter the Border Patrol hotline number. Now, as Connors had instructed, all I had to do was press the call button.

I hesitated. If I were caught, would there be a record of my call? *You've been watching too many spy movies, Jake.* I could throw it in the river. Would there still be a record with the phone company? I closed my eyes and took a deep breath. *Settle, Jacob, settle.*

My breathing had just begun to temporize when another vehicle on the path above came to a brush-swishing stop. *Oh my God, are there two of them?* Or was the first some couple in search of privacy for their mating ritual? They didn't stop the last time. Of course they're going to vary their routine, Jake. I sat motionless as I tried to ride herd on the alternatives ricocheting through my mind.

Call, call! If it's not the BP, you'll just have to sneak the boat into the river as quietly as possible. Besides, if it *is* a pair of lovers, they'll be much too busy to notice. If it's the BP, this is your only chance to send them on a wild-goose chase!

I moved farther downstream to escape the hearing of the interlopers above. I was grateful I'd entered the number earlier, as now a trembling finger could barely find the call button. After a short moment, the answer came: "Border Patrol, how can I help you?" I heard in the peculiar accent of the Mexican border a Texas drawl overlaying the flat Spanish pronunciation of vowels.

I froze. *For the love of God, Jake, speak!*

"This is the Border Patrol. Who's calling?"

I somehow finally succeeded in freeing my voice from paralysis. "Hello," I said in a hoarse whisper. Then a thought pierced my insides. *God in heaven, Jake, water carries sound—you know that!*

I heard the dispatcher once again impatiently ask, "Yes, this is the Border Patrol. How can I help you?"

I tried to make my way as quietly as possible up the bank at an angle that would carry me farther away from both the water and the vehicles above. "Hello," I repeated, and I realized that my struggling up the bank would be picked up by the dispatcher. Then it struck me that my breathlessness would lend realism to the story. "I'm...at the river. I'm about—about a half mile south of Bridge Three."

*Oh God, could they triangulate the call and know where I really am? Extirpate this police-science nonsense from your mind, Jacob!* "I...I see a group of people crossing from Mexico. Looks like about ten or twelve." Then I added the gravy that would seal the alarm. "Two of them appear to have some kind of weapon—rifles. It's too far to tell what kind." Then, before she could ask for details that might expose the lie, I said, "Oh my God, they've seen my light! I have to go!"

I quickly disconnected and fell from crouching to kneeling as the tension throughout my body turned my upper legs to mush. Some amorphous creature rushed through the brush to my left, shooting me up to a statue once again. I listened for the sound of the car. All was utter silence, save for the roar of the river's eddies and currents. The faintest strains of *Norteña* music, with its punishing snare-drum polka beat, wafted in the air from origins unknown.

Then the starting of an engine and lights that cut the night shot me down again, face to the ground. I felt the sharp sting of a jumping-cactus thorn through my jeans and into my shin. It began to work its torturous way deep into muscle. I tried to carefully remove it but only succeeded in impaling more thorns in my fingers. *Can't worry about that now, Jacob. Suck it up.* The spots immediately began to throb, but I breathed a sigh of relief as the two cars pulled away.

Wounded, still in panic at the thought of what awaited me, I started on what I thought was the path back to the canoe. I went straight down to the water's edge and then upriver toward the canoe rather than risk mistaking the angle at which I'd climbed. *God in heaven, did I pull it far enough up the bank? Did I tie it tight enough? Please, God, let it be there!*

After what seemed like more than enough distance, I again began to panic. *I couldn't have gone this far!* Then an angry whisper forced its way from me: "Where the *hell* is that damned boat?" I mentally slapped myself for speaking out loud even in the faintest whisper. *Oh God, Artie, what're you gonna think? What're you gonna do?*

I looked across to see if I could spy anyone on the other side of the river. It was at that precise moment that my good shin came into violent contact with something hard, sending me reeling forward and straight down onto a prickly-pear cactus. An "Ah!" of pain and anger escaped me before I realized that I had run smack-dab into the canoe. Trying my best to pull the spines out of my right shoulder, arm and hip, I quickly untied the canoe, pulled it into the water and started across.

Unfortunately, the pain and hysteria of the last few moments caused me to forget Artie's careful instructions, and I began madly paddling helter-skelter toward the opposite shore. As I came to about the midway point, I descried a group of about five individuals running toward the Mexican shore.

At that precise moment, my haste and carelessness were answered in a sharp eddy that spun the canoe in a violent circle. I was experienced—or lucky—enough to not drop the oar and grip the sides of the craft in an effort to steady myself. But I was caught by one odd current after another and was spinning downriver in a state of chaos when I heard the fateful shots.

Shots. Echo. Silence. Shots. Echo. For a moment, I managed to right the canoe. I aimed it at an angle upriver to the appointed spot. But the force of the current was too powerful. Again I started whirling, and each time I righted myself another sandbar or undercurrent would spin me further downstream.

I shot up over white-water obstructions and violently plunged down the opposite side. The waters rushed over the edges of the canoe and pulled it deeper and deeper with each passing submerged rock, hollow or tree trunk. In the midst of trying desperately to right the reeling mass of aluminum, the pain was wrenched from my consciousness.

Then suddenly, the canoe made violent impact broadside with a sandbar. It careened over and vomited me forth into the muck and pollution that are there the waters of the Rio Grande. I started to swim in the direction of the sandbar, but the undercurrents dragged me below the surface and downstream. Each time I managed to rise for a frantic gulp of air, more shots split the dullness of the night. It was a syncopated pop-pop, pop-pop-pop, echoing across water's natural amplifier. I struggled to claw out some shallow portion of the river but was pitilessly hurled up, over and down in swirling, life-snatching crosscurrents.

Finally, I was slammed with malicious force into a huisache tree that the river's current had forced to bend over it. It lay partially submerged, clinging to shore with the barest of roots. The impact on my head and chest exploded the paucity of air I had managed to swallow, and I struggled to remain conscious and maintain my grip.

I turned upriver to where I had seen the small group hurrying toward the bank. And I saw something that made no sense: *People, people in uniform it looked like. And that one that towers above them—it's Connors! There's no mistaking that walk! What the hell? Where…?* And then all was the blackness of night.

# 11

A smell in the distance coming into view. *I know that smell; I've felt it so often.* I scratch at its undersides to recognize it. It's comforting somehow. *I'm alive, I think.* But everything is so cloudy. I barely slit my eyes open and see a room. It's familiar—and it's comforting, too. I recognize the wall, the pictures, that doorway to a hall.

*God, I hurt! My whole body aches!* It even hurts to turn my head to look around, try to get my bearings. There's a person looking down at me. Who...? Where...? Gradually she comes into focus. "Aunt Agnes?" I can barely squeak out.

"Welcome back to the land of the living. How you feeling, cowboy?" As I clawed my way to semiconsciousness, I found her sitting by my side on a chair next to the bed I'd often slept in as a child. It was an escape from the constant sibling battles at home.

"Aunt Agnes, what...how in the name of...? How did I—"

"I don't know, Jacobson. Your uncle found you on the front porch when he went out to get the paper this morning. He managed to drag you in. Here." She handed me a glass of fizzing, gurgling liquid. "Drink this. And take these. Chew them up. They'll work faster."

"How long...?"

"Sometime last night—or this morning, actually. You don't remember? You told me quite a story about your adventures on the river. You're lucky to be alive, not to mention not in jail. You've only been down a couple of hours. I'm surprised you woke so soon.

I tried to focus while I did as she directed. Swallowing the powder I'd crushed the pills into, a part of the previous night came rushing back. The river! I'd been—"Artie! Connors! Aunt Agnes, are they—?" I exclaimed as I sat up on the bed. My head exploded in pain like pins at a bowling alley hit smack in the pocket. I suddenly became aware of all the scrapes and bone bruises and the swollen, pus-filled sores courtesy of the cactus spines still lodged in my flesh. "Ohhhh!" I protested as my wounds sent me retreating back onto the bed.

"Easy, cowboy. You're not ready to take on the world again. Your uncle and I got you cleaned up, and I pulled as much of the cactus spines out of your body as I could get to. I hope you're prepared, you'll never get rid of the feel of them completely. We cleaned and disinfected your wounds as best we could, but there's no telling what kind of nasty filth got into them from that river. I had to convince your uncle not to call your parents, at least until we got you somewhat set to rights."

The pills I'd chewed and swallowed had left the savor of axle grease, so I swilled down the gurgling liquid.

"I told your parents as believable a tale as I could think of. So if they ask, you went to a party at the Trautmans' and put on one heckuva dog. How you got here is something you'll have to make up yourself. I suppose 'I don't remember' would be as credible as anything. They were pretty worried, Jacobson. Of course, your mother never seems to get frantic—or at least not show it. But you can imagine the state Grace is in. You really don't remember how you got here?"

I fought the gauzy cobwebs swirling in my brain. "I remember the river…being taken by the currents. I hit something, a sandbar or stump I guess, and was thrown out of the canoe. I was being pulled down. Then I…Oh my God, Artie! Connors, did he—?" Again I tried unsuccessfully to rise, but Aunt Agnes's firm hand arrested my progress.

"Like I said, Jacobson, we found you on the front porch. No telling how you got there."

"Is there any word...?"

She looked down at me as the pills she'd given me slowly began to work their magic. "I think it's a little too soon for news about your friends. You've only been here a few hours. Now you lie still and let the potion I gave you take effect. I'll make some inquiries. Rest."

"My God, Aunt Agnes. Artie! I saw him!"

"*Rest.* You can worry about your friends once you've pulled yourself together. If anybody can take care of himself, it's your friend Artie. When you wake up, you're going straight to the doctor. I don't think you have a concussion. The fact that you don't remember how you got here could just be traumatic amnesia, but it does concern me. For now, just lie back and let the pills do their job. Merry Christmas, by the way."

"Oh God, Artie. I let him down, Aunt Agnes. I let him down." I was surprised that the medication she'd given me was working so fast. My speech was already beginning to slur.

"I'm sure there's a good explanation if that's the case. You've always been way too hard on yourself, Jacobson. Now close your eyes and let it all go for now." Aunt Agnes had a soothing command about her, and my mind and body were still in such a state of exhaustion that I quickly drifted into a restless, dream-haunted sleep. "Artie...my God...Conno...Art..."

As I sank deeper into the swirling haze of confusion, sulfurous dreams haunted my sleep. Demons howled in cries of perdition. I found myself on high seas, floating tenuously on turgid waves. An ominous charcoal sky melded into a sea of suspicion and malignance. They whirled together in a torn, battling union. I stretched out my hand farther and farther across a tempestuous and tormented ocean. I reached for Artie, for my baby sister, for sanity.

And there was another figure, a child, but with a face ancient and decrepit, reaching out a tiny finger for me to grasp. I tried to lift a hand toward him. My arms would not move. They lay flaccid and useless by my side. So the child calmly and contentedly smiled good-bye and slowly sank into the sea's watery womb. From far beneath the gray saline waters, that aged child's face watched me with a vacuous stare as he sank farther and farther and finally floated into oblivion.

# 12

That Christmas Eve so many years and tears ago was the last time, save one, that I had seen or heard from Connors McClain. He had suddenly disappeared. And try as I might, I could find no trace of him. I called his home. They had no idea. Or if they did, they put on a very convincing act. I tried calling Andie and found that she was missing as well. Friends, fellow students... Nothing. And Artie? Oh God, Artie! I couldn't imagine this world without him.

*What in the name of all that's holy happened?*

No one knew. Even Artie's fiancée, Anabel, dropped out of sight. I asked some people with contacts with law enforcement across the border. The only thing I was told was that, if I valued my life, to let it go.

"Why? For God's sake, *why?*" Grim silence was my only answer. But I could read between the blank stares. Powers—and in the jungle that is Mexico no one knows who's on which side—knew of my connection to my two blood brothers. And that alone put me in grave danger if I persisted.

With the exception of Grace, my family accepted, as much in self-defense as belief, the tale I told. Grace communicated her skepticism in one piercing glance. Without words, I related back to her my reluctance to tell the real story.

I made my way back to law school, graduated and passed the bar on my first try. But not without locking myself in a room for several weeks to study. I immediately went to work for the public defender's office, riding my white horse of righteousness against the oppressive forces of railroading government. It was, of course, government that I actually worked for, but such irony was then easily buried under young-adult sanctimony.

Gradually, as more inquiries into the fate of Artie and Connors were absorbed into the leaden wall of silence, their frequency faded like old jeans. Desperate urgency eroded to grim resignation.

Besides, there were others, others who were still present, that needed my attention. I had a girlfriend locked in a prison for the criminally insane and, likewise, locked in her own catatonic trance. And my sister, Grace, was withdrawing farther and farther from the world as our father's health slowly deteriorated. The time I wasn't occupied with work I spent either in the State Mental Hospital or home in Aguagria, trying to keep my sister's head above the waters of despair.

Days ran to months and months to dog-eared years as I continued my one-man crusade to bring "justice" to the disenfranchised. So my hours back in Austin were filled with hopelessly pedestrian matters of DWI, driving without a license and public intoxication, spiced occasionally with more serious matters like assault on a female and uttering a forged instrument. They were inevitably solved with pleas, probationary sentences, restraining orders, anger-management classes and community service or the like.

These mostly mundane affairs alternated at home in Aguagria with the soaring artistry of Bach, Mendelssohn and Paganini. But neither I nor my father could entice those rhapsodic airs outside 2001 Saint Thomas Avenue. And their frequency grew less and less.

There were also occasional moments of recreation back in Austin with an attractive ADA. As it would go with most of my relationships from then on, she became as critical of me as she was of my arguments in court. With the questionable faculty of hindsight, I wonder if she had the sense that my heart and soul were another's.

But apart from that, my anguish concerning my friends slowly crumpled into the dull ache of an ancient wound. And so my life began to take on a patina of normalcy.

*Until.* Until one incredibly sultry late summer afternoon, into my professional life walked Stanley Oxendine. And shied by this unique specimen of humankind, my high horse of righteousness would buck me into the swamp of amorality.

Stanley was a mousy little man with shoulders beaten into a pronounced hunch by his life in institutions, hand-to-mouth existence outside of them and, I suppose, the filthy rucksack he carried across his back. He had a milky-white, pasty complexion exaggerated by a life in night and shadow. His yellowed teeth were outlined in tobacco-stain brown, many chipped or missing. From them came breath that could wilt artificial flowers. He stared out at the world with vacant, beady brown eyes that could never bring themselves to meet a fellow human being's. A twisted scar-laden nose branched out desultorily from between them.

He had come to the attention of the Public Defender's Office owing to frequent arrests for trespassing and public drunkenness. Naturally, he was always assigned to yours truly, as I somehow managed to keep myself low man on the totem. I suspect the reason that the most distasteful cases made their way to my pigeonhole had to do with an officewide acknowledgment of my evangelical self-image.

At any rate, when more serious charges of peeping and indecent exposure, including to a minor, were thrown into the mix, I at least had a reason to meet with my client before arraignment. This was particularly true in this case since a magazine with pictures of children in questionable poses was found in his bindle.

"I don't think I can keep you out of jail this time, Stan."

"Ah know, Mr. Kazmerk, Ah know. The Lord knows Ah deserve to be in jail. But Ah'm just...Ah'm just so skeered."

I knew that not once had an article he claimed to have stolen been found in his possession, constructive or otherwise. "Is it that you deserve it, or do you *want* to be in jail, Stan?"

His deer-in-the-headlights look of confusion never failed to elicit my protective instincts. It was curious, my reaction to Stanley Oxendine. At that time still defending with my true sword the rights of those on the margins of society, I was disposed to wrap Stanley in a metaphorical embrace. He had always seemed so innocuous, so obviously the butt of all jokes and bullying, with never a chance at negotiating the rough-and-tumble of this world. So I knew how he'd fare in prison. Ever most polite, I even found his inability to pronounce my last name endearing. "Ah…Ah don't…Whaddya mean, Mr. Kazmerk?"

"Never mind, Stan. Look, I might be able to get the DA to let you plead to the main charge in exchange for dismissing the other, or others. It depends on how generous she's feeling."

"Wha—wuzzat mean?"

"It means you'll spend less time in jail than if you asked for a trial and got convicted. Tell me the truth, Stan. Did you do what they say you did?"

"Mr. Kazmerk, Ah…Ah 'uz washin' mah clothes there at the Duds 'n' Suds, 'n'…'n' Ah only got two pair a' underwear. Ah 'uz washin' 'em both at the time 'n' all mah other clothes too, 'n' Ah didn't have no quarters for the dryin' machines. Mah coat just opened by accident, Ah swar!"

Then guilt would overcome him, and he'd continue in self-mortification: "But Ah know Ah ain't no good. The Good Lord knows Ah deserve to be punished. The devil's in me! Ah kin hear his voice, Mr. Kazmerk!" Stanley's devout faith together with his desire to confess to the most exotic crimes and misdemeanors were well-known within the legal community in Austin.

As I look back on it now, Stanley's curious combination of protestations of innocence for what he was actually accused of, together with assertions of guilt for offenses macabre and sui generis, should have rung alarms. Yes, pulsing beneath my self-image as the Maecenas of the oppressed was an irksome recognition of the ugliness of this world. But I still could not accept its ineradicability.

Actually, I remember always having the urge, which at the time I thought was a response to Stanley's lack of personal hygiene, to run home and take a shower immediately after my meetings with him. Perhaps there was something else that felt unclean. Why was I then unwilling to recognize or even contemplate it?

And Stanley's last comment echoed in my ear: "The devil's in me! I can hear his voice!" Why did that declaration I'd heard the likes of so many times now send a shiver up my spine? Perhaps I'd just suppressed it before.

I was certain that as soon as he got out of jail, I would hear from him again. But I was totally unprepared for the nature of the call. Its arrival some five months later sent a wave of panic through me. A warrant was sworn out for his arrest in connection with the rape of a nine-year-old girl. For a moment I sat benumbed. Even more disturbing than the shock was the nascent feeling of inevitability.

The offense had occurred in an alley that he was known to frequent, and he'd disappeared immediately afterward. *That's rather opportune*, the advocate in me thought. *A place he's known to frequent. Yeah, along with every other homeless person in the city.*

But a wave of tiny insects crawled across my skin when the phone rang the next morning. "Jake?" Lissette, our receptionist, mouthed in hushed tones. "It's Stanley Oxendine." I hesitated as my face seemed to lift off its moorings and waves of colored shadows pulsed before my eyes. "Jake...?" she repeated.

"Put him on," I finally managed to murmur. The click as Lissette patched me through took on an ominous tenor, like the thud of the guillotine.

"M-M-M-Mr. Kazmerk," his haunted, pleading voice whined over the line. "Mr. Kazmerk, Ah...Ah don't know what to do."

"Stanley, where are you?"

"Ah'm…Ah'm in Maxwell."

"Maxwell? Where is that?"

"It's, uh…It's close to San Marcos. What 'm Ah gonna do, Mr. Kazmerk?"

The tone of his voice reeked of guilt and terror. It rifled through my bones like a cold December wind. But why now? It was, after all, only an exaggeration of Stanley Oxendine's normal demeanor. He was always guilty—and always afraid. It could easily have been presupposed guilt for any horrendous crime—committed by any*one*.

So I told myself.

Suddenly the fundamental ambiguity of my position as defense counsel came crashing down. What if he was guilty? What if he had actually raped an innocent child, robbed her of that sense of safety and trust so indispensable for the development of a happy, well-adjusted human being? These are qualities of personhood that can never be restored—never *fully* restored. What then? I felt the impulse from my law-school days to split into alternate personalities and argue the case as though it were hypothetical.

"What're you doing there, Stan?"

"It's where Ah'm from, Mr. Kazmerk. It's where Ah 'uz born 'n' lived till Ah 'uz seven er eight."

In the heat of the moment, my defense-counsel reflexes took command. I swiftly rejected any inquiries into his guilt or innocence. "Stan, you've got to turn yourself in—there in Maxwell. An arrest warrant's been sworn out for you here. Now, do *not* tell me anything about the case over the phone." I felt numb, on automatic pilot. "When you go to the—is there a police station there?"

"Uh…nah, nah, just the sheriff's office in Lockhart."

"Go there and turn yourself in. Do *not* tell them anything other than that you heard there's a warrant for your arrest in Austin. Do you understand?"

"Uh…y-yeah, OK."

"Listen to me, Stan. Do not even say that you know what the arrest warrant is for. If they ask you how you found out, say you heard it on the radio." My self as an officer of the court sworn to uphold the law managed to surface. "No, strike that. You just tell them that your lawyer told you not to say anything."

"But Ah *did* hear it on the radio, Mr. Kazmerk."

"Well, that's fine, Stan. You can mention that, *but that's all!*" I felt myself sinking deeper and deeper into a stinking pit of amorality. "Other than that, you just say your lawyer told you to turn yourself in and say absolutely nothing. And, Stanley, I mean *nothing*, to *nobody*—not the sheriff, the deputies, your cellmates—*nobody*." I felt the annoying exhilaration of being a good advocate claw at my humanity.

"Mr. Kazmerk, they know me here. Ah've turned myself in fer different thangs here too, 'n' they know me purty good."

"It doesn't matter, Stan. *Nothing*, to *nobody. Do you understand?*"

"Yes, sir. Yes, sir, Mr. Kazmerk, Ah do. Ah-Ah-Ah won't say anythang. Ah won't."

"All right. Hang up the phone and go immediately to the pol— the sheriff's office."

"All right, Mr. Kazmerk. Ah'll see if I kin hitchhike over thar. Thank you, thank you." He hesitated and then diffidently hung up the telephone.

As I hung up on my end, a nauseous ball of ambivalence made its way down my gullet. *Reasonable doubt, Jacob, reasonable doubt,* a voice whispered faintly from a space on my left shoulder. It made that shoulder sag under the weight of it. I tried to gag the other voice that screamed in the voice of innocent children the court officer's oath to uphold the law—to ardently seek justice for all. *Justice* for all. This was the conflict that before this moment I had never faced in any soul-threatening way. *Do your job, Jake,* the first voice, now turned coarse and despotic, commanded. *Let the prosecutor do his—or hers.*

Hands I could not recognize as my own searched for lawyers in the area of Lockhart. I finally found one who occasionally dabbled in criminal law between normal duties of executing wills. A voice that was a stranger to me made sure he would go immediately to the sheriff's office to meet my client.

*My client*: those words scraped out my insides. I chased thoughts of a violated nine-year-old child away with the mollifying salves of *zealous representation*. They served to cover the wound of her innocent face, disfigured by the snatching away of her world of trust and safety.

Once notified of Stanley Oxendine's secure custody in the hands of the deputy sheriff, I arranged for his arraignment at the Caldwell County Seat in Lockhart. He would then be transported back to Austin by Detective David Méndez of the Austin Police Department. My request to accompany him, and so ensure that en route he would not make any self-incriminating statements, was roundly denied. Albert Prelip, the local lawyer I'd contacted there, made the same request. It was likewise rejected.

It was on that fateful trip that justice itself and my life as an officer of the court would begin to unravel.

Detective David Méndez was a devout Charismatic Catholic and had gotten to know Stanley Oxendine particularly well over the years. He had actively sought his salvation and directed him to his own church on Austin's east side. I had, of course, often crossed paths with Detective Méndez as a result.

I'd always felt a curious connection with him. He was older than I, and though I liked him, I was always struck with a vexing sense of inadequacy whenever we met concerning a case. This was particularly true when it pertained to Stanley. I felt from him what was perhaps a benign condescension. It was as though he recognized something of himself in me that he had grown past. At the time, it was particularly discomfiting. I look back on it now with that painful feeling of, *If only I'd known then...*

He realized that this time his efforts regarding Stanley had failed and that only Stanley's incarceration could ensure the safety of society. But he also knew that little Cathy Owens, after her assault, had reacted as many confused children might. She went home and immediately burned her clothes and scrubbed herself raw in the shower, destroying whatever biological evidence might have existed. Her identification of her attacker would help, but he knew that only a confession would ensure the necessary result.

I wonder now, as I'm sure David Méndez does, about the power of religious conviction to redeem a life of constant physical and sexual abuse. For my years defending him had revealed that such was the case with Stanley Oxendine. From his stepfather through foster homes and institutions, Stanley's life had been one of unremitting outrage and spiritual slaughter. Perhaps faith could delay or ameliorate the powerful urges that that mistreatment engendered. But it seemed that the devils of Stanley's youth were too powerful to overcome. Or maybe those opposing forces just didn't have sufficient time.

But most vexing of all, I've learned since then that most victims of abuse don't become abusers themselves. What is it then? What could possess a human being to commit such unspeakable evil? At any rate, Stanley's devils were now mine, for where in that concatenation lies responsibility for one's actions? Where is free will?

On the short journey from Lockhart to Austin, Detective David Méndez turned to look at the broken lump of humanity in the backseat of his car. Tears and snot rolled down that wizened face, rutted with the hardscrabble life of institutions and alleyways. "What're the tears for, Stan?"

"Ah...Ah don't know what...The devil's in me, Detective Dave."

"Like I told you before, Stan, the devil's in all of us. We can't resist him by ourselves. We need help. I ain't seen you at Our Lady of Guadalupe in a while. You bin to confession lately? To the meetin's they have there for substance abuse?"

"Aw, Ah..." Stanley took a long time before answering simply, hopelessly, "No. No, Ah ain't. Ah-Ah jus'..." He hesitated as my admonitions lulled absently in his glue-sniffing-addled brain. "Uh, Detective Dave, M-Mr. Kazmerk told me not to say anything till Ah seen him in Austin."

"Well of course you have that right, Stan. You absolutely have that right. Just know that once we git there, I cain't help you. You'll be interrogated by people who ain't your friends like we are. I always thought of us as friends."

The tears now ran down Stanley's face in torrents. "Ah wanna be yer friend, Detective Dave! Ah ain't never had no real friends. But Mr. Kazmerk—he's nahs. And you know, he—he told me…" And Stanley's voice disintegrated into heartrending sobs.

David Méndez then pulled over to the side of the road. "Stanley, I can tell you got something eatin' away at you, something that's got your insides so twisted up it's gonna kill you. Now, I'm glad you have somebody like Mr. Kazmareck in your corner, but he doesn't go to the same church we go to, does he? I ain't never seen him there. I used to see you there. I used to see you coming out of the confessional on Saturday afternoons. But I ain't seen that in a long time, Stanley. Why is that?"

"Oh, Detective Dave, Ah…Ah…Ah jus' ain't no good."

"Stan, we're all children of God, and we can all be forgiven whatever sin we've committed. But I want you to think about the promises you made to the Lord when you came out of that confessional, and in those meetin's—about acceptin' responsibility for your actions. And I want you to think about a little girl, a little nine-year-old *Catholic* girl, Stan. I found out she had just made her first Holy Communion this very year. Did you know that?"

"Oh no! Detective Dave, Ah-Ah…" exploded out of Stanley Oxendine in choking sobs of guilt. "Ah…Ah need to talk to Mr. Kazmerk. Please, Detective Dave."

"Well, we can wait, Stan. We can sure do that. I'd just like you to think about that little girl's parents. How must they feel? Think of that innocent little girl who's had her childhood just ripped away from her."

"Oh, God he'p me!"

"God will help you, Stan. He will. He's tryin' to. He's there waitin' for you to just let Him. But you got to let Him. You know Christ expects us to own up to the sins we commit. You know that, don't you?"

At that moment, Stanley's sobs began to subside as his substance-macerated brain started to perceive the only possible escape from his torment. "Yassir. Yas, sir, Ah do."

"Now, Stan, is there something you want to tell me? God's trying to help you. He wants to take this terrible burden off your shoulders, if you'll just let Him. Let it go, Stan. Just let it go."

And so finally, as tears and sobs subsided into resolution, Stanley Oxendine did exactly that. And I was thrust into a maelstrom of legal and ethical ambiguity.

# 13

It was no surprise that, after visiting Stanley in jail shortly thereafter, I felt the need to go immediately to the Y down the street and shower. I spent an inordinate amount of time soaping up and rinsing and then repeating the procedure ad infinitum. I only realized when I was getting dressed that I hadn't even worked out. I have no idea how long I sat on that bench in the locker room. I was lost in thoughts that circled like hovering vultures. I came to my senses only when Mike, the custodian, broke my reverie.

His voice seemed to come from across a distant canyon. "Say, Mister Jake, you awright?"

I looked up, and my consciousness, still rooted in agonizing choices, lagged behind.

"You okay, brother?" the voice repeated, and finally, my brain registered the images and sounds being transferred.

"Oh...y-yeah! Yes, I'm fine. Thanks, Mike. I was just thinking. I do that on occasion—keeps the mind from atrophying."

"Must be a powerful subject. You been sittin' there since I come by half-hour ago."

I looked at him in wonder. "I have?"

"Yeah, boy. You sure you're awright?"

"Yes. Yeah, yeah. I'm...I'm good. Just got caught up in something I was, uh...mulling over. But I'm...fine."

"Awright," he skeptically but cheerfully answered as he whistled his way on through the dressing room. Mike was a champion whistler, and his concerts as he collected towels, swept, mopped and attended to this and that were always soothing. Except today.

I quickly finished dressing and stuffed the clothes I'd been wearing in my gym bag. The unnerving thought then occurred to me to burn them along with my bag. *Jake, he's your client! You took an oath to give him the best possible defense you can! And he's innocent until proven guilty!...But this! This!*

As time progressed, the devil's details of the law kept up their pursuit. The vagaries of the Fifth and Sixth Amendments bore into my intestines and twisted my insides into a pretzel. For the first time, the little game I'd played in law school of splitting myself into two persons began to take on a macabre tone. In school, it had been a fun little exercise. Now I felt as though a part of me were slipping away, benumbing what was left to be free to spin its web of legal technicalities.

"Technicalities!" it protested. "The right to the assistance of counsel is not a technicality! Nor is the right against self-incrimination! They are two of the most fundamental guarantees of the Constitution!"

My self felt a rot in the pit of its stomach. "I am an officer of the court," it dully heaved.

"You are this man's lawyer, and you took an oath to provide him with the best, most zealous defense you can!"

"*Legitimate* defense."

"And who are you to decide what's legitimate?" my counterself demanded. "Rule 3.01 of the Rules of Professional Conduct: 'The advocate has a duty to use the legal procedure for the fullest benefit of the client's cause.'"

"You're leaving out the second clause in that sentence: 'but also a duty not to abuse legal procedure.'"

"Hah! It was Officer Méndez who abused legal procedure!"

"Two wrongs. Two wrongs! Plus, you're ignoring the rules that follow: 'A lawyer shall not knowingly fail to disclose a fact to a tribunal

when disclosure is necessary to avoid assisting a criminal or fraudu-
lent act.'"

"You—you're not assisting any criminal act. The act has already
been committed, by *someone who's not been proved to be our client!*"

"Right. And when we talk about accessory after the fact, we only
take into consideration the letter and not the spirit of the law."

My counterself waited a dramatic moment and then repeated,
"You swore an oath to God."

"I...I'm not even sure I believe in God."

"Do you believe in anything—in honesty, in personal integrity, in
the sacredness of the justice system?"

"Yes, I do, dammit! And I believe in the truth, in genuine justice,
in the spirit of the law, not just its letter! And this man is guilty!"

"That is *not* for you to decide! You are counsel for the defense, not
judge or jury! You swore an *oath*!"


At the lineup, little Cathy Owens, the alleged victim, hesitated. "I
think it's number five."

"Take your time, sweetie. Try to be sure," Detective Méndez
advised.

The urge within me to step forward and caution against coach-
ing met a brick wall of ambivalence. At last I wheezed out a weak,
"Detective."

Then came the nail in the coffin: "I'm...I'm pretty sure. It was
dark, and I closed my eyes." At this, my body caved in on itself, like a
can in a science demonstration: water evaporated and cap in place,
external pressure collapsing me inward.

As time and the case progressed, I became dissociated, wrenched
loose from the earth. I consulted experienced attorneys, my crimi-
nal-law professors, constitutional scholars and reams and reams of
case law. All of it buried me in supposition and doubt.

That part of me consumed with zeal, coldly chomping at the bit
for experience and—I realize now—for other things I wasn't willing
to acknowledge, listened and read with ravenous hunger. And the

more I heard, the more precedents I absorbed, the more I hungered. It seemed so surreal. I could not recognize the part of me that argued with such vehemence the illegality of the confession and the poisonous fruit of its discoveries.

And then on the fateful day of pretrial motions, I stood before Judge Alton Moore, one of the most conservative in Texas's Travis County. We awaited the newly hired assistant district attorney whose identity, for some unexplained reason, had not been revealed. That secrecy sent a strange sense of foreboding up my spine. Then, as he finally stepped through the courtroom door, my blood turned to ice.

It was Connors McClain.

My lower jaw unhinged and plummeted. Our eyes locked across the great expanse between defense and prosecution. I was suddenly aware of the courthouse smell of antiquated wood, the refuse of timeworn matters that haunted its corners. There were skeletons creaking out of old festering wounds—cases echoing of the innocent condemned and victims who never knew justice. Tears spilled down its ancient dowdy walls and crawled beneath the skin of its pellagric floor.

Connors's eyes at first bled apology and regret. But then that look transformed into a caged defiance—no doubt a reaction to the accusation that flooded from my own.

"Hello, Jake," was all he said. His tone was short and hard, like the whipping of saw grass in a fierce spring wind. The room caromed about his face. *How in God's name is this possible?* was the barely articulated thought that flickered about my brain. *Is this real? Is it a dream?*

I stared, waiting. Beyond his words, there seemed to be nothing else. It was as though all existence vanished but for the two of us. Then a foreign voice seemed to waft from another dimension. "Are counsel prepared to proceed?"

The face turned and offered its profile. "Ready, Your Honor." The silence that followed screamed of betrayal.

"Counselor?" the former voice impatiently, but with a twinge of curiosity, insisted. Again, silence hung in clouds of anguish. "Mr.

Kazmareck, are you ready to proceed?" The face across from me maintained its rock-hewn profile, my attention fixed.

Finally, out of some antipodal space and time, a voice aspirated, "Ready, Your Honor." And it was my voice. But I could not recognize it as such. It seemed devoid of sense—nay, of place. I saw myself transported to the future present, and the voice found its origin in the sterile winds of the wasteland. But I could not perceive myself in it—in them, as it became two. One was the voice of Connors, and I heard myself, which was not myself, arguing in his voice. The other was robotic and atonal, with no register above a monotone.

Out of its depths, it spoke, "It would be a fundamental violation of his inalienable rights under the Fifth and, according to abundant case law, Sixth Amendments, Your Honor." It had the hollow sound of a hammer against pipe, the metallic chink of a cardinal in its quest for sustenance. It seemed to flow out and down and linger upon the coffee stains on the scarred wooden floor.

The other voice, more assertive, more sure of itself, rejoined, "Your Honor, the exclusionary rule does not include voluntary speech. The defendant wasn't being interrogated at the time but was rather engaged in conversation only. And by taking part in that conversation, he implicitly waived his right to counsel and against self-incrimination."

The first voice I was rapidly recognizing as my own countered in gradually strengthening tones. "*Brewer v. Williams*, Your Honor: 'The coercive nature of the conversation was tantamount to interrogation.' And what the detective did in this case goes far beyond the Christian burial speech."

The other snapped back in quick but measured rejoinder, "*Rhode Island v. Innis*, Judge: 'It is only interrogation when an *objective* policeman would think that the comments could elicit an incriminating response.'"

Finally, Judge Moore spoke. "I've read the report, Mr. McClain. Are you implying that this was casual conversation, meant to elicit nothing from the defendant but the same?"

"Your Honor, it's an established precedent that the police have the right to use deception in their search for the truth. *Brewer v. Williams* was a very controversial five-four decision, and—"

"And as such," Judge Moore interrupted, "it's established precedent, is it not, Counselor?"

"Well, Your Honor, opposing counsel has still not clearly shown how the defendant had a right to counsel at that time."

Against my will, the second voice was becoming stronger and more confident. There was some part of myself that I couldn't or wouldn't recognize, that I can only perceive in the present, looking back. But it began to speak with a vigor that now places me on a teeter-totter of ambivalence. "*Massiah v. United States*: 'Once adversarial proceedings have commenced'—and my client was already arraigned, Your Honor—'he has the right to legal representation when the government interrogates him.'"

I could no longer hear the voice across the aisle as any part of me. And I now cringe at the pleasure the faint note of desperation in its tone gave me. "Your Honor, former chief justice Warren Burger warned of the costs those precedents inflicted on a civilized society."

"The costs, Your Honor," my own voice now sharply responded, "might be great, but they would be a teaspoon in the ocean of injustice compared to the violent shredding of the Constitution and everything that we, as officers of the court, are sworn to uphold."

*From where had those words come?* Though delivered with incisive assurance, they seemed to drip down beveled arguments of mist and insubstantiality. They sutured the rent, frayed text of jurisprudence as they escorted embattled justice to the ash heap of stale cigars in backroom equivocations.

"Quite eloquent, Mr. Kazmareck, if a bit hyperbolic," Judge Moore dryly observed. Then, as I heard the words "motion granted," a shiver of uncommon sharpness coursed through me. I immediately exited and gorged myself at the water fountain like a sweat-stained horse at a water trough. Cupped handfuls of the chilly liquid doused my face and dampened my hair in efforts to awaken from the nightmare I found myself in.

Then I heard his familiar voice behind me. "Jake." I turned to face him. "Jake..." He hesitated, uncertain how to proceed. Finally, he settled on a simple "Jake, I'm sorry." I stared in disbelief. "I had to disappear. We couldn't tell you. I couldn't even tell my family where I was. They were looking for me, on both sides of the border. I'm...I'm sorry."

I stared up at him in a stew of emotions, wonder and rage dueling for primacy. Finally, I managed to force out a hoarse "Artie...?" His eyes, cast down in defeat, answered more articulately than all the words in Shakespeare's canon. And so my accusation came: "I saw you. *I saw you!*" His quick glance at me and then away confirmed the tattered threads of my memory of that night.

"Where...? Why didn't...?" The words came drooling out of overloaded, misfiring synapses. His eyes once again met mine. Out of them poured apology, regret. And then...something else. Was it *defiance*? Could he feel some justification for his betrayal? I tried to fathom the contradiction I was seeing. I finally recognized a condescending smugness slowly replace regret. My right hand, with a volition all its own, doubled into a fist, reared back and came lurching forward with Connors's face as its target.

But I had too telegraphed the blow. Connors half blocked, half evaded it with ease. The rush of adrenaline my blow aroused momentarily brought fire to his eyes. But he quickly regained control, and we locked eyes once more, wordless, breathless. And so I passed beside him and marched to the stairs, down and out into the late-autumn air.

I was filled with rage. But as I look back on it now, I'm unsure of exactly where my rancor was directed. At Connors, certainly. But there was, blended in so fine as to be indistinguishable from righteous indignation, revulsion at myself.

For buried beneath my devotion to the defenseless and the vow to uphold the sacred documents upon which this country's justice system is founded, there was a darker impulse. I now recognize an urge more base and primeval: I wanted to win! And from the moment Connors stepped into that courtroom, the passion, the avidity to beat the boy who had teased me and my sister so mercilessly for so many years, had metastasized. It would infect and undermine my sense of ethics for all the subsequent proceedings.

I became what I least respected: an attorney fighting to win regardless of the consequences, regardless of the insult and injury to the victim. Victims, I should say, when including the parents, relatives and society at large—and to the very system of justice itself. The very opening of the Code of Professional Conduct stood like a dust-covered article of furniture in an abandoned house: "A lawyer is a representative of clients, an officer of the legal system, and a public citizen *having special responsibility for the quality of justice.*"

A plea offer for internment in a mental institution was roundly rejected by Stanley. Institutions had been nothing short of chambers of horror for him. But I recognize now that I was not disappointed by his refusal. It would not have satisfied my primitive impulse to vanquish my childhood antagonist.

And when I did win, when I heard the bone-chilling, gut-hollowing pronouncement—"We find the defendant not guilty"—*there* was the monstrous ogre of ego I had to deny. I had to displace it in its totality upon Connors's shoulders. And in the bargain, I heaped upon him my own failing of Artie.

# 14

I didn't speak to Connors McClain through the length of the trial.
I made sure any negotiations were handled through subordinates. Owing to this highly publicized trial, I was no longer the
low man on the totem pole. When it was over, I studiously avoided
him. And he apparently knew better than to try to contact me.

Nor could I return to court. There were no celebrations, no pats
on the back or high-five congratulations in the PD's office. There and
at home was just an eerie silence—a dull, lifeless ache as I sat at the
table in my efficiency apartment looking out the window onto the
coarse, beggarly streets of east Austin.

Given my penny-pinching ways, I had saved enough money to take
time off and drag my bruised and bleeding soul home to Aguagria.
There I could find safe harbor in the loving company of my sweet
Grace. A few nights, with only my aging dog Alex as company, I'd
revisit the crude haunts of my days with Artie and Connors.

Under a canopy of starlit magic, we were invited into the parlor
of deer and fox and ragged raccoon, serenaded at night by hoots and
chirps and feral howls that had once filled Alex with atavistic hunger.
Now in the twilight of his time, there only because he knew I wanted
him to be, he could exhibit only a tired nonchalance. After a few of
those excursions, the memories they inspired wrought too sharp an
ache. So, to Alex's relief, we stayed home.

Every morning from then on would find us in the warmth of hearth and home, Alex grateful to curl up on his personal pillow. There, we'd be treated to the dulcet bow strokes that nursed Bach and Vivaldi and Beethoven and Dvořák from Gracie's violin. It was a time to heal from the slings and arrows of ideals flushed down the black waters of Weltschmerz. It was a period of rest from the pangs of self-judgment.

Finally, the time had come to return to the capital and the work whose sheen now lay buried beneath the grime of real-world choices. And one morning as I attended to routine cases in district court, news more horrible than morbid fancy could conceive flayed away the patina of normalcy: Stanley Oxendine had graduated to new heights of evil, and a Hispanic child of six was discovered in a shallow grave behind the warehouse where he often took refuge.

For a moment I stood frozen, my jaw unhinged. A nauseous ball of disbelief hollowed out my insides. It must have clearly registered, for my supervisor, who'd delivered the news, grabbed my shoulders as though to keep me from falling off the earth. "Steady, Jake. This kind of thing happens: los gajes del oficio; it comes with the territory."

I stared vaguely at her, trying to escape the information from her wounding tongue. I pled desperately with God to make this a nightmare from which I'd shortly awaken. I begged Him to take me back to my comfortable world of absolutes, transport me beyond messy compromises and resignations. I felt the world slewing on its descent into hell. There it lodged leadenly in the hollow swale of sewers.

I charged through the hallway crowd to the nearest restroom. The eggs and toast I'd had for breakfast came violently forth and exploded against the wall seconds before I could reach an awaiting receptacle. My back made forceful contact with the wall behind me, and I slid down, my backside flopping against the tile floor.

After a moment of stupor—or hours, for all I could tell—I heard the door open, a few steps taken and offended noses turn about-face and exit. Embarrassed, I tried as best I could to clean up the mess I'd made. My body violently shook at the greater mess I'd made of the concept of justice.

By the time my trembling abated enough for me to stand, Fulgencia, one of the custodians, had been alerted and entered to finish my paltry cleaning job. "Oh, Fulgencia, por favor, perdóneme."

She quickly stopped me, always grateful that I addressed her in Spanish. "O, no se apure, Sr. Kasmare. Estas cosas pasan. ¿Se ha recuperado? ¿No se necesita una ambulancia?"

"No. No. Estoy…Bueno, no es…este…No, no, es-estoy bien," I stammered, making my way to the door.

"Bueno, cuídese."

I have little memory of my journey to my apartment. Only the sight of children registered. Their innocent laughter played like a horror movie in my mind. For a time, I sat dazed and semicatatonic, staring out my kitchen window at autumn winds wrenching leaves from mostly barren branches. Perversely, I turned on the radio to hear further news. I listened hoping that my former client would, through some divine intervention, be found innocent of this new unspeakable evil.

Days passed, and the angry ringing of the telephone gave way to messages of solicitude. They were followed after by ones of concern, then impatience and finally despair. Alex lay patiently by my side, sensing some shift in the earth's orbit.

Then, upon traitorous television waves came news that was the complete dissolution of my faith—faith in the justice system, faith in humanity, faith in myself. There was Stanley Oxendine on the courthouse steps, and his words still echo in the hollows of my soul: "I ain't ta blame! Ah seen it on th' Innernet! They's thousands, millions, in the world jus' like me! It ain't perverted, and someday you'll all look back and see that it's jus' a different kind a love. Ah didn't mean to kill that little girl—Ah's jus' tryin' ta keep her quiet! She jus' wouldn't stop screamin'! It's y'all's fault! *You just wouldn't let me be who I am!*"

I continued immobile on the floor of my apartment, only occasionally taking Alex outside to attend to his necessities. It had become more and more difficult for him. More and more frequently, I was too late. Finally, he was unable or unwilling to rise. The gray, sooty light of early winter cast a pall on his head against my leg.

He had not left my side since I'd come home. His breathing was labored. My hand could identify each and every bone of his body as it passed across it. Cavernous indentations showed the form of his skull. His fur crackled as my hand passed over it, his skin thin as angel's breath. It whispered in my ear of good-byes and finalities. The vet at his last appointment had told me that it was just a matter of time. "I guess he's just wearin' out," she'd assessed at his continued loss of weight.

From here in the present, atop this mutinous mound of earth, Grace's questioning of the fundamental injustice of our father's death seems transported back through time. It hangs in the room like a gray fog, lingering upon the curves of Alex's ribs.

I looked back over the seventeen years in which he'd shared my life. No one had ever listened with such sympathy and support, never judging, ever loving.

"Who is to blame, buddy? Who?" I mumbled to him, to the walls, to no one in particular. I gently stroked his head and down his back, feeling the warmth of his body slowly dissipate. "What ordurous, disease-ridden self-absolution lies beneath the veneer of civilization? How did we get to this place? How can we find our way out of this empty pit of self-righteous condemnation of *they*?"

"*They* are to blame."

"Who is *they*?"

"*They! Them*—those other people who are in control, the ones behind the curtain who pull our strings!"

"Who's in control?"

"Not me! I have no control over my life! They charge too much. They demand too much. They don't pay enough. They have no sympathy or understanding for my suffering! They all conspire in secret boardrooms to hog all the riches and fun and enslave the rest of us. They make me eat foods that are bad for me. They force me to drink unhealthy drinks. I have to smoke. I can't get through life without that toke of cocaine! I'm too unhappy!"

"Why are you unhappy?"

"Because of them! They put too much pressure on me. They expect too much. Life is too hard! They drive me to drink. They only offer me a dead-end job.

"Did you look for another job?

"Yes, twice!"

"Did you get any training?"

"They didn't help me enough in school. My teachers made it too hard!"

"Well, did you ask for help?"

"I was too young. I didn't have no time. They didn't inspire me. School wasn't no fun! My jobs're boring! I just wanted to have some sex, I didn't want no damn baby! It's too hard to learn a new language. I don't care if I've been here twenty years. I'm too busy!"

"Oh, buddy, how did we get here?"

No tail wagged, and Alex's breath cut shallower and strained like the weight of the world pressed down on him. "I love you, buddy," I gently murmured in his ear. "Do you hear me? I love you more than all the world. You're my sweet baby dog. Can you hear me? I love you so much...so very, very much."

There was the tiniest rise of ribs beneath my hand. Then, a faint rattle. "Alex...? Alex...? Oh God." I listened for some errant breath, some trace of life against my leg, but only cold silence screamed.

"Aw, Alex...Good-bye, ole buddy. I loved you like nothing in this world. Gracie? Dolores? Gracie?"

Angela Balladares, the victim, was unearthed with a finger poking through the garbage bag she'd been buried in. At the moment of her interment, she was still alive. It was the day I quit the legal profession.

Who's to blame? Who's responsible? Who is Ayn Rand?

# 15

Austin had grown at a fevered pace during the years of my absence. At the dawn of the new millennium, all makeshift campsites along wild rivers now huddled in the stagnant fist of civilization. Bee caves were tamed, and flinty waterfalls once joyously slid down in cutoff jeans were now cordoned off by the mighty hand of authority—to protect us from ourselves, of course. We were strapped into seat belts, bicycle helmets and the straitjackets of limited drink size by the beneficent arm of maternal solicitude.

And so the spirit of adventure and discovery was choked into submission, turned worn and infirm as the arteries of wilderness hardened. It now bowed docilely at the hand of charity, and all that pioneer impulse had been smelted down to bathing-suit-clad characters on street corners: exhibitionism and lunacy posing as uniqueness and daring.

As Connors assistant, Trevor DeGrassi, and I made our way from the airport to the capitol building in a government limousine, a question I had studiously ignored began to articulate itself: why had I never confronted Connors McClain? Why didn't I look straight into his eyes and say, in the words of Laertes, "Thus didst thou"?

I was grateful when that noisome thought was interrupted by a message from the chauffeur: "Looks like there's a big backup on one eighty-three—accident or something. I'm gonna try to go around south and come in from Congress."

"That's fine, Jimmy," Trevor answered.

A breath of relief escaped me, as I knew that would delay my encounter with my long-lost compadre. And my reprieve was drawn out by considerable traffic on the alternative route. I turned to Trevor. "Is it usually like this?"

He looked up briefly from papers he was judiciously studying. "It was growing like a weed even when you were here, but you missed a lot of it living so close to downtown." *Man, he even knew where I lived?* I was beginning to feel like a lab rat in a psych experiment. "In the last two, two and a half years or so you were gone, the growth rate skyrocketed. And, of course, so did the traffic. But it can't be anything compared to New York. Or didn't you ever drive there?"

I didn't bother to answer, figuring that my time in the city must have been as open a book as the rest of my life. Instead, I tried to take in the sights. They seemed to be all new—like I was passing through a different city. Only every now and then would some structure look vaguely familiar. Until we got to Towne—er, Lady Bird—Lake, crossed and made our way through downtown traffic. Ahead, the beautiful old capitol building stood out in all its glory. "Well, at least there's one thing I recognize." Trevor just flashed his characteristic close-lipped grin.

We pulled into an underground parking deck and exited the car into the late-spring air. I couldn't tell how much of my sweat was due to heat or nerves. We took an elevator to a floor restricted to government officials' offices. The prospect of seeing the great Connors McClain conspired with the air-conditioning to send a shudder through me. Trevor maintained his wonted discretion and stared straight ahead.

When we entered his well-appointed office, Connors rose from behind his desk—motionless, eyes riveted to mine. We were two statues regarding each other in the silence of failure. In that moment, I realized that I had actually missed him. And that thought filled me with rage.

As I look back on it now, I can see that there were sources of that rancor that I didn't then recognize. True, there was what I believed to be the betrayal of our friend, the ridicule of my sister and me. But I can now see that there was something else, some spiritual itch or ripple. It passed undetected. But now I think it probably added fuel to the fire.

Trevor stepped aside, recognizing his position as outsider. The atmosphere was choked with the weight of history.

It was Connors who finally broke the silence. "Hello, Jake."

"Connors. You've put on weight."

"That's the barbecue, carne asada and trimmings I indulge in at just about every fund-raiser and gala I'm forced to attend." There was a smile of irony that surprised me in his self-correction: "Make that 'that I attend.' Nobody held a gun to my head. The ceremonies are a necessary evil. The food, I'm afraid, is what makes them bearable. I'm surprised the fare at Mount Sinai Hospital didn't put a few pounds on you." Something deepened in his eyes as they locked themselves to mine. "It's good to see you, Jake."

"Wish I could say the same" escaped from me before I could censor it.

He responded with a patient and rather patronizing smile. It intensified my anger. Perhaps to forestall any escalation, he patiently said, "Gimme a little time, Jake. That's all I'm askin'." He then hesitated, as though he were trying to gauge the possible consequences of what he was about to say. In that moment of uncertainty, I thought I recognized something akin to regret. "How's Grace?" he finally asked.

A wave of nausea swept through me on hearing my sister's name on his lips. Then it seemed to resonate outward. It registered on him in the slightest widening of his eyes. I dropped my gaze to the floor and kept it there a few moments to regain my composure. "Coping," was all I could manage to say.

There was a dialogue of things that couldn't be voiced—at least, not yet. The strain was even visible in Trevor, try as he might to be invisible.

Perhaps in recognition, Connors tried a less volatile topic. "I was sorry to hear about your father."

I glanced at Trevor and back, as much as to say, *So you sent one of your minions after me?* But then, of course, if he'd come, he knew what the result would've been.

"Thanks."

His mouth opened to form a question, and the hesitation let me know the tenderness of the subject. "And…?"

"I don't know. It's been a while since I've visited."

"I can provide you with a car if you want to go."

I needed an escape of my own. "How's Andie?"

"She's good. Expecting our second."

"Congratulations."

"Thanks." After an extended period during which our eyes locked in mutual examination, he took a deep breath. "Shall we get down to business?"

I answered in the affirmative without word or gesture.

"You've seen the prison manifest and the picture?"

"I have." Whether it was his mentioning Grace, the image of him on that riverbank or the years of agonizing over what had happened to him, to Artie, to us, all the accumulated venom came gushing forth in one statement: "What I can't figure out is why you give a shit."

For a fleeting moment, the facade he'd adopted as a politician was replaced by a searing malice. It lasted only a split second but was enough to remind me that he was still human. It quickly coiled back into a patronizing and deadly smile. "It must be cozy, Jake, living in your cocoon of absolutes. It must give you great solace to look down on us mere mortals slogging through the mud and selling our souls to at least keep the world idling.

"Oh, but Jake Kazmareck isn't satisfied with chugging along in first gear! No, he's shooting to jump from a dead stop to light speed.

You know what happens when you do that? The engine explodes. That's the story of your life, isn't it? Quitting your calling the first time things went the usual way of the world? Where's your loyalty to your profession?"

"How you've got the chutzpah to talk about loyalty helps me understand your success as a politician."

His lips curled into the smirk of a card shark who's just drawn the ace of spades to complete a royal flush—something not uncommon for Connors McClain. "Oh, so righteous, so quick to judge from your ivory tower of moral purity. How's it serving you now, Jake? How'd it serve you at Abe Beame Middle School? How'd it work out at PS 136?" Then, as his counterattack unchained the predator in him, he closed in for the kill. "And tell me what it did for Angela Balladares."

The mention of the little girl raped and killed by the man I had successfully freed from the penal system thrust me over the edge. Faster than wish or thought, I made my murderous way toward him. Fortunately, and probably more for me than for him, Trevor anticipated my move and stepped between us.

"Naw, let him go. Let him go," Connors magnanimously offered. Though my feckless assault had managed to rouse a rush of adrenaline in him, he gave the challenging sigh of the bigger man who knows he can deck his challenger without breaking a sweat.

As the fight-or-flight hormones raged, I shook myself loose from Trevor's grasp. I paced across the room to the large bookcase on the interior wall, took a moment to calm myself and then walked to the large window overlooking downtown Austin. The scalding blood pumping through my veins was not inclined to cool quickly.

After sufficient time had passed, Connors finally sighed out a calming breath of chagrin. "Hey, Jake, I..." He stretched out his hands in a gesture of regret. "I'm sorry, OK? I know what that case did to you. You just...got my dander up." I was a bit disarmed by the gesture. "Listen, you did your job," he continued. "And you kicked my ass, by the way. You're no more responsible for the consequences than I am."

I looked long and hard down the wide expanse of Congress Avenue, at average people, I imagined, going about their daily lives. And with my meliorist propensities, I imagined them aware of the impact every tiny decision they make has on the future of mankind.

"Aren't we?" I asked, still staring out the window. "If not us, then who?"

"Stanley Oxendine. And no one else."

I finally turned to him. "And it doesn't bother you one bit that the justice system, and you and I who practice it, failed—failed so miserably that it cost the life of an innocent child?"

"I don't necessarily agree with your conclusion or even your premises. But yeah, it does bother me. It always will. But you can't just wash your hands of the ugly mess this world is, Jake. You can't always be the unsoiled, disgusted cynic looking with jaundiced eyes at the bumbling, fumbling rest of us."

"If there's anything I'm not, it's unsoiled."

His face lifted in a thin-lipped look of painful triumph. "You know what a cynic is, Jake? He's an idealist who's had his feelings hurt. Tell me what you could've done different."

"I could've refused to represent him. I could've recused myself."

"Hmm, I'm sure you'd look fetching in an orange jumpsuit while you served out your time for contempt. And don't tell me you would've paid the fine. I know your penchant for the martyr's role."

"What if the next lawyer assigned to the case had recused? And the next one after that?"

"OK, Jake. You want to ascend the stratosphere of ivory-tower hypotheticals? Answer the question yourself. What happens to a defendant if he doesn't get adequate representation? He goes free! Or he will eventually. The only difference—the *only* difference—is that you and I and the rest of the taxpayers I hope to represent in this state would've had to pay every last cent they'd earned to find a lawyer with an ounce of practicality."

"So it all boils down to a waste of taxpayer money, does it? Your politician's slip is showing. I bet that argument sells really well with your constituents."

"It sells because it's right."

"Certainty is so seductive. It's what the people demand, isn't it?"

"Oh, you're a great one to talk about certainties. You've never met an absolute you didn't fall in love with. But the answer is yes, that's what people demand. And although they criticize it in others, they always seem to have a hard time seeing it in themselves." With a half-sigh, half-laugh, he lowered his imposing frame into his leather office chair and looked long and deep at me.

"You want to take the example of my constituents, Jake? Let me tell you about the conversation I had with my next-door neighbor. This was when I was first elected attorney general. He's an elderly retired gentleman, as decent and caring as you're ever likely to meet, the kind that never misses the opportunity to vote—so deeply religious in that old-time William Jennings Bryan way that he doesn't even believe in evolution."

He caught my frown of disbelief. "Yeah, that's right. And he's not alone. People believe whatever makes them feel comfortable. For instance, he tells me, 'Connors, if someday you get to be president of this country, you ought to just fix the price of gasoline. Keep these greedy oil companies from making these ridiculous profits like they do takin' advantage of us workin' folks.'

"Do you have any idea what that would do? Oil exploration would fizzle. Refineries would shut down within months because none of them could make a profit. We'd be rationing in the blink of an eye, so transportation would grind to a halt. And the economy would careen down the cliff of no return. And these people vote, Jake! That's the ugly reality! Now, what would you have me tell him? Or better yet, what would *you* tell him? That his ideas are just plain stupid?"

"I'd tell him the truth."

After a glance at Trevor and a long, exasperated sigh, Connors looked down at his hands folded on his desk. He seemed to be considering the implications of my answer. Finally, he looked up at me with a queer combination of pity with a smattering of respect. "Yeah, you would, wouldn't you? You sure would. No sullying his hands in the dirty business of politics for the above-it-all Jake Kazmareck. I'll tell you something, Jake. You show me a man who's not political, and I'll show you an unemployed bachelor—which only one of us in this room happens to be."

A dry, humorless laugh escaped me, and the smiles on the faces of Connors and his subaltern lowered the temperature in the room significantly. But I could not yet completely let go. "So what do we do? Chalk it up to the quote 'Imperfections of the system?' You say I won't dirty my hands with nonabsolutes. How can you so blithely wash your hands of all responsibility?"

"I don't. Or at least I realize that every time I try a little less of the stain comes off. With each passing year and every nasty compromise, they stink a little more. But as much as the grime and sleaziness pile up, as rank and putrid as my hands smell, at least I know they're in the soil. At least I know they're mixing in the foul-smelling manure, so that something, however imperfect, might grow among the weeds. At least my land doesn't lie fallow. 'All it takes for evil to triumph is for good men to do nothing.'"

I turned to face him. This was the quote from Edmund Burke that I had once told Artie and Connors would be the guiding principle of my life—and for which I took scathing ridicule from Connors. It had been just after I'd decided to become a lawyer and was full of fantasies of riding my spotless charger into battle against the forces of injustice.

Disarmed by the memory, out of me came not an argument but a plea: "Then how do you explain the evil, the *monstrous* evil, created by my doing *something*—something legal and smart and in keeping with all the tenets of classic jurisprudence?"

His eyes spoke with the eloquence of a master of oratory, though the furrow between them seemed to acknowledge the weight that pulled my shoulders earthward. "You know the answer to that, Jake.

Better than I do. You're the one who had a paper on constitutional law published while he was still a student. You were defending against an assault on the Constitution, not a man."

"I'm sure Angela Balladares's father would take great solace from that."

"Don't do that to yourself, Jake. Don't." With a great sigh, he rose. "You're a good man, Jake, one of the best I've ever known. What you did for the kids at Abe Beame Middle School and PS 136, for the voiceless and downtrodden, very few in this world—this nasty, dirty muckety-muck world—could or ever would have done. But you can't function in this fallen corner of creation and keep your virginity. That's pure vanity. It's hubris." He joined me in staring out the window. "It gets lonely up on that pedestal, doesn't it?"

*Lonely. Lonely.* How that word struck like a well-placed fist in the solar plexus. We both turned to each other at the same time. "How could I be...?"

"Well, it's a pretty neat trick with all the people who care about you. But somehow, you seem to manage it. And I don't think you do it with just yourself, brother. You've got to look at the other people in your life with an east-of-Eden eye as well."

"What're you talking about?"

"Well, let's just concentrate on you for the moment. You need to come down from the clouds and accept your place in the sty of humanity, Jake. If you can't, if you persist in avoiding the greasy, grimy, nasty fight...then Artie is lost."

As though through a fog, the mention of our friend at that precise moment slapped me in the face with the fact of my own self-pity. Connors's adage about the cynic truly applied. Seeming to recognize my epiphany, Trevor looked down and away, as though I suddenly stood naked before him.

But Connors's gaze remained steady as African rhythms. "Now, do you think you could listen to me for a minute?" I silently gave him license to proceed. "That freezing Christmas Eve we'd planned out so carefully, so sure of our young selves, Jake. We were so certain that our righteous cause would protect us. Or at least I think you were. Anyway, I found out at the last minute that the cartel was on to our little plot."

The look on my face must have spoken volumes. He answered before I could even process the information.

"It seems Artie's uncle Teo had told his best friend that he was going to *desaparecer* and how he could get a hold of him. Apparently, this friend wasn't such a good one. I couldn't get to Artie; it was too late. It wouldn't have mattered anyway. The cartel knew about his uncle, and now they knew about him. So they were all dead no matter what they did. By the time I'd found out, they were already on their way to the river.

"The only thing I could do was get the federal police out there, hoping they could arrest them before the cartel thugs got to them. As it happened, we got there about the same time. There was a shoot-out. Everybody without a gun, including me, hit the dirt. When it was over, I looked around for you, hoping to God you weren't caught in the crossfire. I finally found you clinging to that tree. I got a hold of you just before you slipped under."

"You took me to Aunt Agnes's house?"

"You don't remember? You don't remember anything about that night?"

"Not after the tree. I barely remember that."

"Jake, I had to disappear. One of the *federales* I was particularly close to told me that they had a mole—make that *moles*—informing on them to the Zetas, that they probably already knew who'd given them away. I took you to a friend, someone I knew I could trust. He said you told him where to take you, gave him directions and everything. You really don't remember?"

"I..." A vague image of being placed in the car, a near collision, the oak tree in Aunt Agnes's front yard were all that flashed across my mind. "Who was your friend?"

"Well, he's dead now, killed by the Gulf Cartel. But his family's still alive, so it's best I keep that information to myself."

"Oh yeah, yeah." I looked out the window, trying to assimilate all this new information. The realization of my monstrous blunder flooded through me. "Connors, I'm sor—"

"No tengas cuidado, hermano. It was a helluva night. It's been a helluva ride since then."

He gazed for a second back out the window as though trying to see what I saw. "Besides, I'm the one who owes you the apology." He turned back to me. "The time I spent in hiding…well, I had a lot of time to think." This time his face broke into a gentle smile. "And I had someone with me to help me do that. I know I made your life miserable, Jake." His tone turned sheepish. Another thing I never thought I'd experience coming from Connors McClain. "Especially with the way I talked about Grace.

"I was jealous is the simple answer—jealous of your accomplishments, of your love of your sister, and more than anything, jealous of how much Artie cared about you. He was always closer to you than me, even though I'd known him longer, even though he'd lived with my family for years. There was some attachment he felt for you that… well, that seemed to go beyond friendship." He paused a moment. I knew what it took for a man like Connors McClain to humble himself this way. "I'm sorry, hermano. I'm truly, truly sorry."

There was a long, embarrassed silence. I couldn't look at him. I was completely disarmed. It never stops surprising me how people can do the unexpected. You think you know someone, and they turn around and do something that shatters your conclusions. Then—maybe out of discomfort—it dawned on me to ask, "Are you safe now?"

"They know better than to come after the Texas AG. The rangers'd have a field day."

I turned to him. "Artie?"

"Yeah, Artie." He walked up to me and stretched out his arms. They seemed to encompass a universe of hurt and sin. "First things first, compadre." He wrapped me in a huge abrazo that I returned in kind. We stayed that way a long time. He kept one arm around me as he sat us on the edge of his desk. "Here's what I'm thinking…"

# 16

I'd begun to wonder how I was going to make a living now that my sterling career as a melon-picker had come to an end. My time in education in the big city had put me in the hospital and come close to putting me in an early grave. The idea of practicing law again gave me *shpilkes*. I would eventually have to search for a métier of some sort. *Hell, Jake, maybe you'll just have to get another job!*

"You don't need to worry about that for the time being," Connors reassured me. When I looked sharply at him, he laughed. "No, don't worry. I won't be funneling you taxpayer money. My family's got property smack in the middle of the Eagle Ford shale deposit. It's rolling in—over a thousand barrels a day: light, sweet crude, natural gas, the whole works."

He recognized the look on my face. "Yeah, I know, I know. It's not charity, Jake. I'm hiring you to execute the plan. You're on my payroll, and I expect results. I wish I could do it myself and not send you into the swamp of Mexican malfeasance. But we need to keep this strictly, and I mean *strictly*, between the three of us. I'm too high- profile, and Trevor's Spanish is too basic."

"I've just started studying, as a matter of fact," added this young man I'd begun to realize I'd judged very unfairly. That rush to judgment merited some self-study. What was it in me that had jumped to such an erroneous conclusion?

"And, in contrast to certain parties here, some of us want to keep our jobs." I acknowledged the allusion with an embarrassed puff of air out my one uncongested nostril.

The plan to liberate our long-lost companion fortunately only involved greasing the palms of appropriate Mexican officials and not helicopters and gunfights. It was a good thing, since my one flirtation with playing the hero that fateful Christmas Eve ended in such failure. As much as I might wish to the contrary, my skills do not include SEAL Team heroism.

So in a car provided by Connors's newfound oil wealth, I would head down to the border and then south into the land of laundered-dollar diplomacy. I scratched inside my ear as the word *subornation* entrained a tickle there. *You're not a lawyer anymore, Jake*, I told myself. Still, it was my word. It reminded me of the peculiar reaction I caught in myself each time I heard the phrase *confounding variable* in my freshman psychology class. As I was growing up, whenever my father was really frustrated or disappointed, his exclamation would always be "Confound it!"

It would take some getting used to, this world of moral relativity.

Tlaquetillo is a mere suggestion of a space on the map, a ghostly echo somewhere southwest of the city of Santiago de Córdoba in the mountainous desert region of Coahuila, Mexico. A few giant steps and a hike from the border, the area is steel-foundry hot for most of the year during the day, the sun a ball of lit magnesium.

But in winter, when the sun droops beneath the horizon and night blankets the sky with starlit majesty, a creeping arctic mass might leisurely settle and turn it blood-congealingly cold. It is dry as a horned toad's skin and imposing in its desolate grandeur. That it was the last place one would look for a federal prison was, I presume, precisely the point.

My success there depended upon meting out the requisite compensation to the appropriate parties. It was definitely not without risk, but Connors seemed sure of his contacts in the area, and I could not fail Artie. The picture Trevor DeGrassi had shown me of my old friend revealed an emaciated, wizened Arturo Cavazos. It was evident that his treatment there had been the stuff of a Bosch painting. It was also clear that failure to liberate him would most certainly cost him his life—if it hadn't already.

Connors had given me the name of a federal prosecutor to contact in Córdoba—a close friend he knew he could trust. As soon as palms were discreetly oiled with cash, the friend would give me the green light to continue on to Tlaquetillo. But I was enjoined in no uncertain terms to make sure he provided secure passage.

Mexico by that time had been effectively carved into warring drug-cartel fiefdoms. Their boundaries were marked with human body parts pointedly strewn on roadsides and battered heads displayed on bridges and makeshift pikes on highways. These measures were also used as provocative incursions into another's domain.

I was fortunate that the prison that housed Artie fell under the aegis of the Sinaloa Federation cartel. Under the control of Joaquin "El Chapo" Guzmán, it was ruthless but practical. Unlike the Zetas, whose territory bordered my route, torture and killing for the Sinaloans had a pragmatic end.

It has been said that humans are the only animals that take pleasure in inflicting pain. The Zetas have taken that insight and massaged it into a fine art. In addition, they had expanded their business plan to include extortion, kidnapping—with mutilation and the tortured screams of its victims as incentive to pay the ransom—and murder for hire, among many others. They really seemed to take great pleasure in their work as well.

First, however, I had to get through *aduanas*—customs—upon crossing the border from a town north of Aguagria. We had mapped out a circuitous route specifically to limit my exposure to Zetas territory. I have no doubt that they would consider my fear of encroachment quite flattering. I hoped I could rely on my skills at dissembling to camouflage the fear I felt upon crossing the border. I had rehearsed over and over the possible scenarios I would face.

I pulled up to the mustachioed customs officer—it seems an inviolable social norm in Mexico that all men have facial hair—and showed him my passport. "Buenos días," I said as perfunctorily as I could to give an air of routine.

"Buenos días, señor." He returned the greeting with a tinge of suspicion under a facade of boredom. I assumed it was meant to keep me a touch off-balance. "¿A dónde va?"

"A Córdoba."

"A Córdoba, ¿eh?" he slowly queried.

"Sí, señor. Y de allí a Tlaquetillo."

"A Córdoba," he repeated with certain smirk of skepticism. "¿Y qué va a hacer usted en Córdoba? Wha' jou do there?"

"I'm going to visit a friend."

"A frien', eh?"

"Yes, sir."

"A frien'. What chur frien' neim?" he asked, I supposed thinking he might trap me in a story that would force me to increase the bribe.

But I knew I held a trump card. "His name is Porfirio de las Casas Hidalgo. He's the unit chief of the federal police there—jefe de distrito de la policía federal." Immediately upon mentioning that particular organization, I felt a stiffening in my interrogator. He made a valiant effort to cover it, his face going blank. "Los federales, ¿eh?"

"Sí, señor. And also with the district attorney there—el procurador, Sr. Santiago Cásarez Montemayor." The latter was Connors's friend who would be my contact. Connors assured me that he would be a good resource in case I happened to incur the displeasure of Coahuila law enforcement. My mentioning of specific names seemed to put the customs agent in a quandary. I imagine that with my having such contacts he was unsure as to whether it would be kosher to solicit the normal monetary incentive.

The art of subornation in that ethical wasteland is a sometimes subtle matter. On occasion, it's as brash as a bull castration. It might even have been unnecessary in the present situation, given the names and organizations I'd mentioned.

But regaining his composure, he continued, "A Córdoba...y después a Tlaquetillo. Pues, no hay nada en Tlaquetillo. There ees nothing there, señor. Besides, eet wou' be *un poco peligroso*...cou' be a leetle dangerous—to go there *a solas*. Things cou' happen on thee way."

Here was the poorly veiled threat indicating that the bribe could also be considered protection money. Since my journey would be taking me through a small segment of Zetas territory, it caused me considerable discomfort. I made my best effort at dissimulation. This was the cat-and-mouse game I assumed I would face throughout my hopefully short junket.

In the coded parlance of the situation, I asked as casually as I could, "¿Tiene usted algunas sugerencias? Do you have any suggestions on how I might avoid that danger?"

"Well, I have frien's too, Señor. Maybe I cou' tell them to wash out for jou."

"Well, I would really appreciate that. Se lo apreciaría mucho." Then, dropping all pretense of subtlety, I continued, "Uh, how much do you normally charge for that service?"

"Pues..." His face betrayed a measure of uncertainty and at the same time victory, having made the gringo squirm. "Lo que usted diga, señor. Whaever jou theenk."

I pulled out my wallet and made an ostentatious show of opening it on a one-hundred-dollar bill and a companion Andrew Jackson amid some Mexican currency. This was per Connors's instructions. It was an attempt to at once show my generosity by handing him the hundred and then to indicate subsequent financial straits. Its intention was as a hedge against being robbed by his friends en route. "¿Será ésto suficiente? I left my one credit card at home—just to be safe. So can I keep the twenty? Para gas, usted sabe."

His acidulous look communicated his skepticism more forcefully than words. "De verdad, señor. Soy emisario, no más. I'm just a messenger."

"And when jou come back?"

"Today. Hoy mismo."

He held my gaze for a moment, just to emphasize his doubt concerning my story. Finally though, he stepped back with the hundred. Then, with a wave of his hand he mouthed a dismissive "Por supuesto, señor. Pase usted. Have a good treep. An' be careful."

I was on my way. First there was the short jaunt past claustrophobic vendors' stalls displaying in sundry bric-a-brac along the main street. Then, before reaching the highway that would ferry me southwest, a welter of familiar smells assaulted my senses: sumptuous aromas of *helote*, boiling corn on the cob, mingled with the pungent stabbing of fresh-squeezed orange juice and the sugary lusciousness of *leche quemada*.

Those luscious aromas swept me back to my youthful forays with family to the town across the border from Aguagria. There I would watch my savvy uncles milk bargain-basement prices from cagy vendors for wooden snakes and other children's toys. Then my taste buds would explode in delight at the toothsome richness of Mexican candy, cloying confections of cream and brown sugar. Now that that city had the dubious distinction of being the ninth most dangerous in the world, such visits had to be suspended.

As I pulled out onto the highway toward Córdoba, I exhaled a tentative sigh of relief. I hoped it wasn't premature. The tiny town that was the sister city of my point of crossing disappeared behind me, warped by the heat waves from the rutted blacktop. Spring in that part of the country lasting about as long as it takes to say an act of contrition, the early-summer sun was already beginning to bake the days with waves of nauseous heat.

Out ahead and extending on either side me, the hardscrabble countryside unfurled to infinity. My racing heart slowed to a gallop with the sheer vastness of the scene. For a time, dust-covered prickly pear and agave were my only companions. Then a tiny adobe hut nestling in the distance reminded me I was still on earth. No creature stirred, save scouring vultures gliding in the heavens.

Once in a while, a car might pass in the opposite direction, raising the hair on the back of my neck. I wondered who might be behind those tinted windows. Or a battered truck ahead, coughing and spitting like an ailing Pleistocene beast, its bed gorged with children, dogs, tools and scavenged lumber.

It or some other battle-scarred mass of metal might slow my progress on the unshouldered two-lane. As I passed, the occupants would stare at me as though I were an alien recently landed on earth. I wondered how much of that aura emanated from me, capturing my present feeling so well.

There is a warring in oneself on entering an unfamiliar land. That is especially true when its openness seems to swallow you to inconsequence. First, it floods you with an exuberance of giddy triumph. Then it shrinks you to a tiny strange quark upon the face of the eternal, lost and lonely at the edges of time. With no self-affirming point of reference, identity seems to evanesce into the heat waves that rise from the pavement.

It forces you to wonder who you are in the inscrutable scheme of creation. It reminds you of the paltry insignificance of your brief passage in it. Here, you can see your minuteness upon this tiny planet, in this insignificant solar system, which is a part of one of many galaxies, in a universe that boasts a limit.

And beyond that limit is what? Nothingness? And what is that exactly? In that stark but eloquent horizon, what a tiny blip you are— I am—in the course of either pointless pantheist philosophy or the grand design of the Deity.

An hour or so into my journey, mountains approached in the distance. They inspired at once a soothing wonder and menacing discomfort. They were comforting for the virginal purity of an untamed country free of human design. Their menace lay in a crude amorality of purposelessness.

A shiver at the sheer majesty of it for some reason drew my gaze to the rearview mirror. Suddenly, my metaphysical speculations were swept aside by the large black vehicle closing in behind me.

As the SUV approached, I could see out of its windows the tips of automatic rifles poking threateningly into the air. It was traveling at a speed much in excess of my own, and my natural inclination was to slow down. *No, Jake,* I told myself. *Don't do anything to draw attention to yourself. Don't slow or, for God's sake, speed up!* The lumbering behemoth rapidly pulled up behind me. My heart began to jackrabbit, and my hands gripped the steering wheel with viselike pressure.

*It's not passing,* I thought. *There can be only one reason for that!* It clung to my rear bumper like a monstrous barnacle. My breath shortened, and my skin produced a gruel that plastered my shirt and pants to me. Then, it effortlessly pulled around parallel, obviously unconcerned with traveling down the wrong side of the road.

*Pass. Please, God, let it pass!* But the mass of metal instead slowed to keep alongside. The passenger window lowered, and a chiseled face cast me a frigid stare. I neither met nor acknowledged it but felt its gimlet-eyed suspicion.

I braced for the order to stop. I offered up a prayer that my end might be quick and free of torture. I waited, neither slowing nor accelerating. The seconds ground on. Finally, out of recognition that refusing to face the face that scoured mine was more suspicious than confrontation, I turned to meet it.

Its Medusa eyes, knifing out of a face of flint, met mine. I held its gaze, maintaining my parallel with the barge that ferried it. Not a muscle of his face made the slightest movement. Then after a few moments that seemed an eternity, it finally registered an almost-imperceptible metamorphosis. It then turned to the driver and, with gentle upward thrust of its chin, motioned him to continue on.

As the armed Goliath sped away and out of sight, I pulled to the side of the road and wiped the sweat from my hands and face. I said another brief prayer of thanks and then continued on.

The land became ever more desolate as I climbed the ragged buttes of the Sierra de la Encantada. Vistas of nothingness stretched to breath-robbing infinity. The sun blazed with bestial intensity. Here in this wasteland, reality seemed to shine in glorious splendor. It was an altar far above the collapsing walls of sin and repentance. It was the realm of *the good.*

In that void, bewitched by the stark majesty of what surrounded me, back went my mind to its metaphysical musings. "Why is there something rather than nothing?" is the eternal question. And how do we define nothing?

If we abandon First Cause to the ash heap of superstition, if we can only conceive of a closed universe that ontologically explains itself, or as one of many in an infinite multiverse exploding pointlessly into existence and some billions of years hence fading to nothingness, do we likewise relegate the law of cause and effect to the chicken and the egg?

How do we explain the universe's wondrous elegance, the perfection of its balance and functioning? What do we do with time up to ten to the negative forty-three seconds after the Big Bang? Do we find the hand of God or some theorem of physics as yet undiscovered?

But most of all, from where do our ideals, our remarkably consistent codes of conduct, this vision of Plato's good, emerge? Is morality simply an adaptation to facilitate social life? Is this "capability and godlike reason" really so mundane? Why have social animals like ants and bees no sense of it? Or do they? Does it likewise come from nothingness? Is it a simple mechanism of evolution to facilitate survival of a reasoning species?

I was about to ask why we were *given* reason in the first place, but the use of that particular verb rather answers itself.

The first signs of an approaching city erupted in a sky gathered in bolts of sooty cotton. They threatened mayhem. From nowhere, it seemed, portentous clouds cast a crepuscular gloom just beyond the crest of a hill. As I crossed the summit, I saw nestled in a deceptively peaceful-looking valley lights flashing on across Córdoba.

Blue-gray mountains laced the far horizon like a tiara circumscribing the city. But above me and approaching in portentous wonder were chaotic billows of moisture. They were so black and menacing they curdled to a charcoal blue. Knifing through them and spilling haphazardly, streaks of sunlight spotlighted accidental peaks and valleys.

A shiver of pending accounts rippled through me with the gathering storm. As I girded myself for a blinding tempest, a few massive drops of rain exploded against the windshield. A howling wind buffeted my tiny car and moaned in protest under a fender.

Then, as quickly as it had appeared, dead calm seemed to suck the storm into oblivion. The heavens parted, and streaks of chaste amber light dripped daintily on the city. The clouds that had so savagely threatened now surrendered to the midmorning crispness of mountain spring. Beneath the desert sun, the city blazed openly in the valley below. I wondered what pulse of wickedness underlay its seeming calm.

I eased the car down a serpentine, unmarked blacktop turned a sickly tan with desert silt. It snaked through eerily quiescent streets, narrow in the ancient Iberian style. It spoke of a city with a veneer of calm. But that tranquility was betrayed by men in uniforms porting automatic rifles, their faces frequently obscured by ski masks. Uneasiness drooped from the branches of its trees and oozed down its streetlamps.

As I had been instructed, the road transformed itself into the main street of the city and led directly to the building that housed the district directorate of the federal judiciary. I parked, swallowed hard in an effort to calm my racing heart and made my way to my first encounter in the land that is not Kansas.

# 17

"**G**ood morning, Mr. Kazmareck. Please come in." Before me stood Sr. Cásarez Montemayor in a charcoal-gray pinstripe suit. Speaking in barely accented English, he had an air of crispness that betrayed a familiarity with the proceeding. "I believe it's still morning," he said as he slipped an old-fashioned pocket watch out of a fob in his vest. A pencil-thin moustache, neat as a hand model's manicured fingernail, cut across his upper lip.

His hand gripped mine with thrift and decisiveness. His economy of movement as he returned to his desk spoke of a conversance with command. He indicated a chair across the desk from him for me to occupy. "Please have a seat. I trust you had an uneventful trip?" His impeccable English had the barest coloration and cadence of his lingua franca.

I was surprised to hear him use a phrase I thought my brother Matt had taken out a copyright on. "For the most part, thanks," I answered, settling myself at ramrod attention on the raw cowhide-covered chair opposite him. His evident comfort with the present business at once bemused me and, strangely, soothed to some degree my anxiety.

It mirrored the feeling that had gnawed at me since entering the city: while there was a palpable sense of danger that hummed in the air, there was also an incongruous air of normalcy. It cast a deceptive feeling of calm, like the eye of a hurricane. I marveled at people going about their daily business as though the time bomb at their feet were just another crack in the sidewalk. Merchants hawked their wares with the familiar "Oi, tss-tss" that had been the constant serenade during my family's shopping excursions across the Rio Grande.

Others paraded up and down the middle of Calle Benito Juárez, enticing and bargaining with prospective customers. They offered once-in-a-lifetime deals on finely crafted model ships, piñatas and cheap jewelry whose silver left a rufous band that multiple handwashings couldn't erase.

An old woman on a blanket in the still-crisp morning air begged alms from passersby. Large swaths of wrinkles cut sunburst-style from her empty eyes—eyes that had lost the hope that industry and self-sufficiency bring. Another sat a few meters away, peddling poorly confected but colorful rag dolls. In contrast, her countenance retained a vestige of dignity purchased by the offering of a good beyond mere entreaty. I knew the one I bought would bring delight to Grace, particularly when I told her of its origins.

Sr. Cásarez Montemayor broke me gently out of my reverie. When he did, it struck me that he had indulged it for a few seconds, as though he had an inkling as to my woolgathering. "How is my friend Connors these days? On his way to becoming the governor of Texas, it seems."

"He's well. And yes, it would seem so."

"Hmm, getting fat and happy, the last time I saw him. I hope he's not also getting too full of himself."

"Not any more than he always was."

An appreciative chortle escaped him as he sat. "I see you know him well."

I remembered Connor's apology. "Actually, he may be learning some humility."

"Huh. That's something I'll have to see for myself." He took a moment to peer into my eyes, and I could see in his a solidity of substance. It spoke of a history of contemplation that had chiseled a few finely wrought wrinkles between thick black eyebrows. "Connors tells me that he would trust you with his life," he said in a way that made clear he expected no response. "And now you and I have no recourse but to trust each other. That's not something I do easily, as a rule."

Despite his choice of words, I didn't detect any hesitation on his part. The question of trust didn't seem to be directed at me. It struck me as more philosophical observation than personal misgiving. And though he sat straight and square-shouldered in his worn leather office chair, there was a hint of world-weariness in his manner. *Connors must have good reason to have the confidence in him that he does*, I said to myself. As I was a stranger in a strange land, this was a hope masquerading as a thought.

"Well, to the matter at hand, shall we? I believe you have an interest in a prisoner housed in Tlaquetillo. A mutual friend of yours and Connors's?"

His brusque reference had the tone of my encounter with the doll merchant outside: a business deal devoid of sentiment. It seemed intentional. I thought I caught the slightest amusement from him at my reaction.

But there was something else lurking beneath that facade of verbal thrift, something he'd become an expert at hiding. It was not sadness or anger exactly but a look—no, it was more like a tiny ripple in the air—of smoldering resignation. It was as though whatever questions that pursue us on our journeys in this vale of tears had been formed at the moment of creation. And their answers would always elude us—grind us between the jaws of speculation.

"If he's still alive, I certainly do."

"Yes," he answered with slightly more breath than was needed for that particular combination of sounds. The word seemed burdened with a kind of ennui. It struck me as his first side step from self-possession. There was some ancient conundrum at the heart of this transaction. It caused his gaze for the first time to stray down and away from the steady bead they'd held my own with. It then darted out the window to the nervous tranquility of the city.

"You have the agreed-upon amount?" he asked with an aggressiveness that startled me. His mien then returned to the inquisitive but sapient stare he'd greeted me with. There was now a tinge of provocation in his tone that set my teeth on edge.

"Well, not with me, of course." I tried to answer as matter-of-factly as possible. "I'm sure that would have been a very poor choice—for the success of the enterprise as well as my health. But I can have it transferred to any account you'd like."

He rose from his chair with an almost-startling grace and took two rather military steps to the window. "The recipients of the bulk of this *incentive* prefer to handle these types of transactions in cash. I'm afraid I'll have to insist on it. Bank accounts can be traced after all."

Fortunately, such a contingency had been anticipated by Connors, no doubt from his many dealings with the authorities on this side of the border. At least I hope he only indulged in this type of transaction here.

"I can have it wired to the account of a confederate here, but I'd need a considerable guarantee of my safety once I have the cash in hand. I'm sure you can appreciate my concern." There was a bit of a chess match in progress, and I felt like I was starting with a few pieces missing from my side of the board.

The first thin-lipped smile of our encounter broke through the steadiness of his gaze. "I most certainly can, Mr. Kazmareck. You'll be accompanied by an armed guard, of course."

"I'd like you to accompany us as well, if you wouldn't mind." *Keep the deadly queen's moves visible at all times.*

The paper-cut smile then shrank to a bare twinkle in his eyes but didn't completely disappear. "That, unfortunately, will not be possible, for reasons I'm sure *you* can appreciate." I felt the heat of alarm raise my scalp a few centimeters. Then, giving just a moment to savor my uncertainty, he finally offered, "But I can send my secretary in my place, if that would be an acceptable alternative."

This was a shuffle not anticipated by Connors. "The young lady who escorted me in?"

"Um-hum," he responded with a touch of what seemed like curiosity. He waited a moment, seeming to enjoy the fact that he had hit upon a contingency we hadn't considered. "She handles transactions of this delicate nature all the time. And you can rest assured that I value her far above her abilities as a secretary. Feel free to check with Connors concerning that fact."

"I hope you can also understand that I'll need some assurance that once I've made the trade, I won't be left to the wolves, so to speak."

With an irony that could have melted the brass upholstery buttons on his chair, he said, "You mean my word isn't good enough?" As our eyes locked in what I perhaps mistakenly perceived as mounting resentment, he saved me from any further improvisation. "How about if she accompanies you to Tlaquetillo and back, along with the same armed escort? Would that allay your concerns?"

"How about if she accompanies me there and then accompanies the two of us back to the border?"

A hollow, acidic chortle escaped him. His manner seemed to betray a recognition of himself in me. "You really don't trust anyone, do you?"

"Not here. No, I don't."

Behind the humor, I now felt a smoldering revulsion. "Good. You shouldn't." And then, "I'll ask her. I imagine she'll agree."

He then paused, staring at me with the same piercing curiosity. Not a muscle of his face moved. I felt rather naked under his scrutiny. But somewhere beneath the conclusions he'd come to concerning my character, there was a searching—a searching for an elusive key to some unfathomable door. He seemed to be reaching for it not in desperation but rather in ambivalent self-discovery.

"I can feel your distaste, you know. I can feel it issuing out of your every pore. I can sense your judgment, the pity for all things Mexican, the wish to return to Oz and be done with the repulsive people you have to deal with here."

I said nothing, aware that any lie might doom the enterprise—and perhaps doom me as well. Then an inoffensive but honest answer occurred to me. "I'd just like to get home in one piece, with my friend in the same condition."

"I'm sure. But I can feel the question burning in you: how can an officer of the law stoop so low? How can a society exist when the fundamental pillars of respect for order and judicial process are violated at all levels of governance? How could civilization sink into such barbarity where extortion and torture are so common that they don't even interrupt the quotidian pursuits of life? I can feel your censure, Jacob." His use of my given name was accompanied by the slightest of pauses. "May I call you Jacob?"

I was suddenly aware that there was a lack of defensiveness in his appraisal of my attitude toward the present enterprise. The resentment, it seemed, was my own projection. And now I discerned an intimacy I found particularly engaging. Was that the purpose of the initial brusqueness...to set me up to feel gratitude for the change? If so, it worked. "You may."

I recognized in the barely perceptible elevation of one corner of his mouth a conclusion—apparently a favorable one about me. His fingers lightly rapped the top of his neatly appointed desk two decisive times. Then he rose and walked in deep contemplation back to the window overlooking the city. "There are so many forces at work in Mexico's downward spiral into—at least in certain regions—virtual fiefdoms."

He turned his head to look at me. "That's how you see it, do you not?" I knew better than to step onto this strip of polemical flypaper. But I felt an invitation to dialogue in his manner, in the casual yet interested way in which he stood at the window facing me. He lit a cigarette and offered me one—I suppose as a kind of communal peace pipe.

"I'm trying to quit, thanks."

"One of my few remaining vices," he answered. "Your novelist and philosopher Ayn Rand says that a man should always have fire in his hand." He gave a shrug devoid of movement. "It's a convenient excuse." Then, taking a moment to peer out of the window at the city below, he continued.

"Have you read Aristotle's *Nicomachean Ethics* by chance?" He turned to measure my reaction to the reference. "Please forgive the perhaps pretentious allusion. You see, I rarely come into contact with people with whom I can discuss such issues. Fortunately, my secretary/paralegal is one exception—on the rare occasions we have to meet outside the office. But I hunger for more than one intellect to hone my philosophical ruminations."

I tried not to betray my astonishment at such a reference coming from this glorified pettifogger. "I've...tried."

He let out a sharp, amused *hmph*. "Yes. It's not light reading, to say the least. I do recommend it, however. It serves as the grain—the warp and woof, you might say—of ethical treatises from Plutarch through Maimonides, past Thomas Aquinas all the way to present-day scholars. It even made its way into certain Islamic writers' texts—efforts to reconcile Hellenic philosophy with the iron and steel thoughtlessness of the *Qu'ran*. Al-Farabi comes to mind.

"I suppose Mexico's present state of dystopia was in some measure foreordained by the manner in which it was formed: Spanish conquest and exploitation. It seems to have contributed to a sort of social schizophrenia—although the term is so misused—between conqueror and conquered. A spiritual conflict that I hypothesize is in the soul of every Mexican.

"And I mean as opposed to how your country developed: through societal establishment rather than plunder. A difference I would point out that was the result of a simple trick of fate. Those early settlers had the same avaricious designs as the Spanish conquistadores. But there was no gold or silver to enrich them, no large population to enslave. And so, incentives had to be given to the underprivileged to work. And the magic of the market took control.

"I often wonder, though: how much of the pioneer ethic of individual initiative will fade as the United States loses its frontier mentality?

It seems the personal liberty and concomitant sense of responsibility for one's lot in life that de Tocqueville, among others, described is rapidly vanishing. How will 'America' fare as more and more people find it acceptable to live off the creativity and productive energy of fewer and fewer—and more and more of those few encourage that dependency?

"It is done, of course, in the name of humanity or Christian brotherhood or whatever other shibboleth might mask a desire for control. And mask it from *themselves*, by the way. It doesn't take a Hitler or Stalin or even an Ellsworth Toohey—just your everyday, garden-variety lover of humanity. And so Oz goes out not with a bang but a whimper.

"Will the next great nation be established when we *Homo sapiens* have the ability to colonize other planets in the distant reaches of the galaxy? Where people are once again left to their own devices for their very survival? Where that spirit of industriousness may once again flourish? I wonder.

"And I wonder if it's possible to maintain in a democracy. It's a system, after all, in which people can vote for themselves more and more privileges they have not worked for or earned. I believe John Adams stated that there was no democracy in history that did not commit suicide."

He acknowledged my astonishment at his erudition with another closemouthed grin. "My father was part of the Mexican diplomatic corps in the United States. I grew up in Washington, DC. I received my bachelor's degree in philosophy from Georgetown University."

Without needing me to inquire into his present situation, he continued. "When the political party that had made my father a diplomat was voted out of office, all the privileges my family had enjoyed suddenly evaporated. It serves as an invaluable lesson in the limits of power and influence, wouldn't you say? And so, here I am."

He recounted his fall from privilege and power with a sense of kismet I couldn't imagine didn't mask some resentment. "Yes, I could be doing other things. But in such a state as the world stands now, my question would be why. Why do anything? What do you think, Jacob?"

"I…" I shook my head in sheer awe.

"Yes, not an easy question to answer, is it? Aristotle argues that the path to the good life, the virtuous life—to immortality, even—is through reason. I might posit that the gospel of John makes the same assertion—or perhaps suggestion. You're familiar with its opening verses?

"I am."

"There is a war at present in Mexico. But I'm not talking about the one between the drug cartels and the government. Rather, it is a war for its very soul. In Aristotelian terms, it would be between what is popularly called 'enlightened' self-interest, perhaps a functional corollary of Aristotle's life of contemplation, and the crude—I would say *irrational*—dedication to the bestiality he calls 'vulgar pleasure.'"

"Is there another kind?" He smiled condescendingly, so I continued, "I believe there's a third option: a life devoted to honor."

There was just a hairsbreadth of hesitation in him. It was like the moment before you take that final step off the cliff or out of a plane with nothing between you and certain death but a flimsy patch of nylon. It registered in his eyes with a cold peering into mine, searching them for the implication. "Yes, you're absolutely right." He regained his composure but with a tiny burr under his saddle.

"To which do you devote yourself?" I asked.

"To which do I devote myself, or to which would I *like* to devote myself?"

"Your choice."

"Ah, but it is categorically *not* my choice, Jacob. That's the problem. Or is it your choice to be here violating your principles by offering me a bribe?" A twinkle in his eyes let me know that I had failed to mask my reaction. "Yes, Jacob, I know all about you. One has to be very careful with whom one deals in the present atmosphere. I know you took a lawyer's oath, and I know that you no longer practice. I even know why. For that reason, above all others, I'm engaging you in the present discourse."

He turned once again toward the window and seemed to embrace in his gaze the entire city. "I suppose, at the end of the day, it *is* our choice. It's amazing, isn't it, what exigent circumstances will drive us to?"

He turned and sat erectly on the windowsill to face me, eyes meandering upward to the ceiling and then back to me. "Aristotle describes virtue as an action that presupposes an intermediate point between a painful deficiency and a painful excess. He gives the example of courage being the golden mean between coward- ice and rash boldness. I wonder about that. To me, virtue is it- self inherently painful or at least uncomfortable. And frequently choosing the happy median implies the compromise of our values, does it not?

"The rational median is, of course, the *prudent* course—some- thing eschewed by William Blake as an 'ugly old maid courted by incapacity.' I would say also repudiated by writers on all sides of the political seesaw, such as John Steinbeck and Ms. Rand.

"In *The Grapes of Wrath,* Steinbeck holds up the government camp as the ideal society, where all self-interest is subsumed into the needs of the collective. And by virtue of that, it exists free of all conflict and wickedness.

"Conversely, Rand's ideal society is her Shangri-la in the Colorado Mountains where all moral virtue is derived from the *pursuit* of self-in- terest. And it results in the same state of perfection: the utter absence of guilt, of jealousy, of sin in general. Interesting that for neither one does original sin exist. The only sin for one is greed and for the other charity. Who do you think is right, Jacob?"

I found myself completely disarmed by his sincerity. "I think only Robinson Crusoe lived in a perfect society, and only before he discov- ered Friday."

My answer elicited a hearty laugh from him. "Your point is well taken: a society, if one can call it that, where no one else exists— where there are no competing needs to take into account. Where there is no sin because there is no morality. Or is there? Rand would say so, as for her, man's highest virtue is expressed in his ability to reason, and reason, as she states, would be absolutely indispensable if one were isolated on some desert isle.

"It is certain—well, let me say that it hasn't been proven to the contrary—that Steinbeck's and Rand's utopias exist only in isolation, where everyone thinks alike. That's the annoying rub, isn't it? People do such irritating and incomprehensible things, like coming to conclusions different from our own. I remember a famous quote from Judge Learned Hand: 'The spirit of liberty is the spirit which is not too sure that it is right.'

"But it's so seductive, isn't it: the vision, the place, *here, on this earth*, where all functions as it should? Where there is no greed, no cozenage, no need for the imposition of order? Where existence is totally free of pain, of fear, of guilt, where there is no sin but rather, as Steinbeck's preacher says, 'just things people do'?

"Men are shorn, like a snake of last year's skin, of all nagging doubts on our journey to Plato's sun. It is that vexing vision of the ideal, always just out of reach. It compels those who do not believe in its realization in an afterlife to pursue it here. Socialism is, after all, the opiate of the secular.

"And in our efforts to create it here, we propagate such evil. Perhaps just as much as when we devote ourselves to Aristotle's 'vulgar pleasure.' It is this, I think, that drives Hamlet to distraction: his prodigious intellect can see with such clarity that ideal but never witness it realized." Santiago paused a moment and then added, "Particularly, and despairingly, in himself.

"For instance, I often wonder what might have happened in Rand's promised land if just one of those *ubermenschen* had decided to fudge just the tiniest bit: if Reardon had decided to add a little tin to his miraculous metal to cut down on production costs; if he believed Francisco D'Anconia was overcharging for his coal. And did the latter pay a fair wage to his mine workers? And fair by whose definition?

"That's where it starts, doesn't it, Jacob? Who decides what is actually a fair trade? I suppose Rand would say 'whatever it's worth to you.' A is A, after all."

A sparkle of pleasure danced across his face. "That has always reminded me of a line from the movie *The Deer Hunter,*" and he continued with a pretty fair imitation of Robert De Niro: "'See dis?' the protagonist says as he holds up a bullet. 'Dis ain't sumpum else. Dis is dis.' I wonder if the person who wrote the screenplay was alluding to that core of Rand's philosophy. 'Existence exits,' as she says, although I believe Socrates and Aristotle said it long before. There is a reality separate from our wishes, our dreams, our strongest desires of how life *should* be.

"You want to know why there is such an epidemic of drug use, of senseless violence, of mass killings of people with no connection to the shooter? Because we've denied that very fact: 'Reality exists.' We want so fervently to believe that we can spend our way to wealth, that our lives and livelihoods, our health and sustenance, will magically appear from some benevolent hand. That life should and *will* cease to be hard. That we can make it...*fair.*

"So when it doesn't happen, when we're constantly challenged and frustrated by the results of our choices, or simply the vicissitudes of life, we feel betrayed. And always, always, we listen to the voices of those who tell us what we so desperately want to hear: that *A* is not *A,* that *this* is really *that,* that we have a right to our daily bread and circuses provided from the hand of some earthly god who confects them out of air. And when it doesn't turn out that way, someone, anyone, *everyone,* is to blame, everyone except I myself, of course. And they must pay.

"At any rate, as far as a fair trade is concerned, Milton Friedman would say that Adam Smith's invisible hand of commerce would make the correction, if one truly needed to be made." He looked at me, not seeking corroboration but gazing across 13.72 billion years of polemical history. "Perhaps...Perhaps..."

At this point, I felt completely seduced by this extraordinary individual. I still could not reconcile his present station in life with his astonishing intellect. I found myself trusting him utterly, something that Connors had expressly forbidden me to do—their long-standing friendship notwithstanding. But I had to plumb the depths of his reasoning. These were questions—and he seemed to know this somehow—that had hounded me all my adult life. "So how do we judge? How do we determine responsibility?"

This time a closemouthed frown of doubt wracked his face. I was surprised at its earthshaking effect on me. He once again rose and turned his eyes toward the window overlooking the city. But he seemed to be gazing upon the entire history of Mexico, of Western culture, of humanity. "Tout comprendre est tout pardonner?" he asked with an implied shrug of the shoulders. It was obvious that he knew the glibness of that phrase.

"That way lies anarchy," I responded.

"That way lies the Santa Muerte, the saint of death that more and more people worship here and turn to not for spiritual but material aid. She doesn't judge. She helps all who pay her homage: thieves, murderers, whores—whores like us, Jacob—no matter what you do or what you are.

"Makes life ever so easy, doesn't it? Be your aim absolute beauty, 'where truth and beauty shine resplendent,' or the meanest indulgences of the primal id, she'll grant your wish. Isn't the largest church in your country the one that promises, 'Love God and He will make you rich?'"

He then exhaled a breath that seemed to end our conversation with an ellipsis of lingering doubt. "Well, I suppose I've taken up enough of your time. I know you're anxious to take your friend home. And you should be—from what I hear, he isn't at all well. I've already arranged things with Daniela, my secretary. I anticipated most of your concerns. She'll take care of disbursing the money to the appropriate parties."

He looked at me with eyes that could have traversed the most impenetrable corner of hell. "Have you ever seen a movie called *La ley de Herodes?*"

"No, I can't say that I have."

"Do me a favor, Jacob. When you're safe and comfortable at home, watch it. And when you do, think of me…and perhaps of yourself."

I paused at the door before opening it to make my exit. "Thank you, Santiago." I hesitated, having one final question gnawing at me. I was afraid to ask not for my physical safety but rather for the spiritual discomfort its answer could bring.

He met my gaze with a posture of inevitability. "Ask, Jacob."

"How much of the money stays with you?"

He answered without a sign of self-satisfaction but rather an onerous sense of futility. "Not one red cent."

# 18

Santiago Cásarez's paralegal and I made our way up the tonsured mountains that lace the edges of Córdoba. We traveled in a worn dust-colored SUV. I assumed its state of disrepair was an effort at being as unobtrusive as possible. Its windows were tinted to visual impenetrability, paradoxically halfway open, drinking in the desert air. With us sat four men hidden behind dark glasses and chiseled stares. They were humorless as the automatic rifles they carried like a fifth appendage.

I had been advised to secure the financial incentive from various Mexican banks to allay suspicions of money laundering. The bulk of it lay in a carpeted suitcase ensconced in some secret compartment Daniela told me it would be safer for me not to know about. The rest of it she kept in her purse, apparently knowing roughly how much would be needed to secure safe passage to our destination.

Though Santiago had been thoroughly disarming and clearly cherished the young lady he had sent as assurance, my nerves granny-knotted. I imagined numerous scenarios in which she could be whisked to safety, leaving me the sacrificial lamb.

Sensing my discomfort, she placed a firm cinnamon-skinned hand on mine and quietly mouthed, "Cálmese. Everything is under control."

"But whose?" Recognizing the rhetorical nature of my question, she answered with a comforting smile and a gentle pat.

We made our lumbering way up and out of the dull brown haze that enveloped Córdoba. The sun knifed through the high pall of gray cast like fringe on the crumpled-teeth hills. The sparsely marked blacktop rose and split two mountain peaks in the distance. Then it seemed to disappear between them like thread through a needle's eye.

The way the meandering two-lane was swallowed reminded me of the moral swamp into which I'd sunk. I tried to comfort my suppurating sense of ethics with news stories I'd read of companies around the world caught in nests of bribery. In many of those countries, such behavior is as routine as a morning cup of coffee.

I turned to Daniela and started to ask, "How does Santiago reconcile—" but she cut me off with a viselike grip and eyes that screamed a silent no. Those simple gestures communicated volumes as to the clandestine nature of the Santiago I'd met. It was apparently at tremendous odds with the personality he presented to almost everyone else.

In consequence, we limited our conversation to my impressions of Córdoba, this arid, stark region of Mexico in general, and my plans once I returned to Oz. The violence of her warning, however, did nothing to ease my anxiety. Neither did the subject of my future, which struck me as being as uncertain as the emptiness that surrounded us.

We threaded the mountain needle and began our descent onto the dusty road, swallowed between vast expanses of parched earth and scrub brush. A few wispy mare's tails and chalky puffs dotted the sky, turning the desert light blindingly astringent.

The lowered windows made conversation a shouting match against the desert wind, eventually enforcing silence. Our four bodyguards, garrulous as mummies, were sunglass-wearing, heavily armed cigar-store Indians. The poorly maintained road's chugholes and cracks whiplashed us to and fro like a car full of jack-in-the-boxes.

After a couple of hours that seemed twenty, the pockmarked road dissolved into the pasty whitish-beige gravel known by its Aztec name of *caliche*. Finally, our four armed statues came alive enough to seal the windows against the choking dust. So we sat in an automotive oven, silent and sweating.

Suddenly, as we came over the last foothill ridge, a scene of utter desolation assaulted my eyes. An infinite expanse of white sand exploded across the landscape, only occasionally interrupted by a wheat-tinctured scrap of weed. The sheer immensity of it wrenched a gasp from me.

"What on earth...?"

"Las Dunas de Bilbao." She was not the least surprised by my reaction.

"It looks like the Sahara."

"Very similar climate. One of the driest places on earth."

Mounds of sand rolled indolently from horizon to horizon, and the isolated shrub straining for life exaggerated the feeling of isolation. It was like a universe collapsing on itself, starved of life. It was a desperate clutch at...what? What is it ultimately that we strive to grasp? Or is it rather something we seek to escape? Or is it both?

You may exit Plato's cave, you men of vision. You may even glimpse the true form of goodness and justice. But know that all, *all* are blinded when they look directly into the sun. Take comfort, though, that the effort, for all its pernicious consequences, is one of courage and beauty. Though our waxen wings melt in the excoriating light of the sun, we must climb as high as our talent and effort permit. And knowing we will ultimately fail and plunge to earth is the glorious tragicomedy of life.

"The prison is not far from here," Daniela said, wrenching my wandering mind back to earth. "It's placed in the middle of this wasteland, much like the island prisons off the coast of Baja. Try to escape those, and you're eaten by sharks. Here you die of thirst and sunstroke. And then you're eaten by those." She pointed to vultures circling in the sky.

"Charming."

"And what goes on inside is even more charming."

"Are you sure Artie's still alive?"

She shushed me once again with the raising of an index finger and answered with her eyes that the mentioning of names was ill-advised. As we grew closer to our destination, her demeanor seemed to harden. The lines of her face took on a chiseled stubbornness. Her bearing matched the surrounding landscape as the dunes surrendered to an expanse of smooth white pool-table emptiness. In the distance it met the razor-sharp blue of the sky that no cloud besmirched.

Like our surroundings, Daniela became uncannily quiet. Her movements seemed truncated and sharp, with a stillness that sent waves of dread tingling down my spine. Ahead, in the midst of that sterile whiteness, a lonely structure came into view. By its side rose a naked, anciently dead tree trunk, sans even a branch to remind that it once had lived.

As we neared, the wooden Indian in the seat to my left even seemed to stiffen. The thought of being so alone, with five beings I did not know, in a place as desolate as the far side of hell pounded danger to my temples. It made me yearn for home, for a Dolores that was no more, for my sweet Grace. It even made me nostalgic for the no-man's-land of the South Bronx.

*You owe Artie your life,* I told myself. *If you lose your own, it's merely payment in full.*

We pulled around the back of the modest stone structure. There, a rusted iron gate hung in overlapping despondency between its ocher walls. Pockmarked mortar occasionally interrupted those massive sand-colored blocks. One barred window accented the structure's mourning.

A sidewinder rattlesnake scurried out of the shadow cast by the rear wall as we stopped. Our four dour escorts opened their doors and hesitated for a moment, looking at the powdery grit where they would step down. "That might not be the only one," Daniela said to explain the hesitation. "And there are Gilas and poisonous scorpions that are camouflaged and very difficult to see."

"This trip just gets to be more and more fun." My comment drew the minutest of reactions from one of the statues escorting us. It was hard to tell what kind behind those wraparound shades. I cast a furtive glance at Daniela as we exited. "The money?" I silently mouthed.

The same index finger rose to tell me to keep silent. "Never show the money until the merchandise is in hand," she whispered to me out of the hearing of our escorts. "The bulk of it is not for the people here. The subordinates here get a small portion, and then we make a stop on the way back."

"Where?" I asked.

"Wherever they stop us."

"That's...reassuring."

A blast-furnace gust moaned around the prison walls—a sound of desolation, magnifying the heat. The rear gate was opened by a dour *anciano* with leathery skin dried and cracked by unrelenting sun and wind. As we entered, the rancid odor of sweat and decay assaulted my nose. I had to stop to gain control over the lunch that threatened to violently exit my stomach. Not a word was spoken as our whole assemblage paused for me. As I regained tentative control, my skin broke out in a clammy sweat.

We were escorted to a small adobe enclosure that apparently served as office and home of the warden or *encargado*. The deal, at least this part, was handled with a few monosyllabic words and looks I strained to interpret.

I was finally struck by the realization that I was really going to see my long-lost compadre. Suddenly the excitement and joy of that fact overcame the oppressive stress of the journey. But it was accompanied by a new tension over the state I would find him in. Would he even be the Artie I knew? What had the isolation, the torture I was sure he'd endured, the illness, the influence of his fellow inmates, done to him? I struggled to contain myself, helped by a hand that took mine and held it hard. Daniela had recognized the flood of apprehension at war with my eagerness.

This deal executed, a few Ben Franklins exchanged as security, we silently exited the building. After a moment I saw a wizened stick figure emerge from a far cell. At the sight, my heart fought a fierce battle between elation and despair. The round-shouldered wraith walked toward us accompanied by the same rawhide-skinned ancient. He hobbled forward with a marked limp and a paralyzed arm that made his progress painfully halting.

It was Artie, though I could barely recognize him. He had the aspect of a limb broken off the lifeless tree outside. I started to move toward him, but Daniela halted my progress with a grip of steel.

"Not yet," she murmured.

I looked at her with yearning. She answered with a look sculpted out of years of painful experience. *Wait*, it said, *it will soon be safe.* And so I waited. Artie must have known as well, because when he finally recognized me, his reaction registered only in his eyes. Not a muscle twitched or gully in his face gave notice. It was a look of primeval pain masked by a feigned indifference. It flashed fury at long-discarded dreams of rescue. *No, no,* they said, *I will not believe! I will not hope again!* I started to speak, but Daniela's iron grip muted me. So, in absolute silence, the exchange was made.

His bowed head stayed still and expressionless. His eyes danced suspiciously from me to Daniela to all others in his field of vision—cold, calculating, prepared for attack from every corner. But he looked no one in the eye.

As we started toward the gate, I tentatively reached to take his arm and whisper a greeting. His panic at the touch ran through me like a bolt of electricity. Daniela seemed to have anticipated this and grabbed his other arm. Paradoxically, the strength of her grip turned him docile, and he let the two of us escort him toward the car. As we neared the gate, he began to feebly resist. "Esperen. Wait," he begged in a barely audible croak. "I can't leave...no puedo dejar a mi amigo, Jesús."

Daniela issued a quiet command of "You have no choice. Cállese."

Too weak to protest more, or too inured to following commands, he hoarsely whispered, "Jesús! Jesús!" We lifted him into the back of the awaiting vehicle. Out of the corner of my eye, I caught sight of the old man, who slowly closed the gate. A tear rolled down his cheek.

In the rear seat of the monster SUV, I started to put my arms around Artie despite the horrible odors that emanated from his mouth and body. But he snapped back hard, slamming his body against the side of the car. His eyes reflected the fear of a wounded animal.

"Artie, it's me, Jake. Your friend, Jake."

He stared as though I were speaking a foreign language. Perhaps it *was* foreign to him now. "Soy tu camarada, Jake." But even in Spanish, there was a feral suspicion that erected a barricade between us—perhaps between him and all the past.

Daniela turned around to us. "It will be a while, perhaps a long while, before he accepts that what is happening is real."

Indeed, he looked at me as though I were some kind of apparition. He looked at the others, too, unable to process what his eyes beheld. So I just looked him over from the distance across the seat. He was missing teeth, and those he had were outlined with a brown gunk from years of inattention. What passed for clothes seemed pasted to his flesh with months of sweat and grime. He shied away from my attempt to place a hand gently on his shoulder. Obviously, he was in such distress that any touch was painful. Or perhaps it was just distrust of any physical contact.

"Wait, Jacob," Daniela cautioned me again. "You're going to have to be patient."

Finally, in a croak of disbelief, he said, "¿Quiénes son ustedes?"

"Amigos," Daniela answered, "y estás a salvo."

He just stared in bewilderment, trying to puzzle out this impossible situation. His head snapped uncertainly as I offered him a bottle of water, eyes flitting from me to the water and back again. Finally, he reached out and took it. Then, as though it were some kind of miracle, he croaked out a throaty "Gracias." And staring at me in wonder, he followed with, "Thanks...Jake? What did...? How...?"

He stared in wide-eyed wonder as I recounted the particulars of his rescue. When I finished, he looked to the others and then back to me. "How the hell did you find me?"

Daniela turned around. "That will have to remain a mystery."

Artie seemed to understand immediately, so I followed his lead and kept quiet. Apparently, maintaining the anonymity of sources was crucial. Artie looked to the others and then to me. "Do you have any idea of the danger you're putting yourselves in?"

"All too well," Daniela answered. "And I'll call in the favor someday."

Moment by painstaking moment as we rode, Artie seemed to grasp the reality of what was happening. At times he became animated, almost euphoric.

Then I asked him about what he'd gone through. He shut down completely. There was even a threat in his voice when he said, "I don't want to talk about it. It was nothing." He stared out the window at the countryside, but I don't know if any of it registered. He seemed to go into a hypnotic trance. He was so quiet that Daniela thought he'd gone to sleep.

"I would be careful of close contact with your friend until he's been isolated in a hospital, Jacob. His eyes have the look of hepatitis. I'm sure he's covered with lice, even with his head shaved, and we don't know what other diseases, perhaps resistant, he's infected with. That prison is notorious. Make sure when you get him to the hospital that they give *you* a full physical."

"She's right. I'm putting you all in danger—in too many ways."

I turned to Daniela. "We need to stop for food, something easily digestible like soup. Maybe just the broth. And to let him shower and put on clothes that aren't rotting to his body."

"We will. But we're not in safe territory yet. About forty kilometers this side of Cuatrociénagas, there's a place within our sphere of influence. We will likely make the final payment before."

Artie stared straight forward, seeming to sleep with his eyes open. I finally sat back, and some of the tension dissipated. "I had no idea it was this complicated."

"Many hands. Many layers of groups in control of other smaller groups that expect their *mordida* as well. Some are in nominal control of this place and that area, of some procedure that is overseen by another group that is franchised by a bigger group. And on and on it goes."

I started to ask how one could possibly keep track of so complicated and, I assumed, ever-changing a system. But utterly exhausted from travel, from stress, from the emotion of retrieving my old friend, I just said, "Thank you, Daniela."

She made no reply but rather turned and looked forward, an inscrutable blankness on her face. Perhaps it was satisfaction, perhaps concern for our safe return. It might have even been resentment for putting her and Santiago at risk.

The setting sun lacquered the western skies with gold and turned the white sands of the Bilbao Dunes a dusty orange. Then, as darkness devoured the day, a gibbous moon blanketed the earth with sheets of pearl. In the distance, it lit up one lone, brotherless tree. Its naked limbs and twigs reflected the moonlight in sparkling rejoinder to the stars, so that it shone like a giant lamp.

Every now and then a thump distinct from the monstrous potholes that jiggered us side to side caught my attention. I finally noticed darker streaks across the road that seemed to correspond with each distinctive thump that was sometimes a thwack. I asked Daniela what they were.

"*Cascabeles*...rattlesnakes. The pavement retains heat, and being *de sangre fría*—cold-blooded—the chill of the desert night impels them onto the road. I doubt they know that they're making a choice between being crushed and freezing to death."

I watched Artie as he slept and was seized by an urge to awaken him. The moon drifted through a few feathery clouds, and its pale beams only emphasized the blackness that swallowed us.

I had never felt so full to bursting. Santiago's haunting words rang in my ears. It wrenched me back to my hospital room in New York and a haunting cry of "We didn't know! We didn't know!" Again, it whispered that hateful phrase that had imprisoned my baby sister in despair.

As the night wore on, I found myself lost in the emptiness of the moon-gilded desert. How could I *not* take the risk, Artie? It is a debt I've owed you, for saving my life, for teaching me to survive, for being my friend and simply because you are. Without warning I looked down, and he was there, before my eyes, transforming into Grace; he was Dolores, he was Shmuel, he was Connors, he was my father. And more than all of these, he was me. And I—*I* was all of them.

Seeming hours passed. Around a curve, the car began to slow. Ahead the lights of a vehicle flashed twice like the eyes of some primitive swamp beast. Barely discernible to its side was a long-abandoned stone structure. We slowed, and our driver flashed his lights twice in answer. Gradually, we pulled to the left side of the road, slowed and then came to a stop some distance before the other vehicle. Artie nervously stirred.

Daniela gave orders in a quiet but commanding undertone: "Quédense aquí, pero preparados." Artie shot up in apparent panic as we came to a full stop. "Quiet your friend!" Daniela fairly hissed at me.

"Artie, Artie. It's okay. It's all right," I hastily murmured as he pulled away from me. It was clear from the look of terror that he was in utter bewilderment as to his whereabouts. "You're with me, Jake," I said in as low and soothing a tone as I could. "You're all right. You've been sleeping." I could see his eyes by the lights from the other vehicle. They had the look of a cornered animal. "Artie, it's Jake. You're all right. We got you out of prison. We're on the way home. We're going home, buddy. You're okay. Relax. You're safe."

Finally, the look of savagery in his eyes eased to a hyper but human vigilance. They darted in every direction to ward off any threatened attack. "Quiet, buddy. It's okay, now. You're fine."

"Keep him quiet. No sudden moves," Daniela issued her final orders before carefully opening her door. The four nameless bodyguards—no longer faceless since they'd removed their shades but still looking glacial in the moonlight—surreptitiously checked their rifles and side arms. Daniela quickly disappeared in the dark as she walked to the other car, hands in the air.

Artie, still bewildered, watched with vulpine eyes. After a moment, Daniela made her way back to us. At her door, she bent over and opened a hidden compartment beneath the car. From it she slid out the carpeted suitcase and then made her way back to the other vehicle. Our four companions sat in motionless silence. I could not sense that Artie was even breathing.

Seconds passed. The apparent leader of the four soldiers riding shotgun made the slightest movement of his head toward the driver. I felt a deathly still response. Daniela was not coming. I could hear Artie's breath quickening and felt his body stiffen as mine turned to steel. The driver soundlessly lifted his hand to the ignition. The man seated across from him lifted his to restrain him.

More time passed. Daniela was not returning. *What could be the problem?* The two guards in the back quietly shifted their weight toward their doors, hands on the handles. I noticed Artie's eyes shooting glances in all directions, searching for a possible escape. Then finally, when I thought all hope was lost, the other car pulled back, Daniela silhouetted in its headlights. It then pulled out onto the road as Daniela made her swift but measured way back to us.

A universal sigh escaped us all as she pulled herself up into our waiting vehicle. "Let's go. Your friend can bathe and eat in Córdoba if you wish. Let's go *now*." And we pulled out in the opposite direction toward salvation.

"Daniela…? You all right?" I asked. She made no answer, her only acknowledgment a slight turn of the head and a steel-jawed exhalation. It told me that talk was now an extravagance. Her silence filled the car with tension, and Artie and I sat rigid across the rear seat from each other.

Our four escorts maintained their wonted reticence. I realized that I had not heard a single word from any one of them during the whole of our journey. The tension in the car was palpable as we made our way from the roadside nightmare. Then, with each passing kilometer, it began its slow dissipation. Muscles could almost be heard unknotting, and breathing became more regular.

Finally, Daniela turned to me. "They wanted more money. They said they would hold me and your friend until Santiago came up with another installment." Through teeth clenched in anger and fear, she concluded, "I had to talk them out of it. I knew what would happen to me if I stayed. And then..."

She didn't need to finish. And I didn't want to know. My concern was getting Artie to a hospital and getting some kind of food in him. I asked Daniela about putting him in the hospital in Córdoba. "Not if you want to keep him alive. Your priority should be getting him out of Mexico as fast as possible."

"Should we take the road straight to Aguagria?"

"Absolutely not!" she snapped. "That will take you into the heart of Zetas territory. If they're not already aware of your friend's transfer, they will be soon. I suggest we don't even stop in Córdoba. If you're captured by them, you can forget anyone being able to rescue you. We'll go straight from Córdoba to Piedras Negras and cross there."

"She's right," a raspy whisper came out of Artie. "I was in their hands until they couldn't find anyone to pay more ransom. Jesús, my friend, and I escaped after being tortured for...I don't know how long. They broke my hip, dislocated my shoulder. We were picked up by police in the pay of the Sinaloans. They thought I might know something about the Zetas and their contacts in government. I let them think that. Otherwise, we would've been killed and tossed out like garbage." Artie's pause weighed with the density of a black hole. "Jesús and I kept each other alive. We kept each other...alive."

"Arturo," Daniela turned with a razor-keen look. "Your friend is dead. You'd best forget him. They'll find out he knows nothing soon enough and rid themselves of him." His reaction seemed to slightly soften Daniela's manner. "I think he'd be better off anyway. No one lasts for long in that prison—and life there isn't life, is it?" Artie's grief suffused the car in palpable waves. "You have a friend here who risked his life for you, and Connors McClain, who risked his career. Take that as consolation. And make it worth it by the way you live."

And with this, I heard a sound I could never in my life imagine coming from my stoic friend. "How...can people be so *evil*?"

*How indeed*, I thought. *How indeed?*

# 19

We dropped off our armed escort in Córdoba, a procedure Daniela assured me was necessary for the remainder of our junket. She, Artie and I then transferred to my car for the trip back to Piedras Negras. I had hoped that our nearing the border and safety would calm Artie. Strangely, it seemed to have the opposite effect. For the most part, he remained shut-mouthed and suspicious, his naked animal fear cutting like razor wire. It seemed to increase the closer we got.

Then, seemingly out of guilt for lack of appreciation, he would thank and then almost scold me for the risk I took. Mostly he just seemed stupefied. He'd answer questions, as long as they didn't require any specificity about what he'd been through. The one time he did get specific, it was eerie. It was as though he were recounting someone else's experience or some movie he'd seen: flat, distanced, coldly dispassionate. Then he seemed to withdraw so completely I worried I'd sent him over the edge.

"How in God's name did you survive that, Artie?"

I felt such a coldness descend. From the passenger seat across from me, Daniela gripped my arm. As I glanced over at her, her eyes bled warning. When we stopped at a stoplight, I took a furtive peek in the rearview mirror. Artie seemed to be in a trance, making some movement with his arms or hands I couldn't see. It must've been excruciating with his shoulder the way it was. But there was no sign of pain—just utter blankness behind eyes that ceaselessly scouted for danger.

"Artie, why didn't your family tell us?"

Silence. Then finally, in a flat, icy tone, he answered, "Because it would've meant my death. And probably theirs."

"That's true, Jacob," Daniela confirmed. "That's the Zetas' normal procedure. You tell anyone, you try to rescue, you don't pay the ransom, and whoever they are holding is dead. And they make it as agonizing a death as possible."

"If they're not going to get paid, why make it so agonizing?"

"Advertising. So word gets around what happens if people don't."

"My God." I turned to Artie. "I guess your family just didn't have the money."

"They paid," Artie answered. "Where my mother and sister got it, I don't know. But it didn't make any difference. They just kept demanding more. Or...I don't know...it's all..."

As he hesitated, I glanced up at him through the rearview mirror. His eyes bulged outward as though random, unconnected images of horror flashed before them. There was some enigma he was trying to puzzle out. "Me and Jesús...we...they...I can't...I remember a gun to my head...so many times. Once..." At the thought I could feel him stiffen and then retreat to his fugue state. "I hoped he'd just get it over with. I thought we were finally free. Then..." The excruciating silence as Artie stopped himself hung on the dark night over Piedras Negras.

"You're free now," Daniela pronounced. "Fix your mind on that."

I caught his look again in the rearview mirror. That same jumble of emotions seemed to slash and snap and grind at each other: relief distrusted, elation weighted down with molten hate. "Thank you, Jake. That's all I can say is thanks. Y gracias a tí, Daniela. Both of you, and Connors." But there was still no warmth in his expression of gratitude. It was as though he were feigning what he thought he should have felt.

"Rest, buddy, rest. We'll be home soon."

We dropped Daniela off at the border after she assured us that she would be just fine with the contacts Santiago had over the eastern part of the state. She made sure we wouldn't be hassled at the Mexican side of the crossing and then departed without further word. Artie seemed hesitant to transfer to the front seat. He did so as though he were escaping from a secure hiding place, rushing to sit beside me and slam the door shut.

But it seemed like the small change from back to front exaggerated his stress level exponentially. And the nearer we got to freedom, the greater it grew. His body stiffened to immobility. His eyes danced from side to side, evaluating every pedestrian, scrutinizing every shadow, every obstruction where danger could hide.

A car horn snapped his whole body around, every muscle a tightly wound spring. Then suddenly, a boy selling chicle tapped at his window. In one frenzied, catlike motion, Artie blasted the door open, and I knew his instincts were to kill. I reached across to grasp his arm to steady him.

Before I could even close my hand around his wrist, his was around my throat. The boa-constrictor strength of his grip made me freeze. I tried to speak, but my voice was cut off. I was just barely able to croak out a feeble "Artie!" I tried to pry his hand away, but his grip was like a vise. I could just barely see his face out of the corner of my eye. It almost scared me more than my breath being cut off. In his eyes was the murderous fury of a wounded animal. I could feel consciousness slipping away.

# 20

Fortunately, I regained consciousness quickly and saw Artie headed for the US side of the bridge. I got to it just as he was being subdued by a number of customs officers. I hastily tried to explain the situation as best I could amid the chaos.

"Please, he's an American citizen!" I yelled as best I could over the myriad commands being yelled at Artie.

"Stay back, sir!" one of the five agents it was taking to immobilize Artie ordered.

I fortunately had the presence of mind to not interfere physically. I was astonished that as crippled as Artie was, he could still fight like a mile-wide tornado. I tried to think of a story I could relate in the fewest amount of words possible. "Please! He's a…kidnapping victim. He was tortured. He's having some kind of flashback!"

Once Artie was completely immobilized, I could finally get them to listen. It took all of my rhetorical skills to convince them he was a citizen. An ambulance was called, and another struggle ensued as they handcuffed him to the gurney. Amid my attempts to soothe him as best I could, he was strapped down to it.

"Do you know what kind of drugs he's on?" the EMTs asked me once we were on our way. I figured, given his paranoia, it was a fairly logical assumption on their part. As I explained the situation to them as quickly and cogently as I could, they grudgingly agreed to give him something to calm him down.

As we neared the Eagle Pass hospital, I finally succeeded in getting through to him. "Artie, you're okay. You're all right. It's Jake, Artie—your buddy Jake. You're safe now. We're going to the hospital. We're far away from the danger. Try to calm down, bud. You're all right. You're safe." After repeating this over and over and reminding him who I was, telling him ad infinitum where he was and where we were going, it finally seemed to register. His look changed from absolutely crazed to a kind of animal alertness.

At the hospital, he was further sedated. Border Patrol agents insisted on his remaining handcuffed until his identity could be confirmed. Once he was completely under control, I gave the hospital personnel a rundown of the situation. We were both isolated and given full physicals.

A couple of days later, I found out that, apart from an infestation of lice and fleas, I was so far in good health. I would have to be kept under observation and retested to make sure that was the case.

Artie, on the other hand, was diagnosed with several diseases. It took a number of weeks for him to be declared disease-free. During that time, he alternated between periods of euphoria, disbelief and the blackest depression and withdrawal I could imagine. Eventually, the depression and aloofness came to dominate.

Owing to privacy concerns, contact with Connors had to be handled with considerable delicacy. That and explaining to my family where I'd been and why I couldn't come home were the only distractions from my preoccupation with Artie's state of mind.

He finally settled into what I can best describe as "distance," broken only by occasional bouts of panic at things that baffled me. No, he was not the same Artie. Not at all. An animal-like suspicion and hostility had replaced the patience and caring I'd always felt from him. He controlled it around me as best he could. He thanked me copiously, but I still got the feeling that he would just as soon be dead as rescued. There was what I would have to call just an *absence*. It unnerved me.

I talked and talked, telling him about Grace and my family and what little I knew of his sister. He asked about his mother, of course, and I had to tell him she had died shortly after he disappeared. I could see no discernible reaction to the news. Oddly, he never asked about his former fiancée, Anabel. When I was sure no one else could hear, I told him about Connors. Connors had made it abundantly clear that his name should never be mentioned in connection with Artie. He could not even send Trevor down.

Once he was declared free of anything infectious, Connors arranged, always through me, his transfer to San Antonio Orthopedic Hospital for surgeries to repair as best as possible his left shoulder and right hip. Cosmetic surgery to replace part of an ear that had been cut off could also take place there. Artie seemed bizarrely indifferent to it all.

After a few months, the initial surgeries were completed, and his appearance at least seemed much improved. "You're starting to look like your old self again, hermano."

The look he gave me pierced like a cold north wind. It was only a brief glance, but I felt hollowed out like a human cave.

"I'll never be what I was," he answered. I realized at that moment that I hadn't heard him call me by my name since his rescue. "I'm not anything. I have nothing to give. Nothing."

He said it so matter-of-factly—like he was referring to himself as an inanimate object. There was no anger in his voice or words. It was more like the amorality of wind, blowing without purpose, without thought, without any genuine substance. That was more chilling for me than all the things I had inferred had happened to him. (He refused to describe them at all.) It was like a dead person talking.

It was during that time that it became increasingly difficult to attend to Artie with any consistency. Crises at home were taking up more and more of my time. Since my father's death, my little sister,

Grace, had been withdrawing deeper and deeper into reclusion—even forsaking her music. I shuttled as best I could between the two.

Each time I could make it up to San Antonio, I saw physical improvements in Artie's ability to walk and use his left arm. But his mental state seemed to get worse if anything. I wondered if it was egocentric to attribute it to the increasing scarcity of my visits.

I talked, mostly by phone, to hospital personnel. Trevor researched psychiatric clinics. Fortunately, there was one in SA that had national, even international, recognition. Trevor arranged, as discreetly as possible, for me to talk to the director, a Dr. John Wilson. Eventually, he put me in touch with the psychiatrist who would be handling his case, Dr. Judith Neuwirth. I filled her in on what I knew.

But as time wore on, family concerns, plus news about my former girlfriend Dolores Martínez, began to occupy more and more of my time and energy. I also felt uncomfortable staying on Connors's payroll, so I tried to substitute teach in Aguagria as much as I could. I felt like the little Dutch boy with my fingers in two dams at once. Or even three, if that were possible. For there was still some spiritual rock in my shoe—barely noticeable, but there. At first, I could bury it beneath attention to family and friends. But as time wore on and the crises expanded to the point of explosion, I felt something personal eating away at my sense of equilibrium.

Where would I find time for that?

During my early adulthood, the zeitgeist of the era was what I now recognize as a selfish illusion: *having it all.*

No, life is about choices. And they're all too often painful ones. I must, unfortunately, make mine.

# Part II

What a new and extraordinary world it was for her! Nine years of all-girl Catholic school, all but one taught by nuns. Now, in her sophomore year, just the size of this public school was intimidating—but oh-so exciting! So many kids, so many teachers, so many new choices. There were classes she could never dream of taking at Saint Ursula's. There was band and orchestra. There were debate and drama clubs. There were so many different sports to choose from. There was cheerleading—even chess, math and science clubs. It was just dizzying!

She wondered if her sheltered life would show. She was sure it would. Would the other kids sense it and reject her? What would it be like having classes with boys? Would she be able to concentrate? Would there maybe be some others from Saint Ursula's coming here? Many of them knew people here and hung out with them sometimes. She'd met some of them—seen them smoking dope a few times. She'd even been offered it herself but refused, knowing her father would be so hurt. She also knew some girls, even in her class at Saint Ursa's, that had had sexual experiences. She even heard some girls talking about oral sex. Gross! How could anyone do that?

She looked around for someone she might know, but there were just so many kids! Most of her girlfriends had transferred to Holy Cross. But since her father's death, the family had no money for private school. "Oh, Papa, why did you have to die?" Despite the tears, she reprimanded herself for selfishness in thinking of her own loss. He'd lost his life, after all. And Mama lost her *husband and best friend, for God's sake. And poor little Chacho, having to grow up without a father. "I'll have to be sister and parent for him somehow."*

*She just wasn't sure how she felt about Saint Ursula's closing. Yes, she felt safe there, but so constricted. Yes, it's sad that a vocation seems to be a thing of the past; she'd heard that most of the teachers at Holy Cross were lay teachers. But is it normal to take a vow of chastity? For your whole life? She knew at this new school there'd be new temptations but was sure she had the strength and maturity to manage them. This was a whole new world!* I must take advantage of it, *she thought.* Look at the new opportunities, all the new people to get to know.

*She'd had an orientation. All the teachers she'd met seemed nice. And they were so different from each other. They seemed to have so much to offer, coming from so many different backgrounds: men, women, African Americans, even one from another country—it was like a banquet! Yes, she definitely decided, this would be an exciting new experience! She only wished she could share it with her father when she got home. Well, she'd share it with her mother and little brother. It wouldn't be the same, but it would have to do.*

*But after a week she'd only made one friend. Then out of nowhere Daniel, the star quarterback of the football team and a* senior *had come up and talked to her! And he was so nice! He warned her that a lot of the girls here could be mean and cliquish. And to watch out for some of the guys, too—that a lot of them might seem nice but were really out to take advantage. He introduced her to some of the other members of the team. They seemed nice, too—not as nice as Daniel, but welcoming.*

*When Daniel called and asked if he could come over with some of the guys just to visit, she couldn't have been more excited. Of course at first she said no, because no one was there besides herself and her little brother. But Daniel promised they'd leave before her mother got home from work and swore there'd be no drugs or alcohol. He said they could just play games and asked if she had Scrabble. She did. She and her father used to play all the time. Finally she had a new Scrabble partner! Partners, actually!*

August 7, 2002. Patient Arturo Cavazos, Chart 1179A—Dr. Judith Lozano Neuwirth, MD, PhD, reporting:

Patient Arturo ("Artie") Cavazos was referred to Sacred Heart Psychiatric Clinic by medical personnel at San Antonio Orthopedic Hospital for suspected posttraumatic stress disorder. Initially admitted to SAOH for a six-month-to-year-long course of rehabilitative surgery and inpatient physical therapy. Course of treatment included reconstruction of dislocated (and poorly healed) left shoulder, plus total replacement of right hip. Pt continues in outpatient PT for both issues. Additional surgeries may be indicated.

Pt is ambulatory, walking with the aid of a cane. (Addendum: There is something interesting in his relationship to his cane. He seems to use it almost grudgingly, as though he resents having to rely on it. I noticed that with each step he places it down gently, sparingly, as though to make as little sound as possible. Curious.)

Movement of left shoulder reported as "restricted," but motion has apparently exceeded initial prognosis. Pt has reported minimal pain, but physical therapists suspect "stiff upper lip" syndrome, as even during very stressful PT exercises complaints were almost never heard. Outward expressions of discomfort were limited to moments when Pt would stop with jaw clenched, sweating profusely.

When asked specifically to rate pain level, comments were limited to "a bit uncomfortable" and "maybe a little" even for quite strenuous exercises. (For some reason, Pt seems averse to rating pain on one-to-ten scale.) If true, it may be expected that this tendency to minimize personal discomfort will factor in during efforts at cognitive therapy.

Main concerns from SAOH at the present time are flat affect and general lack of interest. (Although Pt never shrinks from exercises, this may be attributed to the "good soldier" mentality.) Violent intrusive symptoms have diminished somewhat (at least around others), although Pt still described as panicking when exposed to certain sensory input: a pair of tongs used by hosp'l personnel to retrieve supplies from an upper shelf, the sound of coffee percolating, a can of soda opened, cologne or aftershave a nurse was wearing on one occasion, etc. It will be of vital interest to identify any other "triggers" and what they are associated with.

Pt is also reported by family (one sister) and friends to avoid contact generally. He prefers to be alone, particularly at night; apparently sleeps little. Suspected substance abuse: mainly alcohol combined with pain medication. These are probably contributing to psychic numbing.

Pt history:

Native of Aguagria, TX. Born in Mexican state of Chihuahua. Pt reports that family immigrated when he was ten by simply "heading south and crossing the river." Father was picked up by immigration a couple of years later when he went looking for work; subsequently deported. At first, he (father) kept in touch with the family through his brother's in-laws, who apparently had relatives in Aguagria. After a short time, father was not heard from again. Brother, named Teo (Pt's uncle), reported that he had simply "disappeared." This left Pt as head of family at age twelve. Consequently, Pt started school in US late, graduating high school at age twenty (almost twenty-one).

Trauma apparently incurred while Pt was held captive by a Mexican drug cartel known as the "Zetas." After apparent escape, abuse continued while Pt was held in a clandestine Mexican prison in deplorable conditions. During initial captivity with the Zetas, Pt was subjected to as yet unnamed but apparently horrific forms of torture. (This group is reportedly famous for it.) According to comments from Pt's associates, this was a combination of punishment for "disloyalty" (of Pt's uncle) and as stimulus for family to pay ransom. Entire family was held responsible for uncle's "treachery."

Pt was captured with uncle and his two children during abortive attempt to cross US-Mexican border. Pt's aunt was apparently killed during attempt. The effort to escape was reportedly necessitated by uncle's forced participation in cartel operations. There is no word of them. They were apparently killed while still in captivity.

Mr. Cavazos is supported by friend Jacob Kizmarech (sp?), who has been in (lately sporadic) contact with hospital personnel and has already contacted this institution. Hospital reports that he is the one who inquired about possible necessity of treatment for PTSD.

Mr. Kizmareck alleges that Pt's family, when they initially crossed the border, lived in a dugout by the side of the Rio Grande River (!). He has also stated that there is a "legend" that the family was forced to flee Mexico because Pt killed a police officer who was trying to rape his big sister. Sister's name is Griselda Johnson (née: Cavazos).

(Does this indicate that PTSD actually dates from that event? Or could it be an exacerbating factor?) This is suspected to be related to father's "disappearance" once he returned to the tiny settlement of La Perla in Chihuahua, i.e. police took revenge against father. Might father have been involved in defense of daughter/sister? Or was it simply a case of a pigeon in the hand, holding whole family responsible? Sister is also a source of support, although she lives quite a distance away and cannot visit regularly.

There is also an unnamed benefactor, apparently the source of funds necessary for treatment and living accommodations. For apparently political considerations, source must remain anonymous. Pt refuses public assistance. Mr. Kazmarech reports that Pt insists that he is going to pay unnamed benefactor back.

This may indicate a strong locus of control (i.e., Pt's belief in his ability to affect his own destiny) and will be important in Pt's rehabilitation. According to Mr. Kazmarech, Pt has (had?) "prodigious" (his word) coping and adaptive skills. Mr. Kazmereck states that, during a time when lost in the desert, it was Pt who kept him and another friend alive. This also indicates once-high sociability. These character strengths will be vital in his convalescence. However, it is expected that these traits have been seriously compromised by his experiences while in captivity.

Referral to Sacred Heart Clinic requested by friend Jacob "Jake" Kismareck (from this point forward referred to simply as "Jake"), in conjunction with anonymous friend/benefactor. Descriptions of behavior by Jake indicate severe to complex PTSD: constriction or psychic "numbing," including severe episodes of dissociation or "lost time," and hyperarousal and intrusive symptoms related to triggers that baffle friend Jake: a pool cue, a pair of barbecue tongs, possibly an odor of singed hair, among others.

In addition, Jake reports that Pt's stress level paradoxically "shot through the roof" as they approached the border during Pt's rescue. (Curious that as they neared what should have been perceived as freedom and safety, Pt panicked. Possibility that Pt grew so accustomed to captivity that prospect of freedom was terrifying.)

Jake says that as they crossed bridge, Pt interpreted a boy tapping on his window as an attack. When Jake tried to take hold of Pt's arm to restrain him, Pt grabbed him by the throat and choked him until he passed out, causing an accident. Pt panicked and ran to US side of border (apparently it was closer), and it reportedly took five Border Patrol agents to subdue him. He was restrained, probably in the throes of flashbacks.

He was then transferred to the local hospital together with friend Jake and sedated. Once more under control, he was treated for various contagious diseases, including hepatitis A and B. Chart also indicates tuberculosis was present but somehow cured. This was possibly owing to Pt's imprisonment in a prison situated in the mountainous desert. After being declared noncontagious, he was transferred to San Antonio Orthopedic Hospital, where treatment for abovementioned chronic conditions was initiated.

August 8, 2002. Intake Interview, Pt Arturo Cavazos (1179A) (with therapist's introduction and comments added after listening to recording):

When he walked in the room, I almost felt myself lifted off the floor. It was like a wave that came across the distance between us, a monumental wash of despair. It sent a flush through my scalp. Why? What was special about him? Was it the degree of pathology I sensed or simply the power of his personality? Was it perhaps the magnitude of distress he felt at being here—at needing therapy? Was it some combination of all those factors?

Possibility that it was so devastating because I could sense that before me stood the shattered bits of what had once been a powerful and solid human essence. Whatever it was, I knew this case was going to be different from any I'd handled in my career. Perhaps it was simply the severity; perhaps there are other factors yet to be identified.

"Mr. Cavazos?"

He gave the slightest nod. "Doctor."

I felt compelled to come around my desk to welcome him. Interesting: I usually just offer my hand to shake from across my desk. This time it felt like a barrier I needed to breach. "Good morning. I'm Judith Neuwirth."

He perfunctorily reached out his hand to mine. I could see the stiffness as he did so. His grip was nonexistent. There was coldness and distance. The look in his eyes was curious: I discerned a fierce native intelligence captured in a bottomless pit of despair. I hoped part of it was an acknowledgment of the necessity of therapy combined with a disgust at the need for it. As I'd been told, this was an individual accustomed to being independent and in control. It was evidenced by his discipline during the course of surgery and PT.

"Would you care to sit?" I indicated the chair in front of my desk. I usually say, "Please, have a seat," but in this instance, it felt more appropriate to make it his choice. He sat down at ramrod attention but at the same time with a catlike grace, seemingly at the ready. Hypervigilance was apparent. I came back around my desk and sat.

I tried to start with something light and neutral to reduce the tension. "Please call me Judith. I understand you go by Artie?"

"Arturo."

There was a finality in the way he said it. Like the former name belonged on a tombstone. It rather took my breath away. I tried to regroup as quickly as I could.

"Fair enough. I've never been partial to 'Judy.' My husband tries it every now and then, but I withhold sex, and that usually puts a stop to it." My comment didn't even elicit a patient smile of recognition.

"OK…Arturo. First thing I want to tell you is that, with your permission, I'm going to record all of our meetings. As a matter of fact, I'm recording us now. I'll turn the recorder off if you prefer. This is a collaborative effort, and you're in control. We only go as far as you're willing and able to. However, I'd ask you to please give me the opportunity to explain my thinking."

I waited for his license to proceed. It was not forthcoming, so I just continued. "My reasons are twofold: first, so that I can go over whatever exchanges we have and see if I missed anything—see if anything jumps out at me that I didn't catch the significance of. It'll also give me a better idea of what direction to suggest we go in moving forward. Secondly, during exercises you'll eventually be doing at home, you can listen to our discussions and do the same."

"Exercises?" It was astounding how such a quiet, measured response seemed to cut the atmosphere like a knife.

I considered covering the rationale for exposure therapy at this point but decided against it. I had the feeling that Pt might be so averse to the idea that he would refuse to continue therapy and so keep up his self-destructive behavior. Plus, my usual initial interview protocol seemed somehow inadequate. I judged that making Pt feel safe took priority. Part of that would be emphasizing that as the Pt he would call the shots. Reconstruction of the trauma story could wait.

"I'll describe those, but first let me know if I have your permission to record us."

Silence. This time I decided to wait, making it his choice to proceed or not. Reluctantly, he answered, "You're the doc, Doc."

"Well, that's true. But I don't make the rules. It's up to you to decide what you can handle, how far you can go. That's because only you know you." His eyes lowered at this. I could almost hear in that gesture *I have no idea who I am* or maybe even *I'm no one*. "My role is more like a guide. I can ask questions, make recommendations, suggest areas to explore, but how our sessions go is up to you. It's sort of analogous to the lawyer-client relationship. A lawyer can identify your options, tell you possible outcomes and make recommendations. But ultimately, it's up to the client how to proceed. "Do you want me to turn the recorder off?"

"No."

"Great. Now, before we go any further, will you tell me how you're feeling? How're the hip and shoulder?"

"Coming along."

"Are you in any pain?"

A cold, distant shrug. "Nothing compared." (Ah, a reference to the trauma, however oblique. Perhaps a start.)

"Will you let me know if there's anything I can do to ease any physical discomfort?"

"OK."

I now had the feeling that small talk was pointless. "Art—Arturo, would it be helpful for me to explain the process...what I hope to—what I hope *we* can accomplish together?

"...OK."

"All right. Let me begin by asking you if you know why you're here?"

God, that icy stare and ever-so-slight pause! "Because I'm crazy." He said it as though he were talking about a houseplant that had died.

This was a first—not just the words but something else (what?). I knew better than to start with anything patronizing. "Well, considering what you've been through, I'd imagine anyone would be." I paused while looking him straight in the eye. I wanted him to know that I meant it—that I wasn't patronizing...or pitying.

There was something that flashed across his eyes that told me I'd established a tiny bit of trust, that he appreciated the honesty. I didn't need a verbal response. "Actually, what I would call crazy is a pathological response to a normal situation. I would call what you've been through a normal response to a pathological situation."

He took a moment to consider it. "But I'm not in that situation anymore."

"No, thank God." I caught the slightest reaction in those dead eyes. It was a cold, cold skepticism, a complete loss of faith. *What God?* it said.

"Are you gonna ask me what happened over there?"

"Absolutely not at this point. What I want to accomplish first— what I'd like *us* to accomplish—is for you to feel safe here."

There was, just in his eyes, the faintest ironic smile; it said, *Good luck with that.* "I dunno, Doc. It's over. I think the best thing I can do is to just...put it behind me."

I hesitated saying this. I didn't want it to be taken as sarcastic. "Arturo, has that been working for you so far?" I could see the answer in his eyes, so I continued. "I wish it were that simple. The problem with trying to just not think about it is this: try not to think about pink elephants. What are you thinking about?" I paused a moment to see if my point had been made. It had.

"Those experiences can't be just forgotten. They'll intrude over and over again. And I'm afraid the more you try to suppress them, the more they'll intrude—and in more and more dangerous ways. I believe what needs to happen, to happen *eventually*—that is, when you're ready—is for us to bring those horrible events into the open. So that they can be integrated into a new reality...a new Arturo Cavazos."

His skepticism was daunting. I had to try a new but related tack. "Trauma changes our ways of thinking. And sustained trauma makes those changes deeply rooted. Let me start with an example, one that might seem trivial but that I hope will give you an idea. Have you ever been in a car accident? Or a fistfight?" The change of subject seemed to pique his curiosity just the tiniest bit.

"Both."

"Not at the same time, hopefully." *Pretty poor effort at a joke there, Judith.*

But I managed to draw a dry, patronizing smile—perhaps a gesture of charity. "No."

"The accident—how serious was it?"

"Well, one was just a fender bender. But before that, I was in a pretty serious one. Broke my leg; the car was totaled."

"Scary?"

"…I guess." Obviously the fear was minimal compared with the more recent trauma; his answer was delivered in the same flat tone. I had to acknowledge in myself a bit of frustration. Perhaps because the degree of flat affect was so chilling.

"Did you calm down immediately afterward?"

This seemed to at least give him the slightest pause. "No, actually. My mother told me I was talking really loud and really fast when she got to the hospital. That was about a half an hour later. Maybe more. I wasn't even aware of it." There was a moment he paused here to think. "But I got over that."

"How long did the accident last? How long were you in danger?" I could see a recognition of the point I was making. "And what about the next time you got in a car? Did you feel the same as before? How about the fender bender? Was your reaction to it what you'd call normal? Or was it somewhat exaggerated?"

I could see the realization happening. It was quick—faster than most of my patients. "Actually, I can think of a better example—one your friend Jake told me about." (Make note of the intense reaction at the mention of his friend—registered only in his eyes.)

"You talked to Jake."

"Yes, I did. For a good while. Actually, he was the one who asked for the referral here."

A slight hesitation as he absorbed this. "Huh." It wasn't an expression of surprise. This told me something about their relationship.

"He told me about the canoe trip you took right after you graduated high school." The depth of pain at the memory! Was it a good idea, telling him I'd talked to his friend, mentioning the canoe trip? Well, I was committed. "After the rapids on that trip…what were they called, the rapids?"

There was another pause. It was obvious that this was excruciating for him to remember. I assumed it reminded him of the person he was, the life he had. But however painful, remember he must. "The Rockslide," he finally answered.

"The Rockslide. After that, what was your reaction to seeing rapids, even mild ones? How did you feel getting back into the canoe? After you were safe, did you look at the river the same way?" Again, I could see the deduction being drawn.

"Now, I imagine what you went through at the hands of that drug cartel and in that prison made the incident in the Rockslide pretty minor by comparison—as terrifying as I'm sure it was. And that torment lasted how long? How long were you in danger, on constant guard, your life in constant peril, the prospect of horrific pain at every turn?"

His look said, *How do you know this?* But it seemed to be quickly answered: friend Jake. I could see the terror even this casual mention provoked. It radiated out of deadened eyes. I had to be more circumspect. Given his evident intelligence, I considered that a more detailed anatomical description might be appropriate. Some discomfort at this point was fine, but now there were signs of increasing stress: perspiration, rapid breathing. *Safety, Judith. At this point, it's paramount.*

I felt a keen sense of his psychic makeup—a kinship even (that's interesting; worth exploring). But I must also take care not to jump to conclusions, projecting my own tendencies, making assumptions based on appearances or hunches. Although I can't ignore them either. "Have you ever heard of what's called the fight-or-flight response?"

His eyes narrowed a bit, indicating that he had. "Yeah. As a matter of fact, I remember…" (there was a hesitation here before saying the name) "…Jake telling me about it." (Each time the subject of his friend comes up, it is clearly discomfiting for him.) "He called it the fight-flight-freeze response."

"Yes, that's actually more accurate. When we're exposed to stress, there are two primary parts of the brain that come into play, or at least two that I'd like to consider. The more primitive one is called the amygdala. And the higher-functioning one is the prefrontal cortex.

"In cases of moderate stress, the prefrontal cortex, the part of the brain that evaluates, that reasons, will act as a brake on amygdalar—fight-flight-freeze—responses. But in moments of intense stress, when there are real threats to our lives, chemicals produced by the amygdala—norepinephrine, primarily—will overcome the prefrontal cortex.

"If you saw a lion charging at you, for instance, it wouldn't do much good to calmly evaluate the situation. You'd need to react—to fight, flee or freeze. I wouldn't recommend the first option unless you have a really big gun." (There was an almost complete lack of reaction to the joke.) "You'd need the flood of oxygen to your muscles that rapid breathing provides. You'd need a heart beating at a high rate to get that oxygen to those muscles.

"Now, what happens when the threat is constant…when that primitive part of the brain takes over for long stretches of time… because it has to? Because if it doesn't, if it isn't constantly on guard, always overruling, suppressing that deliberative part, it could mean your death? For instance, what happens when one part of the body is overworked? Or one side? I mean, over years? It throws the body out of whack, doesn't it?"

"Yeah. I've seen that." (Finally, a response indicating interest.)

"The same thing can happen—*happens*—with our brain. You had to overdevelop—the technical term is *hypertrophy*—that primitive, say...*reactionary*, part of your brain. You had to in order to survive. The pensive, contemplative part had to take a backseat. And what's happened to it, that part that serves to suppress those sudden reactions, is the opposite: it's atrophied—weakened through disuse. Like I said, it's a normal adaptation to an extremely abnormal situation.

"Consequently, anything that reminds you of what you've been through—we call them 'triggers'—that primitive part of your brain reacts to before the reasoning part can tell you that it's not really a threat. And it can be anything: an object, a sound, a smell. Veterans, when they first come back from combat, will hit the ground at the sound of a firecracker or a car backfiring."

I gave him a moment to assimilate the information. But he was a quick study. "What we need to do is exercise that prefrontal cortex, to build it up. We need to teach your brain that those things are not really a threat. Not anymore." I was again heading toward a description of exposure but stopped myself. Some instinct told me to. I decided there were more important things to establish first.

"Of course that's only a part, a crucial but superficial part, of all we need to address. The other is a part we therapists struggle to define. Some call it the basic personality structure, the vital essence, life energy. Others call it the human spirit...the soul, if you will. There's usually, especially in extreme cases, a profound loss of faith, loss of a sense of purpose, of belief in a meaningful existence. Some people call it the 'just-world myth,' the very concept that life has purpose, meaning."

I could see how this resonated. The despair radiated out from him like a dense, killing fog—so much so that I began to feel myself dissociate, lift off my chair. I gripped the arms for all I was worth and pushed my feet against the floor to maintain connection, all the while making every effort to maintain a sense of calm and detachment.

"I dunno, Doc. Is there any way to get that back...once it's gone?" It wasn't so much the comment that made me shudder. I had expected that. It was the affect—or the total lack of it. It was the cool, calm certainty, the absolute absence of hope, of possibility, the clarity of the no. It was a no of such finality that I had to grip even tighter, dig my fingernails into my palms, push harder on the floor. My God, I knew this kind of thing happened, but in all my years of doing this, this was the first time for me. I tried to focus on the patient, force myself to be as analytical as possible. I was in danger of having intrusive symptoms of my own.

I wanted to give him hope but not false hope. "Not…in the same way. But we'll work on it, Arturo. We'll work on it. As I said earlier, it won't be the old Artie" (I could feel his pain at the mention of the name, a flush of intense anger) "but a new *Arturo*. And we'll get there. As long as it takes, we will get there."

Something told me I had to present this now. "Arturo…do you believe in God? Do you have any sense of something beyond the physical world? The spiritual, if you will?"

God, that penetrating stare! "I believe there's such a thing as evil."

"Hmm. You've experienced that firsthand."

"Let me ask you, Doc: you've been doing this for what…years?"

"A little over thirteen."

"Cases like mine?"

"Not…quite like yours. But cases of trauma, yes."

"So tell me, with what you've seen and heard over the years: rapes, murders, torture…"

"Child abuse, child sexual abuse, yes."

"With all that, do you?"

I weighed whether it would be wise to answer questions at this point. I decided that it was necessary to establish trust. "Well, let me say that I do find it difficult to believe in a God that would permit such evil…such suffering. But I also have a sense, a feeling of something beyond what we perceive in this world. For instance, I believe there's a difference between the brain and the mind, between electrical impulses in the cerebrum and identity…that we have a will that is separate from those electrochemical impulses."

This discussion, and in particular his reaction to it, was not helping my sense of rootedness. It felt, for just a moment, that he had slipped into that extraphysical sphere—so far away that it seemed the space we occupied had wormholed into another dimension. I was now clinging to keep from being swept into that space, fending off intrusive symptoms of my own, fighting to stay out of that gathering of high-school studs...in my own home, at my invitation.

I had to pull us down to the more concrete. I tried to segue it back as best I could. "You might consider spiritual counseling...in addition to what I can offer. I would be wary of the simple answers that your average cleric tends to offer, however. But before we can take on any of those issues, as I said before, the first thing we need to do is to make you feel safe. We need to come to trust each other. And trust doesn't just happen. Trust is earned."

"Why shouldn't I trust you, Doc? You weren't any part of that."

"Well, first of all, you don't know me. My question would be, why *should* you trust me? Even in normal circumstances, people need a reason to trust someone, don't they? They take a small risk, and if it works out, if trust isn't betrayed, they begin to feel more secure. And they take a slightly bigger risk, and the process continues." This more down-to-earth theme seemed to guide me back to my chair.

Feeling a bit more centered, I continued, "But your present situation, I'd imagine, is quite different. For instance, how long was it that you couldn't trust anyone?" Again, I could see I didn't have to draw the conclusion for him. "Just like the brain learns to be on guard all the time, so it learns not to trust if trust is betrayed at every turn. It'll take time to...reestablish, say, those alternative modes of thinking."

"I've been out of that situation for over a year now, Doc. How long does it take?" He said it not seeking an answer. It was a comment and, again, a chilling one. I could feel that, for him, all eternity couldn't put Humpty-Dumpty back together.

This I had to fight. "I wish it were just a question of time. I wish it were a question of a short time. It's going to take a lot of work and a lot of time. It may take a lifetime. In fact, it probably will. But we'll get there. *We will get there...*as long as it takes." My own expression of confidence seemed to help ground me. Perhaps I said it as much for my benefit as his.

I met his at-once vacant and piercing stare with my best look of certainty. "And the goal won't be to get you back to being your old self. I don't believe in Pollyannaish 'everything's going to turn out fine' attitudes. Those *are* myths. That's something to watch out for with your average priest or preacher.

"We have to—together—create a new Arturo Cavazos. We need to engage that contemplative part of your brain to incorporate what you've been through into some kind of meaningful whole, a new you. But a new you that includes all your experiences—including the horrific."

His reaction radiated skepticism. "How do I find meaning in insanity, Doc?"

"Arturo, I wish I had a simple answer for that. How do we integrate 9/11, The Holocaust, slavery, honor killings, all the expressions of irrational hate in human history into our understanding of who we are as sentient beings? Again, we'll just have to work on it...together.

"And we'll get there. It won't be easy. I have to warn you that a lot of it will be difficult, painful. But I don't get the sense that you're one to shy away from a challenge.

"It may even involve metaphysical discussions of what reality is, why evil exists: Is it a fundamental part of us? Is it an entity in and of itself that overtakes us somehow? Is it a necessary part of having free will—having the freedom to choose between good and evil, right and wrong? Is that choice relative or absolute?

"I don't know the answers. I don't think there are any *absolute* answers. But I can sense a powerful mind in you, and I think just considering those issues, sharing our thoughts and feelings about them, will help. I'm asking you to give me a chance. But most of all, to give yourself a chance."

I had never gone this far with any of my patients in the initial interview. But I could see it was the right choice, as the barest glimmer of hope glanced across his face. It was fleeting, so tenuous that I wondered afterward if I hadn't imagined it.

I decided that this was as good a place as I could hope for to finish up. Besides, I was utterly exhausted. It had been less than an hour, but I knew I'd had all I could take. "Ar—Arturo, we're coming to the end of our time for today. But before we stop, do you have any questions, any other questions?"

I saw what looked like millions of calculations passing through that mind. That tiny aperture of hope in a universe of despair quickly receded to nothingness. I hoped it wasn't just wishful thinking on my part.

"No."

"Then could you answer one question for me?" He just looked at me steadily, waiting. "Why the name change?"

Oh, that look! It spoke of a spirit not broken but shattered, demolished, lost in the abyss. It was like a cold wind that settled where my lungs had been. It reminded me of Volkan's dictum. It radiated out from eyes that seemed no more than the hollow spaces of a skull: "The regenerative powers of the ego are not limitless. The human spirit can be broken beyond repair."

In a voice paired to those empty, empty eyes, he answered, "Artie's dead."

08/08/02 (personal log):

I'd ended the intake with Pt Arturo Cavazos early. The depth of his despair, the utter shattering of his ego had shaken me back to my own time in hell. I hurried down the hall to John's office. On the way, I passed a couple of male employees sharing what I assume was either a dirty joke or a laugh at one of their conquests. I was seized with the impulse to rip their eyes out of their sockets. I swallowed hard and continued on.

I fairly burst into John's office. Fortunately, he wasn't with a patient or some potential donor. "Judith…?" He looked up, curious.

I sat. John just waited. He had a soothing patience about him that I paradoxically sometimes found exasperating. Not this time, though. I think he immediately recognized the state I was in. It was to let me know that I could take all the time I needed. He nonchalantly cleaned his glasses with a handkerchief in the silence. "I don't know if I can do this one, John."

"What one?"

"The one I just finished interviewing, Arturo Cavazos."

He paused a moment. I suppose to give himself time to get a sense of my state of mind—maybe to give me more space to settle. "OK. Why?"

"It's just…John, I just finished the initial interview, and during it I already felt myself start to dissociate. That's never happened to me before! I felt myself levitating, watching the interview from somewhere above, floating around the ceiling. It was…"

He waited a good while before speaking. "…Scary?"

"That wasn't all. On my way over here, I almost had a flashback."

"Almost. But you didn't?"

"John, I've just started with this patient! If I'm in this state already, how will I be when we start exposure therapy?"

"Do you plan to do that right away?"

"Not a chance. He's too fragile."

"Then you have some time to adjust."

It was beginning to get frustrating. "John, aren't you the least bit concerned?"

"Oh yes. I'm...*concerned*. I'm concerned any time one of my best therapists is questioning her ability to work with a patient." He left hanging that his "concern" didn't automatically lead him to conclude that I was unfit for the job.

"He reminds me of my brother, John."

"Oh? In what way?"

This struck me. "Hah. I really don't know. He's nothing like him. Chacho was frail, hypersensitive—almost feminine. I can tell that Arturo is—or, at least, *was*—a rock." I looked up at John. He just looked back at me, waiting. "*Was*, I said."

"Right. What do they have in common?"

"John, I've got, what...thirteen years now working with PTSD patients? I may have seen some that reminded me of Chacho, but I never *identified* them this way."

A look of curiosity passed over his face. "What do you think's different this time?" This was the first time he asked without my having the feeling that he already knew the answer.

"I don't know. There's substance abuse. But that's the case with many patients. Could he be suicidal? That's always a risk in these cases."

"That's true. Any attempts?"

"No. And I don't think if it happened it would be an *attempt*." But I had the feeling that the possibility of suicide wasn't it. And I also had the sense that John didn't think so either. Or that that wasn't all of it. "I really...*don't know*."

We looked at each other, both realizing that this was one of those mysteries that only time and exploration could solve. John's soothing manner had had its effect. Suddenly, I was focused on the case, excited by the challenge it presented. "You want me to stick with this one, don't you?"

"Well, if you want me to reassign it, I will. But I think Mr. Cavazos needs and deserves our best." He smiled.

As I walked down the hall back to my office, I saw one of the two gentlemen I'd seen just a few minutes earlier. *Hah, now they're "gentlemen."* I remembered how I felt earlier and was startled...startled by the strength of my feelings then and startled by how now there were no such feelings. He was just Paulie, now. Paulie, the utility man.

I saw two other patients that day, both female. One had been in an abusive relationship for years, and one was the victim of rape—gang rape, at a frat party in college. It should have been that one that brought up my own assault. But after cognitive restructuring so that she wasn't blaming herself for being "stupid," we'd already tackled in vivo exposure and were able to start memory exposure. And I didn't even flinch. Of course, I'd handled other similar cases.

What was it about this one? What was unique about Arturo Cavazos? I listened to the recording of the initial interview. Damned if it didn't almost have the same effect—fortunately *almost*. But I realized it helped me get a little distance. I listened to it again. Again it had the effect of objectifying the case. I realized I was doing my own exposure therapy. I felt more like the doctor and less like a bystander—or even a patient.

I began to consider my reactions with a bit of detachment. Of course, Judith, you know little about the case at this point. Yes, you have a history and a general outline, but few of the specifics of what the Pt went through. Ongoing assessments—ongoing assessments and teasing out details. I'll have to be careful of pulling him into exposure too soon, though.

August 8, 2002. Preliminary Impressions of Pt Arturo Cavazos (1179A):

Pt presents with severe complex posttraumatic stress disorder. He shows marked symptoms of constriction. He is aloof, affectless. Though he seemed sober enough, I suspect considerable substance abuse: efforts to wall off the traumatic experience and sense of hopelessness, not to mention the need to control violent impulses. It is evident that even having a conversation, even small talk, is arduous for him. I note profound distrust, suspicion and, underneath the flat affect, extreme hypervigilance. I doubt Pt is sleeping much. This, despite pain medication that I suspect is part of the substance abuse. There was possibly a mild odor of liquor on his breath. It is way too soon for any preliminary hypothesis. But fascinating.

I have the feeling there was something beyond the torture he was subjected to. But what? Was he sexually abused? For a man like this one, that kind of humiliation would be beyond unbearable. Was he forced to watch his family tortured? I'm almost certain that a man like Artie Cavazos would feel responsible for them (as I imagine Arturo Cavazos does as well). Was he even forced to be complicit? Again, if so, that would be an issue of shame and guilt and anger (hate) rather than anxiety and fear, and would indicate cognitive restructuring.

But I have to be very careful and examine my own motivations at every step. I know the idea of exposing Pt to memories of what he went through strikes me as unbearably cruel. Do I want to delay exposure for my sake, rather than his? Even the initial interview seemed to resurrect my own trauma. Where to begin, where to begin? Safety, Judith.

I'll probably need to consult John every step of the way, countertransference already an issue. I wonder if John has the time to meet with me before and after sessions. Probably once a week is the best I can hope for. I hope he'll have the time for that. I trust him so implicitly—both as a therapist and as a friend.

But as close as we are, would he have the distance, the objectivity, at this point? I think he would. But I'll have to ask him. Given the degree of countertransference, I might need to go back into therapy myself.

The phone rang. It made me almost jump out of my skin. Who could be calling now? I looked out my window. Darkening. It was almost nine-thirty. I realized at that moment that I hadn't let Donald know that I'd be late getting home—certainly not this late. I hope he was able to get some dinner. He tends to get cranky when dinner is late—as cranky as dear Donny ever gets. Tonight I just couldn't deal with it. "Hello?"

It was that long-suffering husband of mine. "You're still there. You all right?"

"Yes, hon. It's been…quite a day. Just finishing up. I got so involved I forgot to call. Sorry. Did you and Jonathan get something to eat?"

"Yeah. I called for pizza and made a salad. How 'bout you? You eat?"

"Oh, wow, till you mentioned it, I hadn't even thought. I'm starving!"

"Well, there're two slices left with your name on them."

"Oh, great. I'll, uh…I'll see you in half an hour. Twenty minutes if I'm lucky."

"See you then. Bye."

"Bye."

Glad I started the automatic recording of all my phone conversations. Glad it wasn't a patient on the verge of suicide. But the jump back to normal life (is there such a thing?) after today was a slap in the face. Glad Donald called, though; I needed some distance. That hubby of mine—always there when you need him.

Oh God, pizza…and late at night…I'm gonna be big as a whale! I'm off.

August 15, 2002. Meeting with Pt Arturo Cavazos (1179A):

I thought back to my first meeting with Mr. Cavazos. I'd decided to start off with some neutral topics. I still felt that the establishment of trust and safety was going to be a complicated and drawn-out process. But I also had to be very careful of my own fear of engaging him in exposure—because of how difficult it would be for me. And the tendency to consider it cruel—making him relive those horrendous moments. I was pretty sure he was in no state to start yet. But to get to what of his thinking needed to be restructured, I had to know the specific traumatic experiences first. Or did I?

It was another insufferably hot south-Texas day. Dog days. Up on the sixth floor, you could see a bit of San Antonio. Typical for a big city in this part of the country, it stretched as far as the eye could see. An achingly blue sky, with a few listless wisps of white. I saw two patients in the morning. Making pretty good progress, I think. Easy ones, just fear and anxiety, one from an assault and the other from a traffic accident in which his wife was injured. Is there some guilt, since he was driving? Something I'll need to be on the lookout for.

Went to lunch at Luby's and couldn't find a parking place in the shade. Probably employees take all of those. Getting back in the car was dreadful.

So, here I am with just a few minutes before Mr. Cavazos comes in. Am I nervous or excited? Both? This is certainly profiling as the most challenging case I've had. I think it's both.

He enters on crutches this time. Possibly even more constricted than at our first meeting. Got to establish a rapport.

"Good morning, Arturo."

"Morning."

"Please, have a seat. What happened to the cane?"

"Oh, I, uh…had a little fall. It's not the hip. Just twisted my ankle a little."

"Any pain?"

"No."

I doubted he was telling the truth about that. I hesitated asking, but it would be normal to do so. "How'd it happen?"

"Oh, I was, uh...walking out onto the balcony of my apartment. Stepped wrong.

"Ah..." It was obvious he wanted to drop the issue at that. I wasn't sure I was getting the real story. But putting him on the defensive was the last thing he needed. I suspected that intoxication had played a part in the accident. Should I pursue that? He moved his foot to a new position. Obviously there was some discomfort. "Arturo, how exactly did the accident with your ankle happen?"

"Uh...I stepped on the doorframe. Wasn't expecting to. Guess I just forgot it was there. Stepped on it kind of sideways, and my foot went like this." He showed me. Then he held for just a second. I was pretty sure the hesitation was for pain. "I guess I was...not quite sober."

We'd just established a bit of a connection. Was it too soon to take on the issue of substance abuse? "Um-hum. That happen often?"

He was quiet for a time. I decided to give him that time. Then, even more quietly but with a tone of defiance: "I suppose."

"Arturo, I want you to know that I'm not here to judge. I would never do that. I *will* never do that." I remembered my own addiction to sedatives and cigarettes. "I'm in no position to. But one thing I've seen over and over again in my practice is patients taking all kinds of measures to avoid, to try to, let's say, *wall off* those horrible experiences. And that includes substances that numb the brain. But as we've discussed before, trying to keep from thinking about something forces them out—and in unhealthy, often violent ways."

"Is that what I'm doing." It wasn't said as a question.

"I think you might be. Arturo, let me repeat: to survive what you survived changed you. As I've explained, and I'll probably keep repeating it, there are changes in the brain in response to trauma, and changes to whatever else makes us who we are. Especially the kind of extended trauma you experienced. But there is still a whole reality of you before, and now after, that time. We need to integrate both with the reality *during* that time."

There was just the slightest but deadliest smile—perhaps even a touch of pity—in those eyes. I'd lost him again. "This isn't reality, Doc."

Curious. I judged it a feeling worth pursuing. It might be a tiny path to his sharing the pain, the utter desolation I could feel in every breath he took. I would have to find a way to bring it back to ground zero, though. "What do you mean?"

If it were possible, his affect was even more chilling than before. "I mean we're living a dream, here. A dream where things make sense. Where for the most part if you're good, you're rewarded, and bad people get punished. At least, that's how most people think. But that isn't who we really are. Even you said it's a myth. We have a cover of kindness, of care for the other guy, of..." (I could feel his pain intensify, the hate beneath it burn) "...whatever. But when it's a matter of life or death, the idea of pain that never stops...you'll sell out your best friend, your own mother. You'll..."

For just a moment, the constriction wavered. I could feel his devastation wash over the room like a tidal wave. Beads of sweat formed at his temples. His breathing became more rapid. Then, there was a curious gesture he made: hands down on the seat between his knees, one rubbing down the back of the other. As though he were trying to scrape something from between his fingers.

For the first time, I noticed his hands. They were dry, red, cracked. I felt the crushing guilt that had laid waste to his spirit. It again threatened to suck me into altered states, the domain of abusive husbands, child predators, the amorality of war. Again, I gripped the arms of my chair, pulled my legs as hard as I could back against the seat, fighting for grounding, for sanity, for place.

"Arturo, I've worked with veterans. Quite a few over the years. Some were prisoners of war. To a man, they discount these stories of heroes who stand up to torture for years and never succumb. *To a man.*" *Careful, Judith. Don't patronize, don't infantilize.*

I wasn't sure he even heard me. He had cracked a window open to his pain and then shut it with violent force. It was too threatening— at least for now. I had to spend the rest of the session reorienting

Pt, allowing him to regain some nominal control. We spoke of any neutral subject I could think of. I think he realized what I was doing.

Eventually, I would have to find a way to crawl in that window. If it opened once, it might again. It must.

August 16, 2002. Meeting with John:

Had a horrific nightmare last night. I woke up struggling against my husband. In the midst of pushing against his face to try to escape, I scratched him. I was back in high school, and he was one of my attackers. He had the face of the devil in *Rosemary's Baby*. ("He has his father's eyes.")

My God! I haven't had an intrusive symptom like that in years. If this keeps up, I'll have to make some adjustments. It would be better to stop seeing Mr. Cavazos now rather than after we've established a rapport. That could be very disconcerting and have serious consequences. Must consult John again, and right away; will record our conversation.

It was early, so I just came in and sat. John waited a moment. "Good morning, Judith."

"I'm having symptoms, John."

I could tell he took this seriously by the way he hesitated for a moment. "OK. What kind?"

"Nightmare. Donald had to restrain me."

"For how long?"

"Well, just momentarily till I came to myself. But, John, it's been… *years!*"

"Uh-huh." He said it rather noncommittally.

"John, you know how important consistency is. I don't want to develop a relationship with this patient and then tell him he's got to find someone else."

"No, that wouldn't be a good. Wouldn't necessarily doom the patient. I've sent any number to you that other therapists couldn't handle." *Yes, and it's created considerable intraoffice jealously*, I thought. "But, yes, consistency is important." Again, I felt he was leaving the decision in my lap. *Thanks a lot!*

"Judith, how many sessions have you had with this patient—with Mr. Cavazos?"

"Just two. He missed one in between. Just two, John!"

"And how have they gone? What're your initial assessments?"

"Oh, John…Arturo Cavazos is in the most extreme state of constriction I've ever seen. His ego structure, his spirit, is utterly mutilated!"

"That can be terrifying. It's a horrible thing to witness—can bring up a lot of feelings, a lot of memories."

"Yes. That's true."

He waited awhile. I know it was to let me find my own way as a therapist. Then he finally spoke. It was what should have been a rather routine question. "What do you think is unique about this case? *Is* there something unique about it—I mean, beyond the severity?"

"I still have fantasies of what I'd like to do to those guys in high school."

"Now that's an interesting response to my question."

I looked up. "It is, isn't it?"

"Nothing ever happened to them, did it? They were never punished? The case was never even investigated, was it?"

I could feel the rage, the shame, building inside me. "No."

John hesitated and then quietly asked, "Why was that?"

"Because I didn't even report it."

Again, John asked as gently as he could. "And why was that?"

"Oh, John, you know all this."

"Yes, I do. *I* do."

"Well, of course *I* do!"

"Do you?"

I could feel the anger flush my face. "You think I still blame myself, don't you?"

"Do you?"

"Oh God, John! If I'm still at that stage, I have no business being a therapist at all!"

He took a breath and then continued in an annoyingly logical tone, "I'm not sure I agree with you conclusion, but let's consider that. Let's consider the possibility that you shouldn't be a therapist because you still have feelings about the trauma you suffered. What would you say to a patient who told you that?"

I just looked at him, leaned my head back and closed my eyes.

"Let me tell you, Judith. If I needed cognitive restructuring because I came to erroneous conclusions about a trauma I'd suffered—one I'd suffered a year, ten years, twenty years ago—who do you think I'd go to?"

We sat in silence for what seemed too long a time. "I shouldn't have invited them over, John. I knew their reputation around school, around town. That's why I was so flattered by the attention they, especially Daniel, were paying me. Seniors? Football stars? They were gods! Adored by the whole town. I should've...Ohhhh!" It struck me then. I was back, judging myself in retrospect, by what I know now, not by what I knew then. "Oh, John, how could I not have seen what I was doing to myself?"

"Because you were thinking like a traumatized victim, not like a therapist. Welcome to the club."

I was barely fifteen, raised in a strict Catholic family, the eldest of the only two children that survived gestation and childbirth. I'd been in an all-girl Catholic school till my sophomore year when the school closed down for lack of teachers, lack of nuns. Where did the idea of a vocation go? I think Oscar Wilde said something about celibacy being the foulest of the sexual perversions. No, Oscar, not true.

Now I remember all the months and months of therapy, starting with changing my thoughts about that horrible night—and the horrible events it led to. I should've—dammit, no, I shouldn't have, couldn't have! Daniel was so nice. And I was so lonely...at a new school...in a different world! And without a father. Essentially without a mother, I saw her so little. I was so flattered that the star quarterback, the guy all the girls swooned over, was showing interest in *me*. And I was flattered by those girls' jealousy. I enjoyed it too, that envy, and felt guilty about that.

Humph, guilt. It has a bad rap, but I wonder: if a man hits his wife, shouldn't he feel guilty? If you lie in court after taking an oath?

If you use insider trading, cheat old people out of their savings, cheat Medicaid, welfare? Ah well, perhaps that's the devout young Catholic girl in me talking—talking to myself.

"Where'd you go just now, Judith?" John broke me out of my reverie.

"Hmm, back to my time in therapy. Seems so long ago—and not."

"And…?"

I sighed long and hard. Maybe a good sign. "Yes. A little cognitive restructuring is in order. It just amazes me, after all these years."

"So? What thoughts do we need to restructure? Concerning the rape? What it led to? Both?"

"All of the above, I guess."

"Well, let's start with the emotions that occur with your patient— during a session. How many did you say you've had again?"

"Two."

"Hmm. How'd the second one go?"

"I didn't dissociate."

"Positive sign."

"Yeah." I had to think for a second—how was I identifying my trauma with his? "John, this happened to him in Mexico—at the hands of a powerful drug cartel. And then in a Mexican prison. It's so completely different, and yet…"

"…There's not much he can do."

"No. There's nothing he can do about it."

"So it's the helplessness? The inability to seek redress?"

"Yes. And what community can he share his experience with? Who of them would understand, would be able to share his sense of outrage, convince him that his feelings of guilt are unfounded? Where can he go for restitution of a belief in a meaningful world? There'll be no medals, monuments, parades or public ceremonies of recognition. Not for him."

John quietly added, "Nor for victims of rape."

I looked up. He met my eyes steadily. I could feel the tears welling. "At least I had my group, John."

"Should that be *had*...past tense?"

"...Maybe not."

We were both silent for a long time. I wondered where John was finding the time for these meetings with his crazy schedule. "Thank you, John."

He waited a moment. "Can you think of anything else?"

"Of course. Chacho."

"You're still identifying them."

"John...I'm afraid I *want* him to be Chacho."

At this, John sat back. I could now see the concern. "Just keep in mind that he's not."

8/19/02 (personal log):

Started back with a group of rape survivors. God, it is so hard to get into the role of patient! I keep thinking like a therapist, wanting to direct the discussion, encouraging others to talk, to recount their trauma, to express their feelings.

And I keep hearing all the usual self-recriminations: "I should've known better. I was so stupid to have put myself in that situation. Why didn't I fight harder?" All the arguments that rapists use to blame the victim, to justify the rape ("She even had an orgasm—probably her first").

It makes me want to scream—literally! And that's probably because I thought that way for so long. Maybe because, to some degree, I still do.

Although I've been able to describe the original incident (and I'd forgotten how hard that was), I haven't been able to go into my feelings about Chacho. Chacho, my poor, damaged baby brother. Why did he have to wake up? He was just a little boy! To have witnessed such a thing! To grow up with the guilt of having done nothing. But he was too young! There was nothing he could have done.

Did I understand that then? Was Chacho's response, his later desperation, his self-torture and drug abuse, in some way caused by me? Did I subconsciously blame him for not doing anything? Or was it simply that I completely shut down emotionally after that—took care of him by rote? I had no love to give anyone—only grief.

I basically floated through those years on sedatives and cigarettes. At least until I started therapy. I think my mother thought that it was a delayed reaction to my father's death. Perhaps that was just a story she could live with, having to take over the family single-handedly. She couldn't have lived with what actually happened. And then Chacho…

If only my father hadn't died the year before. If Mama hadn't had to go back to work—and work such long hours. If I hadn't felt so alone. We couldn't have afforded private school anymore, anyway. All the poor guy had was me. And then to witness such a thing! At such a tender age! If only...

Oh God, Coolidge thinking. I remember reading a biography of Calvin Coolidge. When his son died, he thought, "If I hadn't run for president, we wouldn't have come to Washington. If we hadn't come, Calvin Jr. would not have played tennis on the courts here. If he hadn't played, he wouldn't have gotten that infected blister; it wouldn't have caused sepsis; he'd still be alive." Ever since then, I've called it "Coolidge thinking."

I haven't been able to respond to Donald. Even kissing and hugging are difficult. The idea of sex is repulsive. The last time he tried to make love to me, I actually dissociated! Went into a fugue state. My God, I hadn't done that in...I don't know *how* long. He recognized it, too. Stopped immediately; didn't even ask for an explanation. Just touched my face, *so tenderly*, rolled over and went to sleep. I hope he was able to sleep. I wasn't.

Oh, Judith, what is this case doing to you? Chacho, my sweet, too-too sensitive baby brother! Please, God, give me another chance. Let me go back, knowing what I know now. Let me save my family, myself, from such horrific tragedy. Let me save my mother from an early grave. Let me shield her from finding her only son OD'd on the bathroom floor, all by herself, that horrible morning.

Oh, Judith, now you've devolved into magical thinking, wishing for miracles. *Think!* You've got a husband who loves you, who's faithful as a rock. Yes, not too much to look at, adding a few extra inches to his beltline every year and sparse up there on top. But then I'm not the svelte thing I was when we met. Too much late-night pizza: padding and oral gratification, I suppose. Sugar and grease are drugs like any other. But oh, that husband of mine: steady, patient and a wonderful father.

I'm afraid that patience has to have a limit, though. God knows someone has got to be a good parent. Oh, I can't believe I wrote that! I can't believe I thought it!

But Donald had to intercede between Jonathan and me. It was only once, and it showed me what damage handling this case could do. The last thing I want to do is alienate my son. I wonder if he's old enough for me to share what's going on. He's pretty mature—the same age as Chacho was when...that's it! That's why I was nagging him so much about the party he'd been to. That's why I was so opposed to him going in the first place. I was afraid he might...

*Oh, Judith, of course you have to explain it to him!* He's got to know. How else can he possibly...? He already knows about Chacho. Maybe he's already got an inkling of what's going on with me. I've been distant, irritable. I've tried so hard not to be overprotective. Have I gone too far in the opposite direction? Thank God for my darling boy. And thank God he's not so hypersensitive, so fragile as Chacho. Oh, just hang in there, guys, please!

But this case, this case. It could definitely merit a book. Could even be my "Anna O." Taking someone who before the trauma was the Rock of Gibraltar, trying to piece together the shards it was shattered into. No, trying to *help him* construct a personality from those exploded particles of ego—guide him back to a sense of community, to a place in it. Remember that word, Judith; it is the patient who does the lion's share of the work.

But I wonder if that's the attraction, if that's why I love this job so much. To take a ruptured, crushed spirit and piece by piece find—help the patient find—a way to put it back together. And not like it was—but into some new form. It's almost godlike, creating a whole person out of fragments. *Have to watch that tendency, Judith. Arturo must put himself back together. You're a guide no more.*

August 22, 2002 Meeting with Pt Arturo Cavazos (1179A):

I had already decided not to mention another missed session. Perhaps at the end of this one, I can just give a generic message about the importance of making all appointments. But it is absolutely essential that I not alienate him. As long as it's just a session here and there, I'll have to accept it. It does make it harder to pick up where we left off, though.

He again came in on crutches. I sensed some contradictory feelings coming from him. He seemed to be a little less wary but even more constricted, even more defensive (if that makes any sense). Perhaps it was that he was now familiar with the place and with me but also aware of what he needed to do—and not at all happy about it. His eyes danced from me to around the room this time. I hadn't noticed that before.

"Good afternoon, Arturo."

"Doc."

When he sat, I noticed that this time his foot was in a cast.

"Still on the crutches."

"Yeah."

I could hear the dismissiveness in his tone. The ankle was clearly something he didn't want to address. I had a suspicion as to why. I decided to poke around a little—see if it might be a way in to his trauma narrative. "Must've been a serious sprain. Your foot's in a cast. Is that why you missed your last appointment?"

"Yeah. It was a little worse than I thought. It's healing, though." I could tell from his manner that it was still too tender a subject. Maybe I could come back around to it. If it is tender, then it might be an issue that needs to be addressed. And it might be an in to more fundamental issues.

I was preempted by a sharp, roving-eyed "What're we gonna talk about today, Doc?" I figured the question was to keep me from exploring the ankle issue. But I thought the impatience might actually be a good sign. It might indicate that he knew we were eventually going to have to talk about substantive issues. It could be a recognition that he had problems that needed to be addressed.

But I decided that establishing a relationship and trust were still more important at this juncture. "Hmm, how about whatever you'd like to talk about?"

A shadow of irony passed over his face. "What if I wanna talk about football?"

"Fine. Who's your team?"

I felt a little disappointment or possibly even irritation from him that I took him up on his offer. Did he sense that I was trying to establish intimacy? And resent it?

"Oh, I…don't really pay much attention anymore. Out of season now, I guess, anyway."

"Oh, preseason's already over, actually." I thought of a different angle. "But when you still watched, who *was* your team?"

"Oh, uh…Cowboys, I guess."

"Uh-oh. I'm a Steelers fan. Grew up in a suburb of Pittsburgh." Got it! I felt just a little relaxation, another step toward establishing a rapport.

Some sort of acknowledgment registered in his eyes. "Well, I won't hold that against you."

Yes! Finally showing some humanity, kidding like that. Opportunity to establish prior life here. "Did you play yourself?"

He hesitated, but this didn't seem quite as painful as the memories with Jake and the other friend. "Yeah. In high school."

"What position?"

"Tight end. Linebacker on defense."

"You played offense and defense?"

"Yeah. It was a tiny Catholic school.

"Wow! I went to Catholic school, too, until my sophomore year." Oh, I have to be careful here. Arturo's perceptive—although I don't get the feeling he senses other people's emotions quite like a few of my patients. But I don't need him to get distracted by my own trauma.

Need to keep the focus on him. "Did you graduate from…what was your school's name?"

"Saint James. Yeah, I did."

"What is it you like about football?" The question seemed to cast a cloud. "Well, kind of a dumb question. Who knows why we like the things we do? We just do." Time to change the subject. "If you don't watch football anymore, what *do* you watch?"

"Now?"

"Now or before. Whenever."

There was an excruciating silence and then: "I don't know. Nothing, really. I hadn't seen a television in so long. There's so much violence…"

"How does it make you feel, seeing that violence?"

God, I could sense the horror, the fear, the barely repressed violence in him. It was too soon. "Arturo, how *are* you spending your time?"

Again, there was resentment at the question, just glancingly expressed in a look away. "Well, the surgeries and appointments—doctors' appointments—and physical therapy take up a lotta time."

I waited a moment. "And after?"

Another painful silence and a gentle shake of the head, shooing away an unwelcome thought. "I don't know. I sit on the balcony of my apartment and look out at the city a lot. It's actually kinda pretty from up there…safe, peaceful. Faces west. I watch the sunsets." There was such a sadness in the way he said it—a faraway ache at such a loss.

I wondered whether to pursue it at this stage. Go round about, Judith. "Did you know San Antonio at all before coming here?"

"I'd visited a few times. Came to a basketball game here when I was in school. Went to a concert."

"Yeah? Who'd you see?"

"Uh…the Eagles, I think it was."

"Oh, I love their music. Do you still listen to them?" Again the question caused discomfort: reminders. Of what, I wondered. Sadness at the loss of innocence, I'm sure. But I wonder if there's anything specific—a specific person, maybe. "Who'd you come to the concert with?" I could feel him shutting down at this question. "The basket-ball game you mentioned—was it a Spurs game?"

"No." There was a pause. Was this too touchy a subject as well? "No, it was a high-school game…against Saint Peter Claver." Another hesitation. *Give him time, Judith.* "Jake played."

I get the feeling that Jake might be my ticket to this patient's inner world. There is a bond here—a bond that might go beyond friendship. Interesting: the last time I spoke with him (Jake, Mr. Kazmarich), just recently, I got the sense of some change in him. It was almost like I was talking to a different person. No, not *different*, but more mature. And with a sadness, but a peaceful sadness (?)…a resignation? Like he had been through some life-changing experience himself. It seemed a good bit of time had elapsed between his initial calls and this last one. If I was right about that, about the increased maturity or perspective, it might prove very helpful with this patient. "Arturo, I get the feeling Jake means a lot to you. Have you been in contact with him?"

Again, there was discomfort, but I had an feeling it might lead to something useful. "He's started calling more often. Came to visit recently."

"He didn't for a while?"

"No, he did, he did. He was just busy with…family issues."

"Oh, I didn't realize he had a family."

"No, no, I mean the family he grew up with: a sister, Grace. And his girlfriend in high school."

"Uh-huh. What's her name?"

"Dolores. Dolores Martínez."

At this point the Pt started to breathe more rapidly. I noticed perspiration forming on his temples. "Arturo…it's hard talking about this, isn't it?"

I let the silence hang to give him the choice to pursue the subject or not. "It's stupid. It shouldn't be."

"Can we explore that? Examine why it might be, or might not be, stupid?"

The first outward sign of irritation. "I don't know! It doesn't make sense." He quickly shut down again. Or was trying to, at least.

"Arturo, feelings rarely do at first glance. First, can you think of reasons it doesn't make sense?"

I could feel his anxiety. And at his, I could feel my own. But I judged this to be a less threatening place to start.

"I don't know...because Jake was my..."

I was pretty certain he was going to say "friend." But I had to be careful not to take the initiative away from him—especially not to think for him. I was disappointed that he used the past tense but wasn't surprised by it. I decided to change it to the present, as though I'd misheard. "Is your what, Arturo?"

It seemed an eternity he didn't answer. My God, if this is so painful, what will it be like when we get into what happened to him in captivity?

His lips mumbled something inaudible. He began to sweat profusely. "Why can't I say it?" Again, he said it to himself; I barely heard. He stood and paced. I decided it was necessary for him at this point—although with the size of my office, it was basically two steps and turn. I can't imagine it was good for his ankle, but this took priority.

"Good question. Why do you think it might be difficult?"

"'Cause I don...I can't..."

I waited as long as I felt I could. "Is there something you feel you'd have to give up by admitting you have friends? Especially a friend who thinks so much of you?"

His answer came in a flood of anger and pain. "*He thinks that way about Artie! And Artie's dead! Dead! Dead!*" He started toward the door. I could see his heart beating through his shirt.

"Arturo, please don't leave. We don't have to talk about it anymore. I can see how painful this is for you. But please don't leave." One of his hands was on the doorknob, the other against the wall. He hesitated. I could see the battle raging inside him. Finally, he slammed his forehead into the door so hard I heard it crack. I quickly called our secretary outside the offices. "Carmen, everything's fine in here. Please don't disturb us—or let anyone else."

I gave him as much time as he needed to get back in control. This was the first time he'd allowed the demons eating away at him to really show. I waited, trying to show respect for the monstrous pain in the step he'd taken. And I waited. And waited.

His head remained on the door, and he made the same curious gesture with his hands: right hand rubbing the top of the left, fingers spread, with the fingers of the right hand rubbing down the webbing of the left. It was fierce and frantic. I had the greatest urge to ask him about it but decided it was still too soon. It might be his way of calming himself.

Sheepishly, but still with a raging volcano inside, he murmured, "I'll...I'll pay for a new door. I'll hang it myself." It was quiet...angry yet embarrassed.

As gently as I could, I answered, "The door isn't important, Arturo. You are."

After another few moments, he finally came back and sat. I knew he was going to shut down. But I wanted to finish as much of the restructuring as I could. "Arturo, could you possibly think of a reason it might—that your feelings might make sense?" I could tell that he'd already given all he had to give. "When we're reminded of something we've lost, or even just *think* we've lost, it can be horribly painful."

I could feel the barrier going up again. He was miles—universes—away. But it was an inroad. Momentary but something to build on. *Let it settle, Judith. Can't take him too far too soon.*

"Arturo, are you all right?"

He looked up. He was almost completely blank—just a trace of curiosity on his face. "Yeah. Bit of a headache." He noticed my bemused reaction. "Why?"

He was acting like he didn't even remember the violent episode. Could he dissociate that completely—that quickly? I wondered if it would be a good idea to remind him. Or make him aware, rather. No, we had too little time left to deal with the repercussions.

"I guess time's just about up, huh?" He said it almost nonchalantly.

It was only a little more than an hour, but I knew he'd given all he had. "Yeah. Pretty much."

He stood, grabbed his crutches and paused at the door. "What happened to your door?"

I just kind of shook my head, dismissing it. "Just got old, I guess." And he walked out.

September 5, 2002. Log entry:

Pt Arturo Cavazos has not kept any of his appointments since 8/20. Missing an occasional one is understandable. Now, I'm quite concerned. I'm aware that the last one was particularly unsettling. Steps in this process tend to be, but I wonder if I'd pressed too hard.

I've been in contact with Mr. Kismareck, Jake, and he is coming in for a meeting on the twelfth, the soonest he could make it. I explained that our telephone conversations were very helpful but that I felt that getting to know his close friends in person would be even more so. He readily agreed and will be spending an extended weekend here.

He persuaded Mr. Cavazos to let him stay with him—at least for the first night. It apparently took some convincing. I was hesitant to approve the plan, worried for Jake's safety as well as the effect on Pt. But some kind of extraordinary measures seem to be indicated. Pt has missed four appointments in a row.

Might the presence of his friend be so unsettling as to drive him deeper into constriction? Or could it have a beneficial effect—for example, make him see that there is life after trauma—that there are people who still care about him? It's a gamble. But Jake reports that the last time he spoke with Pt, he was clearly under the influence: efforts to numb feelings, suppress thoughts. This was almost a week ago. Pt has not answered phone since then, which is particularly worrisome.

I'm concerned for myself as well. I have to admit that the expression of violence and the evident rage behind it was terrifying. Perhaps we both needed a break. But the substance abuse is especially troubling. Yes, on balance I think the visit from Jake is necessary. I suggested staying the night be played by ear. In addition to getting Pt back in touch with his community, it might make him cut back on the substance abuse.

I had a bit of time before my next appointment. I took a chance and went to John's office. As I entered, he was on the phone.

"Oh yes, Elaine, I'll definitely be there—if the good Lord's willing and my caseload don't rise." A self-conscious laugh as he looked up at me and motioned me to sit. "Oh, well, thank *you* so much. You've been so generous with us—I can't thank you enough." Again he stopped to listen and made a "just a moment" gesture.

"Well, I'm glad to hear that. I'm sure as time goes on, he'll get better and better. And, of course, if there's any relapse, Dr. Neuwirth will be glad to have him back." He tossed a conspiratorial wink at me. "Oh, she is, she is—a miracle worker, yes." This time the raised eyebrows said, *The customer is always right.* Or maybe that should be *the contributor.* I completely understood: without Elaine Horowitz's money, we'd probably be closed by now.

Her son David had been my most challenging case before Mr. Cavazos: severe PTSD from combat. He was only one of two survivors when his unit was hit with an IED and a coordinated ambush in Afghanistan. He'd lost an arm and his left leg below the knee. One thing that stood out for me was his description of war. I have it recorded in my office.

(The following was added after my meeting with John.) Here is David's description: "It's like being in a spiritual fog. Nothing is certain. Morality is turned on its head. Killing is not only permitted, it's required. And whatever anyone tells you, however necessary it may be, it cheapens human life...life in general. It can't be otherwise. How else could you do the things you absolutely have to do? Even the rules of war itself have no meaning: if you can save your buddies and yourself by an act of savagery, you do it. And you become, of necessity, a savage.

"There are no everlasting truths. There is only expedience. The laws of civilization no longer apply. All the assumptions you had about life, about yourself, about God, come into question. There's no fighting for God and country. There's only fighting to stay alive and to keep your brothers alive. No one who's never been there can ever understand. There's no longer any order, vice becomes virtue, horridness becomes beauty."

The last thing he said I will never forget: "In war, you lose your sense of truth. In war, there *is* no absolute truth."

But I wonder if absolute truth exists anywhere. We believe violence is bad, but wasn't it violence and violence alone that stopped Hitler? Was it not our very humanitarian impulses that delayed our confrontation with Germany and made WWII as horrible as it was? Was it not those same impulses that allowed the slaughter of nearly three thousand people on 9/11? We thought we were building bridges, training pilots from the Middle East.

Would anything short of violence or the threat of violence have stopped that group of high-school scum? If they *had* been stopped, stopped with violence, would Chacho be alive? Would I now be able to respond to Donald? Would I have more patience with Jonathan?

I remember what Arturo said about this not being reality. Could he be right? Are we here living a dream, a dream of moral clarity? Is war, trauma, torture, sadism our natural state and this, this here and now, a pleasant fantasy?

Daniel was so nice. He seemed so kind—to this new girl, fresh out of Catholic school, with no knowledge that such beasts, such bestiality, existed. Is it all an illusion, this belief in a definite right and wrong, good and bad? Where we're all kind, thoughtful heroes? Where we have purpose? Where there is a point? Is it part of me?

I could see John's exasperation mounting as he spoke on the phone, although his voice didn't betray a trace of it. "Uh-huh...uh-huh. Well, how 'bout we talk that over when I see you at the fundraiser? Well, of course you will, of course you will. But perhaps I could come a little early, and we could...I mean, I know you'll be busy with preparations, but—"

He was obviously cut off. "Oh, well, that'd be great. Yes, I can be there, say...a half hour before we start?" He paused to listen. "All right, OK, forty-five minutes be enough?" He was silent now a good while, listening. He looked up at me with pleading eyes. It was a plea not directed at me but at the universe for deliverance. "Um-hmm. Um-hmm."

Finally he spoke, and not a trace of impatience could be heard in his tone. "Well, that sounds great, M—uh, Elaine. I'll see you then." There was an arrested motion to hang up. "Oh, again, thank *you*. See you then. Yes, oh yes. Bye-bye, now."

After a brief sigh of gratitude, he turned to me. I told him about my last session with Arturo Cavazos.

"It was after that you had the nightmare?"

"The second one. I've had two, John. And no, it was just two nights ago."

"That's interesting. Anything in particular you can tie it to?"

"No. Yes. Well…it's so stupid."

John smiled at that.

"I know, I know. It's probably not."

He smiled again. "You know the drill."

"I had a minifight with Donald. Well, it wasn't really a fight. It was me chewing his head off for such a trivial thing."

"What made it not so trivial? Well, what was it about, first?"

"Leaving the seat up. But it wasn't really that. I'd cooked dinner for the first time in weeks. When we were getting ready for bed, he said, 'Thanks for the great dinner.'"

"How dare he?"

"Yeah, I know, I know. I thought at first I reacted that way because I thought he was being ironic."

John waited a moment to see if I would continue on my own. Then he urged me on with, "But in reality, it was…?"

"The last thing Daniel, the leader of that pack of animals, said when they left was 'Thanks for the great time. It was oh-so sweet.' It's burned in my memory."

"Ah."

"I felt the enormity of Arturo's rage, John. And it's resurrecting my own. It's terrifying on two counts. In and of itself, it's barely contained. And it is *so* violent. Then, what it's doing to me."

John sat back in his chair. He was silent a long time, staring up at the ceiling. The slight turkey neck he'd developed lately disappeared as he did so. He sighed. "You're making progress, Judith. I won't lie to you, we need this case. That anonymous donor is keeping us afloat— he and Elaine Horowitz. And I don't have anyone, including myself, who could attend this case better.

"No doubt his scourges were male, and we want to keep feeling as safe as we can. Pardon my sexism, but women are generally more empathetic than men. But you'll be no good to me, or to him, if something happens to you during one of his intrusive episodes. You must protect yourself. Will you promise me that?"

"Promise."

"Have there been any other episodes, I mean, at home?" I just looked at him. "To be expected, I suppose. How's Donald handling the strain?"

"Pretty well, considering. But John, I can't..." I didn't have to say it.

"Ah. Well, you've started group therapy again, haven't you?"

"I have. But it's so hard to think like a patient, like just a member of the group."

"It'll come, Judith. It'll come."

"And then, how do I take off that hat and put on the therapist's?"

"By meeting with me in between. And I want a report, a verbal re- port in a face-to-face meeting, after every session you have with him. I'm going to reduce your caseload. The last thing I want is for you to burn yourself out with this one. You're too valuable." He made it very clear that this wasn't flattery. It helped nonetheless. "Keep at it—but be very careful. Again, you're making progress."

"But at what cost?"

"Yours or his?"

"Yes."

On the way back to my office, I thought about John's observa- tion that in general women are more empathetic than men. The odd thing is that I agree with him, except in my own case. Donald is much more empathetic, more nurturing than I am. I suppose that's why I was attracted to him. He's always been the nurturer for Jonathan.

He's always been better at reading his moods. And anytime Jonathan has a problem, some personal problem, it's always Donald he goes to, always Donald who helps him with it. I've felt quite jealous about that—although less so with time.

I suppose we each give what we have to give. But thank God for Donald. God knows what would have become of Jonathan without him. And of me...there's no way I could've finished college and gone to med school otherwise. Or kept my sanity—make that *regained* my sanity.

From the time he was born, my relationship with Jonathan has been...I guess *uneasy* is the best way to describe it. I love him with my heart and soul. Oh, what would my life be without those two guys in it?

Perhaps it's a blessing that Arturo has missed two weeks of sessions. God knows I needed a break. Especially after that last one. Did I handle it the way I should have? What if it happens again? It's bound to recur, we've barely scratched the surface.

09/11/02 (personal log):

On this, the anniversary of 9/11, there is a feeling of…how to describe it? Reverence? Sobriety? And I get a sense of comradeship, fraternity, a kind of solemn veneration for the dead…the murdered. It is present here in the office in the quietness of greetings, the extra effort to make contact, the slightly extended looks, the firmer handshakes, the more frequent cigarette breaks.

And always in groups. It's uncanny how everyone—everyone that smokes—seems to congregate at the same time. Although, and I find myself sad at this, the group had gotten smaller over the year (except today, interestingly enough). Now, I find myself tempted to join them. I wonder if a non-smoker would be welcome. I was one of them for many years. God, it's tempting!

In contrast, from what I can gather from news from other parts of the world, the outpouring of sympathy for this country has dried up. *Deutsche Welle*, the BBC, *Le Monde* etc. seem now to be intimating that the US had it coming, that it was the comeuppance for an international bully. Perhaps that is the word of the *intellectuals*, the media, and not of the person on the street. Then again, perhaps not.

This is fascinating from a psychological perspective. Taking the side of the perpetrator has a long and storied past. It is eminently tempting. All that is necessary for the crime to go unpunished (or even denounced) is for the bystander to do nothing. And that is so much easier to justify when the victim is to blame. This is all the perpetrator asks: to look the other way. The victim, meanwhile, asks society (and its individuals) to share her pain. I've known few in my life who are capable of that. (My dear Donny is one of those exceptions.)

And admitting that there has been evil committed requires those of conscience to take action, to empathize, to be outraged, to feel very unpleasant feelings—chief among them, vulnerability, even helplessness. It also forces us to recognize the capacity of humans, people just like us, to commit evil—horrendous, abhorrent evil. It goes against the natural human tendency to ignore uncomfortable topics, to "wash one's hands in innocence."

Even Freud himself came to repudiate his conclusion that female hysteria was the result of trauma experienced as children. To do so would have been to recognize such a sweeping existence of evil in polite society as to be unspeakable. Hah! *Unspeakable*—that's the word.

This was true in the early studies of hysteria (named as a pathology originating in the "uterus"—i.e., unique to women). It is still true today among many ("she was asking for it dressing that way," "she should've known what she was in for," etc., etc.).

It is evident even among those who have experienced the horror of war: on my way home from med school, after I'd decided to specialize in psychiatry, the veteran pilot sitting next to me vaguely suggested that combatants who claimed to suffer from PTSD were malingerers and those who treated them enablers.

People even question Holocaust survivors (not to their faces, of course—well, maybe even then) with "Why didn't the Jews defend themselves? Why did they go so willingly to their slaughter?" And for present-day ethnic atrocities: "What did the Bosnians do to the Serbians? What did the Tutsis do to the Hutus? That kind of hate can't come from nowhere, can it? Can it?" One notes the desperation in the way the questions are asked.

To admit that there is no justification, no genuine provocation, is to acknowledge that hate has no rational origin. It is to take a step toward that world of chaos that Arturo described.

And the perpetrators can always rely on that natural human tendency to refuse to believe anything that makes us uncomfortable: "It never happened." "They're lying." "She asked for it." "They've exaggerated it way out of proportion." "The victim brought it on herself." "The truth is, it's over and done with, and it's time to move on." "We, the accused, are the *real* victims."

In this case, however, the victim was not powerless in the face of atrocity. Traumatized, yes, but not powerless, not bound to silence by a society that might prefer to make a gesture of sympathy and then curl into ignorance and inaction. And so, in their eyes (and even in the eyes of many of this country's own) the victim became the perpetrator. My God, the protests started before we'd even done anything, before we'd even had time to formulate a response!

Like so many of my patients who find a way to blame themselves for the most hideous evils committed against them ("I must have done something to provoke him/them; I'm inherently dirty, so that's why someone I looked up to did this to me"). Even here, on a national level, so many find us responsible ("We don't support democracy. We nurture dictators. We're guilty of discrimination.").

I suppose it gives people a feeling of moral superiority as well: "I'm above the need for retaliation, this jingoistic appetite to exercise power." "I'm too objective to indulge in tawdry feelings like patriotism; I'm an internationalist, a humanist." Cynicism, especially about your own country, is so cool and detached (or cool *because* detached).

It now seems a lifetime ago I found myself in this crowd. As a college freshman, the Cold War still raging, antiwar sentiment continuing at fever pitch, I proudly proclaimed this country responsible for all evil in the world. It was and is mob behavior: if one finds oneself in a crowd espousing a certain belief, the need for inclusion is often too powerful to resist.

So you get to have your cake and eat it: inclusion in a family that stands above pedestrian impulses like love of country and righteous indignation (unless, of course, it is directed at oneself or one's own). And seeing so many engaging in a certain action seems to give it legitimacy. So, the tendency to ignore the victim, even blame her. Unless enough stand up and bear witness.

John has been true to his word. He's reduced my caseload considerably. The cases he does give me are softballs: a traffic-accident victim, although with the level of pathology I wonder if there's more to it. Is there guilt about his wife's injuries? The other driver ran a stop sign, blew a .20 on the Intoxilyzer. Then there's an assault case with no rape involved. Both involve exposure therapy primarily. And there's been good progress on both.

I worry about the burden this puts on the other therapists, however. And I worry about their resentments. I often get the sense that I'm seen as the favored child. This will undoubtedly add to that sentiment. We've had to cut back lately, like everyone in this profession. John was quite honest about it: the anonymous donor paying for Mr. Cavazos's treatment is paying cash.

Whoever this person is, he must have deep pockets. I'm certain it's not Mr. Kazamarek. He's barely eking out a living as a substitute teacher, living with his mother and sister in Aguagria. Although he told me he's considering practicing law again. I wonder what possessed him to give it up in the first place.

Funny that John asked about Donald but not Jonathan. Well, it was me who brought it up. And he's right: our relationship, Donald's and mine, is the foundation of Jonathan's well-being. But I wonder how much more of this Donny can take. Well, he's been there through the worst, the withdrawal, the crushing depression, the episodes of irritability, the lashing out over completely unrelated things. But I thought I'd put those things behind me. Oh, you know better than that, Judith. Dealing with severe trauma is never completed; it's a lifelong process.

Maybe we can get away for a while, just the three of us. The next real holiday is Thanksgiving. Maybe this year we can skip going to Donny's parents' house. Although you never know how many more we'll have—Aaron and Tessa are getting up in years. Maybe we can spend Christmas there instead. They don't really celebrate it, but what the heck? We all look forward to visiting. I think Donald will understand. And I hope by that time to be a little more on top of this. Is that the right expression: *on top, in control*? Maybe *taking this in stride* would be more appropriate. Oh, who cares?

9/23/02 (personal log):

On John's orders, I took a long weekend and managed to slip away with my family down to the coast. It was as though he'd read my thoughts.

And oh, how it rejuvenated me! Galveston is such a pretty town. And the old hotel we stayed in was so charming. The rooms were tiny but so quaint! Out on the beach, that gulf air was just delicious! The constant breeze off the ocean, the lull of the waves lapping at the shore...it just smoothed out all the kinks. I loved the graceful hovering of begging seagulls, the rolling sea stretching to infinity, the sun's patient warmth.

It turned out to be the perfect place to talk to Jonathan about what's going on with me. I was amazed at how nonchalant he was about it. He is astonishingly mature for his age. So understanding. Quite a surprise how easily he seemed to get it. It turns out he already knew more about Chacho than I realized. He seemed to understand my concerns before I even mentioned them. He assured me that he was fine and had no interest in drugs.

It was almost as if he were expecting "the talk." I imagine that hubby of mine had something to do with that. Jonathan even told me that if I needed to talk more about it as things developed, he would always be there to listen. My God, who's the parent here?

It was that night, Saturday night, that the most wonderful thing happened: Donald and I were finally able to make love. I even had an orgasm! Humph, Donny was so pleased with himself, the rascal. Well, fair enough—he did most of the work. But that I could *respond*...finally! What a relief! I spent most of Sunday walking on a cloud, holding on to his arm as we wandered through town—wonderful antiques, art galleries, museums. And the seafood! And some of the best Greek food I've ever had.

It was so perfect: Jonathan had met someone on the beach Saturday, and they had gone to a movie together. It was so wonderful to have that time alone with Donald. Oh, we've got to do this more often! Humph, famous last words. But I've got to make a commitment. My marriage—and my son—depend on it.

It is also clear to me that my own sanity depends on it. The day before we left, I met with my group of rape survivors and was finally able to share the whole story. At last, I was able to fully accept the support of my sisters as a plain victim. I cannot express how extraordinary a feeling it is to actually let go of the need for control. It is truly liberating.

I suppose it's that letting go that made me able to respond to Donald. There is a need to surrender control in order to enjoy sex— at least in its healthy manifestation. It is a union of self with another self, in which two become one. And I suspect that my need for control is the one trait that may somewhat debilitate my abilities as a therapist.

The effects of our minivacation remind me of the studies I've read on combat fatigue. They show that everyone has a breaking point. They also point out that the best remedy is R and R, a break from the insanity. That's something I don't imagine Arturo ever had. Maybe that applies to therapy as well. Perhaps missing all those appointments was good for both of us. Well, certainly for me. And the time away with my family was the clincher. Now I think I can deal with the horror of his story (and, perhaps, my own). The question is, can he?

September 24, 2002. Session with Pt Arturo Cavazos (1179A):

Pt finally came back to therapy—at least for today's session. This is most opportune, since after a postponement I finally meet Friday with friend Jake Kazmareck. Regarding my patient, I decided to tread very lightly. It took courage for him to return after so many missed sessions. I did ask him if his coming back had been at the urging of his friend. Although he answered only indirectly, I was pretty sure that was the case.

He was even more taciturn than usual, and I got the impression it was embarrassment. Possibly, he was ashamed as the "good soldier," for dereliction of duty. That being the case, I judged that those feelings would tend to ensure (or at least promote) future compliance. I also emphasized that his attendance was completely voluntary. I was concerned that any sign of impatience or disapproval on my part might alienate him further.

I asked him how he'd spent the time. From what was not said, I gathered that he'd pretty much passed it in an alcohol- and painkiller-induced stupor. That concerns me a great deal. He is starting to show the signs of addiction: occasional stumbling speech, mild tremors now and then, dilated pupils. But he assures me that he's started cutting back on the drugs, and withdrawal could account for some of the symptoms. This will need to be very carefully monitored. I'm hoping to get some information in that regard from Mr. Kasmareck.

For the most part, Pt was coherent. Affect is still completely flat. At times, when talking about himself, it is as though he's describing a different person—and one he has little connection with. Perhaps that distance (dissociation) will be necessary for him to begin to recreate the trauma narrative.

He actually made a tentative step in that direction. Sometimes it seems necessary to take a step (many steps?) backward in order to make a small leap forward. I believe the French have a phrase for that: *Recouler pour mieux sauter,* or something like that.

I noted the dark rings under his eyes. "Arturo, how much sleep are you getting?"

He shrugged. "I'm not sure, r-really. I sleep for a bit. Wake up. Then maybe after a few hours, a l-little more."

"Is it ever a sound sleep?" He shrugged. "Does the pain medication help at all?"

"It did some at f-first."

"There's medication called Ambien. It's supposed to help with that. I'll give you a prescription. The choice to fill it is, of course, yours. And if you do, I'd recommend you only take it occasionally. I'd like you to take it the first time—that's if you decide to take it—the night before our next meeting. We'll see how you react to it. I can't imagine that lack of sleep can do you much good. Are you having nightmares?"

"All the time."

I wondered if the moment was right. If not, this would be fairly easy to back away from. "Arturo...do you remember anything from your dreams?"

"Images. Smells. Sounds."

"Do you think you could share one?"

"Onions."

The answer came so quick. Like he was already thinking about them. Onions. The smell? The taste? The image?

"I w-went to the grocery s-store once. They had a person at a display. She was cutting them up. I could smell them. I had to l-leave." I was about to pursue this when he suddenly seemed to focus on some faraway object. Then a sudden frown told me that something had registered. "A song."

I waited a moment to see if he would elaborate. "A song?"

"A star. A little star."

Was he referring to one auditory and one visual memory? If so, were they connected? And if they were, in what way? Were they connected to the smell of onions in some way? Or was it "A song *about* a star?"

He seemed to go into a fugue state, almost like self-hypnosis. I could see him drift away. Then, I heard a barely audible, "I hear…I…hear." His eyes widened, body stiffened, hands tightened around the chair arms. His breathing essentially stopped.

I prepared myself for something explosive. Then, of all the things, my cell phone rang. I'd forgotten to turn it off. "Arturo, I'm so sorry!" I quickly muted it. The sound had shot him to a standing position. He stared down at the phone, breathing rapidly, heartbeat skyrocketed. I waited, trying to avoid a repeat of our last session.

Ever so gradually, something seemed to finally click. Was it the phone ringing? What were the implications of that? I was astounded at how quickly he seemed to calm. I watched him go through several distinctive affective phases that seemed to lead to a state of constriction. Then he sat and looked around as though he were trying to figure out where he was. Breathing slowed. He looked at me, just recognizing who I was.

Arturo…? Are you all right?"

He took a moment to think, seemingly surprised at the question. "Yeah. Why?"

"You went somewhere else for just a moment. I mean, in your mind. Do you remember? You mentioned a song, and then a star. When I asked you if it was a song about a star, you said, 'I hear. I hear.' Do you remember that?"

He just looked at me with curiosity. "A song about a star?

"Yes. You said, 'A star. A little star.'"

His gaze seemed to follow his mind over hills and down mountainsides. "Jake sang it."

"Jake?"

"When we were on the river, in the Big Bend. He has a *good* voice."

Why the qualification, I wondered. Suddenly a wave of horror contorted his face. He stood. "What is it, Arturo?"

"I smell…"

"What do you smell?"

"Hair…burning hair. Horrible." Then in a slightly different voice, gruff, commanding, "Cover your nakedness."

Nakedness...? Whose? Is someone's hair on fire? "Who's naked, Arturo?"

He went through another altered state. He calmed and then looked at me as though he'd just come in and sat down. "Do you need to answer that?"

I realized he was talking about my phone. "No. It was nothing important." He was now miles away from whatever he'd remembered. He was here again, looking at me like he had no memory of what had just transpired.

"Arturo, you mentioned a song when I asked you about your nightmares. Do you remember?"

"Nightmares? No. What nightmares? We were talking about nightmares?"

"Yes, when I asked you about your nightmares, you mentioned a song about a little star. Then you mentioned the smell of burning hair."

It seemed to spark some vague, faraway image, like a story someone else had once told him. "There's a Mexican song about a little star. But I don't remember it." He thought for a moment, then vaguely shook his head. "No, I can't remember the words...not even the tune."

It was gone. But I noticed that when he mentioned the nakedness and burning hair, he covered his genital area. So perhaps he wasn't talking about the hair on top of the head. But it was clear that, to be able to even momentarily remember, he'd had to either totally absent himself from the experience or be transported and living it once again—in scattered shards of memory, bits of trauma, like subliminal knifing images on a screen. There was no territory in between. Yet.

He was able to recount how Jake had sung the song on the river. That was very positive. But it was as though he were describing an account he'd read. And he couldn't remember a single line from the song. There was the slightest hesitation when he tried. I got a vague sense that he might know them, but something was blocking his memory. Or maybe he could only remember in that other reality, the one fragmented by trauma. The one he was momentarily absorbed by…then had to escape.

As I review the recording of the session, there appeared to be two moments of reliving the trauma: the initial memory of the song and then the olfactory memory it triggered. How could the song be related to burning hair? And how is Jake related to all this?

Whose voice was that saying, "Cover your nakedness"? It didn't sound like Arturo's normal voice. Although it could have been his in the immediate stress of the trauma. Was it *his* hair that was burning or someone else's? It must have been pubic hair, perhaps combined with what we called *pelusa* in my family: the soft fuzz on the arms and legs. Maybe it was both.

The images the idea conjures up for me are so horrific that I'm grateful he was able to share it at all. I kept waiting for that curious gesture with his hands to surface, but apparently he was too dissociated from the story—or it was a different episode of the narrative. I expect it will take many months of therapy to get to a point of consciously recreating it. I'm beginning to wonder if we'll get there at all.

My hypothesis is that the threatening aspect of trauma recall is exacerbated by Pt's once prodigious self-control. That sense of self-control is—or was—a potent source of pride for him. Consequently, to recall a period of utter helplessness is too shameful to reexperience—at least for now.

I also believe there is a powerful element of guilt. There is some conduct beyond mere submission (which would in itself be horribly shameful for this particular Pt). He must have been complicit—undoubtedly under horrific duress.

My conclusion is that Pt needs someone or, preferably, a group who will share their own trauma narratives, their own shame at helplessness, their own guilt at participation, however coerced. I am concerned that without hearing others share their stories and the feelings they produced, he will never be able to share his own. But with what group? With whom?

September 27, 2002. Meeting with Jake Kazmarick (friend of Pt Arturo Cavazos):

When he walked into my office, I had the feeling of a solid if vulnerable human essence (and that's not contradictory). It struck me that the solidity was recently acquired and gained through some life-changing experience—or experiences. As we shook hands, I felt a sobriety purchased from some self-revelation. It is also possible that I acquired that feeling in part from our phone conversations—and the change in them—over the last year.

What I was totally unprepared for was the information he would share at the end of our meeting.

We sat. "Well, it's good to finally meet you in person."

"Likewise, Doctor."

"Judith."

"Judith. Uh...Artie knows about our meeting?"

"Oh yes."

"I guess it would have been pretty hard to keep it from him."

"And unethical, not to mention probably counterproductive."

"Yeah, yeah. So what do you think, Doc—uh, Judith? How is he? How is therapy going?"

"Well, of course there's only so much I can tell you—actually very little, confidentiality laws and my oath being what they are."

"Of course. Of course."

"We talked briefly about that, about what I could share with you. I found it interesting that he wanted me to paint a rather rosy picture."

"Yeah, that's Artie."

"By the way, do you still call him by that name?"

"Well, I did at first. But I got a pretty chilling response. So I started not calling him by name at all."

"He insists I call him Arturo. I can't go into why."

"I...understand."

I hesitated to pry into Jake's private life, but I got the curious feeling that he might welcome it. And I had a sense—perhaps it was more of a hope—that it would help me with Arturo. "Jake...would you mind if I asked you something personal? I mean, about you, specifically."

There was a lack of surprise in his reaction. "No, not at all. Especially if it'll help Artie."

"I think it might. Any insight into his friends, those who love him, will help me get to know him better." He waited for the question almost as though he were aching to answer it. "I've felt a change in you. There was a hiatus between your first calls—a little over a year ago, I think it was—and the more recent ones. When you did start calling again, I mean regularly, you sounded more certain, more...centered. As the saying goes, 'sadder but wiser.'"

His slightly pained toothless smile told quite a story. "Yeah, Judith. I have gone through some changes, some pretty painful self-revelations. Then, strangely enough, there was a period of euphoria—a euphoria I rather egocentrically projected onto the world at large. I guess I still had some growing up to do." Another smile at pain—or at pain overcome. "Sadder but wiser pretty much sums it up. At least, I hope so. I feel like I'm ready to live in the real world. Or I'm learning to."

From the way he expressed himself, I could tell that he would be a good influence for Arturo. "That's good as far as Arturo is concerned. There won't be any miracle cures. It'll be a long, hard-fought battle—probably for the rest of his life. And I don't need you to go into any details about your own experiences. But your sharing the results helps. Have you talked about this with Arturo at all?"

"Yes, I did. Last night, as a matter of fact. I hope that's all right."

"How did he react? Well, first of all, tell me what you said."

He looked down. A frown radiated from his forehead through his entire body. I thought it was more one of concentration than reticence, but I needed to be sure. "Jake, if this is too tender a subject..."

"No, no. It isn't that. I'm just trying to understand myself why I told him. I did a little research on PTSD, Doc—Judith. And I'm not trying to be his therapist. I just wanted to try to understand his...what? His distance? The one-eighty-degree change in his outlook? His despair? His...just...*absence*. Anyway, I had a vague feeling—maybe it was just a hope—that sharing my own…crisis, journey…whatever you'd call it, might help in some way. I still can't say exactly why."

There was a sigh of considerable pain here. I have to admit that I was so intrigued that even if it weren't helpful for my patient, I wanted to know his story.

"I'm very close to my little sister, Dr. Neuwirth. She's always been one of these hypersensitive, tortured souls. She experienced a horrific trauma as a child. If you listen to classical music, you might have heard her name: Grace Kazmareck. Although she hasn't recorded in years. She's at least playing again."

"She stopped for some reason?"

"Yes." There was another hesitation and what seemed like a side stitch of distress. "She stopped recently after our father died. Well, he was really her stepfather, although I think their relationship was as tight as any father-daughter relationship could be. But I always thought the trouble got started by something someone said about her in school. As I said, hypersensitive. That was when she stopped playing for the public…stopped recording. She wouldn't go to school, hardly ever left the house at all."

He paused for an agonized second. "I finally found out why it was so devastating for her: it was I who'd said it. I'd just repressed it all those years."

This was quite a revelation. I was itching to know the details but knew my first responsibility was to my patient. "I'm curious, Jake. Why *do* you think you told Arturo?"

"I'm not sure *what* I was thinking. I mean, I know Artie's got a strong sense of care for others. Or had. I mean, it's not something he was ever obvious about. You just kind of felt it. Or I did, anyway. He was taken—I thought he was killed—trying to save his uncle and family from the cartel, the Zetas. Like I told you, it was he who kept Con—uh, me and the other guy alive during that canoe trip in the Big Bend."

*Ah, the one with the deep pockets must have been the third person on their adventure.* "Jake, I want you to know that even though you're not my patient, whatever you tell me will never leave this room."

"I appreciate that, Doctor—uh, Judith." Some new conceit seemed to strike him. "It's funny. I wonder now whether I told Artie for his sake or mine. I mean, did I just need to confess to him? To someone? To someone I've always looked up to?"

This time he looked straight into my eyes. "We nearly died on that trip in the Big Bend. If it hadn't been for Artie..." He had the aspect of someone trying to gear up to share some truly frightening conceit.

"There was a point where the other guy and I had a fight that Artie had to break up. That was the only time in my life I felt the urge to kill—the only moment that I felt myself capable. I think it was the desperation, the fear, exacerbated by slow starvation." He paused, and I could tell he was in direct touch with that horrible feeling. "I'm afraid it was the perception of other as competitor...competitor for life. I still shudder at the impulse."

He gazed out the window, looking like he was trying to solve the most puzzling enigma. "Why did I tell Artie these things—that I could have so wounded my baby sister—that I came to a point of...of being willing to kill? I don't *know*. But I remember saying to Artie that we're all capable of horrendous evil—every one of us. I guess maybe I had some sense that part of his...*whatever* was guilt. I was seeking expiation for my sins and at the same time trying to allay his guilt... that I wasn't even sure he had. I don't know. It's inexplicable."

*Wow*, I thought, *here is a complex and dynamic psyche.* "Well, your instincts were good. You..." I started to delineate the origins of guilt and shame after trauma. But I realized this might be revealing too much about my patient. I took a different tack: "Tell me, Jake: how did Arturo react? Not just what he said but his demeanor, his affect."

Again, his sigh and hesitation struck me as an effort to find the right words rather than reluctance to answer—although I could tell it wasn't a pleasant memory. "It's hard to describe. I'd never seen anything like it—from him, from anyone, really. It was cold, cold as ice, flat and empty. It sent a chill like death through me. He said, 'You have no idea what we're capable of, Jake.'"

He winced at the memory. Then his whole body shivered. "You asked about his affect. It was the affect of a cold-blooded murderer—how I'd imagine a contract killer would say it. It shook me so much I couldn't answer."

I sat back. It was abundantly clear how much Arturo Cavazos meant to Jake. It made me want so much to reassure him, to tell him that this is to be expected.

I could give him a general idea of complex PTSD. I just had to avoid mentioning anything specific about Mr. Cavazos. Jake isn't even family, after all. Luckily, I'd considered the possibility and had an outline of the general features at the ready. I judged that Jake would be able to follow the concepts involved.

"Jake, besides organic changes in brain functioning, there are two experiences that victims of intense, sustained trauma tend to go through. I'd like to try to at least give you a feel for them. I think it'll be helpful. My mentor and colleague John calls them the *inversion* experience and the *abyss* experience. The latter has been explored by philosophers and psychologists throughout history. They're both features of severe complex PTSD.

"The inversion experience is just what it sounds like. If you think of the 'self' as the earth and the trauma as an asteroid hitting the earth, there are some superficial injuries and some that penetrate to the very core, utterly destroying its integrity, its structural coherence. The inversion experience turns our understanding of reality on its head. In the case of abuse, it's interpersonal inversion: abuse as an expression of love. In politically motivated torture, it's moral inversion—that is, 'suffering equals justice'; you come to believe that if there's any justice, then you must deserve to be abused.

"It's totally outside of our normal understanding or 'schema' of reality. Consequently, it's remembered, or 'encoded' if you will, not as a coherent whole but as random stimuli: sights, sounds, smells, textures. Trying to integrate those experiences into a connected narrative is in general the goal of therapy.

"But that's *my* job, Jake. Yours is to be his friend. Please note that I didn't say *just*. Having friends that will stick by him through this is crucial. And that doesn't mean putting up with any kind of behavior. In fact, it's been demonstrated in combat veterans that lashing out can increase alienation. The traumatized person feels worse, more estranged from the community, when he pushes people away with bad behavior. He feels more alone, more worthless, the more he strikes out."

"So how do I respond, Doctor? I mean..." I could tell some kind of uncomfortable confession was coming. "Well, one of my greatest failings is my short fuse."

"Umm. That could be a problem. Can you control it when you're around Arturo? It'd be a good idea to control it period, but especially—"

"I'll control it. I do around people anyway. I need to learn to even when I'm alone."

"Well, that would be the healthy thing to do. But it's good that you can control it around people. And it's good you know yourself that way."

There was an uncomfortable pause here. I had to applaud Jake's honesty. To be willing to reveal so much of himself to a complete stranger, even if I am a therapist, takes courage. It takes many of my patients way past our first meeting to share so much; some never do. On balance, there's no question he'll be good for Arturo.

I was about to break the lull in our conversation when he did it for me. "Doctor, you mentioned another something common to PTSD patients."

"Yes, those truly severe cases. It's called the *abyss* experience. Some call it the 'black hole' experience."

"That...doesn't sound pleasant."

"No. No, it's truly horrific. But I think it'll help you to understand. It'll give you a feel for what any victim of extreme trauma is going through. It's central to understanding and therefore healing the disintegrated psyche.

"OK."

"The theory is that the basic, primal self is one of pure feeling. It is separate from the rational, relatively coherent life narrative that we all 'normally' have. It's described in philosophical and psychological texts and alluded to in mythology and archetypal literature: the *Odyssey*, the *Iliad*, King Arthur and so on. It's presented as the demonic or shadowy side of life.

"John Stuart Mill describes insanity as the withdrawal into the abyss. Carl Jung's collective unconscious, at least as I understand it, is that state of being in which we're not separate individuals but rather one organic whole—sensing, experiencing everything as unconnected stimuli, like an infant. And what happens in situations of extreme torture and abuse is experienced as the abyss: rational consciousness reverted to the primitive state of feeling and survival.

"Severe trauma experienced over a long period of time destroys—or you could say is incompatible with—our rational, coherent, sequential story of our lives. It sends us back into the abyss, where there's no rationality, no sense of sequence, where morality and reason cease to exist. All senses become one; all sensory input is experienced as one. There's a feeling of not belonging to the living. We revert, as in insanity, to our most primitive selves. Or, I should say, *self*."

He sat back, eyes slightly glazed, mouth cracked open. "And you can recover from that?"

Here, I hesitated. I didn't want to destroy his hope for his friend. I especially didn't want him to give up on him. "Unfortunately, not always. There are stories of combat veterans from when PTSD was little understood whose spirits remained broken. That's why the incidence of suicide is so high. Or that's one reason." I could see him deflate. "But that's *not* going to be the case here—not if I can help it."

I could tell I'd overwhelmed him. "I know it's a lot of information to absorb—and not very pleasant information at that. Just know that you don't need to—in fact you should *never*—act on it. You leave that to me."

He let out a puff of air. "Don't worry, I will. I wouldn't know where to begin, anyway." He paused a second in thought. It struck me as important, so I waited.

"Doctor, I haven't experienced anything like that, but I did go through an identity crisis of sorts. Having realized it was I who'd said that horrible thing about my sister…it was so contrary to how I saw myself."

"Like you said, we're all capable."

"Yeah." There was a finality in the way he said it. Then, I saw him reorient himself to the task at hand. "In the meantime, what *can* I do for Artie?"

"Be his friend. Outside of therapy, he needs to find his way back into the community, to rejoin the living—doing whatever normal activities you can get him involved in. What is he good at?"

"Huh. Just about everything—short of academics, that is."

"I guess that was due to the late start."

"That and probably lack of interest. I mean, he wasn't at the bottom of the class. He graduated. I guess he just did enough to get by."

"Tell me some of the things he was—is—good at."

"Oh, auto mechanics, home repair, hunting, fishing…survival in general."

"I guess that came in handy on your trip in the Big Bend."

"Humph, without it I'm pretty sure I wouldn't be here, Doctor."

Funny that he can't seem to get used to calling me by my name. It indicates a rather strong sense of authority—of hierarchy, even. Well, he just met me. If he feels more comfortable addressing me by my title, what the heck.

I wondered which of the activities Jake mentioned would be best to try to get Arturo involved in. "Jake, I'm a bit concerned about the hunting. If there was a lot of shooting and gunplay during his captivity, it might be unsettling—might cause intrusive episodes. On the other hand, it might give him a sense of power, of control. But let's not pursue that for now. Fishing might be all right, auto mechanics certainly. Can you think of anything else?"

"Well, he used to make money playing pool. Funny, he'd never play me for money. Humph, good thing. I wasn't even in his league.

You know, I tried mentioning that place we'd go back in Aguagria, things we'd do. It just seemed to make him sadder."

"It's like remembering something about someone you loved who died. The memory hurts because that person is gone."

"Should I not talk about the past?"

"Oh, yes you should. Definitely. Not *only* about the past—we want to give him hope for a future as well. But definitely about the past you shared with him. I mean, don't ever shy away from it. It'll help to spark a sense of connection—show him that he had and, because you continue trying to connect, *has* a community. And by the way, I can't think of anyone better for Arturo."

This seemed to remind him of something. "Actually, Doctor, I think I can. I wanted to ask you about that."

Interesting. Who is he referring to? "Are we talking about the other friend, the anonymous one? Does he engage at all?"

"Yeah, some. But he has to be very discreet. If it got out that he was involved in Artie's rescue, because it was very extrajudicial…well, it wouldn't be good. But no, I'm not talking about him."

He hesitated, and it made me concerned that this other person might be some kind of bombshell. "OK, who *are* we talking about?"

"Uh…before Artie disappeared, he was engaged. I'd lost touch with her. Everyone had. But she—her name is Annabelle—she's resurfaced."

I took a moment to absorb this. It could lead to a breakthrough. On the other hand, it could be such a shock as to send Arturo reeling. "Has she contacted him?" If she has and he didn't mention it on Thursday, he might be taking it in stride. On the other hand, it might simply be a matter of his characteristic reticence.

"No, she hasn't. Not yet. As a matter of fact, she came to me first."

There was something ominous in the way Jake was relating this information. "Well, does she intend to?"

"I think she'd like to, but…Annabelle's quite a lady, Doc—Judith. Very independent. I always thought she and Artie were a perfect match. After Artie disappeared, we thought he was dead. She must've thought so too because she was just…gone."

I could sense that there was a greater complication. I waited to see if he would volunteer it. The longer he held off, the greater the bombshell it seemed. And what could be greater than this girlfriend/fiancée appearing out of nowhere? "Did she tell you where she'd been?"

"Married. She has a daughter."

I just waited. I knew there was more. She wouldn't just show up if she were *happily* married. "Uh-huh, and…?"

"The daughter is apparently Artie's."

I sat back. "Oh my."

"Yeah." He paused to let me absorb the information and its implications. "Doctor, I think I know Annabelle pretty well. If you tell her not to contact Artie, I'm fairly sure she'll stay away. I mean, what kind of effect could it have on him, just to see her again? And then to find out she's the mother of his child and married to someone else?"

This time it was me who sighed—or blew out a breath of wonderment. "Well, I don't think at this point her presence or the news are indicated. That kind of information, all at once, could overload him. And I don't think there's a realistic way of delivering the information a bit at a time. At some point it might nudge him in the right direction—toward a sense of belonging, of community. But that's a long way off." I tried to digest the possible consequences. "How about the husband? How does he figure in all this?"

"That I don't know. Apparently the daughter—I think her name is Leticia; they call her Letty—apparently she only knows him as her father."

"Again, oh my."

"Yeah, it's pretty complicated."

I couldn't help letting out a laugh of astonishment. "I'd call that an understatement." He gave me a moment to mull the situation over. "Jake, I'll need to think about this and run it by my supervisor. Meantime, not a word to Arturo. Can you keep that to yourself—I mean, not even let anything slip?"

"Yes. I've been a lawyer, remember. I know how to dissemble."

"Hah! Thanks, I needed a laugh." His glance at his watch reminded me. "Oh, I've got another patient. Uh, can you still come in Monday?"

"With bells on."

"Good. See you then."

He got up to go. "Thank you, Doc—Judith."

"Oh no. Thank *you*."

September 27, 2002. Impressions on meeting with Jake Kazmerick:

The married ex-fiancée is quite a complication. But the fact of the daughter is potentially explosive. I hope Jake is right about her...what was her name...Annabelle? I hope he was right about her discretion, her willingness to hold off.

On the other hand, the knowledge of having a child—at least at some point in the future (certainly not now!)—might gain him a sense of connection, of belonging to the living. But to get him to the point where he could accept the idea—that's the challenge. He still thinks of himself as tainted, as poison for any creature unsullied by the abyss. As things stand now, he can't even fully accept Jake's friendship.

Could that be part of my problem...my problem in treating him? Could the dissociation on my part whenever he gets in touch with his shame, his guilt...could it be because I still blame myself for inviting those animals over to my house? Blame myself for bringing on my own rape? Do I still consider it a dishonor to my family...to the memory of my father? And especially, do I blame myself for the destruction of Chacho? Do I still feel tainted myself...that it happened because I was dirty to begin with? That I somehow subconsciously willed it happen? The fact that I'm thinking along those lines makes me wonder.

Jake reminds me of Chacho; there is a vulnerability about him. But there's not the same fragility. There's a strength purchased through self-revelation. I wonder what the difference was. He said his sister went through a traumatic experience. But I get the feeling that he had some childhood trauma of his own. I get a sense that whatever it was, it's linked to his relationship with Arturo. There's a big-brother/little-brother feeling about it. I wonder if it was the same for Arturo. If so, is there something in Arturo's past that made him "adopt" Jake as his brother? Who was Jesús? Did that relationship share a similar sentiment? Must ask Jake about that on Monday.

Jake reminds me of myself as well: I can feel the strength of his love for his little sister. Thank God he still has her.

Oh, the shooting pain when I think of Chacho! My baby brother. Oh God, I still feel the guilt of what that episode did to him. And even more, what my withdrawal from him did. I was in my own abyss, certain that I was too tainted to have any relationship with anyone. And I was so full of hate—for myself, at first. It was only after I was able to restructure my thoughts during months of therapy that I was able to redirect it. And then, the regret for having done nothing about it...

Talking in my group—as a patient, a victim—was so uncomfortable: giving up that sense of control as "Doctor"—getting back in touch with those feelings of helplessness, powerlessness...letting myself be supported by my sisters. God, I hadn't cried like that in so many years!

It was a terrifying step to take. But so necessary...and so cathartic. And it's almost equally hard to step back into the role of doctor. But I know that I will be able to do a better job as a result. Yes, I need to continue with it...and meeting with John. Speaking of which, I need to do that now.

September 27, 2002. Meeting with John:

John was busy yesterday afternoon, the twenty-sixth, so I hadn't had the opportunity to meet with him after my session with Pt Arturo Cavazos. This would be our first meeting since my weekend getaway. He looked somewhat refreshed himself. "John, you don't mind my recording our meetings, do you?"

"As long as you don't mind my recording them for myself." He waited a moment, giving me the reins for how our meeting would go.

"Oh, there are so many subjects to cover, John. Mr. Cavazos has come back to therapy finally. I just met face-to-face with Mr. Kazmareck today for the first time. He is one interesting and dynamic personality. I have so much to cover with you."

He shrugged. "It's Friday. All I'm planning on doing is getting home to Melinda and watching a movie—maybe a Marx Brothers: some good wholesome irreverence and inanity."

"Hmm, you'll probably need that after today's meeting." I tried to think of some logical place to start. It seemed all a jumble. "I'm not sure where to begin, John. There are so many issues I need to address."

"OK. Let me suggest a place. How did last weekend go?"

"Oh, John, it was wonderful, just what I needed. Just what the doctor ordered, to coin a phrase. It was good for Donald and Jonathan, too—for us as a family. A lot of the stress just melted away. We stayed at the most charming old hotel, the Galvez—a hundred 'n'eight years old. Apparently Gálvez was the explorer who discovered Galveston Island.

"It was just so relaxing out on the beach, that constant breeze off the gulf. Then we walked the Moody Gardens and went out in the Gulf on paddle boats. Had the most wonderful seafood at a place called Cato's and then, surprisingly enough, some of the best Greek food I've ever tasted at another restaurant. I can't remember the name now.

"When we were back on the beach, I was able to talk to Jonathan— explain what was going on. Of course without specifics. He was so understanding, John! How did I manage to raise such a mature, thoughtful teenager?"

John let a little grin spread across his face. "Must be some good parenting involved."

"I still worry he's too hard on himself sometimes."

His eyebrows rose. "Umm. Could that be a dominant gene in the family?"

I just let that pass. "Then, Donny and I had the most wonderful time. I could finally relax and just be at ease with him...with both of them."

"And...?"

"Yes, I was able to respond to Donald…finally. I think it was opening up in my group that helped me…let him in so to speak."

John tactfully ignored the double entendre. "Funny how that works."

"It was a surprise that I still had feelings of guilt. The ones concerning Chacho are especially strong." He looked up and raised one eyebrow this time. "I know, I know, it's a lifelong process. I guess what really surprised me was the depth of those feelings. I still miss him so. I did feel a great lightening of the burden once I'd shared it."

John picked up a book open on his desk and flipped a page. "You know, that reminds me of something a colleague of mine once wrote. Here it is: 'The ultimate struggle of the victim of trauma is to arrive at a reasonable assessment of her conduct. She must find a balance between unrealistic guilt and the denial of all responsibility. The beginning of that journey is the sharing of the story of her trauma with others. When others listen without ascribing blame, the survivor can learn to accept her failure to live up to unreasonable standards of conduct. Then she can come to a realistic judgment concerning her behavior and a fair attribution of responsibility.'" He flipped to the cover. "Huh. Dr. Judith Lozano Neuwirth."

Oh, that smug little half grin as he put the book down. "John, how in hell did you happen to have that handy at this precise moment? Have you taken up divination?"

He gave another tiny shrug. "I just like to keep up with colleagues whose work I admire."

I let out a big sigh. John's reading of the passage from my book gave me license to tell him what I was planning for Arturo Cavazos.

Again, he seemed to read my mind. "You mentioned being surprised at the depth of your feelings of guilt. Any idea why those feelings, or perhaps I should say the degree of those feelings, have resurfaced?"

"The Cavazos case of course." John just rested his chin on interlaced fingers, his expression unchanging. It was blank, poker-faced, not wanting to give any indication of approval or disapproval. He was obviously trying to avoid urging me in any direction so that I'd come to my own conclusions, take the discussion where I wanted it to go. "I'm thinking of sharing my story with him, John."

He sat back. I tried to read his reaction. Was it surprise? Curiosity? Disapproval? Hard to tell with John. "Purpose?" he simply asked.

"John, it's been almost two months, and I'm still barely scratching the surface. It's his spirit that's broken. No amount of exposure therapy...well, I can't even start restructuring his thinking until I know what horror caused that...*annihilation*. I think he needs to know that he's not alone.

"Combat veterans have groups who've been through the same madness. There are support groups for rape survivors, incest survivors, victims of domestic battery, even natural disasters. Who does Arturo have? What group could possibly understand what he went through? I don't know of any cartel-survivor groups. Maybe there are in Mexico, but he could never go back there."

John took a breath. His look was still enigmatic. "No, obviously not." There was a caesura here, an extended period for both of us to try to assimilate the implications of what I was suggesting. Finally, he continued. "Judith, go with your instincts. If you're pretty sure there's no other way to reach Mr. Cavazos, then I trust your judgment."

He then sat forward, and his look sank into me like spear. "Just be careful. I'm listening to the way you talk about your patient. Notice I said 'your *patient*.' Your affect is straddling the edge of mothering. You've got to keep reminding yourself that he's not Chacho.

"The deeper you get into this case, the more you've got to work at maintaining your objectivity—avoiding countertransference. I can help with that. Again, as time and work allows, I want a report after every session you have with him. And you must continue with your survivor group. Now, do you believe you can maintain that objectivity if you share your own story?"

My instinct was to answer right away. But I knew I had to go through a process of self-examination. John was right: Arturo's pathology brought out the big sister / mother in me. I had to consider the possibility that I was having savior fantasies. And how much of that was due to projecting my feelings—my maternal feelings—for Chacho onto Arturo? I was aware that I saw Chacho in Arturo's utter aloneness in his posttraumatic state. When I withdrew from life, Chacho was left alone. Was I hoping for absolution for Chacho by "saving" Arturo? Oh, my head is splitting.

I took a deep breath. "John, I'll have to continue asking myself those questions the whole time I treat this patient." (I said *this patient* purposely.) "But at least right now, I'm pretty sure I can do it—not by myself, of course. But with your guidance and the relief of meeting with my group, at least at this point, I believe I can."

"Then, as they say, 'go for it.'"

September 30, 2002. Second meeting with Jake Kazmareck:

He walked in rather sheepishly. I assumed it was the result of his rather prominent black eye. "Good morning, Jake. That's quite a shiner you've got there."

"Yeah, well...I've had worse."

Funny, Jake doesn't strike me as much of a fighter. He told me about the fight on the river, but that was when they were kids, and kids in extreme circumstances. If Arturo is getting this out of hand, I'm going to have to take some measures—possibly ones I'd really rather avoid. "Jake, is Arturo responsible for that?"

"Well...yeah, but only accidentally."

I was skeptical. "Accidentally? How's that?"

"It's...a bit of a story."

"I'm all about listening to stories. And I don't have another appointment till eleven."

"Well...last night I talked Artie—Arturo—it is so hard to call him that."

"I can imagine. But I think it's important, Jake, for two reasons. When he was in captivity, he had his sense of autonomy, his independence, stripped from him. Having control over what others call him is a step toward reestablishing that sense of control.

"Also, he needs to establish a new identity, a new self. It will include who he was and what he experienced before, but it'll be added to by his experiences in the present and even the recent past, as horrible as they were. I think insisting on 'Arturo' might be his subconscious way of doing that—of at least starting the process of creating or integrating a new self. And our respect for that will help the process."

"Oh, OK...OK."

I could tell that Jake was able to grasp what I was describing. I'm lucky to have someone who understands the concepts so readily. "So, go on with your story."

"Uh, I talked him into letting me come over."

"You hadn't seen him since Friday?"

"N-no. Actually, not since Thursday night."

"Thursday? Jake, what happened?"

"Well, Thursday when I got here, I invited Artie out for dinner. But he didn't want to go out. And I couldn't convince him. I didn't think it'd be a good idea to pressure him, so I talked him into letting me cook dinner at his place. It wasn't easy. I think he only acceded because he'd turned me down for going out. Anyway, I was sautéing some onions—or I was about to put them in the skillet, and I'd misjudged how hot the pan—the oil—was. When I put them in, they really sizzled. It was like a miniexplosion."

I could tell he was hesitant. To urge him on, I just said, "OK..." with an *and* implied.

"He...went berserk. He knocked me out of the way and grabbed the pan—it had to have burned the heck out of his hand—and started banging it against the stove. Sloshed hot grease all over himself. When I saw him last night, he had blisters on his hands and arms and even on the side of his neck and face. He banged the pan so hard he actually broke it off the handle."

"Why the hell didn't you tell me about this Friday!"

"Artie asked me not to. He was really insistent. I mean, once he got command of himself, he was really embarrassed. I'd never seen anything like that from him. I guess I promised him I wouldn't tell just because he was so out of control. I mean it scared the sh—hell out of me. I don't know...maybe I wanted to forget it, too."

I tried to take this all in. Arturo had mentioned the smell of onions as one of the sensations from his dreams. I was honestly rather irritated at Jake. The incident might have prompted me to call for an extra session with Arturo on Friday afternoon—I had an opening. "Is that when you got the black eye? I didn't notice it on Friday."

"No. That was actually last night. It's just turning now."

"Oh, brother. What happened last night?"

"Well...I'd lobbied all weekend to let me go and see him again. But I think he even scared himself—scared that he might, you know, do something to me. I know what he di—what happened on the bridge is still in his mind. Anyway, yesterday morning I pointed out that I was going back to Aguagria the next day, today, and I really wanted to see him.

"At first he refused. I told him this time we could meet at a restaurant. I noticed there was a little café attached to a pool hall I passed by on my way from his place. It was more of a diner—you know, really relaxed? That's how I described it to convince him. Long story short, I finally got him to agree. I told him I'd go by his apartment to pick him up.

"Well, we actually had a pretty pleasant meal. It took a while, but I tried to think of neutral things to talk about, funny things that happened in school—a time our classmate Willie let out his characteristic yell in the hallway when he hurt his hand, came back with his pants undone 'cause he couldn't zip them up himself. Somebody in the class had to do it for him—all of us were in stitches.

"Then, the time I, without thinking, imitated one of the brothers who always said 'wheres' instead of 'where' and 'commer' instead of 'comma.' He was from New York—most of the brothers were. We used to make fun of him all the time. But never where he could hear—he had a terrible temper. He'd get in these moods. Anyway, I got away with it. He just happened not to notice.

"I talked about—I did most of the talking, which I'm really not used to...except around Artie for some reason. Well, when it was the three of us, our other friend did almost all of the talking. I talked about my sister, Grace...there always seemed to be a thing between the two of them. I mean, not anything romantic. I can't imagine Gracie in any kind of romantic relationship."

He hesitated here, at first seemingly sad at the thought of his sister never having any kind of love interest. Then, as though he were trying to puzzle something out, he said, "It's hard to describe. It was like Gracie was a little uncomfortable with his...what? I don't know... his hardness...his solidness? But at the same time, she found a kind of comfort in it...a sense of safety. Or maybe I'm just projecting. I don't know.

"He asked about Dolores—my girlfriend. I told him we were engaged. He almost smiled at that. But, you know, if he had, I think it would have been a pained smile. It made me want to mention Annabelle, but I remembered you'd warned against that. And, believe me, I understand. He can barely tolerate being around me."

"Jake, this is exactly what Arturo needs. I'm so glad, grateful that you were able to do this. He needs that sense of connection to friends, to the community. But the black eye...?"

"Yeah." He started and then hesitated just a bit. "Well, I really thought that Artie'd relaxed just a bit. I think he had. We finished up and went outside. It was still pretty light. Sun was just setting. There were a couple of guys standing outside the pool hall. They were arguing. Well, one was basically reaming out the other one. I could feel Artie all of a sudden tense up. We had to go by them to get to the car. All of a sudden, the bigger one slapped the smaller one on the back of the head. I mean hard."

I could tell from the way Jake's eyes turned into saucers that it was pretty bad. "Artie just lost it. He knocked the guy down and then got on top of him and started *beating* him. Doctor, if I hadn't been there... Anyway, just as I tried to grab hold of him, his elbow came back and hit my eye."

"Oh my God. And you were able to calm him down?"

"Eventually."

"Were the police called?"

"I have no idea. I got Artie into the car and home as fast as I could."

I sat back trying to assess the implications. Now I had to worry about assault charges, fleeing the scene and God knows what else. "Did Arturo say anything?"

"Not a word. He was like a statue—frozen solid, just slightly rocking. He did do something odd with his hands, rubbing one down the back of the other."

"Like this?" I demonstrated.

"Yeah, exactly. And, you know, when I was there Thursday night, I noticed that he washed his hands over and over—like every fifteen to twenty minutes, it seemed. Even at the restaurant...although he tried to hold off there."

"Yes, leave it to me to figure out what that's about."

"Oh yeah. I will." He took a breath. "Anyway, neither of us said anything in the car. It was all I could do to calm myself down. When we got to his apartment, I got out of the car. He didn't move. I went around and tried to open his door, but he slammed it shut. I figured it was best to just leave him alone.

"That was smart."

"Finally, without a word, he got out of the car and went straight through the lobby to the elevator. I just followed him. As soon as we got inside his apartment, he took a bunch of pills and drank about a half a bottle of whiskey. He fell asleep—sort of—on the sofa. Never said a word. Wouldn't even look at me."

All I could do was let out a giant sigh at all the complications this could cause: police involvement, assault charges, maybe eluding arrest. And that last one would include Jake—abetting? Aiding flight? I suppose he could claim he was just trying to defuse the situation.

But thank God he was there. If the charge turned into murder, I would certainly lose my patient. For him to be imprisoned again...! Dammit! Oh, dammit! That dinner could have been a major breakthrough. Why the hell did it have to end that way?

"Jake, if there's any report of the incident, you know you're going to have to turn yourself and Artie in."

"I know."

"Were there any other witnesses?"

"No. Just the kid. I caught a glance of him as I hauled Artie away. He actually looked grateful. I don't think he'll report it. The other guy was down and out. I know he didn't see us take off."

"Did you talk to Arturo at all this morning?"

"Yeah. I stayed. Made him coffee when he finally came around."

"He slept?"

"Fitfully."

"Jake, have you had any sleep?"

"Oh, I dozed here and there."

"And now you're driving back to Aguagria."

"Yeah. Don't worry, D—uh, Judith. It's just two and a half hours. It won't be a problem."

I was still concerned. But he was young—probably used to going without sleep. "So, how was Arturo this morning?"

There was a hesitation from surprise. "You know, aside from being seriously hung over from the pills and booze...Well, it was like he had no memory of it. He was just groggy as hell."

My immediate reaction was relief. If he didn't remember the incident, it would go toward mitigating the flight. "Officially, Jake, I have to tell you to make a report to the police. Now, you're an adult and can do what you want, but that's what I have to advise."

"I understand." He stood. "Uh...I think I should take off."

"Yes. That's probably a good idea."

He left without a sound. And I sat. Oh Lord, how is this going to affect Arturo? I'd have to consult with John on this. Would Arturo come for his appointment tomorrow? Would he come back at all?

This is making me revisit my conclusions about his treatment. Maybe he wasn't—*isn't*—fit for life in the community yet. Maybe the monsters his trauma unleashed in him are still too close to the surface. Should I suggest...*what?* Incarceration or confinement in an institution would be a death sentence. Any sort of halfway house would expose him to too much stimulation—the possibility of some trigger or triggers that might have tragic consequences. Maybe his self-imposed house arrest is best. Sometimes it seems my patients know what's best for them.

I went straight to John's office. He was with another patient. He wasn't going to be finished until about ten-forty-five, so I tried to use the remaining time to reorient myself. I went outside and walked around the complex. Thankfully, the heat of summer had abated somewhat, and it was still early enough that I could enjoy a stroll. There's a small creek with good shade running through the grounds, and I took full advantage. There was one bird who was singing so pretty I said a little thank-you to it. I let my mind wander to last weekend, the botanical gardens, exhibits, museums, walking arm in arm with Donny, talking on the beach with Jonathan.

Fortunately, I was able to get my brain situated for my eleven o'clock. It went well: patient reported that he'd done some successful in vivo exposure and was now able to drive to and from work without panic. Then we managed to do some imaginal exposure with minimal discomfort. We'll go together next session with him driving to other places he used to frequent. Eventually, we'll go to the scene of the accident.

Back to John's office for the few minutes before lunch—which John usually never takes. He seemed a bit preoccupied this time but still welcomed me. I started to tell him about the incident—or incidents, actually—with Arturo and Jake. But I realized that I'd been really hogging his time and expertise. So I asked him how he was. I pointed out that he seemed a tad distracted.

"Oh...creditors," he answered dismissively.

"You know, John, you're carrying a hell of a burden. Today might be *your* turn to vent."

His first instinct was to just slough it off, but he stopped himself short. With a sizable sigh and a bare nodding of the head, he acknowledged the stress he was under. "All of these fund-raisers and sucking up to donors takes its toll. I've got to acknowledge that. But if we can get the grant from HHS, we'll be all right. I gotta tell you, though, I do miss just working with patients and doing research.

"Might be time for a sabbatical. How's the new book coming?"

"Well, the book's on hold. We're waiting for study results anyway. And as far as taking time off...Not just now. Let's get that grant; then I'll think about it."

"You look tired, John."

"Well, my last patient is…a handful. But talking to you helps. Believe me. How're things going with Mr. Cavazos?"

I hesitated to bring up the recent developments. But John can tell when there's an urgent problem. Plus, he needed to know. Anytime there's a question of dangerous behavior and possible police involvement, he's on the hook as director. I described the incidents. His eyes spoke volumes. He leaned back in his chair, focused on the ceiling and let out a short but potent sigh. He didn't speak for quite a while. "Have you heard from him?"

"No. I plan on calling him this afternoon. I can use the excuse of reminding him about his appointment tomorrow."

"He definitely needs to make that. Any news about the assault?"

"Not a word…so far."

"Well, I know that part of town. It's just a few square blocks that haven't gentrified yet. Fights are not uncommon there. We may just dodge a bullet. That kind of rage is very concerning, though. How're you planning on handling it?"

"For now, just wait and see. As far as the assault is concerned, I don't know what else to do. I mean, I know what I *should* do, from a legal perspective, but…"

"Right."

"But, John, looking at treatment going forward…I think Arturo might just know what's best for himself."

"How's that?"

"I mean, isolating himself—for the time being. He's got a hair trigger. And like you said, prodigious rage. Maybe he's just not ready for being out in the world."

"Agreed. Let's, uh…play this by ear. Let me know how the phone call goes and what state you find him in. For the rest…like you said, wait and see."

I stopped at the door. "Take care of yourself, John. I'm prescribing for you what you prescribed for me."

"Right."

October 24, 2002. Patient Arturo Cavazos 1179A (Summary of last few weeks):

Complications, complications. Pt has spent the last few weeks first in detox and then in recovery in inpatient program due to overdose of prescription pain medication. Something tells me that this was not a suicide attempt. Pt's personality is that of one who would not merely "attempt." It is likely that if suicide were the intention, the action would have been stepping in front of a truck or a bullet to the head. It is more probable that this was a self-medication error—an almost lethal combination of prescription narcotics and alcohol—probably an attempt to "erase" memories of the violent episode.

Efforts to reach Pt by telephone during the weeks of 09/23–10/3 were unsuccessful. Finally, Pt's friend Jake Kasmirich was called. Without any hesitation, he came to SA and found Pt in his apartment in a semiconscious state. He immediately called for an ambulance. Pt was admitted to SA regional, stabilized and then sent to a clinic specializing in detoxification and cases of drug overdose. Mr. Kazmireck has stayed in SA with a cousin and has visited with Pt and been active in his recovery.

Also participating is Jake's fiancée, Dolores Martínez. I believe Ms. Martínez to be a very positive influence. She strikes me as extraordinarily empathetic, yet with a quiet strength that allows her to take Pt's mood swings, aloofness, etc. in stride. She seems very conversant with psychological trauma and has a quite soothing aura. She knew Pt when they were growing up in Aguagria through Jake. How extensively she will be able to participate is unknown, but she is a welcome addition to the "team."

She did report one brief conversation she had with Pt. He had mentioned something to the effect that he wasn't worth the trouble she and friend Jake were taking. She answered that to them he obviously was, that lots of people cared about him. Pt responded, "People don't know me." She answered, "Maybe you don't know yourself, Arturo." She has apparently already adjusted to calling him by that name.

Clinic staff report that Pt has refused medication to ease withdrawal symptoms. Although in obvious discomfort plus nervous distress from withdrawal, he is again manifesting the strength of character noted by friends. I'm somewhat concerned that that kind of "stiff upper lip" self-reliance might bleed into a loathness to accept other forms of support. However, as noted above, Pt's community seems to be widening, and he has not rejected it out of hand.

There have been no legal repercussions as a result of the violent episode. No police report has been forthcoming. Another positive development is that Pt's brush with death has alerted him to the need for active participation in therapy. He is working with another therapist in the inpatient program, and I have visited him twice. It is also my opinion that Pt's realization of the devotion of friends Jake and Ms. Martínez has caused something to click.

So far as I can tell, Pt is still unaware of reappearance of former girlfriend/fiancée. I spoke with her briefly, and while eager to renew acquaintance with Pt, she understands the necessity of delaying that event. She strikes me much as Jake described her: a strong character, independent, practical and no-nonsense. If circumstances were different, she would also make a welcome addition to the team. I find it interesting that not once has she mentioned her husband.

During my visit with Pt, he was able to touch ever-so-glancingly on some aspects of his trauma or at least his feelings about them. He also has a vague memory of the incident outside the diner. This I consider very positive, as the dissociation was not so complete that the attack was totally erased from memory. It is, however, only recalled in fragmented images.

When I mentioned it, he went so intensely still that I was at first alarmed. For a moment, I regretted having reminded him of it. Then he replied, not as affectlessly as previously, "Yeah, Doc, I might've killed him. If Jake hadn't stopped me, I probably would have. I have no business being around people. I'm too dangerous." (I spied a measure of hope in the words *might* and *probably*.)

For some reason, this sparked a memory of his time in captivity. "I remember when they took me and Jes...me and..." I thought he was going to mention his friend Jesús, but for some reason, he stopped himself. He started to make that same hand gesture, then suddenly stopped. A look of confusion came over him, the memory apparently splintered.

He went into a kind of hypnotic trance. Then he continued, almost robotically. "I remember when they took us...me...us to that deserted place to get rid of...us. I remember the gun to my head. I had no feelings about being shot. None at all. It wasn't that I welcomed being dead. It's that I had no feelings about it one way or the other."

He seemed to regress to who he was at that moment; his eyes went dead. "I had no feelings, period. I had no existence. I was less than a vegetable. I was a piece of dirt or a rock. A clod of dirt doesn't care about life—it has no life. I was beyond wanting to die because I wasn't alive. I woke up in a shallow grave, the side of my head caked with bloody dirt. I guess the bullet just glanced across my skull."

So, he'd reached the final stage of complete submission—the loss of the will to live. For a man like Arturo Cavazos to have arrived at that kind of absolute passivity argues that his treatment was unimaginably brutal. In Nazi extermination camps, a prisoner who had reached this point of degradation was called a *Mussulman*. Basically they were the walking dead, no longer attempting to find food or warm themselves, not even making an effort to avoid being beaten.

I was surprised that the first memory he was able to share was one of such extremity. Perhaps that was because it was so passive. Could it be that his fear of the potential violence in himself makes him only able (at least at this point) to remember a moment of utter passivity? Such decimation of will indicates complicity. They must have forced him to participate in the barbarity. We're a long way from being able to address that issue.

But we'd started. So it was with a feeling of relief that I said, "Thank you, Arturo."

He looked at me, surprised. "For what?"

"For starting the process."

10/25/02 (personal log):

After listening to the recording of our meeting, I hoped it actually *was* the start of the process. The robotic manner in which Arturo recalled the scene made me wonder if it would in fact lead to more sharing. I had to expect periods of stagnation, even regression.

It was certainly true for me in my journey. I had never reached the stage Arturo had, but I remember a complete loss of faith, a total rejection of God.

I basically withdrew from the world at large. I got permission to set my own course of study—fortunately my grades were good enough. I had no social life. I wanted none. Having to take a few classes with other students was excruciating. I suppose I remember some people trying to befriend me, but they soon gave up. It was a relief when they did.

Seeing those guys was the most horrific part. They acted as though it was just one of their many adventures, a passing lark. The only way I could make it through was to just shut down completely. Finally, I just refused to go to school at all. Because I was such a good student, I was allowed to study on my own, graduate a year ahead. I guess academics was all I had.

I went through the motions of caring for Chacho—his physical needs. I think my emotional deadness caused him to despair. He must have taken my withdrawal for hatred of him for having done nothing. I imagine he internalized the shame as well. From there, it turned into self-hatred. The most horrible thing I have to remember is that when I became aware that he was taking drugs, I don't think I even cared. I didn't care about anything.

It wasn't until that horrible morning: I was in college. I took every math and science course I could. I wanted nothing to do with the humanities. I didn't believe there was such a thing as humanity. So, by the time I filed for a degree plan, I was told that I had all the credits necessary for premed. It was almost my last year.

I remember it was a Thursday. I didn't have a class until eleven. I woke up to hear my mother screaming. Chacho lay on the floor of the bathroom, needle in his arm. Oh God!

I suppose it was Chacho's death and my mother's pain that woke me up—that spurred me to get help. It started with individual therapy. I remember now how much I blamed myself for the rape, how I'd dishonored my father, how worthless I felt. I was so fortunate that I had a good therapist.

I remember so clearly the moment, the day the cognitive restructuring finally took hold. All my depression, sadness, worthlessness changed to anger—hate! I guess I'll always have that anger. I just learned not to let it rule my life. It still intruded from time to time. Then it gradually receded...became almost an awful memory...like a recurring nightmare from when you were a child.

And then this case happened. And now I have that anger—that hatred—toward the people who did this to Arturo. I could feel it so strongly during his intrusive episodes, when he broke my office door. I could feel maternal instincts almost overwhelm my judgment. The impulse was so strong to stop him, to wrap my arms around him and protect him—rock him like a baby in my arms. So strange to imagine treating such an imposing human essence that way. It's so seductive, that image. But I have to, *have to*, maintain my objectivity. You're his doctor, Judith, an objective, empathetic witness, not his big sister, not his mother. Remember that.

What was it that took Arturo Cavazos over the edge of that abyss? Whatever it was had to be something so horrific that dealing with it will be explosive beyond imagining. Perhaps lethal. I can feel my own fear of subjecting him to the memory. But I think a character, maybe in some Shakespeare play, says, "I have to be cruel only to be kind." I suppose that pretty much sums up my job. The question is, will he be able to withstand it? And also, do I have the courage to guide him there...and pick up the pieces afterward? Scratch that: help *him* pick up the pieces.

November 5, 2002. Meeting with Pt Arturo Cavazos (1179A):

Halting progress has been made. Pt has at least been able to occasionally have visitors to his apartment—but only one or two at a time. The only ones I'm aware of are Jake and fiancée, Dolores. They have also been able to coax him out to dinner—twice. They assured me they would be very careful in doing so.

Jake reports that on one occasion they walked past a blind man with a walking stick. Pt froze in his tracks. Jake could see panic overtaking him. Then, according to Jake, Dolores took his arm and held him, and after a moment they were able to continue without incident. Thank God for her. Perhaps pointed objects might be a way into Pt's trauma.

Pt has also been able to talk about his time in prison following escape from initial drug cartel. (So far, he has not been able to discuss his time while still in their hands.) Conditions in the prison were beyond deplorable: prison was criminally overcrowded, any space fought for tooth and nail—often with tragic results—and often encouraged by the prison guards. Plumbing was frequently stopped up, and human and animal waste would cover the floor. I asked Arturo about the smell.

"After a while, you couldn't smell anything. Food had no taste. You just ate to keep from starving. I often wondered why."

Repairs took days to even commence, although inmates, following Arturo's example, eventually began to make repairs themselves. I wonder if this element of self-care, this small sense of control over his environment, kept him from his earlier absolute submission. Fights, occasionally to the death, were a daily occurrence, and the raping of the more vulnerable was also fairly routine.

I asked him about personal hygiene. Access to showers was spotty, and soap was often unavailable, as was toilet paper. Newspaper was the usual substitute (when *it* was available). Pt had to relearn how to use a toothbrush after his rescue. Continuing dental appointments (crowns, implants) are necessary (and sometimes conflict with therapy).

Pt recounted the following story: "I remember you asked me the first time we met if I believed in God. I always had. I figured that He knew what he was doing and had a purpose for things being the way they were. That it was up to us to learn from our mistakes—that He let us make our own beds. But...I'll tell you, Doc, there were times, especially before, when I was still...I mean before I got away from the cartel...There were times I called on Him, begged Him for deliverance, for some kind of miracle."

I could feel his shame for this appeal to God. His sense of personal responsibility must be immense. Then, the full force of his despair came crashing down like a tidal wave. I again had to grip and push strenuously to keep from dissociating myself.

"But how could God, an all-powerful being, allow such evil in the world?" he continued. "I don't think any priest or preacher has an answer for that."

I let the silence hang to show appropriate respect for his loss of faith. "I have to confess, Arturo, I often wonder myself."

There was just a glance in my direction before he continued. "Anyway, I got into some kind of routine in the prison. But I had to do some things there, and before..." The hesitation was excruciating. "I don't think I'll ever get over those things, Doc. I don't see how it's possible.

"I remember there was one inmate who sometimes disappeared—at night or in the evening. Then he'd be back the next morning. Well, there were a number who did that, actually. I thought at first that they were singled out for some kind of reward...or punishment.

"I finally found out where they went: they were *sicarios*, let out of prison at night to go on hits, mob hits. Then they'd come right back in the early-morning hours. They were the big dogs. They had conjugal visits. But they also had a harem within the prison, of younger, frailer inmates. Sometimes it was voluntary. Lots of times, it wasn't—it was a matter of survival.

"But there was one guy in particular. Every time before he'd disappear, he'd go off by himself and just sit with his head bowed. I thought, maybe he's just preparing himself. It can't be easy, murder for hire. So one time I asked him what he was doing when he went off by himself like that.

"'Oh, I pray,' he said. 'I pray to Jesus.'

"I figured he was praying for forgiveness. But something in the way he said it made me think it was something else. So, I asked him, 'What do you pray for?'

"He said, 'Well, for success.'"

He paused for just a moment. It was either to allow me to try to digest the information or to try to assess the implications of it himself. "He was praying to Jesus for a successful hit. He was asking God's help—asking the Prince of Peace for help in committing murder." He paused to think a moment and then looked up at me. "I think when I heard that, I lost hope all over again. I thought, if this is what we've come to—I mean as a people—then we're doomed."

I knew to let his expression of despair stand. Of course he felt that way. How could he not? It was of absolute necessity to validate those feelings. I knew them myself. "Arturo, I want you to know that I understand those feelings. I understand them all too well. I didn't go through anything like the hell you went through…but I understand."

He looked so *deep* into me—with a questioning frown. It seemed he had a sense of what I was intimating. I met his gaze with rock-hard steadiness. Was it time to carry out my strategy—to share my own trauma? Something told me it was still too soon.

I decided to try a different tack to help him reorient himself. "Jake tells me that you've gotten together with him and Dolores. How's that been going?"

"Yeah, they've come over to visit. They're two of a kind, those two."

There was almost a smile in the way he said it, though his tone was flat. So, I supplied the smile myself. "Yeah, how's that?"

"Ah, they—they both have a sense of what's going on with me. Not just with me. They seem to know what other people are feeling. Sometimes before *they* even do."

"Yes, I get that. They're both very sensitive people in that way. Empathetic."

"Exactly."

I waited a moment, hoping that he'd put it together himself. I finally went ahead and drew the inference: "And they still want to be around you...still value your company." He just looked up at me, knowing the point I was making.

"Arturo, I remember your saying that this isn't reality, this life. I'm just wondering, is this here...now...your friendship with Jake and Dolores, with your sister...Is it—has it taken on any more reality for you?"

He took a long time to answer, pondering. I could see the gears grinding as he looked at me. When he looked down and away, lines of concentration cut across his brow. It was as though he were trying to puzzle out the deepest mystery. "Yeah...I suppose it has." He paused. Then, "I suppose that's progress."

"Sounds like it to me."

But I could tell from his reaction that he still wasn't able to accept it—to accept it as dependable, lasting, genuine. There was still at this point (and of course there would be) an inability to trust it. He was still expecting the bootheel of evil to come crashing down. He'll always have that doubt, that knowledge of evil in this world— the knowledge, the sense, that all happiness can be snatched away in a heartbeat.

"I don't know about hoping, Doc. It's dangerous."

I wonder if it *is* only a myth, that sense of a just world. Horrendous evil does happen to good people, after all. All too often, it seems. Can we only maintain our sanity based on a fantasy? And *is* that sanity?

And what of the coarsening of society? Would my assault have taken place in the 1940s, the '50s? Would the perpetrators have been so blithe about it afterward? And, speaking of evil, was it my innocence that attracted them? Did they thrill at the prospect of destroying that innocence? I can feel my hatred swelling in me at the thought. I must go see John.

It was time to finish up. "Arturo, I think hope is all we have."

November 8, 2002. Meeting with John:

"So...?" John just waited. I knew what for.

"Not yet. But I came close."

"What stopped you?"

John allowed me a moment to think. "I'm not sure. Because I think he's still too fragile? Maybe because I still think all the attention needs to stay on him, if that makes any sense. It's like I don't feel he's ready to share anyone else's pain...their trauma." I was having a really hard time articulating what I was thinking. "It just didn't feel right, John."

John faintly nodded with that bare, quizzical poker face of his. "Well, I'm glad you followed your instincts."

I suddenly felt very anxious and had to stand. I walked over to the window overlooking the creek. I popped another stick of gum in my mouth and then realized how aggressively I was chewing. John just waited. "I'm sorry, John. I know how busy you are."

"Actually, Judith, I'm intrigued. This is a very special case. Not to mention that it's actually paid off some of our debts. The anonymous donor pays regardless of Mr. Cavazos's attendance. To tell you the truth, I'm actually a little jealous. I haven't treated a patient with this degree of trauma in quite a while—if ever. I'd like to include the case in the book I'm writing. Actually, and I've thought about this, I'd like to say '*we're* writing.'"

It took me a moment to realize this was an invitation. "Oh, John... of course I'd love to collaborate! You've taught me most of what I know about this job. And you've had as much to do with Arturo's treatment as I have."

"Well, I wouldn't go that far."

"Yes! I mean with all you taught me. All my technique is—the core of it—is from you. Plus strategizing all these months with me on this case. You've kept me focused...not to mention sane."

There was just a hint of ambivalence beneath his satisfied smile. "Good then, that's settled. You get first billing." I started to protest. "Yes. This is your case, Judith. I'm just the coach. I doubt I even have the energy to get out on that particular field of play."

"Oh, John, you—"

"I've been concentrating on administrative work for too many years now. And I'm past retirement age to boot. We both know I wouldn't have the stamina."

"John, I..." A great feeling of sadness washed over me as I suddenly saw John with new eyes—eyes that now shed that dashing gray-templed image of thirteen years ago. He was a giant then, a fiery ball of energy with a mind that cut through pretense and supposition to the very core of pathology. Now before me was a salt-and-pepper halo surrounding a shiny bald pate. Tired, fleshy eyelids hung over black lashes sinking under the pull of gravity. Where on earth was I while this was taking place?

I could see John wordlessly acknowledging my reaction. With his typical discretion, he refocused us both on the case. "Now, back to our...*your* patient. I get the sense that there's something else that made you hesitate—I mean to share your own trauma with Mr. Cavazos. Am I wrong?"

Why was I so irritated? Was it just at John's question or something else? Anger...that's it. "I think there's a specific countertransference going on. I came close to dissociating again today."

"What do you think you might be transferring?"

"Well...it's more that I think there's the possibility of a countertransference—one that could be counterproductive, even damaging."

"OK. What would that be?"

Despite how well John knows me, despite how absolutely I trust him, this was uncomfortable to air. "My own anger, John. I think there's the possibility that I could project my anger, possibly encourage his as an outlet for my own—as a kind of...commiseration.

"I've done that to Jonathan. I've only lately come to realize it—well, in the last few years. He—I mean Jonathan—has a lot of anger beneath his empathy and understanding. He's taken to smoking cigarettes. And I know it's because the nicotine tends to calm you. I know that from experience. I still miss it."

He just humphed. "Is that nicotine gum you're chewing now?" I didn't need to answer. "Judith, you're one of the few therapists I know who have the self-knowledge and honesty, honesty with yourself, about yourself, to be aware of the urge. Yes, it's a concern. But I know you'll be able to guard against it. Your being aware of it is the best preventative. And as far as the nicotine gum goes, we all have our drugs, our ways of coping. Melinda had to warn me about my scotch intake lately."

"You need a break, John."

"Yes, you're right. I do. Perhaps a very long one. Pretty soon it'll be a permanent one."

"Oh, John, I—"

"Happens to the best of us. And I'm counting on you to tell me when that moment comes. You're the only one I trust for that particular assignment. Melinda's been after me about that, too. I came this close," he made the usual finger-and-thumb gesture, "to snapping at her."

"Well, until that time comes—and it's a ways off, John—let me reiterate my prescription. Thanksgiving's coming up. What are your plans?"

"Oh, Millie's having everyone over on Saturday. We're going to celebrate it then."

"And Thursday and Friday...?"

"Well, I've got a lot of paperwork to finish up..." I could tell my look stopped him. "OK, Dr. Neuwirth," he sighed. "Melinda suggested we do a time-share on Padre Island. I suppose if the doctor insists..."

"Best medicine I know."

November 15, 2002. Meeting with Pt Arturo Cavazos (1179A):

Another week gone, and I still haven't shared my story with Pt Arturo Cavazos. I wonder about my hesitation. Am I just being a careful therapist? Or is it fear motivating my reluctance? If it's fear, then who am I afraid for—my patient or myself? And why, if it's the latter, would I be afraid for myself? *Ah, Judith, for the same reason you hesitated in your group: it's not a pleasant memory.* I must recognize in myself the same overwhelming urge: to try to forget, to expunge those memories, to pretend it never happened. And so, to drive it deeper and deeper into more and more pathological expressions.

The therapist in me says that it is of particular purpose now, as there is some cause for optimism. For instance, he has started to mention his time in the hands of the cartel in the broadest outlines. He seems to be able to recall his own torture better than that of his uncle and family. Apparently it was easier to take his own abuse than to witness the torture of those he cared for.

At this point, he's only been able to describe these episodes in a completely detached, almost trancelike state. I consider that quite understandable. I've tried to be careful during those moments not to take him or allow him to go too far. It is a delicate balance between empowering him to take control of the discussion and keeping him from dangerous intrusive episodes.

Before our meeting yesterday, I had decided that I'd put off exposure long enough. Besides neutralizing their toxic effects, exposure to some of his triggers might ease a path to sharing the horrors they were associated with. Though again, it was a delicate balance. And so, our sessions took a decided turn.

"Arturo, could we talk about some of the things that set you off? And why they do? What they remind you of?"

"What kinds of things?"

"Anything that provokes those startle responses in you: objects, places, sensations, smells, textures…tastes even. Things that trigger those reactions."

"So many things." He'd answered matter-of-factly, almost robotically: "Green fatigues, black sweaters. I saw a guy dressed all in
black, and I wanted to kill him. It's a good thing Jake was there. Cigar
smoke, bottles of tequila, people in moustaches and goatees, gold
chains, sweat mixed with cologne, the smell of onions."

"Yes, onions. Does the idea of onions, or their smell, bring up any
images or feelings for you?"

Just for a split second, he winced. Then he very slightly shook his
head, as though he were trying to unravel some mystery. "Yeah, I...I
don't know why."

"Your friend Jake mentioned that when he first visited, you reacted when he was cutting up onions to sauté. He said it was when he
put them into the pan that you really panicked."

It was obvious that the loss of control was profoundly embarrass-
ing to him. "Yeah, I have a vague memory of that. I don't know if it
was so much the smell—it was partly that. But when he put them in
the pan and they...they kind of exploded."

I waited to see if he'd continue on his own. But I could feel his hesi-
tancy. He started to withdraw. "Arturo, maybe we could start with that.
Not the sautéing, just the smell to begin with. The rationale would be
that it might be something a little less threatening to begin the process.
I get the feeling it is—that the smell is less threatening than some of the
other triggers you've mentioned. Does that sound like something you
could try? Here in the office, with me. And later, maybe at home?"

"Exposing myself to onions?"

"Well, the onion—or the smell of the onion...or maybe even the
sound—might actually stand for something else, some smell it reminds you of. Smells are incredibly powerful evokers of emotion. The
sense of smell is the most basic, the most primitive we have. So odors
tend to provoke some of our most primitive responses. It would be a
step toward establishing new associations with those stimuli—non-
threatening ones. It might also allow you to begin to piece together
the underlying trauma." I noted increasing discomfort. "The idea
worries you."

"Well...yeah. Primitive responses, Doc...they...I mean, that guy dressed in black...I really had the urge. I don't want to...I mean, there was the other guy—the one Jake had to pull me off of." He started to tremble. "And then before, I nearly killed...You know when Jake took hold of my arm...in the car, on the bridge."

"You remember that?"

"Vaguely. Just seeing his eyes bulge."

"And you stopped yourself, didn't you?"

"Yeah..." His pause here carried a great deal of weight. "...That time."

I thought of this as an opportunity to give him the hope a feeling of progress provides. It wouldn't be a false hope. "Arturo, can I point out that Jake had to, or he felt he had to, and did, restrain you, both times. Now, was your reaction to that restraint the same in all of those instances?"

From the squint of his eyes, it was evident that he was trying to clarify the memory. I could see he was also coming to realize the implications. "No. No, the second time I let Jake stop me. I have a hazy memory of him dragging me away. But I don't remember from what. I have no memory of beating the guy. He...or you had to tell me."

I had to consider how to handle this. "Arturo, I think that might be of lesser importance than the difference in your responses. I think the difference indicates progress. You didn't interpret being restrained as an attack the second time. It also implies a measure of trust...in Jake. And perhaps in yourself—a recognition that you were doing something wrong."

A curious combination of emotions seemed to overwhelm him. His eyes widened, as though some realization had suddenly struck. It strangely resembled the look people get when stricken by an attack of nausea. "Arturo, what is it? What just happened?"

He struggled to put it into words. I understood, because it seemed like such a jumble of feelings and thoughts. "Jake is..."

I waited a good while to see if he would complete the idea. But I had a feeling that whatever had overcome him was too essential to let pass. "Jake is...?" At that, I could feel him retreat from the thought. It was too threatening. Was he going to say *a friend*? Was he not quite ready to trust the community, his community? To believe that he had a community? That he could take his place in one?

Perhaps we could come to it round about. "Arturo, maybe that's the place to start. What did you feel when Jake took hold of your wrist—in the car, on the bridge? What did it remind you of?"

He began to tremble. Beads of sweat formed at his temples. "I don't know...panic, fear...hate." I noted increasingly rapid eye movement, respiration. Was it too soon? Was I getting desperate myself? "It's all...mixed up. When I was in that prison, two guys grabbed my arms, tried to hold me down. I had to...I *had* to. And before that, they..." His mind seemed to suddenly jump in a new direction. "It wasn't the onions. It was, and it wasn't."

"...What was it, then?" I could see him grip the arms of his chair with such force that his knuckles turned white. "Where are you, Arturo?"

"I don't...It was when he put them in the oil...in the pan...the boiling oil. The smell...the sound...'Don't let them burn.'"

He said it like a quote. Quoting whom? Himself? "...Yes. Jake said you had a strong reaction to that."

"The bridge...knocking at the door...that tap, tap, tap."

"Yes. Someone tapped on your window. Do you remember that?"

He shot to his feet. "Down the hall...tap, click...tap, click."

*Hall? What hall? This hall?* His trembling became more violent; I could tell it was too much at this point. The look of terror was that of a wounded animal. It was homicidal. It terrified me, but I had to keep myself as cool and detached as possible.

"Arturo, this is too much, and we need to stop. We need to stop now." He backed up against the bookcase on the far wall. His eyes darted in all directions and then looked at me as though I were a complete stranger. "Arturo, you're here...with me. You're safe. There's no threat here. We need to stop, and you need to come back to the present—where you are *safe*."

I had the urge to stand but forced myself to continue seated, thinking it less threatening. "Could you look at me, Arturo? It's Judith. I'm your doctor. You're out of danger. You're in San Antonio, in my office. And there is no threat here." It was clear I was not getting through. The episode this time, if it came to pass, would be catastrophic—and it was clearly incipient.

Only one thought occurred to me: "Artie!" I said sharply. "Artie, look at me!" This seemed to penetrate. He peered at me, as though he were trying to place me, distinguish me from whatever demons were circling. "We're in my office in Sacred Heart Clinic." I was undecided as to which name to use now. Then I noticed just a hint of recognition. "You're safe, Arturo. You're all right."

Slowly, slowly I could see a reduction of the panic. I was glad I'd kept my seat. When he looked at me, I could tell he was finally placing me in the present. I saw his grip loosen ever so slightly on the lower shelf of the bookcase. He was still on high alert, but the dissociation seemed to abate.

As gently as I could, I continued. "Arturo, do you recognize me: Judith, your doctor?" He stared and then looked around the room. Gradually, he seemed to recognize where he was. A look of confusion came over him.

"Wha'...what happened? How'd I get up here?"

"You had an intrusive episode. For a moment, you..." *No, Judith, you need to concentrate on calming him.* "Let's just leave that alone for now. Do you remember where you are?"

"Uh...the clinic. Your office."

"Um-hum. And you know who I am?"

"Yeah...Dr...Dr..."

"Judith."

"Yeah, Judith."

"Good. Good. You're all right, Arturo. You're safe. There's no threat here." His breathing began to slow. "Do you think you could sit down?"

He hesitated and wiped his brow. "Yeah. I don't know how I..." He slowly took his seat.

"It doesn't matter, Arturo. All that matters is that you know you're safe, you know you're okay." I noted another positive sign: this time after the intrusion he didn't withdraw into complete constriction. "Arturo, you're still here with me, aren't you?"

He seemed bemused by the question. "Yeah. Why wouldn't I be?" Now he looked at me in the queerest way. I had a hard time interpreting it. It was a look of curiosity, and at the same time of discovery. It felt like he'd just uncovered something about me that had puzzled him. But he wasn't certain. He was looking to me to explain—*what*, I wasn't sure. But I had my suspicions. "What is it, Arturo?"

"I...You know my trouble, my craziness." He said it as though it were a great revelation.

"Well, I do know something about trauma."

"Yeah, but..."

"But what?"

"You know it more than...more than just..." I was unsure if he was just having trouble articulating it or if he felt constrained by rules of privacy.

It seemed the moment had finally arrived. This was an opening. "I know it more than academically? I know it from...experience?" It was obvious his discretion prevented him from pursuing the subject. "I do, Arturo. You're right." I think I might have been wrong about this Pt's social intelligence. Although it's possible he deduced it logically rather than empathically—from nonverbal signals I'd given.

At any rate, it made me more confident than ever about sharing my own traumatic experience. "I was raped." I tried to judge his reaction. His eyes were just locked to mine. "As a matter of fact, I was gang-raped. It happened a long time ago, but yes, I still have trust issues, anger issues. That's one of the reasons I chew nicotine gum—probably too much. And I do tend to chew...*emphatically*, let's say.

"Even though my trauma was short-lived compared with yours, I recognize the symptoms: insomnia, nausea, startle responses, nightmares. For a long time after the event, I was so constricted I didn't even feel alive. I was just going through the motions—aloof from everyone and everything."

He just looked at me. An understanding passed between us. "There've been studies that suggest that rape victims, combat veterans and victims of political torture have similar symptoms.

"Understand, Arturo, I'm not comparing my trauma to what you went through. But I want you to know that there is light at the end of the tunnel. I'm married, relatively—well, I'd say quite happily on balance. And I'm not blowing smoke. I have a son who's pretty well adjusted given the circumstances. I don't think he's in any danger of severely antisocial or self-destructive behaviors, anyway—although he's taken up smoking. I'm hoping it's just a phase. Anyway, he's a really good kid, if I do say so myself."

Arturo sat back. He looked around and out the window as if he were trying to decipher the deepest of mysteries. "What's the matter with people, Doc? What the f...What possible reason could they have for doing what they do? How can people be so evil?"

As I think about his question now, I actually find something very positive in it. He is apparently distinguishing himself from those predatory people. I'm hopeful that this is a significant step toward finding a place in his community.

"That is a question for the ages. What makes people need to treat others that way? What experiences rot the soul to such a degree? And even, what does it provide them in the first place?

"I think the purpose of the torturer and the rapist is the same: to terrorize, to dominate and humiliate his victim—to utterly destroy the victim's sense of autonomy. Along with the abuser, their motivation is to supplant their will for that of their victim's. Although in the case of the religious fanatic, there's the pretense of it being the will of God. I think that's the product of self-delusion, however—it absolves you of hubris if you convince yourself it's God's will rather than your own."

"But why would someone need to do that?"

"Yes, that's the question. Psychologically, I think, because it allows the perpetrator to feel powerful, and that's a source of self-esteem.

To hold complete mastery over the life of another is, in effect, to be a god. I think that's why begging for mercy might actually encourage the behavior. There are studies of rape victims that support that conclusion. To hold sway over the life of another person is for the terrorist and torturer similar to the rapist's violation of the victim's privacy: her right to choose—that is, her will.

"So to make their every action a reflection of *your* desire is to feel omnipotent. To force them to participate in acts of brutality"—note the immediate reaction to this!—"acts again *contrary to their will,* is to be the absolute master. There've been examples throughout history: the Nazis, Stalin and, closer to home, the SLA with Patty Hearst, the Black Panthers, among others."

At this point, I noted a strong reaction. Pt once again reverted to that familiar hand gesture. He was obviously in distress. "Arturo, something seems to have upset you. Do you have any sense of what that might be?"

"I just…" He seemed to suddenly become aware of it. He stopped and then lifted his hands and examined them. But it seemed the memory was blocked. He started to withdraw, but I didn't get the sense that he was completely dissociated. He looked from his hands to me. "I just…don't understand why people would need to do that."

I thought about pursuing the hand gesture but quickly discarded the idea. If whatever it was associated with brought him this close to panic, it was too soon. John and I agreed that violent episodes were to be strenuously avoided—the dissociation keeps the trauma from being explored as a consistent narrative. (I had to consider how much time we had left in this session as well. The issue of the hand gesture will keep.) I chose instead to restrict the discussion to more objective subjects.

"Well, the heart of the matter in strictly Freudian terms is the unleashing of our most primitive urges. Freud believed that that part of us chafes under the constraints of the ego. It is itching to be let loose, unbridled. On a more pedestrian level, Phil Deluca in his book *The Solo Partner* points out that it's that primitive part of our brain, from our reptilian past, that finds it very satisfying to lash out in anger. He explains that in a relationship that lashing out tends to provoke the same response from the other party. And so things escalate, and the relationship falls apart.

"But I think, even beyond the psychological, there is a philosophical, eschatological component. I mean the fact that as human beings we're aware of our own mortality—that we're going to die and eventually be forgotten. The inevitable conclusion is that if you don't believe in an afterlife, life has no meaning. That's a truly horrifying conclusion to come to. So, the power over the life and death of others gives you at least the *illusion* of power over your own—again, the power of a god. I think that's why it's so seductive.

"I also think that power is a substitute for love—for those who have had the conclusion beaten into them that they're unlovable... perhaps even that violence is an expression of love, as twisted as that sounds. That archetypal narrative is evident throughout the history of literature...Richard III, for instance."

This brief philosophical discourse seemed to calm him enough that we could avoid another violent episode. He'd reverted to hand rubbing, but as I spoke, it became less and less vigorous. Plus, we had already used up a little over an hour and a half. I was spent. And I can't imagine that Arturo wasn't as well.

Now we'll see if I was right about sharing my own trauma with him. But I could see a strong reaction to the last point I made—about power as a substitute for love.

"I nearly killed Jake."

*Wow, that's a fascinating association!* I'll have to analyze where it might have come from. At the time, I judged it necessary to keep it on a personal plane. "But you stopped yourself, Arturo. And then, in your apartment when you panicked, you went after the pan, not Jake. And when Jake restrained you the second time, you let him. You didn't interpret the restraint as an attack."

"Jake is..."

This time I had to urge him on to saying it. "Jake is your friend?"

"He saved me. Why?"

"Why? Well, according to him, because you saved him—on your trip in the Big Bend. And, I'd say, simply because he *is* your friend... and he loves you."

He looked up at me, obviously in conflict, but as though some extraordinary discovery had just struck him. I actually saw a hint of tears forming. This struck me as something monumental. I couldn't let it go.

"Jake isn't my friend," he finally said.

I waited. Was he going back into denial...refusal to believe in the possibility of connection, attachment, a community? Whatever conclusion or realization he was coming to was profoundly painful. But despite the pain, I glimpsed a tinge of hopefulness in it.

"...He's my brother."

November 22, 2002. Pt Arturo Cavazos, 1179A (Summary of last few weeks):

"He's my brother." This admission of connection and caring by Pt Arturo Cavazos is such a huge step that his withdrawal during this, the following week, is perfectly understandable. I must be careful as therapist to be sensitive to his reticence: two steps forward, a step back to regroup and protect himself. It was, after all, a tremendous risk.

Bit by agonizing bit, however, the tale of Pt's time in the hands of the Zetas drug cartel is piecing itself together. It is to be expected that he could only do so in a detached state. While my efforts at hypnosis have failed, Pt seems to place himself in a quasi-hypnotic trance in order to recount abuse and periods of hopelessness.

At this point, it is as though he were describing an account he'd read—of some fictional character. These periods alternate with moments of panic during which I've had to talk Pt down from violent outbreaks. It is becoming easier to do so as time passes. Pt has hinted at particularly gruesome episodes concerning his uncle Teo and cousin Imelda. Details appear too horrific to describe at this juncture.

We have also engaged in in-vivo exposure therapy. So far, we've been able to detoxify at least the smell of onions. (I have a feeling the real pathological association is with the sound or smell or sight of onions—or something—frying.) Pt has also been exposed to tongs (from my fireplace) and a cane that seemed to have a particularly strong effect, among other items.

It was when I accidentally tapped the cane twice on the side of my desk that Pt had an explosive startle response. I remember his expression of "tap, tap," or "tap, click" when recalling the association. Was there someone with a cane? He said something like "in the hall" or "down the hallway." (I'll have to check my notes.) This sound seems to be strongly related with the so far unspecified episodes with uncle and cousin.

Thanksgiving and Christmas are now upon us, and I wonder how this will affect Pt. These are usually times of exceptional stress for individuals who are isolated (not to mention for the rest of us). This is particularly true if there are pleasant associations from the past that have been lost.

Pt's sister, Griselda, has visited, and Pt has a standing invitation to spend the holidays with her and her family. I doubt he'll take her up on it. He still seems ill at ease in a crowd and is just getting comfortable with sister's and friend Jake's visits.

I have scheduled another session with Mr. Kasmarech for this afternoon. He and fiancée will stay with Jake's cousin, as there is more room there than at Pt's one-bedroom apartment. Though Pt is apparently comforted by Ms. Martínez's company, I think this is preferable.

Jake asked me about inviting Pt to his place in Aguagria for Thanksgiving. I told him that the invitation is definitely a good idea but not to expect Arturo to accept. In the likely event he refuses, Jake and his fiancée will suggest a small celebration on Friday at his apartment.

A return to his hometown could be good or bad, depending on how prepared Pt is. Perhaps a day or two around Christmas would be better. Ms. Martínez's house is another alternative. She apparently still lives by herself (effectively with Jake, although I get the feeling this can be hit or miss), so Pt could avoid large crowds and hectic schedules.

I'm also concerned about the hiatus of therapy sessions over the holidays. However, I'm confident that Jake, Dolores and Pt's sister will not allow Arturo to spend too much time alone. Perhaps another break from therapy will be salutary rather than harmful. I know I'm looking forward to it.

Donald, Jonathan and I are spending Thanksgiving with Donny's parents. I'm lobbying to spend Christmas here, just the three of us. There doesn't seem to be much resistance. Perhaps we can even get away for a day or two. Maybe go skiing—that always refreshes me—though I think my favorite part is sitting in front of a fire after dinner with a glass of cognac (or two!). Perhaps we could go between Christmas and New Year's when there's not so much traveling—at least, I'd hope there'd be less air traffic. Guess it depends on how many people have the same idea.

November 22, 2002 Meeting with Mr. Kazmarech:

Interesting that when Jake entered, I noted a bit less confidence than at our last meeting. I wondered what the difference was. He didn't seem at a point of crisis, just slightly less sure of himself—a little more preoccupied. *Remember, Judith, he's not your patient. You have your hands full as it is.* "Hello, Jake. Good to see you again." We shook hands.

"And you, Doctor—Judith."

"Please, have a seat. How've you been?"

"Oh, fine, thanks. And you?"

"Pretty good, thanks." There was the tiniest uncomfortable lapse here. We'd spoken on the phone and met one other time, but that was a while ago. It concerned me that Jake seemed somewhat off-kilter. There was concern for him, of course, but principally for my patient. He'd been such a positive influence on Arturo, him and his fiancée. "Uh…Arturo tells me you've asked him to be best man at your wedding."

There was another vague, almost imperceptible hesitation—not in time so much as in demeanor. "Yeah. He didn't give me a definite answer yet. Anyway, we've pushed back the date."

"Oh? To when?"

"Well, we're not sure." He took a thoughtful breath. I could tell I was going to get an explanation for the change in demeanor now. "Judith, Dolores is…I think it's just some adjustment problems. You know, she was involved in a trauma of her own."

"No, I didn't know that." Suddenly, it struck me. This was the famous case of Dolores Martínez, the girl who killed her mother! *Holy Moses!* Yes, I remember it happened in a border town. I believe she was exonerated after a lengthy period of incarceration. The case made its way through psychiatric circles around the country. I remember a seminar I went to on catatonia where it was discussed at length. Though I tried to cover my reaction, I'm pretty sure Jake caught it. "Is she currently seeing anyone—I mean, a therapist?"

"Uh, my sister, Grace, and I—Grace is her best friend—we got her to go see Grace's psychiatrist once. But he's more about medication and stuff. I've talked to some therapists in Aguagria. None of them really impresses me...or her. I can tell you know about the case. I guess it's fairly well-known in the mental-health field."

"It is." I tried to cover my eagerness to get firsthand insight into the case. Wow, the complexities of this whole situation!

He took a thoughtful moment. "Anyway, it's not just her. You know, at first you're in seventh heaven, nothing can go wrong, everything's right with the world. Then you come back down to earth and realize there's gonna be bumps and curves along the way. We both have some things to work through."

I got the sense that his realistic view of life and relationships would tend to help. But I also had the feeling that while many of his issues were resolved, there was some fundamental doubt still rooting around in his psyche. "Well, that's good. I can tell you will." I hoped for his and Arturo's sake I wasn't being overly optimistic. "And how's your sister? I think you told me she's a musician?"

"Yes, and she's playing up a storm—at home. I haven't gotten her back to recording yet. But we're...we're working on that. Her old label seems amenable. Again, it's a process. And it's got to be because she wants to...when she's ready to."

I knew I needed to concentrate on my patient but was fascinated by Jake's situation. And now, knowing he was engaged to Dolores Martínez! I'll have to be extra delicate with that. *Just let him volunteer information if he wants to, Judith. Don't press.*

But he's such an integral part of Arturo's recovery. And knowing him better might give me some insights. "Jake...I remember you mentioning a period of euphoria. I suppose that was after your epiphany and your reconciliation with your sister. It struck me then that you said you—actually, it's here in my notes somewhere—that you 'egocentrically projected it onto the whole world?'"

"Yes, that's right. Like I said, seventh heaven."

"I'm curious. Was there something specific that brought you back down to earth?"

A humorless smile of self-irony rippled across his face. "Oh yeah. 9-11, Doc." *Huh, first time he's called me that.* "Before that I was glutted with 'happy endings' and 'world peace.' You know, the Cold War was over…" He let that hang, but I wanted to know more.

"Umm. What did you take away from that, Jake?"

There was a rather bitterly ironic chuckle. "Something I'd rather not know, Doctor: that there's no final redemption, that there'll always be people who want to destroy and conquer. I guess that horrific event just brought home that if you're walking on air, you're not living on earth. And earth is the only place we've got. I guess the French are right: 'Plus ça change, plus c'est la même chose.'"

I gave this insight time for both of us to absorb. "Yes, that's an important thing to come to grips with. Those who can't create can only destroy the creation of others." I hoped I didn't let my own wistfulness at the thought show too openly. This was Jake's show, Jake's story, Jake's epiphany.

"Anyway, Doc—Judith, we're here about Artie."

"Yes. We are. The most I can say is that we're making progress. And you've been an important part of that progress—you and Dolores."

"Uh, have you had any more thoughts about our inviting him down to Aguagria for Thanksgiving? I wanted your input."

I had considered the possible implications of such an event. "Well, again, I think the invitation would be okay—actually, more than okay. I'm thinking he'll probably refuse, but offering to include him in a family event would be good. I know his sister, Griz…"

"Griselda. Some of her friends in high school called her 'Greasy.'"

"Oh no. Did she mind that?

"Well, I wasn't really a part of that crowd."

"Right, right. Anyway, she's invited him to spend the holidays with her and her family, and—"

"Oh, that's good."

"Yes, but he refused that invitation. And that didn't surprise me. So you didn't know his sister that well?"

"Not really well. And when she married, she moved so far away. Uh...Seattle, maybe?"

"Spokane."

"That's right."

"And speaking of that, have you heard from Arturo's ex-girlfriend—Annabelle, I think you said her name was?"

"Oh yes. She calls from time to time to ask how he is. I can just tell her about the times I've seen him. And Artie does seem to be more... I don't know, sociable? Human, maybe?"

"Yes. I spoke with her once, rather briefly. Tell me this: do you get any sense that she'd leave her husband and try to get back together with Arturo?"

Again he had to mull the subject over. "I don't know, Judith. I...get the feeling that it isn't a bad marriage, or I don't think she's mistreated or anything. Well, I don't think Annabelle would stand for that." He took a moment to consider. "I honestly don't know what that situation's like."

"Well, I'm grateful for her discretion, anyway."

There followed a period of silence that neither of us felt compelled to break. There were so many complications and permutations to this case. I do hope that Dolores will continue to contribute. That time Arturo was about to panic, the fact that she sensed right away what to do—and that it was successful—tells me that she's a very stabilizing influence. But the trauma in her own history...of course it's going to take time and effort to resolve. *Hang on, Jake. Just hang on.*

I could tell there was something else on his mind that he hesitated to bring up. "Might there be some other issue you'd like to share, Jake?"

He seemed to brace himself with an expansive sigh. "Doctor, I'm not your patient."

"No, that's true. But it might be an issue that would give me some insight into Arturo. And if it's affecting you, it might very well affect him...affect your relationship, which is so important."

He thought for a moment. "Well, like I said, I don't think the problem is all Dolores's. I feel like there's something...incomplete in me."

"Well, Jake, I mean, welcome to the club. Life's a journey."

"I know, I know. It's just..."

I gave him a moment to see if there was anything definite. "Is there something specific that you feel is missing? Anything you can identify? What Dolores went through, Jake, it's got to be—"

"It's not Dolores. Or it's more than just Dolores. It's something in me. It has partly to do with what Artie went through. Somehow I tie it together with 9-11."

"Well, they're both examples of horrendous evil."

"That's exactly it. That kind of evil needs to be resisted."

I paused to try to gather the implications of where this was going. "Jake, be careful. You projected your own exhilaration on the world at large. That's what *you* told *me*. Be very careful you don't project the problems of the world onto yourself. In both instances, it's egocentric."

He locked eyes with me with such a penetrating look. Oh, he would be a difficult patient to keep ahead of. "Yes, maybe. But...'all it takes for evil to triumph is for good men to do nothing.'"

I was knocked back on my heels. "Edmund Burke." He affirmed that by merely holding my gaze. He really got me with that one. Yes, there is a point where psychology must defer to philosophy—a point where one must take action. I was completely flummoxed. "Yes...yes, perhaps that's right. Perhaps it is."

"What makes people like that, Doctor? Evil, mean, sadistic, heartless? Is it because they've been abused, taught that violence is a normal way of life? Are they brain damaged? Are some people just born that way?

"Jake, that's a question that's been asked from time immemorial. I can only give you my personal opinion. I think there are people that, yes, because of genetic makeup, are more easily tempted to abuse, to violence.

"But I also believe that an essential element is the violation of trust. I'm talking about the foundational sense of trust that love and nurturing in the earliest stage of life provides. That sense of trust provided by the first caretaker determines a person's ability to believe he or she has a place in the world.

"Now, it's possible that those without the sensitivity gene, if there is such a thing, would have that propensity toward violence. I also suspect that when that sense of trust, of being valued, is absent, the natural substitute is power."

I could see multiple associations being made, conclusions being drawn. "How about the victims of that violence? Is Artie's reaction typical?"

"Jake, remember confidentiality laws. I can only answer in general terms. But for victims of any kind of prolonged trauma, that foundation of trust is shattered. Dying or wounded soldiers call for their mamas, that most central core of care and respect—or to God. When their cry is unanswered, they despair. They despair of having any place in the world. Of course their reaction depends to a large degree on their pretrauma psychological makeup. Those that were antisocial before tend to act out, have issues with anger. Although irritability is common to all."

"What about the ones that weren't antisocial? That care...or cared? What happens to them?"

"Again, in general terms, they tend toward depression—a hopelessness of having a place in the world, a sense of a purposeful life. They can feel more a part of the dead than the living."

I could see this was pretty disturbing. I let him take all the time he needed. There's usually an appeal for some expression of hope at this point. At first I could see the discouragement I'm accustomed to with family, with friends. But then it seemed a look of determination replaced it. "So, what do we do?"

"You do what you've been doing, you be his friend."

His gaze wandered a moment. Then, seeming to come to a conclusion, he gently nodded a few times and then looked back at me. "Anyway, Doctor...Judith, you have your own patients. And I've taken up enough of your time." He rose.

Though I was fascinated, he was correct. I needed to save my time—and my energy, which has its limits—for my patients. "You take care of yourself, Jake. And consider seeing someone yourself."

"I will. I will."

November 26, 2002. Session with Pt Arturo Cavazos (1179A):

I had decided to be extra gentle during our last meeting before Thanksgiving. Recalling pleasant times that are considered gone forever can be profoundly disturbing. On the other hand, allowing oneself to feel that loss is a step, however painful, on the road to recovery.

Actually, I consider the fact that there was pain involved (i.e., that he didn't describe it in a detached state) to be positive. He's allowing himself to feel, to remember being part of a community (and missing it). If that community is now lost, there is at least the knowledge that he once had that capacity, that connection. It may, if present relationships are allowed to grow, give him hope for membership in a new one. Again, it is a delicate balance.

But I also get a sense that there is some added, unexpressed ache when he talks about his family. I'm not at all certain. I just have a vague feeling that it is something of longer standing than his recent trauma. I'm also convinced that we've only scratched the surface of the source of his pathology.

I've mentioned this mysterious Jesús on a few occasions. While I've only been answered with evasions or silence, it is clear that each mention strikes a chord. Again, it is not at all clear, but I'm leaning toward the conclusion that Jesús is associated not only with Pt's recent trauma but also with something much older and perhaps even more central.

I'm certain that whatever specific trauma is connected with Jesús is buried in the deepest layers of Pt's disorder. Reaching beneath those layers to pathology's core is essential but also extremely risky. As therapist, I must be patient. But I also can't afford to shy away from those painful, even volatile, associations.

Apparently through the anonymous third party's sources in Mexico, contact was made with the prison concerning the identity of Jesús. According to those sources, there was no Jesús on the manifest of inmates or among the guards (!). And yet according to Jake, Pt actually cried out for him during his rescue.

Could Jesús be imaginary? I have to consider that possibility. It would not be unusual for someone under such extreme stress to create an imaginary friend. This might explain the evasions. Then again, I get the sense of someone very real. Of course, for the traumatized individual denied genuine companionship, an imaginary friend can seem devastatingly real.

But with each vague allusion, I'm getting more and more of a sense of Jesús being more than one person. Would an imaginary friend fragment like that? Might Pt have needed different qualities in an imaginary friend in different circumstances?

One Jesús was certainly associated with Pt's time in captivity. But there was also once where the issue arose when speaking of Pt's family's original crossing of the river. Curious. Could Pt have combined diverse personalities into an imaginary Jesús? How could Jesús be connected to family's original flight from Mexico? And if he's imaginary, is this fantasy crucial to Pt's present relative stability and progress? Could the revelation that he's imaginary shatter the delicate balance of his recovery?

For the present, I will keep these topics on hold until after the Thanksgiving holiday—probably till after Christmas. The holidays are stressful enough without pushing Pt toward potentially excruciating revelations.

As I suspected, Pt refused the invitation to spend the holiday with Jake's family. As an alternative, Jake and Dolores will bring leftovers (he says there are always more than the family can consume) up to Pt's apartment Friday and have a separate celebration there. At this point, one or two people are still about all Pt can handle. But I am extremely grateful that Arturo will not spend the entire holiday by himself.

I decided to raise this issue with him. It seemed a bit less threatening than some others might be. "Arturo, how're you feeling about the holidays? You know they can be a difficult time for anyone, what with the stress. And then there's the pressure to be cheerful even when you're not feeling particularly cheerful."

In his typical reserved manner, he answered, "I think I'll be able to handle it."

"Are you looking forward to Jake and Dolores's visit? That's Friday, right?"

"Yeah, Friday. They said to expect them in the afternoon."

"Are you going to go out or what?"

"Naw, they're bringing leftovers from Jake's family dinner. And Dolores says she's gonna roast a turkey breast."

"That should be fun." It was often quite a task getting this Pt to talk—particularly when there was some immediate stress. "Are you just going to stay in your apartment or go out and do something? I mean, after dinner?"

"I think Jake wants to watch a football game."

"Uh-huh. Is that something you think you can handle?"

"Yeah, yeah. I've actually been able to watch some things lately, including football."

"Ah, good. What else? I mean, what else can you watch?"

"Well, Connors prov—uh, I, uh…have a lot of channels. Too many, actually. I tend to limit myself to sports and the Hallmark Channel."

*Connors? Is he talking about Connors McClain, the governor? That's right, he's from Aguagria!* Oh my Lord! So that's why he can afford the apartment, paying for therapy in cash. I hope it's not taxpayer money. Now I understand why this third party had to stay anonymous. From what Jake has said, a considerable bribe had to be paid for Arturo's release. That could be quite a scandal. *Don't let on you put that together, Judith.* "Yes, I can see how that…that content might be a little easier to take."

"Yeah, no explosions, murders…"

"Right. Well, I think that's a positive step, Arturo. Particularly the Hallmark Channel. Their stories tend to be about family and community. Are there any that particularly resonated?"

He hesitated. Did the movie or program, whatever it was, affect him *too* deeply? "Yeah…there was one."

Now it was my turn to hesitate. I could tell that the story had been very moving. That explained his reluctance to tell it. But because it was fictional and deeply affecting at the same time, it might be a good opportunity to reach deeper into his trauma history. "Do you think you could tell me the story? Or just give me an idea of what it was about?"

Again, there was a pause of uncertainty. But I got the feeling that he knew why I wanted him to tell it to me. He seemed to know that these uncomfortable tasks were an integral part of his therapy. It was also clear that he was being the "good soldier" (i.e., not shying away from difficult tasks).

"Yeah." There was another considerable pause. I could feel him gearing up to recount it. "It was about a Vietnamese brother and sister, who escaped on one of those boats—you know, after the North Vietnamese took over?"

"Oh yeah, the boat people. I remember that. Horrible. A lot of people died on those boats, didn't they?"

"Yeah...they did. As a matter of fact, their mother dies on the way—out at sea. The father had been executed immediately after the takeover."

"Hmm. So they're alone—the brother and sister."

"Yeah. They're alone. Before she dies, their mother makes the brother swear that he'll take care of his little sister." At this point Arturo had to stop to collect himself. That he could allow himself to be moved this much indicates considerable progress, however fictional the story. Does he relate it to his own sister? Perhaps the story Jake recounted about the flight from Mexico was true.

"They make it to...Thailand or some country over there. They have to stay in a refugee camp. The conditions are pretty bad. And the brother..." Again, Arturo had to stop. He bit his lower lip in an effort to control himself. "...the brother often goes hungry to make sure his sister has enough to eat—to honor his promise to his mother." He swallowed hard and took another moment to collect himself.

"Finally, they make it to America, sponsored through some program. At first they want to only bring the brother. He had something to do with helping the American troops. But he won't leave his sister behind. Eventually, they're allowed to come over together."

This time I waited myself a good while to let the implications of the story settle. "That sounds like a pretty powerful tale of sibling devotion."

It was a good while before he was able to answer. "Yeah. Yeah, it was."

I questioned how far to take this—now with the holiday hiatus coming up. "Arturo, it seems to me those kinds of relationships mean a lot to you." I sensed a sudden flash of anguish. It told me that this was too volatile to pursue for the present. I knew that in order to control himself he would begin to detach.

"Uh, Arturo, maybe we can take this up after the holidays. It strikes me as a critical issue but one that maybe we should put on the back burner for now. Maybe it would be better for the present to look at the positive things in your life: your friendship with Jake and Dolores, your sister, the time you're going to spend together..."

Ever so slowly, he started to withdraw. I could feel the wall building brick by brick. Did I make the right choice? Could this have been another major breakthrough? Yes, and it could have led to a major crisis. I think he's gone far enough for now. There's no time for real follow-up until after Christmas.

"Arturo, are you and Jake planning anything else during the holidays?" I could tell he was grateful for the reprieve; there was quite a long exhalation of air before he answered.

"Yeah, actually. He mentioned something about a fishing trip."

"Oh, that sounds great. Would that be here or in Aguagria?"

"He didn't say. But I'd rather go somewhere around here—the lake or maybe the Pedernales. I've never fished around here. God, I haven't fished in..." He just shook his head.

"Then I'd say it was high time, huh? What kind of fish do you catch around here? Trout, or..."

"Naw, it's not cold enough for trout; the water isn't cold enough. There's lots of bass, catfish, perch…"

"Do you eat them?"

"Oh yeah."

"Who cooks?"

"Jake is the expert at that—at preparing the fish too."

"You don't just throw them in a frying pan?"

I could see my distraction was working. He seemed to be almost enjoying my ignorance. "No, you've got to scale and gut, and Jake's pretty good at filleting."

"Ah. That would be good for me. I've never enjoyed picking at whole fish—trying to keep from swallowing bones. What kind of gear do you use? A bamboo pole or what?"

He paused for a second. I had the feeling he realized what I was trying to do, and appreciated it. "You haven't done much fishing, have you?"

"I went fishing once. I think I remember pulling up an old bicycle tire."

I almost got a smile. So close…so close.

12/2/02 (personal log):

Whew! Made it through Thanksgiving and airport chaos. I do wish Donny's parents didn't live so far away. The stress of delays and missed flights even showed on the Donster, phlegmatic as he normally is. I guess Donald gets that equanimity from his father, Aaron.

It is so wonderful to have the parents-in-law I have. I almost don't think of them as in-laws anymore. Despite being a shiksa of the first order, I've never felt anything but welcome from the first time Donny brought me home to meet them. I've always felt the same from Donald's sister, Marcia. This, despite the fact that she married into an observant family. Too bad she and David and the girls couldn't make it this year.

Thanksgiving dinner was wonderful. Donald's father has such a quick wit. It seems that everything out of his mouth puts us in stitches. I see some of that in Jonathan, actually. And I'm so happy about that—laughter is such a blessing.

I have to laugh at Tessa, the way she will almost never let him stop eating. Well, he is their only grandson. Good thing he has that adolescent metabolism. The only somewhat unpleasant moment came when Jonathan went outside after dinner to smoke. While it does concern me, it really seemed to upset Tessa. This is the closest she's ever come to scolding me. "Why do you allow that?" She looked at Donald, but I could feel it more directed at me.

It's a question I've asked myself, actually. "Tessa, we're not particularly happy about it. But hard as it is to accept, he's almost an adult. I think we have to give him some room to make his own decisions, his own mistakes. After all, he's not taking drugs. He's doing well in school. He even told Don that he's usually the designated driver for his friends.

"Actually, we've been trying to convince him to try this new thing, or relatively new, called electronic cigarettes. E-cigs, they call them. I did some research. They don't have any of the tar or carbon monoxide or other noxious chemicals, and you only exhale water vapor."

Aaron's only contribution was "So if it's not bad for you, what's the point?"

"Well, it delivers a modest amount of nicotine. I've honestly considered them for myself. From what I've read, nicotine by itself is not a harmful substance. You know I chew nicotine gum."

"No, I didn't know," Tessa answered, and not approvingly.

I hesitated to continue the discussion, but Donald kept it going. "Mom, I think we all have our drugs. Look at the size of your husband. And I'm not too far behind. Food can be a drug, depending on what you eat."

Aaron couldn't let that go without a comment: "Hey, speak for yourself, old man." He patted his ample tummy. "This is solid muscle. What you got too much of between your ears." It was good to hear Donny laugh out loud.

"What nonsense. Food is not a drug!" Tessa protested.

"What Donald is saying, Tessa, is that we all do things that are... not the most healthful. We all need things that help us get through the heartaches and disappointments that are an inevitable part of life." I had shared with Tessa the substance of my own trauma. I assumed that she'd told Aaron. Understandably, this cast a momentary shadow over the conversation.

Fortunately, Aaron was there to quickly dispel the unease. "Like marriage." He then turned to Tessa, who'd given him a withering look. "To the wrong person, I mean. At least I've heard that. I, of course, wouldn't know."

Used to Aaron's teasing, she turned back to me. So I continued. "Caffeine is a drug for that matter, but I've read studies indicating that it's actually quite beneficial. It has what are called antioxidants that fight cancer, and it's been shown to improve mood. Like everything else, in moderation."

"Now I know why my beautiful wife won't say a word to me until after her second cup of coffee," Aaron said.

Tessa, of course, had her own bag of rejoinders. "If you had to deal with you in the morning, you'd understand."

"Shall I get you another cup of coffee, dear?"

After a sour look at her husband, Tessa just sighed. "Well, I was going to offer dessert, but I don't want to be an enabler."

"Tessa, I don't consider you an enabler," Aaron teased, "just my drug connection."

After the laughter died down, Tessa answered, "All right, Mr. Wit, what's your poison, pumpkin or mincemeat?"

"Yes!"

December 2, 2002. Phone conversation with Jake Kasmerick:

Despite missing our one connecting flight home and getting in late Sunday night, I felt refreshed and ready to take on my patients again. I'd been advised that Arturo had a follow-up operation on his hip—pain and stiffness had suddenly increased. For Arturo to complain at all, I knew the pain had to be intense. He would be out for the first week in December at least. I was anxious to know how his Thanksgiving had gone with Jake and Dolores, so I'd arranged for Jake to call me Monday afternoon.

"Hello, Jake. How'd it go with Arturo?" I was a bit concerned when he hesitated slightly before answering.

"Well, it went…pretty well."

I sensed some ambivalence. "But not great?"

"No, no, it was good…it was good. I think he enjoyed it. He was fairly relaxed, actually. So was I."

I was a bit bemused by the qualification about himself. "OK…" There was a brief pause in the conversation that I found a little unsettling. Jake seemed to have something he was hesitant to share. If it concerned my patient, I needed to know about it. And anything that affected Jake would have an ancillary effect on Arturo. "Jake, you know you can discuss anything with me, don't you?"

"I…Doctor, I just…Is there any possibility that I could come up to San Antonio and speak with you in person?"

"Jake, you're welcome here anytime! You don't even have to ask. Just give me a little notice and...of course!" I was intrigued. He hadn't said a word about Dolores yet. I got the feeling that this had to do with her.

"Look, Arturo has a number of tests and follow-up surgery this week. Then he'll be in recovery and inpatient PT, so I've got plenty of time. The best day would probably be Wednesday. Let me check... Yes, I only have one appointment from nine to ten thirty, and then I'm free the rest of the day. Will that work?"

"Well, I'm committed to teaching this week. But I'm taking off the following Wednesday through Friday. I have a meeting with the district attorney's office in Austin Thursday. Would Wednesday the eleventh work?"

"Uh, yes, I suppose. It'd have to be afternoon. I have an eleven o'clock that day. Is this a job interview in Austin? You switching sides?"

"Yeah, maybe. But hopefully not to litigate. I'd like to stick to research and investigation if I can. Of course, it'd be nice to be on the winning team for a change." There was another pause, but I felt like he had more to say. "I'm not sure about much, at this point."

It was interesting: an expression of uncertainty, but not with the same feeling of self-doubt I got in my earliest conversations with him—before his epiphany. It seemed more philosophical conundrum than personal insecurity. If I was right about that, that it was a spiritual rather than emotional doubt, I wondered if I was the right person to address it with. But I'd done that with many of my patients—Arturo certainly, and others who'd gone through that loss of faith.

Whatever the case, it will certainly have an impact on Arturo. "Jake, can you give me an idea of what this is about?" There was another hesitation. I couldn't tell if it was a matter of taking time to think or the delicacy of the subject.

"I'm not sure I can, Judith. It's not completely clear in my mind. It's partly about Dolores and me...and how our problems affect Artie. I mean, Dolores won't leave that house—I mean move. It's where the incident with her mother happened. But, on the other hand, it's a tie to her father. It was only a few months after they were reconciled that he died. It's a strong connection to him, and even to a dog she was very attached to.

"She's talking about wanting to get to know her father's side of the family. I'm encouraging that. There's a great-aunt just across the border in Mexico that was very close to her father—helped raise him, actually. But she's in ill health and can't travel. I don't know about Dolores visiting her. Aguagria's sister city is now the ninth most dangerous in the world...right there across the border."

"I take it you're not effectively living together anymore."

"No. No, we're not. And she hardly leaves her house. Basically just to visit Gracie and me, run errands and the like."

"So I gather this situation is what made Thanksgiving not as pleasant as your other visits?"

"And it's not just her. I...I just don't know."

This was most unfortunate. Not only Jake but also Dolores was having a very beneficial effect on my patient. I would hate for him to be without her empathetic, soothing nature. Aside from Arturo's sister, who can only afford to visit on rare occasions, these two friends are all the community he has at present—with the possible addition of the governor. How much he can participate is an unknown.

And Jake and Dolores, in addition to being devoted friends, were an example of unity—an anchor, if you will. I thought about inviting the two of them up, but something told me I should see Jake alone. "Well, then, let's meet on Wednesday the eleventh—say, one o'clock?"

"That'd be perfect. Uh, could I take you to lunch?"

"We'll see about that. But if we do, I'm taking *you* out. You can't be making millions substitute teaching."

"Well, I feel like I owe you for—"

"*Don't* feel that way. You have no idea how much you've helped me with Arturo. I'll see you Wednesday of next week. Oh, by the way, have you spoken to Annabelle about calling me? This would be a good time to meet with her, too—or at least have a conversation. I spoke to her once but very briefly. And it was a while ago."

"Oh, right. Sorry, I've been a little preoccupied. Uh…I'll call her today, give her your number."

"That'd be great. Have *you* spoken to her lately?"

"Not for a couple of weeks. She seemed a little distracted then—a little worried about something, maybe. And she sounded a little more anxious for information about Artie. Doc—uh, Judith, I…Well, she's a woman of few words, but I got the feeling she's getting impatient about seeing Artie."

"Oh boy. Well then, do me a favor and tell her to make sure she calls me. Or maybe I'll just call her. You gave me her number."

"Yes. I did."

"Yeah, I have it somewhere. Oh, that's right, I put it right on the front of Arturo's file. Yes, here it is. All right, I've got a patient waiting in the lobby. Wednesday the eleventh, then."

"OK, uh…bye. Thanks, Judith."

"Thank *you*. And take care of yourself, Jake."

"Yeah."

I found it interesting that as soon as I hung up—well, even while we were still talking—I was thinking about Donald and Jonathan. Oh, how wonderful it is to have such loving people in your life—to have the stability and self-affirmation and just plain fulfillment of that! I deal with so many broken relationships, broken lives. I think we tend to forget what a gift it is to have that certainty, that connection—until we either lose them ourselves or see others who do.

December 11, 2002. Patient Situation Summary—Arturo Cavazos (1179A):

There were apparently complications with respect to Pt's original hip replacement. He will be in the hospital for the rest of this week after his corrective surgery of December 3.

It is my intention to take advantage of the time to meet with friend Jake Kasmirick this afternoon and with former fiancée, Anabele (I found out this is the correct spelling of her name), on Friday.

In our telephone conversation Monday, I again found her to be much as Jake described her: straightforward, practical, with no illusions about Mr. Cavazos's fragile state. I realized that she has shown remarkable forbearance in not contacting him. However, I also had the distinct feeling that beneath her self-possession there was (or is) an urgency.

There is at least one very hopeful item. During our phone conversation, I brought up the question of Jesús. I'm coming more and more to believe that this person (or persons) is a major part of Pt's trauma narrative. Ms. Volpe's reaction to the mention gave me the feeling she has some insight. She is the first of Pt's circle who was given pause by the name. I hope to be able to tease out the details during our face-to-face.

I also find it telling that there was still no mention of her husband—almost as though she were trying to ignore his existence. This could be volatile.

They are obviously of means, living in one of the more exclusive Dallas suburbs. The only information I have about him came from Jake: that he is originally from a town close to Aguagria and was a friend of Ms. Volpe's (Anabele's) family.

Jake also found out that he has an import/export business (apparently a quite profitable one). Has Anabele shared with husband what she will be doing in SA? I doubt she has. Will she bring her daughter? If so, where will she (daughter) stay during our meeting? I have no wish to pry, but I must consider the interests of my patient.

My greatest concerns are the loss of the stabilizing influence of Ms. Martínez (Dolores) and the question of Mr. Kazmirick's involvement. I do not foresee his retreating from participation—only the possible debilitation of its positive effects. This would be owing to apparent troubles in his relationship with Ms. Martínez and some as yet unidentified (and unresolved) personal conflict. For the sake of my Pt, I believe it is crucial that I address whatever the issue is.

I must confess that I am also intrigued. Mr. Kazmirick's is one complex psyche. I'm still inclined to believe the issue more spiritual than psychological (perhaps exacerbated by his relationship problems). He seemed fairly settled when first becoming involved in Arturo's treatment. Of course, like he said, when a great weight is lifted from your shoulders, all seems right with the world. Once the catharsis is over, unresolved conflicts have a way of resurfacing.

I have visited Mr. Cavazos once in the hospital. A week's interruption of treatment is unfortunate but doesn't present a serious setback. A two-week hiatus is problematic. In this instance, however, it is looking like we will have but one session (here, at least) between now and 2003. Well, again, two steps forward...

Another concern, however, is that he is being given narcotics for the pain. He had weaned himself off of them (or at least seriously reduced their use) and refused them when the discomfort started returning. It is unknown whether as pain increased use did as well. At any rate, they were administered intravenously after surgery.

In addition to easing physical pain, I am worried that they will contribute to psychic numbing. This will undoubtedly lead to some regression. There is also the danger of reinstating his addiction. I don't know if he was ever completely abstinent, but I'm certain that his use had been considerably reduced.

Jake has also visited Pt. Unfortunately, I have no evidence that he was accompanied by fiancée Dolores. I'm hoping I can still call her that—that is, that they still plan to marry. On the other hand, if she is going through some crisis, or some considerable psychic discomfort, she might not be the soothing influence she was. That would be a truly unfortunate loss. It will be the absence of one pillar of support and the possible weakening of another (Jake).

Meeting with Jake Kazmareck:

When he entered, there was a look of determination on his face—an urgency. There was a new firmness in his handshake. I sensed an insistence to get down to business.

"Jake, I have the feeling you have something specific on your mind."

"I do, Judith."

Still, I sensed a hesitation. "Well, have at it." He bit his lower lip in thought. "Jake, whatever affects you affects Arturo. Let it go."

He paused, and his eyes narrowed as though he were trying to concretize some abstract thought. "Ever since our conversation about 9/11 and the etiology of evil, there's something I can't stop thinking about."

"OK. What's that?"

"I told you about it when we first met. It was during that canoe trip in the Big Bend."

"With the rapids."

"Yes. But it's not the rapids that sticks in my mind."

"OK, what does?"

"The fight between me and the other guy, when we were all feeling the strain of hunger and isolation—the fear of…well, death. Like I told you then, it was the only time I've actually felt the urge to kill."

"That can be a horrifying feeling."

He looked steadily at me as though this was the heart of the issue. "But not for some people."

What was going on here? Was he equating himself with those monsters who kill without compunction? "Jake, let me say that you're not alone. Not by a long shot. In extreme circumstances we're all capable. It doesn't make you one of the bad guys."

"It made me feel that way then."

"That's only because you have a conscience, an ability to empathize."

He looked away and down, again seeming to try to capture a thought that remained elusive. Finally, his eyes returned to mine. It was a penetrating gaze. There was an urging, almost a demand in it. "Let her rip, Jake."

"Again, Judith, I'm not your patient."

"But Arturo is, and anything that has the potential to adversely affect your friendship will definitely affect him. Tell me."

I could see he knew I meant it. He took a breath and began. "Well, I hope this is not more of my egocentrism, but...all this utter savagery: what happened to Artie, 9/11, honor killings... my sister, Grace, was a victim of a suicide bombing in Israel when she was a child." He started to continue and froze with his mouth open, the thought inchoate or ineffable or just struggling to be articulated.

"I guess it *is* egocentric, because I somehow relate it to the fact that I always held back in fistfights. There were a lot of those growing up on the border. I don't know...maybe it's just a natural part of growing up. But that time on the river is the only time I felt...that *beast* unleashed." He took a contemplative breath that formed itself into a frown. "How do people live with that? Knowing that they're capable of such...horror?"

I sat back to get a good look at the human specimen before me. Where was I to go with this? *He's right. He's not your patient, Judith.* But how much is his mental health tied up with Arturo's recovery? How much can I reveal about Arturo, his pathology, his state of mind, his prognosis, the course of treatment, without violating my oath? Then again, will my patient's recovery be impaired by my holding back? I'd already crossed a boundary in revealing my own trauma to him. Do I continue breaking—or at least bending—the rules with Jake? If so, to what end?

John said to follow my instincts. They were telling me now to pursue this. I could only hope they weren't leading me astray. I could see Jake was reading my ambivalence. It looked like he had a question burning to be asked. "What do you want to know, Jake?"

"I…" Again he hesitated, boring into me with a look at once inquisitive and familiar. "The way you said that I wasn't alone. It seemed…I mean I got the feeling that it was based on more than just professional observation. It's none of my business, it's just…" He threw up his hands in a shrug of retreat. "Well, it's none of my business."

*Here we go.* "No, it's not," I said, with a *however* implied that he might not have perceived. He nodded slightly and lowered his eyes. "But…you've been more open with me than most of my patients. You've taken a lot of risks, Jake. A lot of risks. So the answer is, yes, it's more than what I've observed."

Now it was my turn to take a breath, figure out how much I could tell and how I would tell it. Having gotten to know Jake over the preceding months—well, over a year now—I knew I could count on his discretion. I think I actually felt that from the first time we spoke on the phone. And nothing since then has given me reason to doubt it. Still, I was breaking all the rules—or at least some major ones. But then, a unique situation always calls for a reevaluation of those rules. Desperate times, as they say.

I was inclined to start at the end rather than the beginning. "Jake, you say you don't know how to live with the beast in you—or even with the knowledge that that beast exists. My greatest regret in life is repressing that beast. I was raped—raped twice actually—once by a pack of animals in high school and the second time by myself… because I did *nothing*."

I could see the regret and embarrassment for pushing me to relate my story. But now that I'd started, it came like a tidal wave. "Yes, I'd invited them over. Yes, it would have been 'he said, she said.' But at least I would have done *something*. At least I would've acknowledged my own humanity, my own right to make my own choices and be treated with dignity—and held those who violated those rights accountable. At least I could've stood up and said, 'This was done, and it was wrong! It deserves to be redressed!'

"It's my having done nothing that still tortures me. I'm sure it was that that really made me retreat into a shell—that had such disastrous consequences for my family.

"Yes, speaking out is different from actual deadly force. But do you think I wouldn't castrate those animals if I had the chance?

"And you know what? The world would be a better place if I did. You think that was the only time they struck, that there weren't other victims before...and worst of all, since? There's a maxim we use in this business, principally for women who stay in abusive relationships, but it applies across the board: *The best predictor of future behavior is past behavior.*

"Yes, I know the urge—all too well. It's a necessary part of us, Jake. I say, God bless it. Actually, you reminded me of the necessity the last time we met, when you cited that aphorism of Edmund Burke's. And sometimes the only way to stop evil is with violence. Only violence stopped Hitler. Only the threat of violence stopped Stalin—and didn't stop him as soon as it should have—before an estimated twenty to one hundred million people were slaughtered under his orders. The list goes on and on."

"I suppose it still applies today."

"Yes. It does. A psychopath doesn't change. You can't grow a conscience. I wish you could. But however much I wish, however firmly I believe, won't make it true."

"'Reality exists.'"

"Exactly."

There followed a long period of silence. Jake closed his eyes for a second. It struck me as an effort to absorb the information, to assimilate it into his philosophy of life. He took a deep breath and exhaled a formidable sigh. An understanding passed. I kept my eyes riveted to his. Finally his returned to mine, a decision made. He stood. "Thank you, Judith."

"Again, Jake, thank you."

12/13/02 (personal log):

As I approached John's office door, I was stopped dead in my tracks. Was that him singing to himself? I realized that my shock was that I actually used to hear it all the time but hadn't in…years, it seemed. It was such a joy to hear that I hesitated to interrupt it. So I just stood at the door for a few moments smiling to myself, wondering what on earth could have happened. Finally, there was a pause in the concert. If I know he's by himself, I usually just walk in. But I felt compelled to knock this time.

"Yes, come in, Judith." Apparently his assistant had let him know that I was coming. He'd even seemed to anticipate that I would break the routine and knock. I guess there're few surprises between people who've known each other as long and worked together as closely as we have. But this was certainly one for me.

I had to stop and look around. "Am I in the right place? Did we somehow get a new director while I wasn't looking?" He was still in the process of rearranging his library—actually, just putting up books that had lain in various positions around the room for what seemed like an eternity. I was used to papers covering just the suggestion of a desk and having to clear them off at least one chair to find a place to sit.

There were normally books with Post-it notes strewn through them opened to various pages in numerous positions with personal notes scribbled in the margins. Now, it looked like a picture out of *Good Housekeeping*. There was no four-inch-thick pile of papers atop the shredder waiting to be disposed of. The trash can was actually empty and a few papers neatly placed in stacked trays on his desk.

"Have I stepped into an alternate universe? What have you done with John?"

"Oh, I'm just a post-vacation replacement. Please, have a seat. You actually have a choice of chairs this time, and no need to dig them out of the debris."

"And to what do we owe this miraculous regeneration?"

"To the right prescription from my personal psychiatrist. Melinda and I and two of our kids and grandkids spent an extended vacation on Padre Island. Took my grandchildren fishing, crabbing and just exploring. Even played video games, although I tried to discourage that as much as possible.

"Great. Whad'ja catch?"

"Eh, who remembers? And the day after I got back, I got the initial OK on the HHS grant." He sang, "We're in the money, dah-dah, dah-dah-dah."

"John, that is wonderful. You just look…"

"Like a million bucks? All green and wrinkly?"

It was so wonderful to hear John actually joke that I just laughed out loud. "So we're going to be all right?"

"Oh, better than all right. Aside from the grant, the fund-raiser Elaine Horowitz sponsored was a smashing success. She's got some deep pockets from around the state and even foreign countries interested."

"That's wonderful news, John."

"So let's get down to business. I understand Mr. Cavazos is, or was, undergoing surgery?"

"Underwent, yes."

"Successful?"

"It seems so. He's been in recovery and inpatient PT all this week. Pain's decreased, and mobility's almost back to normal. Of course, he was put back on oxys for pain, and that concerns me.

"Um. Have you visited?"

"Twice. There's been some regression, but not as much as there might have been."

"So…what's been the effect of sharing your own story?"

"I'm pretty sure it's been positive. I think it gave him hope that there's life after trauma. I also shared it with his friend Jake." John raised his eyebrows at that. "Yeah, I know, I know. But we may be losing the calming influence of his fiancée/girlfriend.

"Jake was in a spiritual crisis of some sort. Well, no, *crisis* is too strong a word—*query* or *quest*, maybe. Anyway, whether it was brought on by her withdrawal I don't know, but I do know we can't afford to lose his contribution. That relationship between Arturo and Jake is crucial. You said to follow my instincts. Well, they told me he needed to know that his situation was not unique."

"What was the nature of his, of Jake's, crisis or query? I mean, aside from relationship problems."

I had to think for a moment. "Unusual. What he told me had to do with an incident that occurred when he, Mr. Cavazos and the third party, the one paying the bills by the way, went on a canoe trip in the Big Bend. It was just after they'd graduated from high school. They came close to starving to death, and a fight broke out between him and the third party. He said his impulses were murderous—exaggerated by panic, I presume."

John mulled that over. "Any idea why it's become an issue now?"

"I have a theory. Once I'd restructured my thoughts about my rape, I castrated and killed those animals again and again in my mind. As you know, this case brought up those feelings again. It's a pretty terrifying thing to recognize in yourself. And for me it was just fantasies. I never had the opportunity to act on it. I don't know if Arturo has shared any of his story with Jake, but I don't think he needs to. Jake saw the effects firsthand. And I get the sense that their ties go deeper than just friendship."

"Like...?"

"I'm not sure. Not yet."

"Well...keep me posted."


Meeting with Anabele Volpe:


She walked in with a firm sense of purpose. She was even taller than I'd imagined when talking with her on the phone—a solid, imposing presence. I found her manner of dress interesting. It was of impeccable taste but had some ambiguity in it. The fact that she was of means showed in the white silk blouse with a tasteful adornment that hung sumptuously down the front. Complementing it was a gray skirt and jacket of the finest cashmere. But around her neck and hanging from her ears were the most beautiful malachite and onyx pendant and earrings. They were obviously of Mexican Indian design. The contrast was truly elegant.

She came straight forward to shake my hand when I addressed her. "Ms. Volpe, thank you so much for coming." Her grip was impressive.

"The pleasure is mine, Doctor."

"Please, call me Judith. Shall we sit?" As she did so, the erectness of her posture spoke of an indomitable strength and confidence. While it was apparent that meeting with a therapist was quite a new experience for her, I got the sense that I would not need to be overly delicate. "First let me thank you again for your discretion concerning Mr. Cavazos."

She barely nodded her recognition. "I want to help in any way I can."

"I appreciate that as well. I imagine staying away has not been easy."

The look in her eyes told me in no uncertain terms that that was an understatement. But her answer still had its characteristic restraint. "No."

I hesitated, wondering whether to try to make her feel comfortable first or to immediately tackle the issues in question. She saved me having to make that decision.

"Judith. Let me say to save time that we can get some things out of the way immediately. Yes, I'm married. Yes, I have a daughter that is Artie's. She's with her father—the man she knows as her father—while I'm here. They're very close. What I'm going to do about that, I don't know.

"I know Jake told you that my husband has an import/export business. I've known for a while that the main import is illegal drugs. I also recently found out, although I'd had my suspicions for a while, that it was my husband who betrayed Artie to the Zetas. He did it for two reasons: to clear the path to me and to become a major distributor for them.

"My knowing that puts me in danger. I left my daughter with him so he wouldn't be suspicious. But my concern above all others is for her. If it means staying with him, then that's what I'll do. He has money, power and influence. He has a whole...*bufete*...law firm at his disposal. I have money of my own but not nearly the kind he can throw around.

"Worst of all, I'm not a citizen. I don't even think our marriage is legal. I don't think he would hurt me, but if the organization he works for finds out what I know about them...Well, you can imagine. That's another reason I may have to stay with him...again, for my daughter."

*Wow!* I was knocked speechless. Obviously there would be no need for delicacy with this woman. But what complications to the situation! Knowledge of them would send my Pt reeling. I was momentarily stunned. "Uh...does Jake know any of this?"

"No, I'm pretty sure he doesn't. He shouldn't; that kind of knowledge is dangerous. I'm even worried for Artie's sake. The Zetas know he escaped. They know where he is. They're animals, Doctor—eh, Judith. They hate unfinished business; Artie is unfinished business for them. Whether it's important enough for them to possibly expose themselves here in the US by going after him I don't know.

"I do know they eliminate threats and competition here; they just try to be more discreet than in Mexico. I even worried about sharing this with you. But I made sure everyone thought I was going to visit family by flying to Aguagria and then coming up here in a car rented under the name of a family friend."

My mind was racing with possibilities at the same time as I was struck dumb. I started grasping at straws. "Anabele...can you not go to the authorities?"

"As an illegal alien?"

Boy, this was so complicated. How could someone be in such an inescapable corner? "You couldn't make a deal? Maybe share some of the information you have in exchange for citizenship?"

"Before I'm killed? Before my daughter is taken away? Before I'm arrested for being here illegally? The cartels have a whole system inside the prisons."

Now I was truly at a loss. Again, the personal problems of my Pt's circle, even if he didn't know they existed, were gravely complicating his treatment.

She seemed to recognize my dilemma. "Judith, the only reason I'm telling you all this is to let you know that Artie's not completely safe. Your job is not to fix my predicament. I'll deal with that. We're here about Artie.

"You asked me about Jesús. I promised Artie's sister, Griselda, that I would never tell anyone. And I haven't…till now. But I know it's something you have to know. I can only hope you'll be very careful with it. Jake tells me he has a lot of confidence in you."

"That confidence is mutual—with him and now with you."

She just paused a second with an implied acknowledgment of my expression of faith. "Artie never told me the story of his family's crossing—even though I told him mine. I had to find out from Griselda. I gave her my word I would never share it. I knew never to press Artie about it—to not even mention it. Over time, I even felt an unspoken promise to him to keep it to myself. Griselda and I never even spoke about it after that one time. But I got her permission to share it with you.

"Artie is a very private person. He didn't even tell me about his plan with Jake and their other friend to save his uncle's family. I don't know…maybe he had a…*presentimiento?*"

"Premonition."

"I think he just always had that reflex: to protect, to care. He always opened the door for me and helped me on with my coat. He knew I could take care of myself, but it was just how he was." She had to pause for a moment, and I was surprised to see her eyes moistening. It was like watching a massive stone wall disintegrate. But they were fierce tears—tears of iron and flint. "And I loved him that way."

As she paused, I could see a determination sweep away the tears. Her jaw set as she inhaled with a shudder. "Anyway, what I found out from Griselda was that when the family crossed, she and Artie had a little brother. His name was Jesús. Chuy, they called him. It was always understood that Artie looked out for him. His parents didn't even need to tell him. He just always did from the time Chuy was born. Even though Artie was her little brother, he even took care of Griselda, she told me. I guess he was just born with that way about him. You know why they had to leave Mexico?"

"Well, Jake told me there was a legend..."

"It's true. He killed a policeman that was trying to rape her. Another thing I knew never to ask about." The barest pained smile flashed across her face. It spoke of such a profound love that I felt a catch in my throat.

She took a breath and continued. "But you need to know about Jesús. When they were crossing the river, Artie was carrying him. Griselda said the two of them were behind her and her parents. When they were little more than midway, they heard him cry out. He was stuck in the mud some distance back. It was like quicksand—it sucked him down. He'd pull one leg out and then sink down with the next step. He'd lost his grip on Chuy, and the child was way too young to swim. He went under and downriver. Artie finally pulled free and went after him. His father did too. They spent hours trying to find him. Finally, Artie's father had to drag him away. Griselda said he fought his father like a tiger.

"I always thought that's why he was so close to Jake. Jake was like his brother. He was always very protective without ever being obvious about it. I mentioned it once. He didn't answer, didn't say anything. I could tell it was uncomfortable for him. That's what made me think he associated him with Jesús. And I know Jake looked up to him.

"I was kind of surprised he let Jake help him with his plan to rescue his uncle. But then, his aunt and uncle and cousins were family. Family was so important to Artie. Where we grew up, family was all you had.

"After the rescue attempt, I thought he was dead. We all thought so." She let out a silent sigh that rent my heart. "How is he doing, Doctor?"

Boy. After what she'd disclosed, I felt horrible about shutting her out. But we take an oath for a reason. "Anabele, as Arturo's doctor there is very little I can legally and ethically share—with anyone. But I can't tell you how much you've helped me or how much my having this knowledge will help me help Arturo."

"It's so strange to hear him called that—although I did myself sometimes. But I was the only one. It's like you're talking about a different person."

"Well, actually, in some sense I am. My job is to help him construct a new identity. And I'd very much like you to be a part of that new person he becomes. But we've got to take things a step at a time. Too much all at once could overwhelm him—especially with so many complications. And not just with you."

I expected her to ask me who else I was referring to, but she didn't.

"I understand that, Judith."

"And I also appreciate your understanding and restraint, Anabele. Under different circumstances, I know you'd be a great addition to Arturo's circle of support. Someday I'm sure you will be."

I saw a cloud pass over her. It looked like she had a *presentimiento* of her own. "What is it, Anabele?"

She looked up at me and just gently shook her head. "No, nothing…nothing." There was a momentary pause. I could tell how painful it was for her to stay away from Arturo. I was also worried about the danger she was in. I was angry at not being able to do anything about it. I think she sensed it. I think it was to save me discomfort that she stood.

"Well, I need to go. If there's any other way I can help, please let me know. You have my secure e-mail. And, by the way, there's no *e* on the end of my name. I know everybody, including me, pronounces it like the Anglo name, but it's really," (and she gave it the Spanish pronunciation this time), *"Anabel."*

"Oh...oh, *Anabel*. OK." I rose, and we shook hands. I felt there was a warmth in it that wasn't there before. "Take care of yourself, Anabel. And again, thank you *so much* for all you've done."

"You can pronounce it Annabelle. It's what I'm used to. And you're welcome. I wish..." She shook her head with a bitter smile of self-irony. It said *wishes will not change facts*. And she quietly exited.

After she left, I had the queerest feeling. Of course I was grateful to her for clearing up the identity of at least one Jesús. This was huge. It actually brought on a feeling of exhilaration—it would give me an in to what is perhaps Arturo's most central point of pathology. There was also worry for Anabel, of course, and for her daughter. There were so many feelings tumbling over each other. It made them difficult to identify.

But I was startled to find anger in the mix. Of course, there was frustration with feeling so helpless about Anabel's predicament. But something told me there was a more personal resentment.

I tried to analyze the different elements of Anabel's story. With Arturo having such a powerful sense of responsibility for others, the loss of Jesús—and the fact that he might blame himself for it—would be excruciating. But doing a self-analysis, I determined that that wasn't the source of the odd feeling. It wasn't connected to Jesús. It was my reaction to finding out that the legend was true—that Arturo had killed a man who was trying to rape his sister. How old could he have been? To kill a fully grown man with a machete...?

It was at that moment that I clearly saw the source of my own unresolved pathology. All this time I thought I'd only withdrawn from Chacho as part of the "just" world I'd lost faith in—rejected. But no. No! I blamed him! And some part of me had to know how unfair that was.

I marched straight to John's office.

Meeting with John:

As soon as I entered, John knew this was a crisis. He let me pace in silence. He let me vent. He let me cry without a whiff of judgment—without a word or even a facial gesture giving away what he was thinking.

All my feelings about Chacho came spewing forth on top of each other: the love...I did love that little tyke...the hate, the guilt, the anger at him for what he did to my mother, to me, to the memory of our father.

Finally, I came to the crux. "John, I feel such guilt! It was my not being there that destroyed my baby brother! Because I blamed him. He was just a boy! And...and...I'm even angry at him now for making me feel that way!" He waited a moment as I stopped in front of his window. "How can I restructure my thinking about that?"

He waited a moment. I was sure it was to give me time to gain some nominal control. Then he quietly began the process. "That's a good question. Imagine a patient came to you with that cognition. How would you do it?"

The suggestion stopped me dead in my tracks. He was at once forcing me from unbridled emotion and into objectifying my case— considering it rationally. Damn him to hell! What came out of me was more complaint than statement. "I don't...*know!* Oh, John, I can't."

"You *do* know. And you must. What's the first thing you'd do?"

"Oh..." I stamped my foot, angry at myself as well. "I'd...let the patient express her feelings...yes, like you've been doing for the past..." I glanced at the clock above the door. "Oh, John, it's late on a Friday. You want to get home. What's Melinda going to...?"

"Judith, you can't read my mind; you have no idea what I want. I have my energy and optimism back because of the vacation you prescribed for me. Not only I but Melinda and my son and daughter are eternally grateful for that advice. I can now return the favor, and you're not going to deny me that pleasure. Now, where would you start?"

I turned from the window to look at him. "Oh, John, you're—"

"*Where*...would you start?"

I sat on the chair next to the window in the corner of the office. I closed my eyes with my head down, took a breath and exhaled in halting shudders. I knew John was right, and it was infuriating that he was. I took a few more breaths in the hopes that I could center myself. But I was so angry at having to do so that I started through gritted teeth, resenting John with every word I uttered. It came out like I was reading from a primer: "What reasons might there be for believing I *was* responsible?"

"And they are…?"

"He had no one else."

"Is that true?"

"John, my mother was so busy. She was so tired when she got home."

"And so it was your responsibility? How old were you?"

"Fifteen."

He let that hang a moment. "Any other reasons you might be responsible?"

"I pulled away from him, John."

"Only from him?"

"No. But I didn't have to blame him."

"Did you blame only him?"

This made me look up. *No*, I thought. I blamed the whole world. I hated a world where people could do such things…where they could get away with such things. I hated God for permitting such things to happen. I hated my mother for not being there. I hated my father for dying.

"Judith, I want you to imagine having a patient: fifteen years old—in today's world that would be more like twelve. She's been sheltered, almost isolated. She's extremely close to her father and loses him at that age. Then out of nowhere, she's brutally raped, fatherless for a little over a year, basically motherless as well now, with a child suddenly dumped in her lap. She has no time to mourn that loss of innocence, that sudden knowledge of evil in the world—and of being a *victim* of that evil.

"Then, she has to take on the responsibilities of caring for a child. There's no time to care for herself. She has no support, no one to guide her away from blaming herself, no one with whom to share her grief, the depth of her pain, her loss of faith in people, in herself, in God. Imagine the patient, *not yourself*.

"Now, if that patient told you *she* felt guilty for not being there for her little brother, for blaming him even, what would you say? No, what would you *think*?

When the facts were presented to me, all I could do was cry my eyes out. I cried for Chacho. I cried for myself as well, for the naïve child I was who had her girlhood ripped away. I mourned that girl I was, placed in the position of sister and surrogate mother when all her emotional resources were just...gone.

And John let me cry. I felt him mourning with me. Those tears purged such pain, such loss, such anger. I must've cried for...I don't know how long. I couldn't look up until I'd let loose the last tear I had in me. I stood and looked out the window for a long time. John just waited. Finally I had some kind of control. All the anger turned into sadness. "Thank you, John."

"You know you're not out of the woods yet, right?"

"I know. I have group tomorrow."

"Thank God for that."

"Yeah, thank God for that."

12/16/02 (personal log):

As soon as I got home Friday night, Donald knew something was up. I had a suspicion Jonathan did too. I just latched onto Donny to keep from floating away into empty space.

"Hey, you okay?"

I just held on. When Jonathan came in the kitchen, I pulled him in and held on to the two extraordinary men in my life as tight as I could. Somehow they both knew to just hold me...not ask any questions, just hold on. Funny, most any other kid would be scared if he saw his mother clinging to him that way, not saying anything, just holding on. It's supposed to work the other way around. Well, I guess he's too old for that now.

I'm so lucky John was still at the clinic, fortunate that he was able to give me some perspective, talk me out of dangerous self-blame. Because of that, my embrace of my guys was more determined than desperate.

Donny suggested we go out to dinner, even though I could see he'd already started it. There was mozzarella and parmesan ready to be grated, onions chopped, spinach at the ready. I only had to think for a moment. "No, sweetie. I want to stay here tonight...just the three of us. I'll cook the pasta. Let's all three of us make dinner, can we?"

"Of course."

"Sure, Mom. I'll get started on the salad."

We had a wonderful evening. Later I found out that Jonathan had canceled plans he'd made to go study with a friend that night. I think it was such a delight, so special, because it was nothing special. We were just a family enjoying each other's company. We talked and laughed all through dinner. Donald told me about the new building he's designing and the team of engineers and contractors working on it. All of them excited about it, apparently.

Jonathan told us about the trend he's started at school. It seems that the electronic cigarettes he's finally changed to are becoming the cool "in thing." He did a few impressions of his teachers—nothing *too* disrespectful, thankfully.

Then we watched a movie. Owing to the season, we watched *It's a Wonderful Life*. It's amazing that as many times as I've watched that movie, it never seems to get old. Those two scamps made fun of me when I cried at the end. But it was such gentle teasing. It just reminds me of what a wonderful life I have—what a privilege it is to have these two guys in it.

Family life nowadays is so different from what it was when I was a child. My parents never shared any of their problems or conflicts with me—certainly not with Chacho. I suppose it was just the culture of the time. Then, in so many ways my parents were throwbacks. Things were already changing, but they were older, from a different era. Their idea was that kids needed to be sheltered from adult responsibilities. They shouldn't know that their parents have insecurities, worries, heartaches. Might I have been more prepared for the world if they hadn't so protected me from its realities? I wonder.

Jonathan had a lot of anger as a child—oppositional, prone to temper tantrums. Oh, I was so worried about him then. Was it a reaction to the distance in me? Was it my fear of being close...resentment at having to mother Chacho? Just being plain unprepared? And then again, how much of it was organic, his simple constitution?

Somehow he seems to have grown out of it. I'm sure a lot of the change was Donald's work. He was always firm but patient. Thank God for that. It helped me be less reactionary myself, less prone to desperation, to panic. It seemed the more I took those tantrums in stride and responded with time-outs and reason, the less severe they became. Would it have been easier if I'd quit work and stayed home? Oh, the dilemma of every mother. It was such a blessing that Donny could do so much of his work at home.

That night, when Donny and I got ready for bed, he held me close and without saying a word made it clear he was ready to listen. I told him everything. I suppose I violated patient confidentiality, but he couldn't have understood how the issue of Chacho came up so dramatically if I hadn't. Of course, I didn't use any Pt names. And he understands how crucial that confidentiality is.

It's amazing to me how Donald knows to just listen—without trying to fix anything—to just listen and be there. When I'd finished, I could tell he was tentative about any kind of intimacy beyond holding me. But he didn't need to be. After that kind of purgation, I craved it. I think he did too—he just wasn't sure I'd be ready after all the feelings I'd gone through. So I initiated things. And oh, did he respond! It was the perfect climax (pun intended) for such a day. And afterward we just held and stroked each other. He was so tender. I felt like I was in the coziest cocoon, safe and warm and protected from all my self-recriminations, floating on a cloud of pure, unadulterated peace.

My group met the next day, and for the first time I was truly eager to share. I even asked to speak first. As I suspected there would be, there were some who didn't understand my feelings of guilt. Interestingly, it was those who struck me as the angriest. Is it that anger interferes with the ability to empathize? Do you have to acknowledge your own sorrow before you can tolerate others'? Or is it the lack of the ability to empathize that makes you so angry? Do they feed on each other? But even from those, there was support, however qualified or just uncomfortable.

John was right—I wasn't out of the woods yet. But I felt I was on my way. Recognizing all of the subtleties and confronting the source of my guilt over Chacho was like lancing a boil: if you don't get at the root and treat it carefully afterward, it can recrudesce. I'll have to continually attend to it. I'll have to accept the help of my community and always rely on it.

I also found that sharing the way I did allowed me in large measure (at least for that session) to actually listen to my fellow members—to listen as a sister and less like a therapist. That in turn made me feel even more a member myself. I felt more comfortable there than I ever had. I think it will be easier from now on. But I'll have to remember that there is a cost...that these progressions depend on taking risks, on doing uncomfortable things. Humph, that's something I tell my patients all the time. "Doctor, cure thyself!"

I found out today that Mr. Cavazos's orthopedic surgeon scheduled a follow-up appointment on the seventeenth in the afternoon. I have two other patients in the morning, so this means I will only see him one last time before the holidays. It strongly suggests I not try to make any new inroads. Rather, I will have to prepare him for spending his first post-trauma Christmas alone—well, his first while in therapy.

Thanksgiving by himself was difficult enough. But he has told me that the Christmas season was a much bigger occasion in his family. He has my number in case of a crisis, but given his personality, I fear it more likely he will turn to painkillers and alcohol than his therapist.

Of course, Jake has promised to maintain contact with him and visit for an extended period—during which I hope their planned fishing trip comes to fruition. Doing normal things with people he's close to is the best defense against that substance abuse—probably even more so than therapy.

I'd only had two opportunities to meet with him during his surgery and convalescence. And he was aided in his constriction by pain medication, so they weren't particularly fruitful. And then such a long hiatus... I tried to suggest a meeting on that Wednesday and Friday, but he'll probably need Wednesday to recuperate from physical therapy, and he flatly refused a Friday session.

And now, when we were making some progress...now, when I feel so much of my own pathology is on the mend.

How much do I still associate him with Chacho? John said to keep reminding myself that he's not. Now with that last piece of pathology associated with my little brother acknowledged, I can feel myself separating them.

They say you can't save every puppy in the pound. I have to be realistic about how much I can do. But it's so frustrating to have made progress and then watch it fade.

Then again, the last interruption in treatment actually saw some positive effects. Perhaps that will be the case this time. I can only hope. Yes, if Jake comes through...if only Dolores could still be contributing. But then being away from therapy for a while, doing normal, enjoyable activities, having some semblance of a normal life even for a while, could be therapeutic. Perhaps for both of us.

Yes, Judith. Let him go fishing, and hopefully do some other normal, enjoyable things. You go skiing with your family, maybe do some shopping together (as much as my guys hate it! Well, not so much if it's for a limited time), maybe even spend a couple of days with Aaron and Tessa (maybe they can come to San Antonio?). That might do us all some good.

December 19, 2002. Session with Pt Arturo Cavazos (1179A):

I was expecting some regression owing to the extended interruption of therapy. I'd met with him only twice while he was in the hospital. They had been mainly maintenance visits. The hiatus had kept us from starting to address the more horrific parts of his trauma.

During one of my visits, I renewed my suggestion that often patients find it less threatening to write out a narrative before trying to recount it orally. On that occasion, I provided a notebook for the purpose. If he decided to do it (and I stressed that it had to be his decision), I suggested it be only one episode, one memory, to start with.

As he was able to recount more and more, it would help piece together the chaotic sights, sounds, sensations of the trauma into a more coherent narrative. Its coherence would tend to detoxify it. This, in turn, would aid our being able to discuss it verbally and start us on the path to its inclusion in the construction of a new self. He had reluctantly agreed to try—a reluctance I inferred only from his blank expression. I'd asked him to call me if intrusions occurred as a result. I wasn't surprised that I never received a call. I was fairly certain it was not because there were none.

I was, however, somewhat surprised at the extent of the renewed constriction. Pt was almost as aloof and affectless as during our initial sessions. However, I was heartened to see that he'd brought the spiral notebook with him. He held it folded in one hand, down against and almost hidden behind one leg. When he sat, he gripped it tightly in both hands, curled up and hanging down between his legs. It was as though he held his nakedness in those hands. If he actually followed through on the suggestion, it would go a long way toward explaining the recurrent symptoms. I would need to reestablish a sense of safety.

Until the break in our meetings, I'd been quite hopeful at the tentative piecing together of at least the lesser parts of the trauma narrative. There was even a halting initiation of the mourning process. But I have to expect these sorts of reversals. Recovery is not a linear process.

I still remember John's description of it when I was just starting work. He characterized it more as a spiral: issues thought to be addressed and resolved tend to recur. The therapist could only hope that each time an issue is readdressed it will integrate itself more fully into a coherent narrative. These will be the raw materials for the construction of a new self, integrating the trauma into all the other elements of Pt's ego structure—that is, life pre- and post-trauma. I must remind myself (and Pt) that it will be a lifelong process.

I must also be constantly aware that my task as therapist is to be disinterested and neutral. There can be no personal agenda or "saving" the patient. It is my responsibility to always keep in mind that my role is to help, advise and support the recovery the *Pt himself* is striving to achieve.

Since the central experience of psychological trauma is disempowerment and disconnection, I must empower Pt to direct his own recovery. No intervention that takes power away from a Pt can hope to be successful. While this can only take place with the creation of new connections—that is, reintegration into the (or *a*) community— it can only occur if the Pt feels safe in his environment.

I believe that my recognition of resentment at Chacho's passivity will contribute to the fulfillment of those objectives. It is hoped that, as a result, countertransference will be less of an issue. It rather astonishes me that I am still prone to the Cinderella complex (that is, being rescued by the handsome prince). (Is that part of my countertransference? Do I imagine that if Chacho were Arturo, I might have been saved?) Perhaps it is a remnant of my sheltered pretrauma youth. I was always my father's "little princess."

At any rate, I must also keep in mind that my own ego integration will never stop being a work in progress. I have to be on guard to avoid identifying Pt with my poor, hapless little brother. (Should I still be thinking of him that way?) I must also be on the lookout for any residual fantasies of replacing one with the other. But I do feel that that task will be facilitated (with the help of John and my group) by that insight.

Priority number one: reestablish Pt's feeling of safety.

"Welcome back, Arturo. How're you feeling?"

"I'm all right. You?"

His reticence and lack of affect were apparent. (Were they perhaps covering resentment? Hostility? He was almost flippant.) I remembered that any new stressor can cause the recurrence of symptoms. If he *had* written out a part of his trauma story, which seemed likely, that could explain the distrust—even resentment—of me in suggesting what was certainly a painful exercise. Of course, it could be something else: a trigger that reminded him in some substantial way, or possibly some new unsettling information.

It is absolutely essential to remember that the victimizer is ever present in the mind of the patient. He was omnipotent, and he demanded (and still demands) silence. I sensed in this instance a renewed transference to me as therapist: I had reverted in Pt's mind to being a figure of authority and therefore dangerous, suspect. I had to remind him that, as Pt, he was in control; *he* was the authority. So I let the silence continue, even though I'm sure that, in itself, was stressful.

Almost completely (but not quite) masking a touch of impatience, he finally spoke. "Aren't you gonna ask me anything else?"

"Arturo, this goes the way you want it to. I'm just here to help."

He hesitated. I could feel the resentment. "You think silence is helping me?"

I considered how to handle this, worked my way around to the truth. "I honestly don't know, Arturo. Would you like to tell me what *you* think?"

"I think this is a waste of time."

Though this was said with basically no affect, it felt like a provocation. *Do not react, Judith.* "Well, I know very well it can feel that way. Frustration is an inherent part of the process."

*Make sharing an act of courage.* "You know, Arturo, it takes a lot of guts to talk about such horrific experiences. Actually, to talk about one's feelings at all takes courage. I think that anyone who has the heart—and the survival skills—to live through what you did can do anything he sets his mind to. All I'm suggesting is for you to let me help guide you through a process that *you* control, that *you* initiated and I'm pretty sure *you* want to complete. I'm just a witness. And you know my own trauma.

"Let me say that I've felt anger, even hatred, for the people who did this to you. But not when we're together. In order to help, I *have* to stay objective.

"But I don't think you want them to win. They want you to be silent. They want you to give up. They want to have destroyed your life. That way they're still in control."

I could tell this resonated. There was fear and blind hatred lurking behind those steel-cold eyes. An epic battle was going on inside him. It was a positive sign that he was able to contain it without dissociating. I could feel the temptation in me to shelter him from such a painful process—from remembering such horror. I waited…and waited.

Finally, I sensed a renewed self-control in him. And I felt he was still here with me. "I notice you brought the notebook I gave you in the hospital." He wouldn't even look down at it.

Again I was faced with opening up a process that would be interrupted by the holidays. But I have openings tomorrow. I could even meet Monday before Aaron and Tessa arrive. I could make time after Christmas. It had to be his decision to go forward. He did bring it with him; that might indicate a desire to share.

"Let me just ask you, Arturo. Would you *like* to share what you've written? I can meet with you tomorrow to follow up. We could also meet Monday, even Saturday—all three days, should that be necessary."

Finally he looked back at me and then down at the notebook. His fear of opening it emanated outward like a tear in space. But I also sensed that he was going to make himself do it. Was it out of defiance? If so, I believe that would be a very positive step: to get beyond their authority, to establish his freedom from their power.

First he slowly unfolded it and held it down and away from him. He started to tremble as he pulled back the cover. Sweat formed at his temples—so soon. Thank God we still had a good hour to go. His voice shaking, he began, "I hear the tap, click...tap, click...tap, click. Faint at first and then growing louder, closer."

I had an impulse to ask about that sound, but I knew better than to interrupt him so soon.

"El Mutilado is coming."

*The Mutilated One? Just listen, Judith.* His body hardened. He gripped the notebook so fiercely that I thought he might rip it apart. I wasn't sure he was actually reading it, his hands were trembling so.

"He has one metal leg below the knee and a piece of metal for a walking stick that would always go 'tap, click' as he came down the hallway. He always paused at the door. I wondered if it wasn't to savor the fear coming from us."

Despite the use of the past tense, I could feel him being transported back there, in the room where they were kept. I decided I could venture a very quiet inquiry. "What do you feel at that moment, Arturo? What do you hear, smell, see?"

"My legs go weak. My stomach turns. It shoots a sickness through my body. Every time El Mutilado comes, it means some new torture. My cousins' cries fill me with hate. Jesús pisses himself."

*Ah, the second Jesús!*

"The smell makes me hate. My uncle cries silently. No. That was an...another time, I think. They took him earlier. I'm not...sure. His brokenness...if I could just get loose, I could kill...so easily. I'm glad my aunt was killed in the firefight. She's protected from the suffering, the torture.

"The door opens. I smell...tar, or oil...hot, like just drained from a hot car."

As I listened, I had another powerful urge to ask about Jesús. This was the first time he'd mentioned him on his own. I must've been right: there was a second Jesús. Could he have imagined his little brother there with him? In his anguish, his desperation, recreated him as a companion?

"Jesús is there?"

"He's just a boy…twelve, thirteen maybe. I tried to protect him, but…"

Ah, he *must* be a separate person, a second Jesús. But Arturo must have identified them. His little brother wouldn't have been much older than this Jesús had he lived.

"Salvadoran." There was then such a shooting pain through him. "Sweet kid. There, in El Salvador, he had the choice of joining a gang or having his family's home burned down, with all of them in it.

"They hopped the freight trains headed *al norte*. All the cars were filled with people fleeing, trying to get here. They're between cars, on the roofs, in open boxcars, hanging from different parts. Some fall. Some are killed; some lose a foot or an arm.

"At different points as they entered Mexico, they were taken prisoner by different cartels. The Zetas got him. They forced his mother and sister into prostitution. They made him a mule and his brother a lookout. They tried to escape."

"Arturo, can you describe El Mutilado…what he looks like, anything he says?" I saw a wave of terror grip him. "Arturo, it's all right if you can't. It's all right. We can come back to that later."

After several breaths, he continued. "He's small—gray hair, white beard. He only has one eye. One side of his face is…it's covered with scar tissue, like he had acid thrown on it. He smells. He smells like onions frying in butter."

*Ah, that's where the onions come into play.*

"He seems…I don't know. He doesn't seem angry or hateful… just like he's doing his job. Like it's routine. Like he'd just as soon be drinking in a cantina with friends."

*The banality of evil,* I thought. I could see the muscles in his legs ripple and lift him slightly off the chair. "What's happening, Arturo?"

"They unchain me from the wall…take me down the hall."

At this point I notice that he doesn't seem to be reading anymore.

"The smell of oil grows stronger. El Mutilado is behind me: 'tap, click'…'tap, click.' The hall is dark…cold cement floor, but I can feel heat coming from the room ahead. As we get to it, the smell is…tar. It smells like roofing tar. We go in. They have my uncle suspended over a huge vat. I can just see over the rim. It's boiling oil. My uncle is screaming, but he's gagged. I try to break free, and I'm cracked on the side of my face with a rifle butt.

"But I'm handcuffed behind my back. Even if I could get to my uncle, what could I do?" He repeats this with such a feeling of disgust and hatred: "What could I do!

"The guards are drunk, ecstasied up. But not El Mutilado. He's completely calm. It's like he's supervising a work crew. There's no feeling at all—no joy, no hate, no regret…nothing.

"He calmly asks what I know about their operation. How did I know about the shipment? Who's informing? Who gave the false tip? He's done everything he can to break me: beat, burned, cut…with all the tools he brings with him: tongs, razors—wires heated and placed around my…electric shocks. If I tell, they could go after my friends, and their friends…family.

"I became a challenge to them. They couldn't stand that there was someone they couldn't break. El Mutilado gives a little nod. They lower my uncle toward the boiling oil. I'd been told by other prisoners that that's what they do to people who betray them: drop them in boiling oil. He's close enough now that his skin starts to burn, his hair. I can see he's soiled himself. The smell…"

Such a look of revulsion.

"Now they want to know more about me. They pull off my uncle's gag. He's told them everything, he says. Finally, he tells them about Jesús…Jesús, my baby brother. Now, they have what they need."

At this point I decide I have to intercede. "Arturo, I need you to keep in mind that this is a memory—that what happened is in the past—that you're here now, in the present, at Sacred Heart Clinic… here with me. *And that you're safe here.* No one can hurt you or anyone you love here. Do you hear me? *You're safe.* But I think it's time to—"

He looked up at me. There was just a moment of vague recognition. Then, that curious gesture with his hands started. With it, a cold, murderous grumble: *"I want to kill them! I'll kill them all!"* The hand rubbing became more frantic, more fierce.

"I know, Arturo. I know. Of course you do. I want to—" *No, Judith, that's over the line!* I wanted him to stop now, but it seemed like he needed to continue...finish something. It's got to be his way, his choice.

"We're walking back down the hallway. I'm almost blacking out. I hear my uncle scream through the door. The most blood-curdling... There's an explosion, a sizzling. Then, it's silent. So deadly silent. The smell catches us. It's the most horrible thing I've ever smelled. All the strength goes out of my legs. I'm suddenly on the floor. They hit me with their rifle butts. I don't feel it. They drag me, kicking and hitting me all the way. I don't remember anything till I wake up...back in our room, chained to the wall."

He was rubbing his hands so hard I was afraid he was going to rub the skin right off. "All right, Arturo. Can you come back to the present now? Could you please look at me? Do you know who I am? Do you know where you are?"

He didn't respond but stared at me as though he was trying to place me. Slowly, ever so slowly, his breathing calmed. The hand rubbing attenuated slightly. Finally, something in his eyes told me he was coming out of the memory.

"You're here at Sacred Heart Clinic, with me, Judith. That's all over, and you're safe now." The back of his left hand was lobster red. Bits of skin were visible on the webbing. "You're safe, Arturo."

He finally looked straight into my eyes. It was such a penetrating stare. It had a frown of curiosity, with a shade of pity. "None of us are safe, Doc. As long as there are people like that in the world, we'll never be safe."

It was a chilling sentiment, said with devastating certainty. It bore into the entrails of an ordered world and exploded it.

Then, it personalized. "At first, I tried to think of how I could save the others. But then, after a while, after the torture, the mutilations, the murders...I finally just wanted to survive." For a moment, I saw a putrid self-disgust overwhelm him. I was afraid he might throw up. "I hate myself for that." He paused again in reflection, the self-revulsion apparent. "Then finally, I didn't want anything. I wasn't. I just wasn't anymore."

It was all I could do to keep myself from just wrapping my arms around him, holding him until the horror had receded to memory. I had the urge to remind him that prisoners of war have the connection of their brothers-in-arms to sustain them—that he had essentially no one. I wanted to say that no human being, no one who's not a god on earth, could have felt differently, could have done better. I wanted to say, "You did the superhuman. No normal person could have done all you did. You have everything to be proud of. Everything."

But I could not. It was the last thing as therapist I should do. It was the last thing he could tolerate. I had to empower him, not infantilize him. I realized that his statement was the beginning of mourning, and I couldn't interfere with it. It was a step in taking responsibility for his own recovery, a moment of self-empowerment.

I decided a neutral therapist might attempt to restructure the conclusion. "Didn't you try to save your uncle?"

"...I suppose."

"What stopped you?"

"They did, by cracking me on the head."

"Uhm. Anything else?"

"I was handcuffed." I could see the pain at his recognition of helplessness.

I tried to deliver this as calmly and rationally as possible. "Arturo, I've had patients who blamed themselves rather than acknowledge their own helplessness. It's an intolerable feeling. And you're a person who's been in command of most any situation. I've had patients who hated themselves for not having superhuman powers. But none of us do. None of us."

From the distant emptiness of his gaze, I knew I'd not heard the worst. My God, what greater horror could there have been? Whatever the case, this was more than enough for now. He was so totally drained I knew he couldn't stand any more.

I decided to use the remaining time to let him reorient himself. "Arturo, what you did today, and writing it down in the hospital, took enormous courage. I can't imagine how painful it must have been. I want you to know that my reaction is pure admiration—astonishment—just at surviving it first and then at recounting it, reliving it.

"And how much you loved your uncle and your cousins is clear as day. It's a tremendous loss. But not nearly as horrible as losing yourself. I think today was a huge step in reclaiming that."

I could see he was reevaluating his self-condemnation...considering the others in his life. We needed to follow up as soon as possible. And he needed to know that. "Arturo, you need to rest. But I recommend we see each other tomorrow. Can you come in, say, around ten thirty or eleven?"

He just vaguely, almost imperceptibly, nodded.

"Good. Till then, you have my number. Please don't hesitate to call—any hour, any moment. Will you do that?"

Again, the vacant nod. It would have to suffice.

"Arturo, I know your uncle and family are irreplaceable. But you have a sister who you told me calls you almost every day...a friend in Jake that does the same and visits often. You've also told me that your other friend keeps in touch...as much as he can."

He looked up. It struck me that there was something else, something not of past trauma but of the present. I'd told Carmen not to interrupt if our sessions went overtime. This one definitely was. If I was right about a recent stressor, I concluded that addressing it now might have more than one beneficial effect: it would reorient him to the present and hopefully relieve some of the stress it provoked.

"Arturo, did anything in particular happen over the last few weeks—I mean aside from the time away and recalling the episode you described, writing it down?" A momentary closing of his eyes and a shallow breath made me think I was right. "Is there anything connected with the surgery...your doctors, nurses, physical therapists?"

There was no reaction. "Was there some trigger that reminded you?" Again, nothing.

There was one thing left to consider. "While you were in the hospital, you had visits from several people. Was—?" He looked up at me. It was just a darting glance before he looked away. It told me I'd hit it. "Was it something about Jake's visit or visits? I understand Dolores didn't join him this time. Did it have anything to do with that?" A quick exhalation of air through his nose told me this was part of it. But I got the feeling there was something more.

Finally, he spoke. "I worry about Jake. I mean...I get a feeling that they've put off the wedding indefinitely."

*What an astonishing instinct of care for others.* And how heartening it is that it's still present. "Arturo, I think it's wonderful that you're concerned about Jake. But...could you tell me how Jake's and Dolores's problems make *you* feel?" I was surprised by his response.

"My sister visited, too."

"Yes. Is there some connection there?"

"When she was here, I had the feeling she wanted to tell me something—something she felt she shouldn't."

I waited to see if he'd elaborate on his own. After a moment or two, I decided that I needed to ask. "Do you have any idea what that might have been?"

"I do now, because I asked her. I asked her if she and Anabel, my girlfriend from before, had stayed friends, still kept in touch. I don't know why I thought it was that, but it was. I could tell just from her reaction. I asked how she was. She told me Anabel was married, had a daughter."

"And...how did that make you feel?"

"How did it make me feel? Not much, really. Everybody thought I was dead. I am, pretty much. What would a dead person have to offer anyone?"

That comment confirmed that the regression was still quite severe. I had to contain my own disappointment—it's to be expected. *Neutral, disinterested, Judith.* I tried to keep my tone rational, objective.

"Arturo, being reminded of someone we were once very close to, loved even, can be very disturbing...painful. Especially if we feel we no longer have anything to offer. But tell me this, do you think you give anything to Jake, to Griselda? What was it Dolores said to you... that maybe you don't know yourself? Do you think Jake and Griselda would keep coming, keep calling, keep being involved, if you didn't give them anything in return?"

His expression was a wall of inscrutability. I had to continue. I couldn't leave my patient in this state. "Arturo, let me just say that you're not the first patient I've had that's felt dead—completely dead. There's a certain appeal, a sense of safety, in thinking that way. It's seductive. Because if you're dead, you don't have any feelings. There's no pain, no disappointments. And perhaps most of all in your case, you can't hurt anyone else. If you give up hope, then there's nothing to lose.

"As I told you before, I've been there myself. And I didn't go through nearly what you did. I know that even with the small part you've shared with me. It's not only horrifically painful to dredge up these memories—it takes incredible strength to let yourself feel, to let yourself care again. But I've got a hunch that you know how much you mean to Jake, to Griselda, to your other friend. And you just now expressed concern for Jake. I'd say that's an important step, a milestone even."

I paused for a time to let him absorb the concepts...see if the empathy was registering. A certain setting of his jaw told me it was—at least that it wasn't rejected out of hand. That accomplished, I gauged that some distraction might be in order, something connected that would remind him of his community—that he was part of one. "Jake tells me the two of you are going on a fishing trip over the holidays."

He closed his eyes in pain and shook his head. "I called that off."

*Maintain neutrality.* "Ah. Does Jake know?"

"I told him. But he still talks about it."

*Got to make sure Jake keeps it up; being alone during the Christmas holiday could be disastrous.* "Tell me, Arturo, you think he'd be disappointed if you didn't go?"

He looked up at me. There was a little flash of recognition or maybe suspicion at what I was trying to do. I could see the uncertainty of just how to take my ploy. It wafted from recognition of a feminine manipulation to grudging gratitude for the nudge. I knew the internal battle all too well: ("People *say* they want to be my friend, but it's because they don't know the blackness of my heart.")

Through his andiron constitution, I could feel the desperate need for companionship fighting against the fear of his worthlessness being discovered. I held my breath for the decision. Then, there was the slightest tentative handhold up the abyss of despair. "Yeah, I guess he would."

*Whew, a Hail Mary comes through at the last minute!* Since it worked, I thought I might be able to milk it a little, just to make sure it took hold. "So, you and Jake'll bring me back some of your catch?" I thought I'd done it but needed a little insurance. "My husband loves fresh fish. And he loves to grill. I suspect that men are only interested in cooking if there's danger involved."

Though not a muscle in his face moved, there was just the faintest trace of a smile in his eyes—an opaque ray of sun peeking out from leaden skies. It hung by a fraying thread, but we'd taken a step out of hope's grave.

"Filleted?" I added. And the corners of his mouth crept slightly upward against their will.

December 23, 2002. Follow-up with Pt Arturo Cavazos (1179A):

I was able to contact Jake Kasmareck after the session with Pt Thursday. I urged him to insist on the fishing trip he and Arturo had planned. He heartily agreed. It will serve two purposes: to let Pt know that there is life after trauma and to let him know that there are those who care, people he can depend on. And the last thing he needs is to spend what is for many the most important family holiday completely alone. Consistent connections are a key element of his recovery.

I was pleasantly surprised when Pt showed up the following day, Friday the 20th, for the extra session. His assent to my suggestion had been the barest of nods. We limited references to the narrative of the previous day to how he felt about having revealed it. This was a session for salving the open wound.

Later, as Pt is better able to recount it as a coherent story, so should the shattered bits of his ego inch their way together, forming a more and more solid structure. I must remind myself that I've probably not heard the worst.

This can be the most dangerous phase in the recovery process. As the history of the trauma is revealed, the inevitable consequence is profound grief over the loss. Depending on the level and duration of said trauma, that grief can be crushing. I'm concerned that this will be especially true for a man like Arturo Cavazos, a man so private and self-contained.

Another considerable danger at this point is fantasies of revenge or compensation. I'm almost certain that where this Pt is concerned, the former is the more likely. Revenge fantasies, however, can cause intrusive symptoms much like the original trauma. (I'm acutely aware of this, having experienced it myself.) This can further dehumanize the patient, making him or her feel less capable of forming genuine human connections. And they can never change or compensate for the harm done.

The goal is to transform rage into righteous indignation. That particular feeling is an indication that the patient feels him or herself to be a part of society. It can be an impetus for a positive social response, such as publicly bearing witness, organizing protests or demonstrations or enacting legislation. Which of those might be possible in this case, I'm unsure. But any public effort will in turn increase integration into the community.

It is during the mourning process that the patient is at greatest risk of suicide. Pt has already expressed feeling of being among the dead. The crucial antidote is a kernel of belief in his ability to form loving relationships. Arturo is extremely fortunate (as am I as therapist) to have the connections of friends and family, not to mention the history of strong pretrauma bonds.

I wonder if he ever had the chance to grieve the loss of his little brother. It will be quite a delicate operation to address that issue—if indeed it needs to be. I suspect it does. I must discuss this first with sister Griselda. I hope that, being a more ancient wound, it will be somewhat easier to deal with. I also have a strong suspicion that it's connected to the main traumatic experience.

Concerning the revelations recounted during Thursday's session, I asked Pt if he remembered the details of the story. His response was to be expected: "Yeah" (with an "unfortunately" implied). The aversion was apparent, so I assured him that I was not going to ask him now to retell it or anything like that. I explained that his memory of it, though understandably painful, was actually positive.

"I know it doesn't feel that way, Arturo. But reconstructing the story and remembering it will help us make it just a part—a horrible part—but just a part of your life. It won't define it. Have you had any reactions to having related it to me?"

"I had a nightmare last night. I woke up standing on the bed. I was trying to escape black figures coming after me." As he told me about the dream, I could feel a terror of explosive power. "They were two-dimensional human shapes, like shadows. Whatever they were made of seemed to be bubbling. Fighting them was like fighting something liquid or gas. Whatever I hit them with just went through, and they re-formed around it."

He recounted having to get up and turn on all the lights and the television to remind himself where he was.

"And was that successful?"

"Yeah, after a while and a couple of stiff drinks."

"OK, fair enough. But, Arturo, please remember that you can call me anytime night or day."

"Yeah, I just…thought I could handle it myself."

"OK. Were you able to go back to sleep?"

"Oh, I dozed some in front of the TV."

I considered for a moment his leaving the TV on. That could indicate a greater willingness to connect with the outside world. Perhaps it's a less threatening step on the path toward increasing human connection. "Do you remember what was on television? Did you watch any of it?"

I noted a tinge of uncertainty. "Yeah, I was looking for a weather report. Somehow watching the weather seems to calm me. I try to avoid the news."

"Honestly, so do I."

Another pause. "But I caught a bit of it while I was waiting for the weather." He hesitated. "It seems like we're headed for another war."

I debated whether or not to discuss this. But Pt had brought it up, and showing interest in current events was definitely positive. I judged that as long as we were only considering war in the abstract, it might actually be beneficial. "Yes, it does. What do you think about that?"

He shrugged. "If we were talking about invading Mexico, I'd volunteer in a heartbeat."

"Um, I can imagine."

He regarded me with what looked like a certain curiosity. I was intrigued. I felt like he was considering me as a person and not just as a shrink. If I was right, it would be another positive sign: a sense of other as a whole person, rather than threat or nonthreat. His question and the way he phrased it made me think so even more. "How 'bout you, Judith…" (Ah, using my given name, not *Doc* anymore.) "… what do you think?

Now besides taking an interest in the world, he was asking for another's opinion: a further indication of broadening human connection. I decided to follow the path he'd chosen. "Honestly, Arturo, I'm not sure. Will we be able to bring the one in Afghanistan to a successful conclusion? Are we overextending ourselves? Do we have a right to invade a country that hasn't attacked us? Of course, like in Afghanistan, it's not about conquest—it's about getting rid of dangerous people and groups."

"I can sympathize with that."

"Yeah. The question is, is it justified? I'm more certain in the case of Afghanistan. But the fact that a Nobel Peace Prize winner like Elie Wiesel supports the invasion gives me pause. He's a survivor of the Holocaust. Wrote a book about it called *Night*. I wonder…what if we had invaded Germany at Danzig, at the Rhineland, at the Anschluss, at the Sudetenland? How many lives would have been saved? The families of my parents-in-law might still be alive. You know they're Jewish."

"I wondered. But *Lozano* is Hispanic, right?"

"Oh yes. I come from a very Catholic Latino family. Remember we talked about our parochial schools?"

His brow wrinkled. "We did?"

Interesting that he didn't remember. "Yes, it was early in our time together. That might be why you don't remember. I'm sure things in your mind were more…chaotic back then.

"Anyway, my husband's family has essentially become mine. They treat me like a daughter. Pretty much just adopted me. They lost all their relatives in the Holocaust."

"Oh man. Are they survivors of those camps?"

I could tell Arturo was very interested in my story, and taking an interest in anything, particularly in other persons, is a sign of considerable progress. "No. Both of them were rescued as children, actually. They were from different French families, snuck out of Paris and taken in by Protestant families in a remote, mountainous region called Vivarais-Lignon. When the war was over, or after Allied troops liberated Paris, they went back looking for their families. They were all dead. Murdered."

I could see the associations he was making dance across the furrows of his brow, so I continued. "I don't know. Could we possibly save some Kurdish or Shiite children from the same fate? Is it our responsibility? If not ours, then whose?"

He looked away into the distance. I thought it prudent to let him ponder. It looked like he was trying to unravel the deepest of mysteries, connect disparate questions. Finally his gaze came back to me. "You know, I remember Jake saying something about doing nothing to stop evil in the world."

"Yes, he quoted that to me as well. I don't remember the exact words. It's something like 'Evil thrives or spreads when good men do nothing.'"

"Yeah, that's it." He thought for a long while, seeming to consider the implications. Then he gently, distractedly nodded his head. "That's it."

12/30/02 (personal log):

On balance, the Christmas holiday has been a wonderful opportunity to get some distance and some relief from the pathologies I deal with day in and day out. Aaron and Tessa's visit was all too short but so enjoyable. It reminded me how very fortunate I am to have married into Donny's family—now, my family.

We had a wonderful traditional Christmas dinner. Tessa helped me prepare it, and as we did, we had a great opportunity to talk and get to know each other even better. She seemed to sense that I needed it.

She told me a little about life in France before the war. Her family actually celebrated Christmas, although certainly not as a religious holiday. Her memories were somewhat sketchy since she was still so young. But she did remember a pastry that her mother and two aunts made for dessert. She'd forgotten the name of it but did recall that it was the part that she particularly looked forward to. "Oh, it was so sinfully rich," she rhapsodized. "I wouldn't dare make it today. It would clog Aaron's arteries so much I could be tried for murder!" Then, mischievously, she added, "Say, that's an idea."

Fortunately it wasn't terribly cold the next day, so we went for a stroll on the Riverwalk before they flew back to Orlando. It's amazing how we all enjoy each other's company. Even Jonathan never ran out of things to say. I was so happy that he never seemed bored with all these old people.

As a matter of fact, he and his grandfather gabbed like old buddies. I was somewhat surprised at Jonathan's knowledge of history, not to mention his interest in Aaron's personal story. It seems he had to do a report for history class and was trying to decide on what. I think he's chosen his topic.

Aaron and Tessa described what a change it was to try to integrate into families that were so reserved and undemonstrative. Even with their own children, there were almost no displays of affection. And the few that occurred were very restrained.

They told us how they had to hide in the woods sometimes, even in the dead of winter, when German occupation forces or French collaborators came looking for them. Tessa told us how she had been taken to the Swiss border by a *passeur* but how they had to turn back and return to Vivarais-Lignon.

The next day Jonathan, Donny and I made the short jaunt to Ski Apache in New Mexico. We'd considered Canada, but having only three days, we decided to go close to home and have more time for skiing. The first day was ideal, just above freezing, a bare breath of wind and crisp as a crouton, with sun screaming hallelujah. We all went nonstop till late in the afternoon. Oh, was I sore! But so satisfied!

The next day was a battleship-gray-sky day. Only the suggestion of a sun occasionally peeked through rolling pillows of charcoal and silver. The wind gusted temperamentally, raising clouds of white powder that twinkled whenever a ray of sun broke through the gloom.

Donny and I eventually loosened up to do a few runs. Jonathan, of course, took to the slopes without a trace of stiffness. Actually, I think my favorite part was watching him snowboard. He is so graceful, so accomplished. (Not that I'm biased or anything.) But oh, how it scares me when he does acrobatics—as beautiful as it is.

We got back with an extra day to rest and recharge. Today I am ready to take on the world.

December 30, 2002. Meeting with Jake Kazmareck:

When he came in, I sensed a question in his handshake. It wasn't so much a question for me. It was more a note of determination with a bit of wonder at its core. There was concern, but it didn't strike me as sadness or even discouragement. It was more akin to curiosity, an uncertainty that he could trust it (whatever *it* was).

He came in with a small Styrofoam cooler.

"Is that my fish?"

"That's your fish, gutted, cleaned and filleted. I'd frozen them, but they're just on ice now, defrosting. So it'd be best to have them tonight."

"Thank you, Jake. That is so thoughtful. My husband's expecting them."

"Hey, we aim to deliver."

"So...? How'd it go?

"It was good. It was good." I waited for the complication, the qualm. I could feel there was one. "We fished all morning. It was a little chilly, but we went prepared. We talked about old times. I tried to keep the conversation on some of the funnier things we pulled at school, some of the adventures we had. Artie seemed to enjoy it or at least be okay with it."

"That's good." There was a lull. He just looked at me, almost inviting me to ask. "What's the qualifier, Jake?"

"Well...the really good thing was that there were actually three of us. The other member of our trio joined us for a while."

"Ah, the one that's footing the bills here?"

"Yes."

"Uh-huh. Wasn't that a little risky?"

He looked at me with a kind of benign suspicion, as though he wondered how much I knew—if I'd realized who the third party was.

I couldn't afford to waste any time playing games. "The answer is yes. I've figured out who the anonymous companion is." I could feel a relaxation come over him with the news. He actually breathed a sigh of relief. I surmised that he actually wanted me to know but didn't want to be the one to break the vow of silence. "Don't worry, Jake. Your secret's safe with me."

"Does anyone else know?"

"Not that *I've* told. Why did you want me to know, Jake? You did want me to know, didn't you?"

"Yes. I did."

It must be an involved situation. He hesitated, taking a deep breath that he exhaled contemplatively, his upper lip bitten in concentration. I was intrigued. Jake had been so forthcoming, even concerning his personal life.

As I thought about that, it suddenly struck me that he hadn't mentioned Dolores in a while. I was so hoping—for his sake, certainly, but chiefly for my patient's—that they could work things out. Dolores seemed to have such a positive effect…on both of them. But the kind of traumatic event she went through has to have residual effects. I do hope she can find someone to help her with it. Eventually, perhaps I might be able to. I doubt that knowing Jake would affect my objectivity.

"The reason is rather complicated, Judith. As governor, Connors is kept informed on the major drug routes and traffickers in the state. He insists on being briefed by the attorney general. It turns out that one of the major traffickers is apparently Anabel's husband, Enrique Volpe. Quique, they call him." He paused, expecting this to be quite a bombshell.

I wasn't quite ready to reveal anything Anabel had told me. "Uh-huh."

Slightly bemused by my reaction—or lack of it—he just continued. "To add to the…*mess*, Anabel recently made contact with Connors's wife, Andie. They'd gotten to be pretty close friends back when they were going out with Artie and Connors. I guess they lost touch after Artie…well, we all thought he was dead.

"When Anabel called, Andie had the feeling that there was something on her mind besides wanting to renew their friendship. In the course of reminiscing, Anabel started asking a lot about Artie— about how he was now…if he was safe…if Connors could offer some protection."

"Protection from what?"

"She wouldn't say. But according to Connors, Quique is the main trafficker for the Zetas across the eastern and midwestern US."

"Hmm, the group that held Arturo captive."

"Yes." He said it rather ominously.

"Jake, you didn't discuss this in front of Arturo, did you?"

"Oh no! Not a chance. Connors and I both know better than that. No, when I was in Austin for the interview, I met with him—with Connors. That's when he told me about Quique Volpe and Anabel. She'd pretty much dropped out of sight after Artie. I knew Quique vaguely. He was from a town close to Aguagria. I had no idea he was involved with the Zetas.

"Anyway, Connors called me about a week later to let me know about Anabel's getting in touch with his wife. But no, we didn't let on at all to Artie. Connors is even better at dissembling than I am. Hell, he's a politician—he's gotta be."

I waited a moment to see if Jake would drop the other shoe. "So...? If neither of you let on, is there another complication? Is Anabel talking about getting in touch with Arturo?"

He had to think a moment, looking like he was trying to figure how best to piece the story together. "That I don't know. But after Connors left the two of us at the Pedernales, there was one point where Artie was silent...well, more silent than usual. I tried my best to keep up the conversation. But I could feel there was something he wanted to say or ask about. I had the feeling it was something I wouldn't want to answer. While I was wracking my brain for more to say, he finally just blurted out, 'How's Anabel, Jake?'"

"Huh. And what did you say?"

"I just looked over at him. He kept looking at the river. I just told him the truth: that as far as I knew, she was fine. Of course, then he asked me if she hadn't contacted me. I knew if I lied, he'd know it. I didn't see the harm in telling him she was married and had a daughter, lived somewhere in the Dallas area.

"He already knew. His sister, Griselda, told him."

"Oh, no wonder...Well, why would he...? Well, of course, to get more information. No way I was gonna tell him the daughter was his. I could tell he wanted to know more. He asked how old she was...the daughter. Maybe he wondered.

"I braced myself for the question. I knew I'd just tell him that I didn't know—hope I could get away with it. Fortunately at that point he got a bite. Reeled in a fairly good-size guadalupe bass—biggest catch of the day. You got that one."

I sat back. "I'll tell my husband we got the best of the batch."

He slightly shivered, like a chilling wind had just insinuated itself down his spine. "Doctor—Judith, I-I've got a funny feeling about all this. Where do we go from here?"

"You just go on being his friend. Let me take care of the rest."

"What if Anabel does get in touch? What if she tries to get back together with him, leaves her husband? She'll have to tell him that Letty is his. And what will Quique do? I imagine he's pretty used to having his own way."

"We'll deal with that—*I'll* deal with that if and when it happens. Just be his friend, Jake. Be his friend."

January 03, 2003. Pt Arturo Cavazos (1179A):

Damn! Dammit to hell! A major complication has arisen. Pt is presently in CHRISTUS Santa Rosa Hospital, being treated for drug overdose and exposure. As best I could piece the story together, he was found on railroad tracks by a lineman, unconscious in sleet and subfreezing temperatures. According to EMTs he was barely alive, pulse and blood pressure at dangerously low levels.

Naloxone hydrochloride was administered, and he apparently became semiconscious while being transported to hospital. He mumbled that he was waiting for the train. Obviously, his intent was suicide. In the midst of waiting, he had passed out on the tracks. The ER doctor I spoke to said that with the blood-alcohol and opioid levels he came in with, it was a miracle he was alive at all.

I repeat, damn!

But I must keep my head about it, principally for my patient but for my own good as well. No, turn that around: I can be of no use to my patient (or anyone else) if I don't take care of myself. I've been in constant consultation with John as to how to handle this. As John has advised (and I know pretty damn well), Arturo must remain a client, not a friend or family. With this particular patient, that is a real concern.

The misgivings Jake expressed at our recent meeting apparently came to pass. I've only been able to get a sketchy outline from Pt so far, but it seems former girlfriend Anabel Volpe did come to see him. During my visit in hospital, Pt said something about her coming to warn him, but he's been vague about what. I have attempted to contact her with no success.

I have spoken with Jake, and he will be coming to San Antonio tomorrow. He has agreed to inform Governor McClain and Pt's sister Griselda. I'm hoping Pt will be in a state today to give me details of recent events.

I must acknowledge my own disappointment—if for no other reason than to deal with it so that it will not interfere with my ability to treat Pt. I believed we had reached beyond the initial stage of remembrance and mourning and were taking baby steps into reconnection with ordinary life. As a result of this episode, it is possible that a great deal of that work has been undone.

I must focus first on making an accurate assessment of Pt's present state. It is imperative that I communicate with Ms. Volpe. What was the nature of the warning? Is Pt still in danger? If so, what kind? It is hoped that today Pt will be sufficiently recovered from his overdose to recount the events of the last few days. However, getting two perspectives on those events can only help to provide a clearer picture.

Pt's treating physician has now advised me that he is awake and, though still feeling the effects, more coherent. Dr. Winslow gave me a rundown of medications administered. Pt should be in a suggestive state, one medication approximating the effect to sodium amatol. I have brought a tape recorder and will record our conversation.

When I entered the room, Arturo never even raised his eyes. His face told quite a story. It was as dark and empty as when we first met. Hopelessness suffused the room like a toxic gas. I couldn't let it drag me down. But it would also be counterproductive to not acknowledge Pt's feelings. Asking how he was would be downright insulting.

I just sat for a few moments trying to honor his evident pain. It was also a necessary gesture to make it clear that I understood how difficult it would be to speak of it. Whatever the trauma was, he needed to know that I would mourn it with him.

Finally, I felt that sufficient time had passed. "Arturo, I can tell you've had a serious setback. Do you think you can tell me what happened?"

He was still as a granite wall. He stared down so intently that it seemed his gaze could burn a hole through the mattress and bed frame. He stayed that way so long, saying nothing, that I felt my own resolution wavering. Perhaps it was for my own sake that I continued. I'm very aware that not every case can have a successful conclusion. This, however, was one I was not prepared to give up on. Not yet.

*Neutral and disinterested, Judith; it's the only way.* "Yesterday, while you were still under the influence, you mentioned your former girlfriend, Anabel." His only reaction was a closing of the eyes. I could feel the pain exude from his every pore. When he finally spoke, his tone was quiet as a gallows.

"You're wasting your time, Doc."

I had to think a moment about the appropriate response. "Well, I guess that's possible. But it's my time to waste. Will it hurt you any to tell me what happened, so that I can make that determination for myself?"

There was another interminable silence that I had to tolerate as best I could. I know it was more excruciating for him than for me.

Hell, if we were back at the beginning, then so be it. But we'd developed a relationship over the previous five months or so, so it *wouldn't* be from scratch. I had to prepare myself for the possibility that I would make no headway today. It comes with the territory. Perhaps I would have to do the talking for now.

"Arturo, a big stressor, a really unfortunate incident, can reignite all the feelings of hopelessness. I've seen it in many of my patients. I've known it in myself. Some episodes can send us back to what feels like ground zero. But people who care about you are on their way here. You're not alone in this."

"That's the problem, Doc."

"OK. How is that the problem, Arturo?" *Keep saying his name. Keep giving him an identity.*

"I would've killed her."

He still had not looked at me—had not even raised his eyes. "You would've killed who, Arturo? Anabel?" His silence told me that was it. The decision to tell me the story had to be his. *Make it a request.* "Arturo, I can see it's a horrible thing to have to recount. Jake'll be here tomorrow; maybe after you see—"

"I don't want to see him!" He'd finally looked up at me but then swiftly looked away.

*Gently, Judith.* "OK. Do you think you can tell me why?" Silence. "Arturo, when we do things we're not proud of, we may feel unworthy.

Is that why you don't want to see Jake? I'll tell you, he wanted to come immediately when I told him you were in the hospital. That was yesterday. I suggested he wait until you were fully...in possession of your faculties."

He emitted such a bitterly sarcastic explosion of air. "And when in hell is that gonna be? I'm not in possession of anything, Doc...of any part of myself, of any part of being human. This is the second time I've tried to kill someone—and this time I'm afraid... No, actually, it's the third, isn't it? But it's just one of many times I've wanted to. But to nearly choke the life out of a woman...a woman who..."

"Who what, Arturo? Who cares about you? Loves you?" Silence. "What happened, Arturo? Did she want to get back together? What did she say?"

Just for a second, he started to answer. Perhaps he *will* be able to tell me today. *Wait for it, Judith.*

"Is...is she all right?" Finally! Showing concern. Showing humanity.

"I don't know. She's not answering her phone."

Again the eyes closed in excruciating pain, but it smacked of a pain of inevitability.

I had to scramble. *Think, Judith.* He said *almost...would have.* "But you said you *would* have killed her. That tells me you didn't."

After another long period of silence, he began the story. "She came to warn me. The Zetas want me dead." He gave a humorless chuckle. "Hell, finally we want the same thing.

"They were putting pressure on her husband—he works for them, she said. They were pressuring him to finish what they'd started. They didn't want me telling my story. And they're just sick people."

Another painful pause. "She told me she had a daughter...and that the child was mine."

"Arturo, that's an awful lot to deal with all of a sudden—especially in your present state. But if you're in danger, I know you have someone who can protect you."

"That's not the problem! It's the world that needs protection from me! If the Zetas kill me, they'll be doing the world a favor."

I chose not to respond, hoping he'd continue with the episode with Anabel. But after another long silence, I was afraid I was losing him. "What happened, Arturo?" Silence. "I know it's hard. I know it's unbearably painful. I know it seems now like a waste of time…because it seems hopeless. I'm asking a hell of a lot. And if you can't—"

"After she gave me the news, she asked to stay. I told her it was too dangerous. She'd already said they were looking for me. And the state I was in, it…" He just shook his head in despair. "I told her to go straight to Jake and our other friend. He has a lot of influence."

"Governor McClain, you mean."

He cast me a momentary glance. There wasn't a great deal of surprise that I knew. "Yeah. Yeah. Anyway, I told her to take her daughter and go to him immediately. She said she already had, that her daughter was with Andie, Connors's wife, that he'd already sent protection for both of us."

Just for a second, I considered questioning his reference to the daughter as "hers" rather than "ours," but quickly discarded the idea. There was enough pressure on him as it was. What was most urgent was to know what had occurred between the two of them. "Then what happened?"

It took a long time for him to answer, but I didn't urge because I could see him starting and stopping. His mouth would open to speak, and then he'd turn away and stare fixedly at nothing. I could feel him starting to dissociate, give in to the medications intended to forestall agitation. Perhaps it was going to be necessary in order to get the full story. We could return to it later when he was in a more present state of mind. When he finally continued the story, it was detached, aloof.

"I told her to leave. She asked me to come with her. I said no. I knew that, besides the cartel, she needed protection from me. It wasn't safe for her to be with me at all." There was another debilitating hesitation. I was a bit surprised by it considering his dissociated state. What he said next was said with the finality of death. "That's obvious now."

I had to break him out of the comfort of despair. "What happened next, Arturo?"

I was grateful he could recount this; it had to be unbearably painful. "She asked…she asked if she could just hold me. 'Just for a little while,' she said. She could tell I hadn't slept. 'Just until you fall asleep; your eyes have that look, Artie,' she said. I was surprised that her calling me Artie didn't…didn't…"

"…hurt?" I suggested.

His silence and a movement of his eyes in my direction told me that was it.

"There was no way I could tolerate that—I mean her holding me," he continued. "She knew without my answering. So she said, 'Then let me just stay until you do. Then I'll leave. I promise.' I knew promises were sacred to her. 'You need to sleep, Arturo.' Why did she go back to calling me Arturo? But she'd called me that sometimes back in the day. It was like a…like a…"

"Pet name?" Again, he didn't answer, but the pain that registered on his face told me that that was what he meant. It was rather unique that some memories or words seemed to rock him out of his detached state.

"She was right. I'd just dozed occasionally in the last forty-eight hours. I don't know why. I just had a feeling something was coming. Guess I was right.

"I told her I couldn't sleep without taking something. I filled that prescription you gave me, Doc. But sometimes I've woken up on my balcony, even in the elevator, downstairs in the lobby, not knowing how I got there. Who knows what I might do in that state. So I'd stopped taking them.

"She said she'd stay with me while I slept—wake me up if I started to wander. 'Anyway, if anything happens,' she says, 'the guards in the lobby Connors sent will handle it.' I was skeptical, but I was starting to almost hallucinate from lack of sleep, so I finally took one of those pills, whatever they're called. They work fast. I don't have a memory of anything after that until…"

He paused, but he was still in a dissociated state. "I woke up...I thought. I heard that song. El Mutilado was singing it...behind the door...coming down the hall. 'Tap, click.' But his voice was different somehow. I don't know how to explain it: it was coming out of him, but it sounded different. Suddenly, he was there in front of me, singing that song.

"In the dream, I managed to wrench the chains out of the wall. I grabbed him by the throat. I squeezed. He just laughed. He was somehow laughing and singing the whole time I was choking him. Then he said my name. Or...I heard it from somewhere. Anyway, the voice was still different. 'Arturo,' he...it said. 'Arturo...' Why was his voice different? Then finally I heard, 'Artie, Artie, it's me.' He never called me that. It was always Arturo...always so formal yet familiar somehow. I finally saw it was Anabel I was choking. 'Artie, it's me, Anabel.' Even though I was choking her, she said it in such a calm, determined voice.

"I immediately let go, backed away. I hit something solid and slid to the floor. Once she got her voice back, she said, 'It's all right, Artie. It's all right. I was singing a lullaby: "Estrellita." You told me that Jake sang it when you were lost in the Big Bend. You said it was soothing. I hoped...it's all right now, Arturo. It's all right.'

"She was keeling beside me, started to put her arms around me. I stood, backed away. I would've killed her. I would've..."

As gently as I could, I said, "But again, Arturo, you didn't."

"The rest is...just images: grabbing a bunch of my pills, going out of the building the back way...a liquor store I think...train tracks... smell of creosote, diesel...whistle of a screech owl...dogs barking."

His eyes closed in a rapture of pain. "Why couldn't I have ended it? Why couldn't...?"

At this point it was clear that I needed to use the rest of his energy and my time to help him reorient himself. It was a long and arduous process. I felt I only partially succeeded. At the end, when I had to leave, he'd almost completely receded into a fugue state.

There were two new guards posted outside his room. And the hospital had put him on suicide watch, so I felt he'd be safe until tomorrow. I crossed my fingers and said a little prayer. But I—we—had to get to the bottom of that song. Did his tormentor sing it as well? He must have. What kind of darker meaning can it possess?

01/06/03 (personal log):

"When sorrows come, they come not single spies but in battalions."
This is what Jake in utter desolation quoted to me from Shakespeare
when we met this morning. It was in response to even more devastating news: Anabel's body was found in Pt's apartment with a single
gunshot wound to the back of the head. She was bound and apparently tortured before being executed.

I'm almost certain this will crush the life out of my patient's
chances of recovery. It has had something like that effect on both
Jake and me. And, oh God, what she must have suffered! How can
this have happened? Where in God's name do we go from here?

There is also the question of his responsibility. But for Arturo to
torture anyone seems beyond the realm of possibility—least of all a
woman, and one who's meant so much to him. He's volatile. The attempt to strangle based on a paranoid delusion I can understand. But
torturing and shooting? Execution-style? That's so impersonal, the
opposite of strangulation in the heat of passion.

Is it possible her sudden appearance was so jarring that it led him
to act out what was done to him? Why? What motive could he possibly
have had? It just doesn't make sense. Of course, extreme emotions
rarely do at first glance. But again, this was cold-blooded murder.

And there was no hint of any of that in Arturo's memory. Of
course, there are cases where a wife or girlfriend is killed and the
perpetrator has no memory of the incident. That would be the result
of traumatic amnesia. The memory is blocked by remorse or simply
by the savagery of the act. The perpetrator simply can't believe he's
capable, so his mind blocks it out.

At first, I remembered very few of the specifics of my own rape—
more than anything, I just remembered the look on Chacho's face. I
will never get that out of my mind. But there were images, unrelated
sights, sounds, smells: the water stain on the ceiling, beer spilled on
the coffee table, my blood on the couch. I remember scrubbing and

scrubbing to get it out—and when I couldn't, just turning the cushion over.

Fortunately state investigators at the highest level are on the case. I'm sure this is thanks to Governor McClain. They seem quite knowledgeable and are certain that the murder was not an act of passion. They rather believe it is tied to the murder of Anabel's husband in Dallas, which occurred the day, or possibly hours, before her own. They're pursuing the theory that it is drug related. They have some information to that effect, the details of which they say they can't share.

There is also other evidence pointing to Arturo's innocence. According to time of death, the murder would have taken place around the time Arturo was found unconscious on the railroad tracks.

But how will the news affect him? I tremble at the thought of telling him. But I must be there. I asked John if he thought it would be a good idea for Jake to be present, or even to break the news himself while both of us are there. I wondered how much my considering that option came from my own fear. No, I will have to do this alone.

Damn sadists! Damn drugs! Damn heartless, murdering, raping savages to hell!


When my office phone rang a little after five o'clock I had the urge to drop it out a window. I needed today of all days to be with my family. I'd had a consultation with John that had at least centered me, but there was still a cavernous space that only my men at home could fill. A fierce north wind moaned vacuously around the building underscoring the feathery blankness in me.

"Dr. Neuwirth, this is Connors McClain."

For a moment, I was stunned. The governor? Why would he risk contacting me directly? I wonder if Jake might have mentioned to him that I'd figured out who the anonymous donor was.

"Doctor...?"

"Uh, Governor McClain, this is...quite a surprise."

"I imagine so. This will have to be the only time we speak. That's if the precaution does any good. Nobody so far's been able to prove I'm involved in this case. But there are suspicions about rangers being assigned to bodyguard duty." I heard a very decisive sigh. "Have you told Artie yet?"

"Uh…no, no, I haven't. I…I'm seeing him tomorrow."

"OK. Well, I figured it might help if you knew some of the leads we're pursuing."

"Uh…yes. I've gotten a few, but…yes, the more information I have…not that I think there's any way to soften the blow."

"No, dammit, there's no way to do that. How is Artie? Or how was he the last time you saw him?"

"Uh, he was still under the influence of medication, including the self-medication he practiced. Uh, Governor, I'm…kind of constrained."

"I understand. Jake's explained to me about confidentiality." He paused for an uncertain or frustrated moment. "Then I'll just tell you what I know."

"OK, thank you."

"And excuse my French, but those murdering sons a' bitches entered just after my rangers found out that Artie'd slipped away and went after him. Now, this is information that *you* can't share. Do you understand?"

"Yes, sir."

"They were hired guns in the employ of the Zetas drug cartel. We have an agent in deep cover in Mexico. The only other person in that snake pit who knows about him is my friend there who arranged Artie's rescue. We found out that Anabel's husband, Quique Volpe, was ordered by the cartel to find and eliminate Artie. Obviously that was because he knew too much. We don't know if Quique actually told Anabel or if she just suspected.

"But when the order wasn't immediately carried out, the cartel sent their goons to his house. Apparently, when he either wouldn't or couldn't tell them where Anabel was, they killed him. Then they went after her, figuring she'd go to warn Artie.

"Damn miserable luck! They must've made the rangers and waited till they were gone. And damn me for finding a place for Artie where the walls were solid and little sound travels between apartments. I thought it'd be better for him."

"Governor McClain, I'm sure it was. Nobody could have foreseen—"

"Yeah, yeah." I could feel his pain at the turn of events. I could tell he blamed himself for not ordering more protection. I'd never thought of the human side of a politician before. It was quite a revelation.

"There were a lot of reasons we knew it was hired assassins: The way she was bound. God help me, the torture. And then the investigators found a sofa pillow with a hole and powder burns." I could now feel the hate, even before he added the following: "I swear to God I'm gonna get those bastards. I'm gonna get 'em if it takes me the rest of my life."

There was a period of silence. I was stunned by the intensity of his feelings. I had no idea what to say. Finally I just said, "Governor, I...I'm sorry."

He didn't react to my expression of sympathy. He finally just said, "Take care of Artie." And he hung up.

January 07, 2003 Session with Pt Arturo Cavazos (in hospital):

All night I agonized over how I would break the news to Arturo. Alternatives flitted through my mind like a swarm of gnats. Quickly discarded, they later resurged with a different face. Every possibility seemed to end in horror. Hovering like a vulture in the background was the option of delay. But for him to find out by chance would be a stake through the heart of sanity.

I'd gotten word that he was going to be released today—this very morning.

As I neared the hospital, a stinging mix of sleet and rain bit angrily at the windshield. It worked together with apprehension to slow my progress toward the hospital entrance. Every frozen drop stung like the thoughts that darted through my mind. They pursued me up the elevator and echoed through the hallway outside his room.

I paced among bored nurses and officious orderlies, passing an elderly gentleman walking with a walker. A physical therapist followed, clutching the wide posture belt around his middle to steady him. I wished there were some such implement to brace the spirit.

When I reached Arturo's room, I realized I had walked the entire square of the floor. A nurse asked me if I was looking for someone in particular. I paused outside the door to steady myself. *Where are the guards?* I wondered. I asked the nurse. One had gone to bring round the car, while the other was mapping the exit route.

Finally the persona of neutral and disinterested therapist took over. I'd given bad news, sometimes horribly disturbing news, to patients in the past. To be of any use, I had to maintain my objectivity.

When I entered, he was dressed, sitting on the chair at the foot of his bed, his cane across the arms in front of him. He looked up at me. It was a steady, penetrating look. It was a look that told me bad news was expected, that there was no other kind anymore, that nothing horrendous would surprise him. There was no hope in that countenance. It contained a spirit so inured to tragedy that it made me falter for a moment.

I entered and sat down on the bed next to him. He stared straight forward. The best way to pull a scab off an infected wound is to rip it all at once. "You didn't kill her, Arturo." The only reaction I got was the slightest lowering of his eyes—a furtive expression of relief. They quickly rose again to mine, set in a face of stone, as if the eyes themselves knew the news to follow could only be abhorrent.

My mind was still whirling with how I would impart that news. His gaze was riveted to mine. It said, *Nothing you can tell me can hurt anymore. I'm beyond pain because beyond caring.* Still I hesitated. I knew the news would be the rock rolled to seal the tomb of his despair.

It was selfish, that hesitation. Yes, I'd grown particularly fond of Arturo. I hated so much to see such a once powerful and decent human being finally defeated. But to lose this patient I had invested so much of my time, my energy, my very identity in was to lose a part of myself as well. To see progress that I had a part in dashed to splinters would be a personal blow. It would be in some part my failure.

Finally, I could see no escape. But I will not meekly accept defeat. It would be another submission to those animals. I will fight to the last breath. Perhaps that bare expression of relief he displayed is a grain of sand on which to rebuild the fallen structure. I must cling to that.

"According to investigators, you didn't even really hurt her." I braced myself. "But...I'm afraid someone else did. They think it was assassins sent by the cartel. They killed her husband, too."

The only outward sign of a reaction were his eyes leaving mine, staring forward. He remained a statue—so still, so impenetrable. It felt as though all the air were sucked out of the room—all objects, the walls, the ceiling, the floor collapsing into him. He seemed to travel so far beyond reach that it sucked my breath with it.

"Arturo...?" It was like reaching for the Milky Way. "Arturo, I'm sorry." It didn't seem like the news broke anything in him. It was more just a confirmation, the final shovel of dirt on his grave.

Then there was the tiniest of reactions. His head lifted and cocked a few centimeters, as though he heard something in the distance. I waited to see what it might be.

Finally I heard it. It was the patient walking up the hallway with the walker. He wasn't sliding it, as patients who are learning to walk again often do. The walker was lifted. The back legs came down with a dull sound. Then the forward legs came right after with a sharper click.

Droplets of sweat formed at his temples. "Arturo…?" It was disconcerting, the depth of his concentration. "Arturo, that's just a patient walking with a walker. Arturo?" I could tell he didn't hear me.

The sound came gradually closer. I didn't think Arturo could stiffen any more than he already had, but it was like he went from wood to marble. It suddenly struck me that this was the sound El Mutilado made when he was coming to the room where the prisoners were kept. It was that ominous "tap, click," "tap, click" Arturo had described.

This was not the place or time to be transported back to that horror. "Arturo, could you look at me? Arturo, please look at me. It's Judith, your doctor. Arturo, you are here, in San Antonio, in the hospital. That's just a patient walking with a walker. Arturo, can you hear me?"

The sound stopped not far from the door to his room. I hoped that would break him out of his hypnotized state. Then I remembered that that was exactly what happened when El Mutilado came: there was that moment of silence before he opened the door.

"Arturo!" I demanded, trying desperately to shake him out of his reverie. Then louder, as strident as I could make it, "Artie!" But he seemed beyond the reach of anyone or anything, trapped in his mind in that room. I tried snapping my fingers in front of his face. I even slapped him. He didn't even look up at me. In desperation, I searched for the nurses' button.

Then the strangest thing happened. So quietly I could barely hear it, he started singing, "Es-tre-lli-ta, de lejano cielo."

It is such a sweet melody. But the way he sang it chilled to the bone. For a moment, I was mesmerized.

His hands started making that signature gesture. Then he grabbed the cane lying across the chair, wringing it furiously. In a voice not his own, he said, "Mátalo! Si quieres salvar a tu prima, mátalo!"

"Arturo, who's telling you to kill? Who is that speaking? Is it El Mutilado? Who is he telling you to kill?" I judged that wrenching him out of this nightmare was paramount. *Where the hell is the nurses' button!*

I grabbed him by the shoulders and shook for all I was worth. "Arturo, what you're seeing is not real! You are in the hospital here in San Antonio. Arturo, listen to me!" He stood, pushing me back like a rag doll.

Had he taken on the persona of his scourge? I looked around frantically for something I could use to break him out of this spell: a needle, ice water, anything.

There was suddenly a deadly neutral voice, as though he was watching it happen but to someone far removed. "Imelda, my cousin. Es una niña, no más; she's just a child. El Mutilado heats his iron walking stick with a blowtorch as he sings. He touches it to her. She screams."

Arturo's voice switched to that of El Mutilado: "No, estás fuera del tono; you off-peetch. Canta bien, hija." Then in his own voice: "He turns to me." Then back again as El Mutilado: "Jou wan' to save jour couseen the pain, Arturo, you mus' keel thee boy. He ees jour brother, and jou must keel him. To save jour couseen, you must take the iron stake and keel him."

In his voice: "She's screaming in pain. I'm standing over Jesús. The guards force another piece of rebar into my hands. I throw it down. And so he burns her."

El Mutilado's voice again: "Peeck eet up!"

His voice: "He starts to burn her, so I pick it up. I try to go after them, but my feet are still chained to the wall. I strain with all my might. The guards just stand there. They're enjoying it. El Mutilado is calm, just doing a job. He burns her again as he sings, softly, gently. She screams. It's horrible. I can't stand it. I can't…

"El Mutilado says so coldly, so logically, 'How can jou leesten to jour couseen suffer so? Jou know what jou hev to do.'

"I raise the piece of iron. Jesús looks up at me. How can they make me do this? How can I choose? I pull with all my strength against the chains, and I feel something snap in my hip. It brings me down. El Mutilado calmly sings, and burns Imelda. The smell…the smell of burning hair and flesh! She screams, and all he says is, 'Jou steel off-peech.'

"I can't stand. I get up on one leg. Imelda's screaming, screaming. I have to stop it."

I went to slap Arturo again, but he raised the cane. I yelled his name over and over. *Where the hell was that damned nurse!* I went out into the hall and called for help. Finally they heard me. The nurse came. "Get help!" I yelled at her.

In El Mutilado's cold, scratchy voice, Arturo says, "Keel thee boy. You mus' keel heem."

Then in his own voice: "Imelda! Imeldaaa!" And he brought the cane down onto the chair with such force that the cushion split. He brought it down again and again.

Then he dropped it and backed away, making that same gesture: one hand scraping down the other. *That's it!* I thought. *He's trying to scrape bits of skull and brains and blood from his hands!*

I knew it was wrong, but I approached him. I stood in front of him and grabbed him by the shoulders. Suddenly his hands were around my throat. But he didn't tighten. He just stared. Then his head slightly cocked. I could see he was trying to place me.

"It's Judith, Arturo. Your doctor. You're here in San Antonio in the hospital. *Please try to understand.* You're out of danger. You're safe. You've been through an unspeakable horror, but it's over now. *There's no danger. It's over.*"

He just stared at me. It was in a way that made me think that somehow I was getting through. Then his look gradually changed. There came to be some element of pity in it. He lowered his hands to my shoulders. Then he spoke. There was not a shred of feeling in his voice. It was a corpse talking. "It's never over, Doc. Never." It was so chilling I was struck dumb…paralyzed.

One of the guards rushed in and tried to restrain him. Arturo threw him across the room. His head banged against the metal arm of the chair. He was out cold. I was frozen against the wall. Even as he brushed past me and then the orderlies at the door, I knew I couldn't stop him. I couldn't follow, or even speak.

01/13/03 (personal log):

It's been over a week, and I've yet to receive any word on Pt's where-abouts. Although he's missed appointments, even whole weeks of them in the past, there was a finality to the way he left the hospital—a determination. To what, I have no idea. I can only hope it is not some revenge fantasy.

I've not heard from or been able to contact Mr. Kazmarick since he arrived at the hospital the same day and immediately left in search of Pt. I presume Governor McClain has state agents searching as well.

I must admit that maintaining my objectivity vis-à-vis Pt was be-coming more and more of a challenge. I cannot deny considerable disappointment, both professional and personal, should my efforts have failed. Perhaps it had become *too* personal for me. I've been working with John on that.

On the other hand, I've not seen any news reports of suicides. Nor has there been any word from the governor's office. Something told me that Jake's pursuing Pt was not a good idea, but my efforts to stop him were fruitless. I can only hope that he might convince Pt to come back. But my instincts tell me that's very unlikely.

It is inevitable to wonder what you could have done differently. Was it wise to share my own trauma with him? Should I have been more proactive in keeping Anabel away? Might there have been a bet-ter way to present the news of her death? One can make oneself crazy with second-guessing.

I've been over it and over it with John. He's helped me restructure some of my thoughts of "failure." Yes, I was making progress. Yes, it was an extreme case. Certainly the most difficult I've faced. And no, I'm not God—I couldn't have prevented the unique circumstances that led to his psychotic episode. And I do have some tough cases, in-cluding David Horowitz, in my win—make that my *success*—column.

I was sitting at my desk, trying to concentrate on paperwork (and not being very successful), when Carmen buzzed. I didn't have another session till this afternoon. I caught myself in desperate hopes.

"Carmen?"

"Judith, there's a man here to see you. He says to say he's the governor. He looks like him."

I was momentarily stunned. Why on earth would Governor McClain come here? Why would he risk being connected with the case? He's certain to be recognized out in the lobby. "Send him in immediately, Carmen." I hoped I wasn't too brusque with her. I'll need to explain later.

There are some people that just exude a sense of command. It's not arrogance. I'm not sure it's even conscious; it probably becomes second nature. It's just an assumption, inherent or acquired, or perhaps some of both, that others should (and will) follow their orders. I felt that as soon as he walked through my office door. I could immediately see why he was so successful as a politician. I must admit I found that sense of power attractive. "Governor McClain, this is... quite a surprise."

He shook my hand with a firmness that told me he considered me an equal and a colleague. "I'm sure it is, Doctor."

"Please, have a seat. And please call me Judith." He sat at attention. I'm sure I did as well. Beyond the prodigious sense of command and intelligence, there was something else emanating from him. Having only talked to him on the phone, I couldn't tell what it might be. "Uh...Governor, aren't you concerned about..."

"I'm afraid it's too late for that, Judith. The news of my participation in the rescue of Arturo Cavazos will be in all the papers tomorrow. That's if it's not on the news tonight. I'll be officially resigning this afternoon."

I was devastated. There'd been talk of a presidential bid. "Oh, Governor, I...I don't know what to say."

"Nothing *to* say." His lips curled up in a humorless kismet smile. "That, as they say, is life. You've just gotta learn to hit the curve ball. By the way, since my political career is over, you could help me get used to being called Connors again." He smiled the smile of a pleasant memory this time. "Or Connie. That's what Artie always called me. I miss that."

"Governor—uh, Connors, do you know what happened to him?"

"Yes, I do. Now it's my turn to tell you that there's so much I can say."

"OK."

"At this moment, he's visiting that friend of mine in Mexico."

"He went back to Mexico!"

"It's all right, Judith. He's all right…for now, at least."

"It's not now that I'm worried about. Couldn't you or Jake or the two of you have talked to him?"

I found his amused dismissal of the idea rather annoying. "Judith, when Artie Cavazos makes up his mind to do something, I'm not sure God Himself could change it. Anyway, he won't be by himself. He and my friend, the one that arranged his rescue, have a project in mind. We're working on some of the details now."

"What kind of project could they—you be—"

"*That's* something I'll have to keep to myself—for your sake, for mine and for theirs. Suffice it to say that Artie's found a way, as I believe you told Jake, 'to convert his pathology into some kind of positive social activity.' My friend Santiago has as well: the woman he sent as surety to accompany Jake and Artie from prison to the border met with a very unfortunate fate on her way back. I know she meant a great deal to him."

My jaw hung wide open at the implications. "Governor McClain, do you know anything about Jake? Where he is?"

"I'm honestly not sure. My attention, and consequently my agents' attention, was focused on Artie. I know Jake's not in Aguagria. But that's all I know."

"You don't think he followed Arturo into Mexico?"

"I don't know. I sure hope not. The Zetas seem to know all about our operation, including who was involved. I've got agents looking for Jake now as well. I've asked Santiago to be on the lookout for him. His intelligence covers a pretty healthy area of the country, but he has to be very circumspect. His image is quite at odds with who he actually is. What they're planning may very well blow his cover."

I took a moment to try to digest this. He accommodated it. "Gov—Connors, what will *you* do now? Will you be able to practice law again?"

"Hmm, doubtful. Questionable I'd want to, anyway. But I have things to keep me busy: a project like Artie's and Santiago's requires funds, after all. As you can imagine, I have a lot of connections…a lot of favors to call in."

My brain was sputtering in efforts to process the implications. I couldn't help being fascinated at seeing the man behind the political facade. I tried to get a feeling for that man. And what really was beneath the nonchalance concerning his fate. I had the sense that he knew what I was trying to do and allowed it—maybe even welcomed it. Finally I just blurted out, "You know, I voted for you."

He smiled. But I didn't get the feeling he was flattered. "I appreciate that. Appreciate you telling me."

"You won't miss running to be the de facto leader of the world?"

"Oh yes I will. It's in my genes. It's in the marrow of my bones. But there's always that nasty thing called reality: some dreams just never come true. What is it Joni Mitchell says—they 'lose some grandeur' at least?

"Life could never be accused of being fair. What happened to Artie is the height of injustice…"—he finished the sentence spewing venom—"for such a damn fine man. What's happening to Jake and Dolores isn't fair. What happened to Dolores in the first place is just sickeningly mean. I suppose it's not fair that I'm being judged by the letter and not the spirit of the law." A bit of sunlight popped through the window onto his enigmatic smile. "But the truth is that life has been more than fair to me."

He stood. A cloud of something passed over him. It wasn't sadness exactly. It wasn't as weighty as world-weariness. There was a kind of self-deprecating wisdom in it. I got the feeling by the way he looked at me that it was something he felt we shared. "Trying to make life fair is where we get into so much trouble."

He reached out his hand. "Good-bye, Judith. Thanks for all you did for Artie—and by extension, for all of us." This time the handshake was held a little longer and firmer than it would be for mere acquaintances.

"It's my job."

The upward curve of his lips at this had a bit of mischievousness in it. "Right."

And he walked out of my life. And somehow I knew I would not see or hear from him again.

02/10/03 (personal log):

It's been a month now, and I've finally heard from Jake Kazmareck. It seems he did follow Mr. Cavazos into Mexico. I'm glad he made it out alive. I imagine Governor McClain's friend there had something to do with that.

Jake asked to meet with me, and I readily agreed. He'll be here this afternoon, expected anytime now. Although it does not appear that Arturo will be coming back for treatment, I'm anxious for some kind of closure. And just from an intellectual perspective, it will be of interest to know what path he's actually taken, what state he's in.

His case has raised many interesting issues for me—hopefully for the psychiatric community as a whole, and those who treat PTSD in particular. On both counts, it is a shame that I couldn't bring the case to *some* kind of conclusion—if any genuine conclusion were possible. I'm hoping Pt had some discussion with Jake concerning his decisions.

I must note that my intellectual curiosity indicates I've achieved a degree of objectivity. I'm sure my meetings with John have helped with that. I'd love to be a fly on the wall during Pt's discussions with Mr. McClain's friend in Mexico—or be able to tap phone conversations between the three of them. I know this case will stick with me for the rest of my life.

I am, of course, concerned for his welfare as well. Arturo Cavazos is without a doubt the client that has touched me the deepest. Would more time have eventually healed him? As I've often told myself, the process is never over. I suppose the crucial question is whether he would at some point have been able to function well in society. How well? It's so agonizingly relative. It's always a question not of *well* but *better.* Some people with basically no serious trauma are unable to adapt to life.

I have to recognize that I'm also eager to see Jake again. I've grown fond of him over the last…what, year and a half now? His devotion to my Pt was truly touching. The intelligence and sensitivity he demonstrated in working with him was a decisive factor in his conva-lescence. I do hope he can work out his problems with his fiancée (or girlfriend now, I suppose). I wonder if I could find some way to work with her. Could she possibly come here, even once a week? Could Jake bring her?

I'm also concerned about Jake's involvement in the rescue from Mexico. Will it preclude his being hired by the district attorney's of-fice in Austin? In Aguagria, for that matter? If it doesn't and he moves to Austin, what will become of Dolores and their relationship? Might the distance actually help—that is, for her to have time by herself? I'm sure Jake will visit often. Could she drive herself to San Antonio? Would she?

But above all, what will become of Arturo Cavazos? What could he and Governor (well, now just Connors) McClain's friend in Mexico be doing? What could the "positive social activity" be?

My mind is turning cartwheels trying to assimilate all the implica-tions of this case. It is extraordinary the feeling of emptiness I'm left with at Arturo's departure. There is something beyond the challenge it presented, the uniqueness and extremity of the pathology, the feel-ing of a job half-done (if I'm kind to myself, maybe two-thirds).

I wonder what it is in me that will so miss the power of his person-ality, the very force of his will and intelligence. It has also left me with profound questions about this thing called life. How can a man be subjected to such horror and then, when there is faint light shone on the darkness, be once again the object of such tragedy?

And there is more, so much more. There is something singular in the bond between these three friends—something so tender and so pure. I wonder about how it came to be so. No doubt their experienc-es on that trip down the Rio Grande had much to do with it, forced as they were to depend on each other.

And I wonder if the bestial impulses unleashed in the fight they had might paradoxically have served to tighten the bond—at least in the long run. Not too many people get to see the ugly underbelly of the human spirit, particularly in themselves. Abhorrent as it may be, it is something unique to be shared. Might a shared sense of shame serve to unite us in friendship as effectively as joy? I wonder.

Whatever the case, I am sure I will find consolation, even redemption, in the strength of that friendship. It will always remind me of the precious gift I have in a loving husband and son. Could it have been God's blessing? Or is it mere chance?

I find myself actually heartbroken at the apparent dissolution of Jake's relationship with Dolores. It seems there is trauma in all walks of life. Perhaps there are only differences in degree of traumatic stress disorder. Perhaps it is a lifelong process for all of us—one that is never completed.

And if there is no life beyond this one? If this universe is some entity within a black hole or the product of the collision of giant membranes in the larger universe that is infinite and eternal, if it exists only in its perception...then what could possibly be the point? Is that the ultimate trauma—that there is none? I shudder at the thought.

When Jake entered, there was again something new about him. He called me by my name from the start without any stumbling over my title. He did it confidently, if rather soberly. I'd felt that his insistent use of my title was the result of my being somehow exalted in his estimation. He seemed to address me now more as an equal, a colleague even. It actually felt more comfortable, if less esteemed.

"So, Jake...first of all, tell me how you are."

"I'm okay, Judith. I'm...okay." He said it as though he had only recently reached that conclusion—and that it was provisional. But it seemed genuine. There was some new confidence purchased from something—some decision or choice made. I wondered what it could be.

"And Arturo?"

"Art...I guess I can go back to calling him Artie now."

I felt some kind of implication in the way he said it. "Uh, that sounds like it has a finality to it."

"Not for Artie, Judith. Just for Artie and me...at least for now."

"Jake, what happened?"

"Oh, nothing bad. He's just gone down a road he won't let me follow.

I thought I knew what he meant but was anxious for details. "How do you mean? What road?"

There was such a faraway look that came over him as he prepared to explain to me what he knew of Arturo's plans. I wasn't sure if the distance in his gaze was only about Arturo. I thought that maybe the decisions Arturo had made about his future had affected Jake's own. But I would have to await his explanation. "Jake, it's not some kind of revenge plot, is it?"

He took time to think about it, looking like he hadn't been able to decide. The wrinkle that split his brow deepened and ran higher up his forehead. He pursed his lips in considering the question. "I don't know, Judith. I honestly don't know. First, because he wouldn't really go into it. And then trying to read Artie Cavazos is a task best left to nonmortals."

"Hah. I see what you mean."

"He did tell me something along the lines of he'd be doing his part to oppose evil—to not do 'nothing.' You get that allusion. I guess my citing that Edmund Burke quote all those years ago somehow resonated.

"I asked him how I could contribute. He said the best thing I could do for him is to forget about him. That made me mad. I said, 'You know I can't do that.'

"He just answered, 'You're gonna have to, Jake.'

"You know, Judith, I was kind of torn. I mean, I felt some of the old Artie in the way he said it. I was pissed off at being excluded, but at the same time...he was decisive, confident, in a way he hadn't been since we got him back here. He seemed to have a sense of himself again.

"I told him I wouldn't go unless he gave me a damn good reason. God, the look he gave me! It said that there was no way in hell I was cut out for it, whatever it was—that I'd be more of a hindrance than a help.

"It captured everything we were to each other, that look. I could feel what we shared on that trip in the Big Bend—the moments of fear and despair as well as the ones of triumph. There were *all* our adventures, all the things he taught me about survival, the help I gave him with his schoolwork. I could see the nights we spent under the stars, the crimson sunrises and blazing sunsets, the dull sameness of mesquite and cactus, the lonesome coo of whitewing doves.

"It encompassed all we could have been if there were no people like the Zetas. It even included that moment of savagery in me—of the necessity of that savagery for what he was going to do. It said, 'To fight animals you have to become one. I can't watch that happen to you.' I saw in his eyes my own inability to accept that part of me—that horrible but essential part that opposing evil dictates.

"I saw a profound love, a wish for a future for me that he couldn't be a part of. I saw all the things we'd done together. And not only the serious things we'd shared. No, I saw all the laughter and silliness when we were kids, the fun we used to make of the brothers who taught us, the stupid chances we took as teenagers, so sure we were immortal. It was all there: the fish we caught, the deer we..." He hesitated a moment, and I saw a rather ironic smile slip across his face. "...*they* killed.

"And there was, of course, his gratitude for my going after him. And I said back to him with a look that it was small recompense."

Jake then paused for a moment contemplating all he'd just said. I took advantage of it. "I think there may be something else, Jake."

His eyes came back to mine, curious. "What?"

"Did you know that when his family crossed the river, he lost his little brother...while the boy was in his care?" His look made it obvious that he didn't. "There was also a boy with him when he was in the hands of the Zetas. I could tell that he'd come to feel about him like a brother. They forced him to kill that boy. That was the ultimate horror he faced."

I didn't wait to see if he would make the connection. "You're the only brother he has left, Jake. Whatever he's going to do down there, he couldn't afford to lose you as well. And I don't mean only your death. I think he's afraid of you losing who you are…by what you'd have to do."

His eyes closed in pain, but I could tell it was a good hurt. When he finally opened them, he characteristically said, "I reminded him that he had a daughter here. Again with just a look he said, *Can you imagine me raising a daughter?*"

"What's going to happen with her?"

"Connors and Andie would like to formally adopt her. That's if there're no relatives that want to be considered. They have two other children, but it wouldn't be any kind of burden—not financial, at any rate."

"Ah. Well, Connors strikes me as a pretty stable person."

"Yeah, and Andie is wonderful with children. She's a pediatrician."

"You know, Jake, it surprises me you haven't thought about helping from here. You have a friend here in Connors, and he's told me that whatever Arturo and the friend in Mexico plan to do will need support and coordination on this side of the border. And there's the child. She's a part of Arturo and Anabel, and she's going to need all the support she can get."

There was a fairly sizable silence as we regarded each other. My curiosity was piqued by the fact that Jake hadn't reacted to my suggestion. "So…wouldn't helping your friends by working with Connors here be a contribution?"

"Yes, it would. Actually, make that *has*. I've already helped some with getting it off the ground."

"I hear a *but* in there."

"I…have a different idea about confronting evil."

I waited. I wondered why he hesitated. What could it be that he was being coy about? "OK…"

"I've enlisted in the marines. I'll be heading to Parris Island at the end of the month."

Utter silence. It's a good thing there wasn't a feather or whisper of wind because either would have knocked me down for the count. I tried to raise my lower jaw to no effect. This was beyond the last thing I could have imagined.

"Jake, I..." I wondered if there were any words I had in mind to follow those halting ones. "Jake, that's the last thing..." It was really hard to get the words out or the thoughts clear. Finally, I just sat back in awe. "Are you sure you're cut out for that?"

His face said he expected—knew—that this would be my reaction. "No. As a matter of fact, I'm pretty sure I'm not." Then there was a slight smile of recognition. It felt rather annoyingly superior. Perhaps he was pleased with himself for being able to surprise me. Or maybe it was just that he thought he'd had an insight that hadn't occurred to me. He was almost condescending. "But then...who is?"

I was too dumbfounded to answer immediately. It took me quite a while to consider all the implications in what Jake had said—what he'd done. All I could think of was, "Jake, what if they don't find what they're looking for over there?"

He'd obviously already considered that as well. He smiled. "Like you said, Judith, 'the best predictor of future behavior is past behavior.'"

"But, Jake, that's for individual cases of..." He raised his eyebrows as if to say, *Can a rule that doesn't apply across the board be a rule? Would Hitler have changed? Would Stalin have changed? Can a twisted mind, a savage mind, be stopped without violence?*

I had no answer.

# EPILOGUE

August 16, 2006 Patient Jacob Kazmareck, Chart #212C. Judith Lozano Neuwirth, MD, PhD, reporting:

Ah, the strange twists and turns that life can take. Jake Kazmarick was the man intimately involved in the treatment of my patient and his good friend, Arturo Cavazos. Now, he is going to be my patient.

To fully explain the prognosis and course of treatment, I will have to fill in some of the history since that time. Jake has been back from deployment in Iraq for almost a year now. During the preceding three years, I also treated his then and now again girlfriend, Dolores Martínez, for her own posttraumatic stress disorder. She eventually moved to San Antonio and is studying child psychology at UTSA.

It is quite a circle of history: Jake was instrumental in arranging treatment for Mr. Cavazos, who was very reluctant to engage in therapy. And now, Mr. Kazmareck has finally agreed to treatment only at the urging of Ms. Martínez.

Jake has from an anatomical perspective adapted quite well to the prosthesis of his lower right leg. Amputation was necessary as a result of automatic fire that mutilated his calf and shattered the tibia and fibula. His psychological adaptation to the prosthesis, as well as to civilian life, however, has not been so smooth. Ms. Martínez reports considerable constriction. Ironically, that was *her* primary symptom, and one that adversely affected their relationship.

Dolores also reports sometimes withering irritability, long periods of withdrawal and startle responses. Pt spends considerable time alone, never gets truly restful sleep and can only tolerate (and then only grudgingly) the company of fellow veterans. If it weren't for Dolores, prognosis would be quite poor. Mr. Kazmirick is most fortunate to have her (as am I). She has told me, and I believe her, that she will be involved through thick and thin.

I have recently taken over the directorship of Sacred Heart Clinic, my friend and mentor, John Wilson, having finally retired. It is quite an adjustment. However, John has made himself very available for consultation. Our book, *The Id Paradox*, has had considerable advanced sales and will be on the shelves this month. Owing to the demands of authorship and my assuming control of the clinic, I will for the present restrict myself to one patient, Mr. Kazmerick. I must point out that I am only able to do so because of the enormous generosity of Connors and Andie McClain.

Sadly, the reason so much of their money comes to this clinic now is the termination of Mr. Cavazos's project in Mexico. This is owing to the violent deaths of Santiago Cásarez and Mr. Cavazos himself, the two principal actors and organizers. The news of Mr. Cavazos's death was quite a blow—not surprising but painful nonetheless.

I've just been informed that Mr. Kasmarick is now on his way from the lobby to my office. Of course, with his permission, I will be recording our session.

He steps in my office. I see quite a different man.

"Hello, Jake. Here we are again. It's good to see you."

# ABOUT THE AUTHOR

Jan Notzon is a novelist and playwright who has made Charlotte, NC his home since 1994.

In addition to *The Id Paradox*, he has also authored the novel *And Ye Shall Be As Gods,* which recounts a brother's fight to rescue his beloved sister from the clutches of despair and his lost love from the prison of catatonia. His first novel, *The Dogs Barking,* is a coming-of-age story set in a sleepy backwater Texas border town in the 1950s, through the dislocation of university life in the '60s and on to the raw, frenetic power of New York City.

He has also written seven full-length plays, a one-act, *The Forsaken,* which was produced in two different venues in New York City. His play *The Cosmological Constant* was workshopped and presented as a staged reading at Actors' Theatre in Charlotte, NC by the Applebox Production Company. His play *When Good Men Do Nothing* was a finalist in the Dramarama Competition in San Francisco. He has also written one children's story, *The Gift of Arbol Ceiba.*

Jan has also worked as an actor, appearing on Matlock, The Young Indiana Jones Chronicles and, most recently, in *Beverly Lewis' The Confession* on The Hallmark Channel, a work directed by Michael Landon Jr., with Adrian Paul and Sherry Stringfield.

He is at present busily, sweatily at work on his fourth novel.